ACCLAIM FOR

Homesick

"One has only to read the first page of Guy Vanderhaeghe's
H̲̲̲̲̲̲̲ ̲̲̲̲̲̲̲̲̲̲̲ international
̲̲̲̲der-Post

̲̲as was once
̲̲Halifax)

̲le and love
̲ *Citizen*

̲dscape and
̲on. . . . He
̲exuberant
̲ee Press*

̲ence. . . ."
̲hroeder

̲eople, their
̲ a difficult
̲d real."
̲ver Sun*

̲are, poetic
̲very effec-
̲ of family
̲. . . . His

̲gston)

BOOKS BY GUY VANDERHAEGHE

NOVELS
My Present Age (1984)
Homesick (1989)
The Englishman's Boy (1996)

SHORT STORIES
Man Descending (1982)
The Trouble With Heroes (1983)
Things As They Are? (1992)

PLAYS
I Had a Job I Liked. Once. (1992)
Dancock's Dance (1996)

HOMESICK

Guy Vanderhaeghe

EMBLEM EDITIONS
Published by McClelland & Stewart Ltd.

Cloth edition published 1989
Trade paperback edition published 1999
First Emblem Editions publication 2001

National Library of Canada Cataloguing in Publication Data

Vanderhaeghe, Guy, 1951-
Homesick

ISBN 0-7710-8691-1

I. Title.

PS8593.A5386H6 2001   C813'.54   C2001-930021-2
PR9199.3.V384H6 2001

We acknowledge the financial support of the Government of Canada through
the Book Publishing Industry Development Program for our publishing
activities. We further acknowledge the support of the Canada Council for the
Arts and the Ontario Arts Council for our publishing program.

ONTARIO ARTS COUNCIL
CONSEIL DES ARTS DE L'ONTARIO

SERIES EDITOR: ELLEN SELIGMAN

Cover design: Ingrid Paulson
Cover photograph: Erik Rank / Photonica
Series logo design: Brian Bean

Typeset in Sabon by M&S, Toronto
Printed and bound in Canada

EMBLEM EDITIONS
McClelland & Stewart Ltd.
The Canadian Publishers
481 University Avenue
Toronto, Ontario
M5G 2E9
www.mcclelland.com

1 2 3 4 5   05 04 03 02 01

To Margaret, as always

ACKNOWLEDGEMENTS

I would like to thank the Canada Council and the Saskatchewan Arts Board for their generous financial assistance during the writing of *Homesick*.

I would also like to express my thanks to my editor Ellen Seligman for her careful and thoughtful labours.

Portions of this novel have previously appeared in the following: a slightly altered version of Chapter 1 was read on CBC Radio's "Speaking Volumes" and "Aircraft"; Chapter 3 previously appeared in *Books in Canada*.

Homesick

I

An old man lay asleep in his bed. This was his dream:

He is young again, once more an ice-cutter laying up a store of ice for the summer. The Feinrich brothers and he drive their sledges out on to the wide white plain of the lake. The runners hiss on the dry snow, metal bits in the harness shift and clink, leather reins freeze so hard they lie stiff and straight as laths down the horses' backs. Before them the sky lightens over purple-shadowed, hunch-shouldered hills.

When the sun finally rises, so does the wind, bitter and cutting. On the lake there is no place to escape it, no trees, no sheds, no bluffs to hunker down and hide behind. On the lake there is only flatness, a rushing space that squeezes eyes into a squint.

There it is now, the first long drawn-out sigh of breath tumbling over the hills, the faint breeze setting snow snakes writhing out over the ice and hard-packed drifts to meet them. By fits and starts this wind gathers force, the skirts of coats billow and snap, its fierce touch penetrates every layer of clothing, drives nails of cold through coveralls, trousers, woollen combinations. It raises gooseflesh and tears the manes of the horses into ragged, whipping flags. It pounds the drum-skins of tightly drawn parka hoods.

They halt. The horses stamp on wind-polished ice. Down from the sledge, standing on bare, clean ice he can feel the cold rise through the soles of his boots, seep through stockings, sting toes. Walking over the ice he can sense the yaw and pitch, the tilt, the gentle undulations that cannot be seen but must be felt, things the eye skates over, fails to register. It makes him feel uneasy, unsteady. He thinks of the waves which ran one after another in slow succession to shore until winter laid its dead hand upon their backs, binding up the heaves and swells, arresting motion. He sees the long rivers of fracture, the widely flung tributary cracks.

He chops a hole for the saw. The axe makes a terrible ringing on the ice, a clash like metal striking metal. With each blow, shards of ice leap like sparks in the air. He opens the lake for the ice-cutters, water spurts and gurgles in the wound. By the time he raises the axe above his head, the water splashed on the blade freezes in a glassy sheath.

The saws squeak. The first block is lifted dripping and gleaming. A square of black water opens wide at his feet. His feet are numb with cold.

So he dances. Dances to heat his feet. A polka right there on the huge ballroom floor of the lake, an imaginary partner cradled in the curve of his arm as he whirls round and round, boots clattering and heels flicking, the Feinrichs laughing and clapping time with their cow-hide mitts. Faster and faster he goes. The horses' nostrils smoke surprise, their eyes roll, their heads jerk as he flashes by. Faster, faster. He throws back his head and sees the last faint stars, the pale silver moon spin with him. Dance with him.

Then he falls. A sudden stunning breath-robbing descent through searing cold and blackness. It blots away moon and stars. A slow, buoyant, bubbling rise which ends with a bump under the ice.

He stares up. Ice. He is under the ice, groping and scrabbling with his nails, searching for the cut-hole, a way out. He snuffles and

2

gulps the thin scraps of air captured between ice and water, kicks his legs frantically. He butts his head madly, desperately against the ice. Water rolls and churns over his shoulders. Out, out, out.

At last, exhausted, he can only hang in the water, suspended in silence and cold. His boots are buckets, pulling heavy on his ankles. His trouser legs balloon with cold and water. It is a silence like he has never heard, a cold like he has never felt. He grows colder by the second and guesses this means he is dying. This is a different kind of cold under the ice, you don't go numb with it. The colder you get, the more it hurts. The more you die, the more you feel.

Every inch of him aches with it. He is cold through to the sap and marrow of his bones. The quiet is no less terrible.

Then he hears something. Above him, people walk. Crunch, creak go the footsteps.

"I'm down here!" he shouts. "I'm down here!"

They don't heed his cry. They don't stop. They pass over.

"For the love of God!" he shouts. "I'm down here! Under the ice!"

The crunch, creak fades away.

His last struggle against the ice begins. It is all rage and foaming water.

Alec Monkman woke in his bed, pillowcase bunched in an arthritic fist. Despite the violence of his grip, the ache and throb of skewed and swollen knuckles was lost beneath all the rest of it. Yet the pain was there, lurking deeper than bone, deep as the deepest waters of sleep from which he had fought upward in terror, cold and shivering, only to find more ice.

Monkman kept his eyes fixed on the feeble, milky light across the bedroom; stars hedged round by a window-frame. Underneath the ice he had sought for some sign of light, a glimmer to guide him.

Jesus Christ Almighty, maybe one of these nights he will drown and it will be left to Stutz to discover him in the morning, deader than Joe Cunt's dog.

3

He had never had any affection for water. Strange then that his first job should have been building bridges. Not that he had had any choice; his Dad had got him the job. His father had work on a bridge construction crew and got him a place by lying about his age. He was fourteen. It was his father's opinion that children ought not to get accustomed to living off their parents' charity, and that fourteen was just about the proper weaning age. So Alec had been put to work driving a gravel wagon two months after the decisive birthday.

Sitting on the seat of that wagon he had seen his first man killed. He had glanced up and seen the half-breed fall from a trestle, sixty feet down to the river. The breed had looked like a spider dropping on a spinner, arms and legs splayed out and working like crazy. The men said he knocked himself out because of the way he fell, face down and on his belly. It kicked the air out of his lungs and did him in, stole any chance of survival he had. Nobody could reach him out in the river, the race of water was too strong, sweeping him around the bend and out of sight before anyone could move.

They had unhitched Alec's team and he and three others had chased down the river after him on the horses, only catching up when the body hooked on a snag. They found him with the white water tumbling over his shoulders and his long black Indian hair fanned out from his skull, rippling and waving in the current.

He had never forgotten how water swallowed you. Never completely trusted it, even when it was eighteen inches thick and solid. One winter was all he could bring himself to cut ice.

Stutz knew about the dream. He had asked Stutz what he made of it. "It's the arthritis," said Stutz. "It makes you ache in your sleep and you dream the cold."

The dream, or a variation on it, visited Monkman every week or so. Sometimes when he floated upright in the icy water, the life trickling out of him, it wasn't footsteps he heard above him but singing far off in the distance, the faded harmony of childish voices. Other times the ice was absolutely clear, a pane of glass, and he could stare up through it at the sky, the moon, the stars.

No one dream was any easier to bear than another.

He shifted his eyes from the window to the clock. A bit past one o'clock. Not so very late.

Monkman climbed out of bed, pulled on a pair of socks, padded downstairs in his underwear. He could not help himself. He needed the sound of another voice to break the loneliness of the ice. Before he had even prepared his excuse for calling, he had dialled Stutz's number and the phone was ringing. It rang nine times and then Stutz answered.

"Yes, Alec?" Stutz knew who would be the only person phoning at that hour.

Monkman cast desperately around in his mind, scrambling for a plausible reason for disturbing him.

"Yes, Alec?" repeated Stutz patiently.

Monkman seized upon the first thing which offered itself. "You know Vera and her boy are coming tomorrow. Can you pick them up?"

"Is that the bus?"

"Yes, on the STC."

"Morning bus or afternoon bus?"

"Just a minute, I'll check." The old man squinted at the calendar tacked to the wall beside the telephone. He read what he had scrawled over the date, July 2. "Afternoon bus. One o'clock."

"One o'clock it is then," said Stutz.

There was no exasperation or resentment in Stutz's voice that Alec could detect, and for that he was grateful. He cleared his throat and, embarrassed, tried to explain. "I just wanted to clear that up. My memory isn't what it used to be and I kept thinking I'd forget. I didn't want them standing waiting with their luggage. So I just wanted to clear that up. Wouldn't sleep otherwise. Seems I can't sleep with things on my mind anymore. Must be a symptom of old age." He laughed in such a way as to alert Stutz that his reference to old age was not to be taken seriously, was a joke.

"What is it, Alec?" asked Stutz in his calm, deliberate voice. "Is your arthritis worse again? Is that what keeps you from sleeping?"

Monkman glanced at his gnarled hand clutching the receiver. Looking at it made him aware of the pain. "I suppose," he said. "Yes, that could be it."

That settled, Alec Monkman hung up the receiver and considered Vera's return. Thought of how so long ago she walked out on him without so much as a by your leave. Walked out on him, a widower, and her younger brother Earl, leaving the boy without benefit of a woman in the house. All the letters she wrote during the war (all of them addressed to Earl) could not make up for that. And then from 1945 until late 1946 even they stopped coming, didn't start again until she sent her wedding announcement, this time addressed to both of them, although now there was only one of them still at home to read how she had married her Jew down east. It was like Vera to make a big production mentioning that. As if he cared she married a Jew.

So now the silence between them had been broken. Sort of. Twelve years of hit and miss Christmas cards, the occasional photograph of her and the kid. And always tagged on to the end of the scanty, bloodless news the same question, the reason she wrote at all: Do you have Earl's address?

And always he wrote back: No, I believe he's moved again. Kind of a drifter, your brother.

He thinks of her as she was when she left at nineteen. Passionate and headstrong. He can't deny the beauty of these qualities. Her mother had them too.

His Vera with a child of her own. He can scarcely credit it. How old is the boy now? Eleven? Twelve? Daniel is his name. Daniel Miller.

It's typical of Vera to claim that it's only because of the boy she wants to come home. "It is because of Daniel that I ask you to help us. I am afraid the city means trouble for him," she had written. The only letter – *real letter* – he can recall receiving from her in all those years. Signed Vera Miller, which struck him as pretty stiff stuff served up to you by your own daughter.

He had not hesitated to say, Yes, come. After one of his dreams, company in the house would be welcome. He could not go on as he had been these past few months, telephoning to Stutz all hours of the night.

Why now, at the age of seventy-three, should he take to drowning in his bed?

2

O n the last part of Daniel's and Vera's journey, the leg which carried them from Regina to Connaught on a little-used local line, the bus was nearly deserted. There were only four other passengers: an old man with a barricade of soiled shopping bags behind which he lurked; two teenage girls, one fat, one thin, who took turns admiring their reflections in a compact mirror as they practised french-inhaling and blowing smoke rings; and a proper-looking young man in a white shirt and dark blue tie who sported a crew cut.

Vacant seats provided Daniel with an opportunity to escape his mother for the first time in two days and the boy had crossed the aisle to stretch himself out on two of them and nap. Vera remained where he had abandoned her by the window, holding herself absolutely erect, an imperious upward tilt to her chin. In spite of how awful she had felt for the past two and a half days, Vera preserved her aloof posture because she had a theory that people who kept their spines straight didn't get talked at and bothered on buses.

Vera Miller was a tall woman who had never once despaired over her height. Even though she was five feet eleven inches she was not afraid to wear high heels. She took secret satisfaction that her hands were large and powerful-looking. She never wore jewellery and although she was thirty-six and her thick brown hair was showing grey she refused to consider dyeing it. She had good teeth and a bad nose, one with a conspicuous bump on the bridge because she had swung a door open on it when she was six and broken it. Her eyes were a biting, restless blue.

My God, she thought, a fifty-six hour ride from Ontario to Saskatchewan on a Greyhound coach. No sooner the bus pulls out of the depot than my sick headache starts and carries on non-stop two and a half days. Of course, I can't say whether it's the bus keeps my head thumping or the sight of Daniel over there, what he's managed to turn himself into the last ten months. If his father was alive what would he make of all that ridiculous hair? Knowing Stanley, probably just laugh. Duck's ass – there's truth in the name. At least Daniel knows what I think. I didn't spare him. "That's no hair for a twelve year old," I told him. "It makes you look like a pimp angling for a promotion." You try, or say anything to keep them decent. I thought maybe threatening to make him wash the grease out of his hair every night before he went to bed, telling him I wouldn't have my pillowslips ruined, might persuade him to give it up. But he's his mother's son. Stubborn. Chalk that one up to him.

Daniel, Daniel, after all those years holding out, you make me beg for help. The pickle you got yourself into, behaving like that. I swore I'd never do it. I swore I'd never go back to Connaught. I swore I'd never ask the old man for a nickel or a blessing. There's not many people keep a promise they made at nineteen as long as I did. And I'd still be keeping it if you hadn't gone off the rails on me.

I'm not like some people; I'm not good at swallowing my pride. It sticks in my throat. Funny how some people have no notion of pride. Pooch Gardiner, poor old silly bitch, certainly doesn't. When I let it slip Dad had got himself comfortable in his later years she couldn't feature how I hadn't got my snout in the trough. "Fool's pride," Pooch called it. But then Pooch isn't one to look too closely where a dollar comes from. "If your old man has a little money," she said, "why shouldn't he help? You're a widow, aren't you? And Daniel's his grandson, isn't he?"

Which is to miss the point. Asking him for anything is to admit failure, to admit I couldn't make it on my own. But I did make it on my own, for seventeen years. Nobody can take that away from Vera Miller. I buried a husband with a seven-month-old baby in my arms and I supported and raised that baby on my own. Until now.

Vera Miller is pride. That's what I am, pure and simple. Because without pride and hope, how did I ever make it this far? How else did I drudge at all those shitty jobs all those years – chambermaid, practical nurse, checkout girl – without letting myself think I was nothing but those things – chambermaid, practical nurse, check-out girl?

One thing, I never surrendered my dignity. I did my job but you never caught me kissing the boss's ass, or pretending to his face that I was eternally grateful for the big favour of being allowed to work for him.

Checkout girl was the worst. Six months after I'd gone to work at the supermarket I remember Pooch saying to me, "Well, Vera, now you've had a chance to size it up, tell me: What do you hate most about this christly job?" Pooch said it was how her ankles swelled. Said she'd had nice ankles before all the standing, punching the till.

I said, "What I can't stand is that if I were to stay here until I was sixty-five I'd still be a girl. Notice how you always stay a girl? I call the store manager Mr. Anderson and he calls me Vera. That's what gripes me. I ran away from home so I could stop being some-body's girl and I find nothing's changed. I'm still somebody's girl."

Pooch said, "They can call me what they like, so long's they pay for the privilege." That's typical.

Of course, when I broke the news to Pooch where I was moving to, I saw the glint in her eye. She was glad to see me taken down a peg after all of my brave talk. I knew what she was thinking, although for once she was gracious enough not to say it. I have to thank her for that.

Maybe it's hope I need more than pride just now. Because I've got to believe this is right for Daniel, if not for me. Because if I fail Daniel now, I fail his father too, and all that was fine and good and noble in Stanley. All of him that was aimed at higher things.

So I've just got to see it as another sacrifice, taking him home and settling in under Father's roof again. I've sacrificed plenty before, for Daniel. And I did it because I had faith in him, I knew he was every bit as brilliant as his father. I was right, too, knew it when they had me to the school to discuss skipping him. It was because I had given him advantages like the Book of Knowledge. There were compliments, too, on how I had raised such a fine, intelligent boy. "Alone as you are," the principal had said, "it's something to be proud of."

The look on their faces when I refused. They weren't expecting that. But I knew it never does any good to have your head turned by praise. Keep your eyes on the prize. They tried to change my mind. That principal even started to talk more slowly, as if I were too dim-witted to follow what he was saying. "The thing is, Mrs. Miller," I can still hear him say, "is that we find that boys and girls like Daniel – if they aren't continually challenged, why, they lose interest in school, become bored. Their marks may even drop. Now Miss Robinson and I have discussed this matter very thoroughly and we're agreed, as professionals, that it would be best for Daniel to move on to Grade Four at this time."

That kind always knows what's best for you and yours. Even though they've never stood in your down-at-heel shoes to look at the problem. Because all those complicated tests they'd given Daniel had measured everything except what concerned me. His character. Maybe it's unnatural for a mother even to admit thinking it, but that I had doubts about.

It didn't take Mr. Principal too long before he thought he knew why I was hesitating. "Mrs. Miller," he said, "if it's buying a new set of textbooks for Daniel in the middle of the year that's troubling you . . . some arrangement can be worked out through the school. There's no need for you to feel any financial embarrassment." I suppose I've got to give him the benefit of the doubt and grant that he was trying to be nice. Still, it was sort of insulting. They think just because you're poor all you ever think about is money.

Well, I wasn't about to give him my reasons. To suggest maybe Daniel was lazy and soft by nature. It seems to go hand in hand with cleverness. Maybe because everything comes too easy to the clever ones, they never learn any fight. Nine times out of ten it's them who quit on you when the going gets tough. With Daniel I couldn't tell whether he'd collapse on me or not. What if he found the work too hard after he was skipped? Would he give up and fizzle like a bad firecracker?

There was nothing to gain risking it. Not after I'd got him that far, all the way to the top of his class. Because one thing was for sure. I knew a checkout girl's wages weren't going to take Daniel anywhere. That was as sure as Carter's got liver pills. If he was going to go to university the way his father would've wanted, it was up to me to see he got a scholarship. I'm sure I did right to hold him back the way I did.

Pooch said I was crazy to worry about an eight year old getting into university. She didn't know the half of it. I started worrying when he was six. But then Pooch couldn't harbour any hope of that Lyle of hers doing anything to write home about. Unless it was from jail. And as far as Pooch is concerned her responsibility is over once she's cleaned and fed him.

As far as Daniel goes, my job is never over. Come home dog-tired, make supper, do the dishes. Then get him to do the drills. The flash cards I made from old cigarette boxes with the arithmetic problems printed on them in black grease pencil. All done so that learning arithmetic would feel more like a game, more like fun. Shuffle those cards like a real deck of cards, snap one off at him. "16 x 16! Come on, Daniel! You know that! Think!" Start counting. He had five seconds to come up with the answer. Just like a game show on the television.

He had more in his head than all the other six year olds put together. The two of us memorized the capitals of all the provinces and all the states. We did weights and measures. How many quarts to the peck, rods to the mile? We did every president of the United States and every prime minister of Canada. The kings of England. He could spell every word in his speller.

Sure he complained. Whined. They didn't have to learn any of this stupid stuff in school. All I used to say is, "Knowledge is something nobody can take away from you. They can repossess your car but they can't repossess your knowledge." But what used to really gall him was the way I made him learn those poems they gave him for memory work. Perfect to the punctuation. Two of us chanting together. "I sprang to the stirrup comma and Joris comma and he semi-colon new line I galloped comma Dirck galloped comma we galloped all three semi-colon." Full effort for full marks was my attitude. Make the teacher sit up and take notice.

I read him to sleep every night before he learned how to do it for himself. Those were the nice, quiet, peaceful times. I could smell him in his bed, fresh and clean from his bath. Children's classics. That's what the librarian called them. She helped me pick. I had read hardly one of them myself. All we had in Connaught when I was growing up was a few broken books thrown in a cupboard at the back of the schoolroom. I remembered reading *Little Women* as a girl so I took that out from the library first. And *Black Beauty*. The rest I let the librarian choose. *Westward, Ho!*, *The Black Arrow*, *Kidnapped*, *Little House on the Prairie*. I even got to read *Anne of Green Gables* finally.

The bus slowed jerkily, came to a halt at a railway crossing. The driver flung open the door and sat listening for the sounds of an approaching train. Everybody leaned forward in their seats and listened too. There was nothing to hear but the muffled throbbing of the bus engine. The coach stood crouched in the silence of empty distances, unhindered lines of vision. Everything disappeared into the blank horizon. The grid road upon which they sat dwindled away to nothing there. Below the nose of the bus rails burned, hot silver laid on a bed of slag and cinders.

Suddenly out of the stillness, wind. A dust-devil whirled up dirt and grit from the road and scurried it through the open door and into the coach. The young man in the crisp white shirt and tie covered his nose and face with a large handkerchief. The driver slammed the door against the dust-devil and the bus abruptly snarled and thumped its way over the planks of the crossing.

Medical student. That's what he reminds me of with that hanky over his face like a mask. He looks exactly like one of those interns and residents from my days at the hospital, back when I was hustling bed pans and wiping old bums there as a practical. I'd bet dollars to doughnuts he's a medical student. It would explain a dapper young man like him riding a bus. They get paid nothing.

I was sorry to leave the hospital. At least I felt I was doing something good, something worthwhile there. But how could I carry on after the old woman downstairs up and moved out on me to go live with her daughter? Had nobody that would babysit shifts. And you can't leave a kid by himself for eight hours a stretch. Nine, counting trolley time there and back from the hospital. Chambermaiding at the hotel worked out better. I could be home at quarter after six so he was alone only a couple of hours after he finished school. Of course, it wasn't much of a life for him, being made to go straight home and lock himself in the apartment. He hated me phoning on my coffee breaks every afternoon around four to check up on him. But he also knew that he'd better be there to answer when I called. Every time he let it ring more than twice I was in a sweat. Saw him dead under the wheels of a truck, or riding off in a sex fiend's car.

Maybe I was too hard on him, not allowing him to have other kids in for company. Could be I was wrong to be so strict on that count. But you never know what the little buggers'll get into when somebody isn't watching them. And two or more are always more naturally inclined to mischief than one. They encourage each other. Playing with matches, poking wire coat-hangers into electrical sockets. Imagine coming home to face the outcome of that.

I did what I had to. No excuses. It wasn't easy for him but easy is for those who have choices. I don't see as I did. Latchkey kids is what they call them. All the women's magazines deplore it.

You never know what's going on in a kid's head. The whole winter of his first year in school he spent drawing maps when he was alone by himself after school. Back at six-fifteen every night and having to bang the bejesus out of the door to get him to come unfasten the chain and let me in. Every evening the same. Like he was in a trance.

"Hi, Mom" was all I got. Needed to be reminded to give me my kiss. He was more interested in getting back to the kitchen table and his maps than saying hello to me. At first I thought it was homework. But it wasn't. These weren't maps of actual places like we did when I was in school. No tracing the U.K. from an atlas, marking places and products on it. Sheffield and steel, York and wool. No, these islands came directly out of his head. They were invented islands.

I give him credit for a beautiful, artistic job. You'd half-wish they were real so you could pay them a visit. Always snaky rivers twisting down from mountains to the seas, maybe a volcano puffing smoke, golden beaches. A vacation paradise.

Every bay, cove, river, stream, mountain, inlet, peninsula he gave a name to. Fish River, Parrot Point, Treasure Cove. The seas were always wild and stormy. He bore down so hard with that blue crayon of his he left ridges of wax on the paper, like real waves crashing towards the beaches.

It's time to eat and he hasn't cleared away his junk, just sits hunched over his map, colouring. Hasn't set the table like you've asked him to a dozen times. Flipping the light switch on and off to get his attention, even though pretty soon the light seems to be blinking in time with that little vein pulsing in your temple. "Mother attempting to make contact with space voyager. Mother to Master Daniel. Come in, Master Daniel."

Stares at me like I'm out of my mind. They have no sense of humour, kids. Not mine anyway.

If you didn't laugh, you'd weep. Thank God I've got a sense of humour. Of course, I was blessed with the kind that mostly gets you into trouble. Every so often getting dressed down by the store manager for giving lip to a customer. "Vera, if you don't learn to curb your tongue I don't care how fast you can punch those buttons, you'll have to go," is what he used to say.

Pooch offering advice. "Do what I do, Vera, just think what you'd like to tell them. That's what I do." Which was okay for Pooch because she couldn't work up a suitable smart reply in under an hour and by then they were home and had the groceries unpacked and in the cupboard. But, speaking for myself, remarks slipped out before I realized it. Part of my trouble all my life, a vinegar tongue.

People misunderstand. Take the first time I saw Daniel. The nurse showing him to me and saying, "Oh, isn't he the most darling, beautiful boy!"

Hardly. They're never beautiful right after they're born. Ugly as sin. I mean, what if Royal Doulton was to make a china figurine of them, all red and gruesome like that? They couldn't sell it. Not if it was true to nature. I never put it like that to the nurse though. What I said was the baby resembled Mr. Gandhi.

She was shocked and offended, that young woman. Shocked and offended for all of motherhood, I believe. Probably thought I was unnatural, unloving. But, as I said, it's either laugh or weep. At the moment the sight of that tiny struggling thing with its bruised-looking skull and smear of hair had turned loose a rush of love all hot and thick at the back of my throat, so hot and thick it was threatening to melt me into tears if I didn't do something to stop it quick. Which is how I arrived at Mr. Gandhi.

Nobody could accuse me of loving him too little, more likely the opposite. Had to be careful after Stanley died that I didn't make too much of Daniel. How many nights spent hovering over his crib while he slept? Just standing there in the dark in my nightgown, feet two blocks of ice on the floor. A terrible ache in my shoulders from gripping the bars of his crib so tightly, gripping them because if I left my hands free I wouldn't be able to trust them not to go fussing with him, picking him up, touching him.

Past one o'clock, past two o'clock, past three o'clock. Waiting for him to cry. Or just whimper so I could snatch him up and hold him. All hunger for the smell of him, for the burrowing warmth of him, for the kick and jerk and jump of life in his limbs.

Love. It's not fair that Daniel has been cheated out of his father's love. He never even knew him. I want him to love his father. But how could he love what isn't even a memory? All he's got is my stories to build love on.

"Daniel, when you were very small and your Dad and I went out he was always worried you'd catch cold. So I'd have to bundle you in every blanket we owned just to keep him quiet. Blanket after blanket after blanket. When I was done, nobody could have guessed there was a baby at the centre. I asked him, 'Satisfied?' Up went his hand to stop me and he disappeared. In a minute he was back with an old overcoat of his. 'There's a nasty wind,' he said. 'Maybe if you put him in this?' And you know what? You almost fit. Wrapped in all those blankets, at four months old you were almost a size forty. My size-forty baby, I called you."

I tell him in what respects he's like his father. I encourage him to set his sights high. "Your father may have run a men's wear store but he had read more books than most university professors. You've got his brains and his brains were not third-class brains, not even second-class brains. They were the top-drawer variety. So see what you can do with them."

Not much in the past ten months. His final report card had a D, 5 C's, 2 B's, an A. But that's not the worst. Having him brought home in a patrol car took the cake. Suspected of smashing headlights on parked cars, although they couldn't prove it. Finding the stuff hidden in our storage bin in the basement of the building, stuff he hadn't the money to buy. Pocketbooks, a hunting knife, batteries, gloves, aftershave. I knew it was stolen. Why this crap? What use to him was it, aside from the pocketbooks and maybe the knife? Boys always want to own a knife. But batteries? Gloves? Aftershave?

You can't tolerate a thief, nor a liar. No, none of it was his. He was keeping it for a friend. He lied to my face, a barefaced lie.

What friend? Who? Lyle Gardiner?

No, not Lyle. Lost where he was going for a second. Tom. Tom Perkins.

Liar. Sneaky little bastard. No such person.

I acted mad, played mad, although I was really cold with fear. Once they start going to ruin on you, who's to predict where it'll come to an end? Police at twelve. What's next? Especially in a city, with so many invitations and opportunities to do wrong. Get him away, was all I could think.

Connaught was what I thought, thought it because I had no other place to think. The old man assuring me he'll find me a job, find us a place to live, everything will be set, no worries. And in a small town you can keep better track of a kid, watch him.

There's no denying this isn't what we called damage control in the Army. Extinguish the fire. Man the pumps. Damage control stinks of defeat. I'm not a salvager by nature. Unless you've let things go wrong, there's no need for salvage. And I'd no business letting things go wrong.

There's a world of difference between the going back home and the leaving. The leaving was a kid's run headlong down a steep hill. Legs going faster and faster, flopping looser and crazier in your hips and you not heeding because it's not your legs, or even your windmilling arms you trust for balance. It's the freedom and wildness, the scream of delight, the risk of it, the I don't give a shit for skinned knees of it, which keeps you from falling and harm.

The going home is nothing but a long hard climb up a hill to no surprises, to I told you so, to him and his boring little town. But that I can take, and gladly, if it puts Daniel straight again.

Vera consulted her watch. In an hour they would be arriving in Connaught. Now, so close to her birthplace, she searched the landscape for anything familiar, anything she recognized. Barbed wire fences strung on peeled poplar poles, summerfallow fields stained white with alkali where the sloughs had already dried despite it being only early July, all went by. The grain crops were stunted. On the rises where hot winds first draw the ground moisture, the wheat was faintly streaked with yellow and even shorter in the stalk than elsewhere. The heat pressing down out of the cloudless sky had ironed all movement from the fields, not a breath of wind wrinkled the crops. There was only an illusion of movement where, in the distance, the farmhouse, a granary, a shelter belt wobbled in the distortions wreaked by the burning air.

That junk in storage could easily have belonged to Pooch's Lyle, she thought. Right off the bat I knew that one was no good. If circumstances had been different I'd have forbidden Daniel from having anything to do with him. But what with Pooch working with me and the two of us living in the same building I didn't have the guts to say I didn't want her boy associating with mine. Especially since Pooch helped me get my suite in the building by putting in a word with the super.

Yet there's no denying Lyle Gardiner is a little weasel and the worst case of smart-too-soon I've every encountered. Of course, Pooch is responsible for that. No respect for herself when it comes to men. Never even makes a pretence of hiding from Lyle what she's up to. She laughed when she told me that Lyle charges her retired fireman boyfriend fifty cents for every hour he keeps away from the apartment when the fireman drops in to put the fire out. Discusses everything in front of the kid, even her period. I'd sooner hang myself in a closet than let Daniel in on any of that. Lonely single women shouldn't talk personal things over with their sons as if they were husbands. Pooch does. That's what's made Lyle so unnaturally old. A creepy, smirky fourteen year old going on forty-five. Used to stare at my tits when he talked to me. Didn't look me in the face, just stared point-blank at my tits. Called me Vera, instead of Mrs. Miller.

I can just imagine the stories that Lyle filled Daniel's head with. Stories of what men and women get up to together. Sickening ones is my guess.

Daniel's never seen any of that. With the exception of Stanley, I haven't had much luck with men in my life. Still, with the way Daniel's been carrying on lately I've got to wonder if this Male Influence business I read about in all the women's magazines isn't a factor. Could be reading those articles in *Redbook* and *McCall's* and *Chatelaine* and *Good Housekeeping* is like eating candy that makes you feel sick, but I can't help it. All those psychologists writing on the break-up of the family, divorce and what-not, keep emphasizing a boy needs a strong Male Influence in his life to ensure healthy, normal development. There's times I believe it and times I don't. Lately, mostly I do. They say it needn't be his natural father. All he needs is an older man to look up to. Could be an uncle, a family friend, an older brother.

Not having one of those kicking around the place is another reason I suppose for going back to Connaught. I don't mean Dad. He couldn't be trusted to raise a cat. Look how he terrorized the life out of poor Earl with his shenanigans. I wonder about this Mr. Stutz. During the war Earl thought a lot of him; I could read it between the lines in the letters he wrote me. Brother seemed to worship the very ground this Mr. Stutz walked on. So he must be something special because Earl wasn't one to take to people. Too shy and too timid. I think Earl was afraid of most people. What was it once that Mother said to me about Earl? That he ought to have been born a girl so he could marry and be taken care of for the rest of his life. He was an odd duck, Earl. Which makes me think that if Mr. Stutz could make a favourable impression on a wary one like him, it's possible he could be a Male Influence for Daniel.

Daniel was waking. He yawned, scrubbed his face with his hands, rolled his shoulders. He was a slim, fine-boned boy with the promise of extraordinary height if the rest of him caught up with a pair of long, skinny legs. His narrow, foxy face appeared slightly sullen despite being sprinkled with cinnamon freckles. Or maybe it was his hair that suggested sullenness; a twelve year old patterned on James Dean. He combed it now, using the window as a mirror, raking it with a rat-tail comb until every tooth mark stood out in his thick, lank reddish hair darkened with Brylcreem to the colour of an oily old penny. When he had finished, he stuffed his hands in his pockets, lowered his neck into the collar of his jacket, planted the soles of his shoes on the chair back in front of him, and jiggled his legs so fiercely that his trousers shimmied up his calves, revealing his sagging white socks. Not once during all this did he allow his mother to catch his eye.

Look at him sitting sassy. Trying so hard, so soon to get old. Now everything's an occasion for him to try and put distance between us. Even his socks, that jacket. The jacket's casual but decent – not cheap either. But if I like a thing, he won't.

"I'm not wearing a golf jacket," was what he said. "Have I ever seen a golf course? Who do you think I am? Arnold Palmer?"

I tuned him in on what he should and shouldn't wear but that doesn't mean I won. He's got the jacket on, but look at it. Cuffs turned back to the elbows and collar turned up to the ears. To provoke me.

"You explain to me the percentage in looking like a hoodlum," was what I said to him.

To think his father had operated a men's wear store; wore a suit and tie every working day of his life. Put a briefcase in his hand, walking down the street he could've been mistaken for a lawyer. I told Daniel, "People draw conclusions about you according to how you dress."

Looking at him you've got to conclude he's another Lyle Gardiner. The sort of brat who lives with his mother in a one-bedroom apartment and sleeps on a fold-out in the living room with his socks and underwear lying on the floor. A kid who thrives on wieners and canned pork and beans, who drinks Coke with his breakfast toast, who reads nothing but comic books and falls asleep in front of the television watching the late movie on a school night. That's what my kid looks like.

And how to make sure that he becomes the other? Like that medical student up front with his short hair, clean shirt, tie, purpose in life? Appearances do matter. From the look of him the medical student is the only person on this bus I'd risk a pleasantry on. With a young man of that type you could have a sensible, intelligent conversation. That's because people like him are taught reserve and tact and courtesy in their homes from knee-high on up. Not like the majority of people on a bus who no sooner drop in a seat beside you than they light into a description of their latest bladder repair operation, or some equally gruesome and edifying topic. It causes my head to hammer all the harder just to think about it.

Exactly the kind of people Pooch and Lyle are. And when I'm at my worst, I don't deny it, people like me. The difference being I know better and Pooch doesn't. As I told Daniel a thousand times, "We may have to live with these people but we don't have to act like them." Although I have difficulty remembering that, what with a bad mouth, swearing and all. An Army habit that's hard to break.

But as I said to Daniel, "Me, I'm a lost cause. It isn't me we're preparing to succeed. It's you. So as the old saying goes, 'Don't do as I do. Do as I say.'"

When I look at him over there I've got to trust it'll all come right. It has to, with so much of Stanley in him. Not just the intelligence either, but the rest too. That funny shade of strawberry red hair; the tall man's stoop to his shoulders even though he isn't tall yet. The spitting, walking, talking image of his old man.

Other people, Pooch for one, can say he takes after me, but I don't see it. Unless it's the eyes, which are blue like mine, only brighter. Set against that pale skin they shine like all get out. When he was small I'd call them his stars. "The stars are out and shining," is what I'd say when he woke up from his nap, just like he has now. I wonder what his reaction would be if I tried that on him again? Say it good and loud so everyone on the bus can hear.

They come out and shine at what they oughtn't to come out and shine at, those eyes. By Christ, that was the straw that broke the camel's back when I stumbled on that peekaboo. Sunday, I was cleaning the apartment. No rest for the wicked. Of course, as soon as I got ready to wash and wax the floors who turns up like a bad penny but Lyle Gardiner? Nothing for it but to send both boys upstairs to watch television at Pooch's until I got my floors done. Let Pooch entertain them and then when I was finished we could send them downstairs to amuse themselves at my place and Pooch and me could have fifteen minutes of peace to put our feet up and have a coffee. Or a coffee and a bit, as Pooch puts it. The bit being liqueur. Courtesy of Pooch's boyfriends. So she was well-supplied and most Sundays got into her stock. I never took more than a sprinkle of Tia Maria in my instant to make it drinkable, but some Sunday afternoons didn't Pooch get awful carefree drinking coffee?

I did my final buff and was off. Knocked on the door but the television was roaring so loud you couldn't have heard cannons fired off in the hallway. So I walked in. It's not often you get treated to a scene like that, Pooch in her easy-chair, still in a housecoat in the middle of the afternoon, both of her big yellow feet resting on a hassock spread with newspapers and her three sheets to the wind. Giggling and holding a glass of liqueur with her pinky out. I suppose she thought the extended pinky made her look gracious and was the accepted way to sip Drambuie out of a Melmac mug that had been the bonus offer in a box of dish soap.

"Don't tickle! Don't tickle!" I can hear her crying it now in her phoney girlish voice.

The two boys on their knees around the hassock, snorting with laughter, painting Pooch's toenails. Each with his tiny brush. Daniel doing the left foot in pink; Lyle the right in red. And Pooch so far gone she had no idea that with her legs drawn up like that on the hassock the boys could see clear up her housecoat. And her without panties on.

"Don't tickle! Don't tickle!" It was enough to make your stomach turn. I'd never have believed it of Daniel, scooting a peek. I could hardly believe it of Lyle, who a moment before I'd have said couldn't have fallen any lower in my estimation and now had. What boy with a shred of decency in him would laugh and think it funny to have his friend look at that?

"What do they think of us?" I caught myself saying aloud. "It can't be this, can it?"

I better leave all that now. Dragging it up only makes my head hurt worse. Two aspirins every two hours for two days and not a bit of improvement. I swear these temples of mine are a pair of blacksmith's anvils.

Here comes the medical student up the aisle. Even doctors have to pee, although they never look it. No harm in a friendly smile to establish there's another human on this godforsaken contraption.

The young man returned Vera's smile. He even hesitated by her seat. He looked as if he wished to begin a conversation but didn't dare.

Now that's a nice smile. Not brassy. A nice smile like that comes from taking proper care of your teeth. But he's shy. You can tell that.

"Buses. What a way to fly," Vera said.

The young man kept smiling, picked at his tie clasp with the nail of his index finger. "You don't like buses?" he asked diffidently.

"Do I look like I'd like buses?"

He did not reply. Only stood swaying in the aisle, watching her.

Vera waited for him to speak. When he didn't, she finally inquired, "Going far?"

"Oh, not very."

Another moment of silent awkwardness. "Well, I won't keep you," said Vera, a little disappointed. "Have a nice trip."

"Thank you. You, too."

Yet on the way back from his visit to the toilet the young man paused by her seat. He had steeled himself to speak. "Ma'am," he began hesitantly. "Ma'am, I couldn't help noticing when you spoke . . . well, I thought maybe you had a problem. I think I have something that might help."

"Why yes," said Vera, surprised, "as a matter of fact I do. I have this terrible . . ." But already the young man was gone, headed back to his seat.

Imagine him spotting that. That I had a headache. Of course, they're trained to spot symptoms. Now he's off to get some new painkiller out of his bag, a sample probably. The drug company salesmen are always pushing samples on them.

He was back and clearly excited now, shyness evaporated. "I knew it. I had a feeling. I could tell." He thrust something at Vera. A pamphlet. She took it. Stared at a bold type headline. TIRED? SICK? BROKE? JESUS IS THE ONE FAIL-PROOF REMEDY.

"You know," said the young man eagerly, "I never thought the Lord would make use of me to proclaim Him so soon, this being my first field mission. But, ma'am, if you would allow me to sit beside you and if you would join me in an earnest prayer of appeal,

I know your burden would be relieved. Would you do that now, ma'am? Would you join me?"

Suddenly Daniel was at his elbow. "Hey, you," he said, jostling the young man rudely to one side, "this is my mother and my seat. I'd like to sit down if you don't mind."

3

———◆———

Alec Monkman sat at his kitchen table wearing a straw fedora with a striped hatband of grey and burgundy. The hat was clean and neat and obviously new; he had purchased it in honour of Vera's coming a week before at Kleimer's Men's Wear, one of the stores he didn't own. Strangers might have assumed that Monkman didn't own it because of its name – Kleimer's – but they did not know that names did not signify much in Connaught. When Monkman had bought a business he had never bothered to change its name. His garage, of which he had been proprietor for fourteen years, was still Collier's Auto; his hotel was still known as Simpson's Hotel. Whatever vanity he possessed did not assert itself in a wish to see his name painted on a sign board, or even more luxuriantly spelled out in gaudy neon light. Alec Monkman seemed immune to the desire to commemorate his success. The house he lived in, shabby and cramped, with long hair-like fractures creeping and fingering their way across the plaster walls of all the rooms, was the same house his daughter Vera had walked away from seventeen years before and today was returning to. It was just as it had been then, with this exception. Two years before, the room off the kitchen that had always been the baby's room, the place where they had put the youngest child's cot because it was warm there near the old, black, nickel-plated stove, had been turned into an indoor bathroom.

He wondered what Vera would think of that. Perhaps it was an odd thing to wonder, since he had not seen his daughter in seventeen years, or ever seen the grandson she was bringing home with her. But he was an old man now, seventy-three, and of all the alterations in his circumstances and surroundings he had made in nearly twenty years, it was the most recent he was likely to recall and seize upon. There had been a misunderstanding with the plumber and he had come home to find himself the owner of a pink toilet. He had let it pass. He had even found it funny, laughed about it with Mr. Stutz, inviting him to step in and try on the new facility for size. Now he was worried Vera might think him gone foolish in the head with a pink toilet.

Mr. Stutz was at the STC stop at present, waiting for Vera's bus. He could imagine Stutz, slow, solid, patient under the tin sign emblazoned with a bounding antelope which was the symbol of the bus company. The sign was fastened to the wall of his, Alec Monkman's, hotel. In the last year he had earned the government contract to peddle bus tickets and sell coffee and sandwiches to travellers. Won it, he supposed, on the strength of clean washrooms. He had Mr. Stutz to thank for that, the cleanliness of the public washrooms in his hotel.

Well, they were both waiting, he and Mr. Stutz. Mr. Stutz there and he in his kitchen. He had resolved not to go to them, but instead have them brought to him. He was making a point. It might be a good idea, too, if he wasn't discovered in the kitchen hovering by the window when they were brought to the door, but in his bedroom, so relaxed and easy that it was possible for him to snooze minutes before their arrival. Showing eagerness over her return would not be wise. If Vera ever felt she had the upper hand she would not hesitate to use it. He'd seen her operate before.

So for the time being he sat by the window in a many times

painted captain's chair whose every scratch and chip, depending on the depth of the wound, revealed a different layer of colour, green or yellow or blue, which, like the rings of a tree, offered testimony to the chair's age. He was occupying himself with solitaire, laying out the cards on a welter of overlapping coffee rings and a scattering of toast crumbs, playing every one with an old man's maddening deliberation, each card held poised and quivering in sympathy with the slight current of tremor in his hands, his lips pursed judiciously and his attention divided between the game and the dirt street that ran past his house.

It was July and early afternoon. Already the sun had driven lawyer McDougal's spaniel underneath his master's caragana hedge, a hedge badly in need of a trimming. The sight of the caraganas stretching up to touch the eaves of the lawyer's house, ragged and wild and infested with sparrows, always irritated Monkman. Several weeks before, when he had met McDougal on the steps of the post office, he had said, "You ever get it in mind to cut that hedge of yours, Bob, you'll have to get the loan of the fire brigade ladder truck." McDougal hadn't liked that. But then McDougal wasn't obliged to. No more than he, Monkman, had to like that flock of shitting sparrows which roosted there and crossed over from McDougal's property to settle in his garden every afternoon and peck among his vegetables.

He stared at the dog lying there in the shade. His eyes were still sharp, no trouble there, thank God. From clear across the street he could make out the slight flutter of the spaniel's flanks as it panted in the heat. Nothing else moved. The dusty leaves of the wilting elm in Monkman's front yard hung limp and still, white in the hard glare of the sun.

There was no doubt that the day would be a scorcher. The garden would need water by tomorrow. He would have to take the truck and tank out to the creek, fire up the five horsepower Briggs & Stratton gas engine he had left there and pump another tank of water. Lately he had been having trouble getting the engine to catch; his arthritis made it difficult to grip the toggle and he was no longer able to put the kick in a pull-cord he once could. Just another one of the annoyances that came with growing old, but one it was impossible to avoid without resigning himself to the death of his garden. The extended dry spell had led the town council to ration water and those who wanted more than their allotment had to find it themselves.

Monkman was not sure how a garden had come to be so important to him, more important even than his businesses. His businesses he scarcely paid heed to anymore. He was content to let Mr. Stutz oversee his interests and keep an eye on the help. The books and taxes he left to Cooper the accountant. But the garden was different. Perhaps it was experience teaching him, teaching the man who had embarked on a new career late in life and out of despair, that there was more challenge to keeping life in cabbages and onions than in keeping it in a movie theatre or hardware store. Over the years he had learned that in a small place like Connaught it was hard to go badly wrong in business. Because if it had been easy, he would have been finished long ago. No, all that was necessary was to see that the roots of an enterprise were firmly set. That done, in the absence of any real competition it could hardly fail to survive. Maybe not flourish, none of his businesses had really flourished, but they had all survived and that was enough for him. Unlike a plant, a shop or store needed no strong encouragement to live; once established it took a fool or act of God to kill it. But gardens he had found were a different matter. A man had to breathe some of his own life into a garden. A garden knew no other aid or kindness in this hard place of shattering hail and scorching heat, uprooting wind and early killing frost, except that which a man could offer.

When his wife was alive the garden had been no business of his. Monkman had spent no time in it beyond digging the potatoes in the fall if the ground was heavy and wet. Martha had kept a garden so she could eat her own canned vegetables during the long winter, all put up to her taste. She had always complained there was no flavour in anything bought in a store.

For years and years now there had been nobody to preserve the carrots and beets and peas and beans. Alec Monkman ate what he could fresh and gave the rest to his customers and neighbours. (He had begun this practice years before, keeping ten-pound sacks of potatoes heaped beside the gas pumps at his garage so that people were free to help themselves.) Although at first this oddity of his was remarked upon, with time the town's folk became accustomed to the sight of a mound of orange pumpkins in the lobby of his theatre, the boxes of carrots and onions and ripe tomatoes stacked by the front desk of his hotel. All of it was there for the taking. Monkman made no distinction between those too old or too ill to tend to their own plots and those too shiftless to bother to. All he wished was to be relieved of an old man's embarrassing and prodigal surplus.

There had never been a surplus when Martha was alive. Of course, there had been the children too, more mouths to feed. Everything had gone into jars, she had been a demon among the steaming pots, ladling and scalding and sealing with hot wax. God knew that thirty years later there was likely still dusty stores of canned fruit and vegetables in the cellar because after her death he had not been able to bring himself to go down there and clear the shelves. It was more than he could do to set a foot on those stairs. For months his heart had hurt him at the thought, closed up on him like a fist. So he and Earl and Vera had eaten out of tins.

He thought of how she had lain all crooked at the bottom of those stairs. The naked bulb swinging to and fro at the end of the cord nailed to the beam overhead had made light and shadow play across her body in such a way that he had been tricked into thinking she was moving there on the floor. But that was all there was to that, a trick of the light.

Now, as whenever he caught himself thinking of his dead wife Martha, Alec Monkman gave a start and his hand sprang up to his head. It encountered a hat. The hat was there. He pulled it off and swore. "Goddamn it to hell!" He was angry. What was he doing, wearing a hat in the house again, after all those years? What was happening to him?

He sat staring at the hat, his large hands holding it delicately by its brim as if he were balancing a plate of raw eggs in the shell, intent on keeping them from rolling off the edge and smashing at his feet. Monkman sat like this for some time, lost in reverie, then suddenly, with a disgruntled gesture, he dropped the hat on the table.

His fine white hair, thick for a man his age, had been disturbed when he had jerked off his hat in disgust. It stood ruffled up around the crown of his head, making him look like a caricature of shock. He was not shocked, only tired. Fatigue confused him. He scratched one bristling eyebrow and then the other with the thick nail of a forefinger; then pinched the long, fleshy blade of his nose between his two thumbs, a characteristic mannerism whenever he was perplexed. His large, clumsy body, shaped by years of hard labour and finally corseted in the fat of subsequent indolence, sprawled a little more in his chair, an elbow carelessly disarranging the cards laid out for solitaire. He had forgotten about the game.

His wife had stormed against his habit of wearing a hat in the house. He had seen nothing wrong in it, having trouble remembering what his own father had looked like without a hat. When his father had been in his seventies he had taken a picture of him standing in Round Lake, water up to his armpits, a cigarette in his mouth and one of those salt and pepper tweed caps on his head. That was what the old boy called going for a swim.

But Martha had seen hats worn in the house as the height of ignorance, boorishness beyond belief. "Where were you born? In a barn?" she would ask sardonically when he neglected to remove his. It developed into a test of wills. Her will, her opinion, had remained unshakable right up until the day nearly twenty years ago when she toppled backwards down the cellar stairs with a clutch of canned preserves pressed to her breast, falling dead of a stroke amid the crash of breaking Mason jars. The shock of that had come close to entirely undoing Alec Monkman. Martha was only forty-four. Women of that age did not keel over dead of strokes. Where was the sense in such a thing?

He gave up wearing hats in the house. It was the surrender of a long, stubborn resistance. There was not a time that his children could not remember him eating his dinner in a sweat-stained fedora tipped back on his head, or listening to his favourite radio program in a cap pulled down over his left eye. After her death they saw him sit bareheaded by a silent radio, the ribbon of untanned skin beneath his hairline which had always been hidden by his hats exposed on his forehead like the brand of the biblical outcast. And for twenty years after Martha's funeral he had never entered the house without at once removing his hat and hanging it on the hook by the door.

But recently, as if by magic, he was finding hats appear on his head. He did not know how it happened. Coming up his street, as far away from home as Kruger's yard, he began to mumble to himself as he ran his fingers lightly over the fleur-de-lis topping Kruger's iron fence, calling himself to attention, reminding himself to hang his fedora on the hook by the door. People who saw his moving lips assumed he was having a chat or argument with himself, as lonely old men do. He was really chanting, over and over again, "Hat on the hook. Hat on the hook. Hat on the hook." Monkman had no idea what went wrong. An hour after going indoors he would pass a mirror, or reach up to scratch an itch lurking in his widow's peak and discover – a hat! He struggled to puzzle out an explanation. Could it be that he had intended to go out, put on his hat, and then, distracted by a ringing phone, the crying of the cat to be fed, lost track of his original intention, only to wander his house in a hat? Or had he, despite his precautions, despite his chant, simply not remembered to take it off? Was that possible? It was strange. Often he could recall in vivid detail the hat swaying slightly from side to side on the hook before coming to rest. He could see it all, plain as his hand held before his face. Then a doubt. Was that today, or yesterday? Maybe it was yesterday he had watched the gentle rocking of the hat on the hook. He could not be sure.

Sitting in the hot sun which poured upon him through a dusty pane spotted with the marks of a rain stillborn a week ago, he told himself: Vera is coming today and I have a pink toilet and wear my hat in the house. He understood how he had been saddled with the toilet but the hat he was not certain about.

Years ago Monkman had heard someone say – a minister maybe, although he wondered how, since he didn't attend church, although it could have been at a funeral, or an occasion that demanded an address at the school – that man's thoughts of the past are largely made up of regret and his thoughts of the future largely of fear. It was one of the few true things he had ever heard a preacher say and he had chosen to remember it. In the past few months he had taken to reminding himself that with so little future left to him, surely he had less to fear, more to regret.

He sensed that the business with the hat was linked to the fact that recently Martha was often in his thoughts and those thoughts were sweet. Something or someone was trying to speak to him. He was certain of it. Did they both want the past? Alec his Martha and Martha her Alec in a hat?

Considering that, it slipped his mind who he was really waiting for that hot July day.

4

———◆———

Mr. Stutz, weighted down with luggage, led Vera and Daniel into his employer's house. He did not trouble to knock. After fifteen years together both he and Alec Monkman walked in and out of one another's houses with the same freedom as they poked their noses into one another's lives. If they had been encumbered with women this could never have happened; a woman's sense of privacy would have been outraged, there would have been a stop to it. But as someone in Connaught once said, neither Stutz nor Monkman needed a wife. They had a marriage of sorts already. Sometimes this surely seemed so. Their squabbles shared characteristics with those of long-established couples. They hinted at a rich background of past grievance, were conducted with fearsome tenacity, yet managed to avoid topics that would make for a permanent rupture. Mr. Stutz no longer invited Monkman to attend church and Monkman no longer badgered Mr. Stutz to join him in a drink.

Stutz was surprised to find the kitchen empty. Where was Alec? He thumped down the suitcases he carried and Daniel unslung a duffel bag from his shoulder. "Alec?" Stutz inquired, walking to the entrance of the living room, Vera trailing behind. His ruddy face was moistly shining as if it had been rubbed with butter, which was the way it always looked in hot weather. Summer was a trial for Mr. Stutz. A big man in the midst of a fleshy middle-age, he panted through June, July, and August, the sun bleaching his blond eyebrows fairer and fairer and burning his face redder and redder until when Labour Day rolled round he was all scarlet and white.

"I expect he's upstairs napping," he said, peering into the curtained living room. "He doesn't seem to get much sleep nights lately." Vera did not respond to this remark. She did not respond because she had not heard it. Mr. Stutz, realizing his information had gone unabsorbed, turned back into the kitchen and left her staring into the dim room, standing with her pelvis tilted forward so that the cardboard box she held was supported on the points of her hip bones. For two days this box had never been out of her sight. Over the objections of the bus driver she had insisted it ride in an overhead rack where she could keep an eye on it and be sure it wasn't lost. In it were birth certificates, a cancelled insurance policy, old bank passbooks, her Army discharge papers, two hundred dollars' worth of Canada Savings Bonds, and six school exercise-books in which her husband had kept a diary. These were, as she had said to the driver, important documents that had to be watched.

Now, however, the documents were unwatched and forgotten, jostled out of her mind by two murky brown reproductions of nineteenth-century book illustrations across the way, on the wall. They struck her a disturbing blow. Vera knew with absolute certainty that they were hung in exactly the same positions as that day seventeen years ago when she turned her back on them and left her father's house. Today she faced them again. The long-horned, shaggy-coated Highland cattle still drank deeply from a burn, misty mountains rising behind them in a romantic backdrop. An expressive-eyed, cupid-lipped, cloudy-haired Lorna Doone still simpered. Everything was so familiar, it was as if the intervening years had suddenly been dismissed. This dismissal made Vera feel cheated and angry. She had not lived through so much hardship to find herself back where she had begun, back in 1942, furious with her father. He had always claimed to hate those pictures which her mother had admired for "being tastefully understated." He had described them as dark and gloomy. So why hadn't he taken them down, changed them? Changed *something* in all these years?

Vera set down the cardboard box and stepped into the living room. The old fake candelabra with its flame-shaped electrical bulbs still dangled from the ceiling. The sofa with the carved cat's paw feet still stood where she had left it, although now it was spread with a blanket to hide worn upholstery. Even her mother's Singer sewing machine was where it always had been, in the bay window for the user to get the benefit of sunlight. Except now the sewing machine was folded down into its cabinet and a litter of torn envelopes and bills on the cabinet top suggested her father was using it as a desk. Nothing new in the entire room, aside from a television in the corner. She was back in the past. All of it more or less the same, except maybe for the smell. That was different. A bachelor smell of sour potatoes, dirty socks, stale cigarette smoke. A heavy, brooding stuffiness that made Vera think of windows painted shut, impossible to pry open.

Vera sensed someone had entered the room. She turned around to see Mr. Stutz standing a few feet off, hands clasped over his belly, looking as if he were hers to command. Once again, as she had when he met them at the bus stop, Vera found herself speculating which was Mr. Stutz's famous glass eye, the one which Earl had written her about so often during the war. The left, she decided. Despite the gloom of drawn drapes, Vera believed she had detected an unnatural glint of light in it.

"It smells in here," she said abruptly. "What kind of cleaning lady has he got himself?"

"Not a very good one," replied Stutz, a slow smile breaking on his face. "I guess I'm what you'd call his cleaning lady."

"You?"

"Well, not regular," he explained. "Just when things get a bit out of hand. The old fellow doesn't mind cooking for himself but he's not much of a one for the cleaning up. When it gets bad I'll wash the dishes, maybe run the vacuum back and forth, do his laundry. Thing is, these old people got a tendency to be awfully untidy."

"You shouldn't be doing that," said Vera firmly. "You ought to have told him to clean up his own mess or else hire somebody to do it for him."

"He's had some of those," said Stutz, "but they always got into trouble with him for moving things. The old gentleman is particular on that point. He likes things to stay where he left them. I generally just clean around his stuff. He prefers that."

"Whatever his nibs prefers. I see that hasn't changed either. He still expects things to be organized to suit him and only him."

"There's some old dogs I wouldn't go trying to learn new tricks," said Stutz. Vera wasn't sure how to take this. As warning, advice, or reproof.

"I'm not a dog trainer, Mr. Stutz. Never had any desire to be."

"I just came to ask if you wanted him called," said Stutz evenly.

"I suppose he ought to know we're here."

The two of them returned to the kitchen, Mr. Stutz brushing past Daniel who leaned against the kitchen sink, turning the hot water faucet on and off, alerting the adults he was bored. "That's not doing the washer any good," Stutz said to him as he pulled open the door to a narrow staircase. He poked his head up it and shouted, "Hey, Alec! Your company's here! Get up!" When he got no immediate answer he pounded on the wall of the stairway with his fist, making it boom hollowly. "Hey, Alec! Get up!"

"What?" The voice was muffled, distant.

"Get up," repeated Mr. Stutz. "Your company's come."

They heard coughing, a shoe dropped on the floor. Several minutes passed and then the stairs began to creak as Alec Monkman started his heavy-footed descent. Listening to his slow, deliberate progress Vera found her heart beating quickly. Her mother had described her father in his youth as a wonderful dancer, amazingly agile and light on his feet for such a large man. "It was like dancing with a big cat," was how she had put it to her daughter. Coming down the stairs he did not sound like a big cat.

And then he was there, poised in the doorway. It had been six years since he had sent her his last photograph. He looked different. For one thing, he had new teeth. Teeth too large, too white, too regular and even. They seemed to prevent his lips from closing. They shone almost as much as the glass in his spectacles. Another thing. He had taken to carrying his head thrust well forward, as if he were straining to see through, to penetrate, a thick fog. It was impossible for Vera to tell whether he had gone grey or bald because of the straw fedora he wore. She judged the hat too small. Like Oliver Hardy's, it made him appear fatter, grosser than he really was. It was downright unflattering.

Monkman lingered in the doorway several moments more, teeth gleaming as he studied his visitors. Then, abruptly, he took the final step down into the kitchen. "So, Vera," he said in a loud, harsh voice, "you made it safe and sound."

"That's me, safe and sound."

He shuffled nearer, still peering, neck craned. "It's good to have you home, daughter," he said at last, reaching out and awkwardly patting her shoulder.

Handles me like a horse in a stall with a bad reputation for kicking, she thought. Nevertheless, she realized her own hand had gone out to rest gently on his forearm. She quickly withdrew it. "How've you been keeping, Dad?"

"As good as can be expected for a man who leads a clean life and pays his taxes. I have sore joints on bad days." He held up a hand and stiffly flexed his fingers. "But a man my age – that's got to be expected." He paused. "Yourself?"

"Can't complain."

"I was thinking, standing in the door," said Monkman, "how you've come to resemble your mother. It brought me up short there. I believed I'd come face to face with a ghost. I don't recall your resembling your mother when you were a girl."

"When I was a girl I had red hair. That might have had something to do with it."

Monkman laughed. "It's been a long time. I'd almost forgotten. Red hair that came out of a bottle."

"Yes. Out of a bottle. You hated it."

Her father gave her a measuring look. "I might have. My memory's not what it once was."

"Mine is. You did," said Vera.

The old man shifted ground. "Is this the boy then?" he asked in a hearty voice, turning to Daniel.

"Yes." Vera nudged Daniel forward. "Daniel, say hello to your Grandfather Monkman."

"Hello."

"Now how do we go about this?" said Monkman. "I don't know how I introduce myself to a grandson I meet for the first time when he's practically grown. Do I shake hands, or what?" He threw his daughter a sly glance. "I think maybe that would be best, don't you, son?" he suggested, extending swollen fingers. The boy gingerly grasped them and Monkman pumped his arm once, twice. "So what do you go by?" he asked. "Daniel, Danny, or Dan?"

"It's Daniel," intervened Vera.

"Pleased to meet you," said the boy.

"Who does he look like?" Monkman said aloud, apparently to himself. "I'm looking at him and thinking someone but I can't put a name to him."

"Daniel looks like his father," said Vera firmly.

"Can't be him I'm thinking of. I never met his father." Monkman smiled at the boy. "I wasn't invited to the wedding," he explained. His next question was directed to Vera. "Would I have liked his father?"

"It's hard to say. But I don't think he was your type."

40

"And what's my type, daughter?"

"You're your type."

The old man adopted a confidential tone, drew closer to his grandson. "Your mother likes to let on I'm hard to get along with. But nothing's further from the truth. Stutz here has been working for me for fifteen years and he's never heard a harsh word from me. Have you, Stutz?"

"No, never just one," returned Stutz on cue.

The two men laughed at an old joke, well-rehearsed.

Pleased with himself, Monkman fussed with his hands, scratching the back of one, then the other. "What do you say we have a drink to celebrate your homecoming, Vera? There's a bottle of Crown Royal under the sink, seal's never been broke. I've been saving it for an occasion and I guess this is one. Stutz won't join us – religious principles – but it wouldn't hurt you, Vera, to have one. It'd help you relax after your long trip. And the boy could join us. Very weak, mind you, plenty of water in his, just a drop of whisky. All for the sake of the ceremony. It couldn't hurt."

"Don't let us stop you," said Vera. "But Daniel and I won't be having a drink."

"Oh, Jesus, no, I suppose not," said Monkman, winking conspiratorially at Daniel. "To hell with that then. But later can I feed the boy? I thought the four of us could take supper in the hotel. I told Rita to put roast pork and apple sauce on the special tonight. That's Rita Benger, the cook. You'd remember her. She's Charlie Benger's sister that went to school with you. Charlie Benger with the limp?"

"Can we discuss supper in a bit?" said Vera. "I'd like to know what arrangements have been made for Daniel and me tonight."

"Arrangements?"

"Yes, arrangements. Like where we're to stay. Also, I'd like to know where and when I start work."

"Why, you'll stay here," responded Monkman with determination.

"Until we find a place to rent."

"This is Connaught, daughter. There are no places to rent. I've got the two bedrooms upstairs that I thought the boy and I could have. That'd leave you the one down here. More privacy for you that way."

"I didn't count on this," said Vera, drawing together her lips. "I'll see for myself if there aren't places to rent."

"Suit yourself. But looking won't change anything. There are no places for rent. Unless you're interested in a fire-trap suite over the poolroom."

"All right then," she said grimly, "there are no places to rent. What about work?"

"We'll settle that in due course. Catch your breath."

"What the hell do I live on while I'm catching it?" demanded Vera, suddenly exasperated. "All the money I have in the world is two hundred dollars in Canada Savings Bonds in that box," she said, pointing. "I can't afford to be a lady of leisure."

"Christ, Vera, relax. The trouble with you is everything gets blown way out of proportion. Always did. You and the boy are home now. You're taken care of. You've got nothing to worry about."

"I didn't come home to be taken care of. I'm not a child. I came to work. You promised me a job."

"If I promised you a job, you've got a job. I'm your father. What do you expect me to do? Cheat you? Put your mind at rest. You've got a job for chrissakes."

"What kind of job?" Her voice was flat, controlled.

"An easy job. You said you wanted to be able to spend more time with the boy so I got you one. We'll talk about it tomorrow when you're not so tired and irritable from your trip."

"I want to talk about it now. What kind of job?"

Monkman hesitated. "Housekeeper," he finally admitted, reluctantly.

Vera's face flushed. "Housekeeper to who?"

Monkman appealed to Mr. Stutz. "Is she serious? 'Housekeeper to who?' she says." He swung back on Vera. "Christ, for who do you think? For me. And for him," he added, nodding to Daniel. "For once you can be a full-time mother. You can look after your boy."

"And you."

"That's such a hardship? You wash his shirt, throw mine in the machine, too. You boil him a potato, boil me one, too. Where's the strain in that?"

"That's not where I expect the strain to come in."

"So where does the strain come in?"

"I'm a grown woman. I'm thirty-six years old and I want to have my own money. I mean to have a salary, not a housekeeping allowance. I don't intend to snitch nickels and dimes from household expenses so I can buy myself a new bra when I need one. I want a wage. I'm not sixteen years old like before."

The word bra caused Mr. Stutz to cast his eyes down to the toes of his boots.

"I was a poor man in those days," her father announced.

"I get a wage or I'm dust. I'll cash one of my bonds and climb back on that bus tomorrow and head right back where I came from."

"Look at her, Stutz!" cried Monkman. "Look at her! There's fire for you! Exactly like she was when she was seven, skipping rope with the other little girls. Going over that rope with her jaw set solid as iron and her pigtails cracking up and down like buggy whips. Little Miss Determination. When I saw that, I said to myself, Lord help and protect the man who gets her."

"Let the Lord look after whoever He has to. I'll look after myself. Do I get a wage or not?"

"What was it your mother did down east?" Monkman inquired of Daniel. "Trade horses? I got a feeling I'm about to be skinned. I best remember you don't sup with the Devil unless you own a long spoon."

"I'm not joking," said Vera. "I'm deadly serious."

"Well then, how much?"

"Room and board for Daniel and me and a hundred a month. When I find a place and move out – two hundred a month."

Monkman shot Stutz an ironic smile. "Sound fair to you, Stutz?"

"This is family," he said. "I don't put my nose into family business."

"You got any idea what minimum wage is in this part of the world, girl?" demanded her father. "Any idea at all?"

"I don't work for minimum wage. I'm not a minimum wage person."

Monkman pushed back his fedora with the tip of his forefinger. "Stutz," he said, "why don't you take the boy and his luggage upstairs to his bedroom. We're going to have a money discussion here and I don't want you getting any exaggerated notions of your worth from my daughter here."

Daniel looked questioningly at his mother. "Go along," she said, motioning to the stairs with her head. Stutz and he disappeared up the stairs, toting a duffel bag and suitcases.

"Daughter," said Monkman, "you can have your money. But let's not get into the habit of public wrangles. I don't like them. I prefer a soft voice in private. Besides, this isn't just about money, is it? What else is eating you?"

"I want one thing clear," said Vera. "Daniel is my son. I'll have no interference from you. I saw what you're up to."

"What the hell kind of nonsense are you talking now, Vera?"

"Trying to get on the good side of him and put me on the bad. Offering him a drink. Winking at him or pulling a face whenever you made a reference to me. I won't be turned into a witch or a fool, or talked around as if I wasn't in the room."

"Jesus, didn't somebody come prepared to stomp snakes? I meant nothing by it."

"I won't allow you to put yourself between me and Daniel the way you did between me and my brother."

"You're dreaming, daughter. I never came between you and your brother."

"Not much. Then why didn't he write when I sent my wedding announcement? Because you wouldn't let him. He was always under your thumb."

"Don't be ridiculous. I did no such thing."

"Then why didn't he write? He wrote once a week during the war."

Monkman stirred from one foot to the other. "Maybe you should remember who stopped writing first. He went down to the mail box once a day for almost a year after the war, looking for a letter from you. There weren't any."

"I had my reasons."

"Maybe somebody else is entitled to reasons, too."

"I got my suspicions why he didn't write."

"She has her suspicions," Monkman told the ceiling.

"You say you never stood between us," declared Vera furiously. "Then how come every time I asked you for his address I never got it?"

"You never got it because I didn't have no address to give. He's always on the move. I never know where he is, Alberta, the States. Those drilling rigs never stay put. He doesn't have an address."

"A man without an address," said Vera sarcastically.

"That's about it."

"And he never visits?"

"No more than you ever did."

"That's not like Earl. What happened? Did you two have a falling out? Is that it?"

Monkman avoided meeting her eyes. "No," he said.

"If you didn't, it's a miracle. The way you treated him."

"I was drinking then," said her father. "But I never run out on him. Just remember who was the one done that."

5

―――◆―――

"If there's a grass whip in there, pass that out, too," Vera ordered, leaning into the doorway of the tool shed, a hoe in her hands.

"A what?" said Daniel.

"City boys. Is there a scythe then? You know what a scythe looks like, don't you? You've seen pictures."

It was her first Sunday in Connaught and Vera had decided to pay a visit to her mother's grave. The decision had been made on the spur of the moment when her father announced after breakfast that he would be gone most of the morning, checking crops on the farm he had rented to an unreliable tenant. If Daniel and she hurried, they could be back home before he returned from his tour of inspection.

The long, awkward, rusty blade of the scythe poked, felt, sniffed its way out of the door of the shed. Behind it Daniel appeared, blinking his eyes and trying to wipe the ghostly, clinging sensation of cobwebs from his face.

Vera hefted the hoe. "All right," she said, "these ought to do the trick knocking down weeds. Because if I know your grandfather half as well as I think I do, he'll have neglected to see to her grave. It's likely ass-deep in nettles. A disgrace, which we will remedy."

Daniel, who was not particularly eager to spend a Sunday morning grubbing weeds in a cemetery, especially after learning it was situated a considerable walk outside the town, said, "If you want to do this, why not wait until he gets back? He'd drive us out there."

"Because I don't want him involved."

"Why?"

"Because it's my mother," Vera stated with dreadful finality, "and I don't want him involved. *Get me?*"

He got her.

Shortly before ten o'clock they started for the graveyard. Vera led them off with an air of purpose, slapping a pair of work gloves against her upper thigh in time with every stride she took, her hoe shouldered like a rifle. Daniel lagged a step or two behind, the scythe cradled clumsily in his arms. The streets were deserted, sunny and silent, pervaded with the sweet, aching stillness of Sunday morning in a small town. Some still slept in their beds. In churchgoing houses, boys were spreading newspapers on the floors in preparation for polishing shoes to be worn to Sunday School. Other children were having their hair washed, their mothers dippering soft water from the reservoir in the wood stove in warm, soothing floods over bowed heads and hair stiffened and peaked with lather. Working men drank a second cup of coffee in their undershirts without hurry, drew meditatively on cigarettes while they listened to Uncle Porky Charbonneau on the radio read them the Saturday funny papers. Only occasionally was the deep, slow, steady quiet broken by the excited barking of a dog, or an automobile with a hole in its muffler.

Past the peaceful houses Vera and Daniel marched, past the yards hedged with lilacs and caraganas and smelling of grass and shade. They turned into Main Street and there the sun lay harsh and glaring on the cement sidewalks, the stucco storefronts, the

47

plate-glass windows. The druggist had forgotten to roll up his torn awning and it was lazily puffing and popping in a breath of breeze. There was evidence the farmers had been to town the night before for Saturday night shopping. Plenty of cigarette stubs, Copenhagen snuff cans and Lucky Elephant Popcorn boxes lay in the gutters opposite wherever an auction poster had been tacked to a streetlight pole. Only a single car was parked on the street. It stood where it had all night, outside the hotel, directly in front of the beer parlour entrance. Huff Driesen had been too drunk to drive home to his daughter's and was sleeping on the sofa in the hotel lobby.

"I wish I had a can of white paint and a brush," said Vera. "All she's got for a marker is one of those iron crosses and by now it won't have a fleck of paint on it. It'll be nothing but rust. You have to whitewash those things regular – once a year, or they go to pot."

Daniel did not respond. It was a way of expressing his reluctance to join wholeheartedly in her expedition. All the same, he had to be careful not to provoke one of his mother's famous explosions of temper by an outright exhibition of defiance. He was treading a dangerously fine line, but he'd had some practice at it.

Once they had crossed the railroad tracks, only a few derelict shacks straggled on either side of the road. Here, outside town limits, by-laws did not apply and the yards held chicken runs and chicken coops, or lean-tos sheltering a cow. In front of the last house a gaunt red horse tethered to a discarded tractor tire lashed its tail to discourage flies and despairingly nuzzled ground that had been cropped black and bare of grass. A flock of small children hunkered in a patch of dirt before their door and stared as Vera and Daniel went by. The youngest, a boy of about three, suddenly yelled, "Pigshit!" in a challenging manner.

"Ignore him," said Vera.

Then they were in open countryside, pasture and poplar bluffs. Vera pointed to a prominent rise about a mile distant. "That's it. That's the Protestant Cemetery."

Despite the earliness of the hour, Daniel could sense the heat building insistently. There wasn't a cloud in the sky. He was thirsty. He squinted at the rise. It seemed an awfully long hot walk there and back. Nor was it any piece of cake hauling the scythe. It was nearly as tall as he was.

"Your grandmother would have expected her grave to be kept clean and neat. She was a lady that demanded respect, and in my books the dead are owed every bit as much respect as the living. It's not too big of a sacrifice to spend a little time tidying on a Sunday morning, is it? And God knows the last time that happened."

Daniel fell farther behind his mother and the sound of her voice. He was dawdling, swatting the heads off Canada thistle with the scythe. The keen blade went through weeds and the tough prairie grass like a hot knife through butter. Roadside and ditches were spotted with colour. Purple clover, wild blue flax, yellow goat's beard, white yarrow, and cow parsnip were sprinkled everywhere. Over the bright flowers bees hovered and droned and brighter butterflies flitted. The air was electric with a crackling and buzzing and thrumming of insects hidden in the undergrowth. Daniel felt as if he were moving in an atmosphere charged with static, walking on legs that the heat was draining of energy, turning water-muscled, draggy, listless.

His mother, on the other hand, seemed to be stepping out more and more briskly; the head of her hoe was bobbing and jerking smartly up and down over her shoulder. She kept up a running commentary on his snail's pace, tossing out remarks. "It's surprising how soft city boys get and afraid of work. Take my advice, Daniel, and leave off whacking the weeds in the ditches and save your strength for the ones up top. Anyways, weeds on the road allowances are a municipal responsibility. They're no concern of yours."

He adopted the wisest course, gave it up, slitted his eyes, propped the scythe on his shoulder, and shambled along in the dust a little more quickly.

They began to encounter traffic; farmers from south of town headed for church. First came Catholics bound for ten-thirty Mass; a little later, worshippers at the United Church. Both denominations were equally and impartially cursed by Vera, even though they reduced speed to avoid spraying Daniel and her with gravel and to gain themselves a look. Vera described it as "a slow-motion gawk." Car after car and truck after truck went by at a crawl, passengers unabashedly crowding forward behind the glare on the windshield to gaze curiously at the curious pair. Even though they were never recognized and identified, this did not prevent the man behind the wheel in his Sunday best from waving. Country manners demanded a salute even to strangers, although apparently women and children were under no obligation to offer this courtesy, only the driver. As the automobiles slid by, churning up clouds of fine, shifting yellow dust, the man of the house raised a hand in greeting as the others gaped and craned their necks. Vera nodded curtly back while she muttered ill-naturedly under her breath, "Fill your eyes. Two clowns minus the circus, but it's free – which is the price a farmer likes."

Finally the parade of cars dwindled away to nothing and they were once more alone on an empty road. A hawk sat on the crossbar of a telephone pole next to a blue-green glass insulator, highstepping it from one foot to another, opening and spreading its wings, folding and refolding them. When they were twenty yards off it took flight, casually, without alarm. In back of them the church bells of Connaught began to peal: the Catholics' real bell, tolled by the church janitor, then the United Church's up-to-date summons to worship, recorded bells played over a loudspeaker. By now the graveyard was near at hand. Vera led them off the main road and on to a narrow trail which crept up the cemetery slope, a trail just wide enough to accommodate the one-way traffic of bereavement. Although the hill was not very high, it was steep, and both Vera and Daniel found themselves leaning into it, their eyes on their feet and the fine, floury dust which rose about their ankles with the impact of each plodding footfall. At last Vera was beginning to show the effects of the heat and the climb. Her arms, bare in a sleeveless blouse, shone with a film of sweat and Daniel could plainly hear the sawing of her breath.

"God," she said, "a stroll up this bugger makes you feel ready for the permanent lie-down up top."

Up top, however, it felt a little cooler; the air was moving. Vera cast her eyes about her as she recovered her breath. "It's a little iron cross," she explained to Daniel. "The grave was on the edges somewhere. She was pretty much off by herself."

They began a search. "Look carefully," said Vera. "It was only a little iron cross. It may have fallen over, or been choked with growth." She was striking at tussocks of dry grass with the hoe, hoping to hear the sound of metal striking metal. "Somewhere on the edges," she repeated. But after two complete circuits around the graveyard they still hadn't discovered what they were looking for.

Daniel had a thought. "A lot of people die in twenty years," he said. "She wouldn't be on the edges anymore. I mean she's likely surrounded by now. Dead people all around her."

They drifted farther in, amid the crowd of headstones. "It's a little iron cross," his mother kept saying, "and if he painted it every year, it could be white."

Daniel suddenly called and beckoned her. "Hey, Mom, was Grandma's first name Martha?"

Vera hurried over to where he stood. Where he stood was not before a little iron cross but a five-foot-high slab of white marble, blazing ferociously white in the sun. It was something to which the word monument could fairly be applied, at least in Connaught. Twelve months ago it had provided Alec Monkman with a topic for proud discussion with Mr. Stutz. "Now they're making a special delivery from Regina in a covered truck, Stutz. I don't understand the principle of that – a covered truck – it's going to get rained on sooner or later, isn't it? But the fellow who sold it to me was most specific on it being delivered in a covered truck, mentioned it more than once. The best. Real guaranteed Pennsylvania marble. I don't know how they intend to unload it, weighing what it's got to, but that's up to them. They're the experts. Just as long as they don't chip or crack it."

There it was, rearing up from the earth, wide as a double door, thick and deep as a bookcase. Sprays of lilies and woolly lambs were carved in relief. Chiselled into its bone-white face were the words,

Martha Serena Monkman

1895-1939

Loving Mother and Wife

The grass on the plot showed evidence of recent cutting and the weeds had been pulled. There was even a jar of flowers. It was true these were brown and dry but in such arid heat flowers would wither and curl in a day, mummify in a week. Vera reached down, picked up the jar, and shook the dead petals and stalks out at her feet. She handed the jar to Daniel. "Go get some more," she said tersely. She didn't look at him. Her eyes remained fixed on the grave and the block of marble.

"Some more flowers?"

"Yes. Some more flowers."

He did as he was told, without arguing. There was something about her face. Going out the gate, he glanced back. His mother's spine was slumped and her arms hanging loosely at her sides.

Daniel had no idea of where she expected him to find flowers on such a godforsaken, parched and barren hillside, but find them he did, clumps of orange-red blossoms emerging from hairy, grey-green leaves. As he stooped to gather them, grasshoppers came spitting up into his face from the short grass like grease from a hot skillet.

In a short time he had collected a fist-sized bouquet. Returning to present them to his mother he found she was still standing before her mother's grave, looking for all the world as heavy as the tombstone itself.

"I have the flowers," Daniel called out to her, holding them aloft as he approached.

Vera turned. There had been a change. It was in her face and bearing. She no longer slumped and dangled; she had bucked up her spine and worked herself into an anger. Daniel hoped it wasn't him.

"I don't know what these are," he said apologetically.

"Scarlet mallow," answered his mother softly. The softness didn't deceive him. "Scarlet mallow and stone lilies. Put them in the jar. It's time to go."

He was kneeling, putting the flowers in the jar when she bolted down the hill without him. Maybe it was because of his slowness or clumsiness with the arrangement. He had to run like the very devil to catch up. She didn't say a word to him all the long way back, but from the look of her, from the way she pounded that poor road, making the dust spurt with her feet, Daniel decided Sunday dinner would be pleasanter for all concerned if she had found what she had gone looking for, weeds and rust.

6

In 1939, Alec Monkman's wife died. Her death was a watershed in his life; after it he became a success. Success was late in coming to him. Until he was fifty-two Monkman was just Connaught's drayman, a bull-necked, slope-shouldered pair of overalls who shovelled coal and wrestled heavy freight, explaining himself with a wry smile and the old saying, "Strong back, weak mind." His business worth consisted of a dilapidated truck used for summer delivery, a sleigh and team of Clydesdales which he drove in winter when the roads were bad.

Grief was responsible for his success, grief made him daring and reckless. Monkman had always kept a stern eye on the bank book, had always been a careful, saving man. But the death of his wife robbed money of its significance. So when Rudy Kollwitz's arthritis made it difficult for Rudy to run a projector and impossible to splice a broken film, forcing him to put his shoebox of a movie theatre up for sale, Alec withdrew all his savings, negotiated a mortgage at the bank, and bought The Palladium cheap, taking all of Connaught by surprise.

His purchase of the movie house had nothing to do with its soundness as an investment, which nevertheless was considerable with a war going on and people hungry for newsreels, and hungrier still for entertainment to push the newsreels out of mind. No, he only believed that running a picture show would help fill the interminable spaces which his evenings, deprived of Martha, had become. The movie theatre would give him something to do, he told himself. It gave him too much to do. He grew pale and drawn with the strain of doing. By day he lifted and shifted ton upon ton of dead weight; by night he sat tense in a projecting booth high above the rows of heads communing with and adoring the bright images he cast into the darkness.

It was a family affair, The Palladium. Alec ran the projector and Vera sold admissions and popcorn. Earl, who couldn't be trusted to do much because he was flighty and couldn't keep his mind on things, sat in the foyer, kicking his heels on the rungs of a chair, watching the people troop in. Generally he slept through the second showing of the picture curled up in a seat in the back row of the theatre. Alec had tried to persuade Earl to stop at home but he wouldn't. Ever since his mother died he was afraid to be by himself. He said alone in the house he heard things. When he was downstairs he heard his mother walking upstairs, and when he was upstairs he could hear her moving in the kitchen, opening and shutting the cupboard doors.

Monkman did not know what to make of this talk of ghosts, except that the boy wanted mothering. Mothering would put him right. The year Vera finished her Grade Ten he took her out of school to run the house and mother little Earl. After all, she had more schooling than he had ever seen and he knew of no earthly reason for her to venture further into the realms of geometry-trigonometry, *Hamlet*, or Latin.

For this his daughter never forgave him. She tried to persuade him to leave her in high school, to permit her to graduate. Vera assured him she could manage it, school, the house, Earl. He would not hear of it, would not yield. "It's too much for a girl of sixteen," he said, "to run a household and go to school. You'd end up ruining your health. I won't have it, Vera. That's all there is to it."

To Vera it felt like a death sentence. She loved school. It was the one thing which lent her life a sense of movement. Turning back over the pages of a notebook in June she could say to herself, "Here is all I know now that I didn't know before. This is how far I've come." The notion that one thing built on another, that the second theorem of geometry was predicated on the first, and the third on the second, was a comfort to her. Vera was attracted to order and valued knowledge that could be measured – so many lines of "Lycidas" committed to memory, so many French verbs conjugated. French was Vera's favourite subject. Walking home, striding into a blustery March wind on long, ungainly legs, she would imagine herself pacing the windswept deck of an ocean liner, speaking French to a dark man. "*Je ne sais quoi,*" she would say softly to herself, and then laugh a sophisticated laugh, rehearsing the future. But her stupid, stubborn father snatched that away. "Earl needs you," he argued. "He's just a little kid. He needs a mother."

So get him one, Vera thought. Do I look like a mother?

"He's not happy," her father added.

Vera had always been his blunt and fearless child. "Little wonder," she said.

"What the hell's that supposed to mean?"

"You ought to quit riding him around the country at night. That's what I mean."

"Watch your step, miss."

"You don't want to know – don't invite me to tell."

For the moment she could see he was ashamed. Well, he ought to be. Doing as he did. Sometimes she truly believed he'd gone clean off his head. When her mother was alive Vera had never seen him drunk even once. Not at a wedding, not at Christmas, not at New Year's. Now, once a month, regular as clockwork, he could be expected to go on a scandalous rip, using whisky to light a fire in his belly against the encroaching darkness.

Drunk he was a different man, a lunatic. Stumbling and ranting, he would kick in the pickets of the front fence, rampage through the garden, tearing up all the stalks of new corn, roaring that winter was coming, get the corn in, even though it was only June. One night he wrenched all the cupboard doors off their hinges, trampled them to splinters under his boots, and fed them into the woodstove. With the stove lids left off, Vera was sure the house would catch. Every time a gust of wind whistled down the chimney and twisted its way through the tin pipes, the fire blazed up roaring and spitting sparks. As she tried to push the stove lids back into place with a broom handle, leaning back from the flame and heat, Vera thought she heard her father whisper, "Let's see her slam the sonofabitching cupboard doors now, Earl."

These things were terrible but worse were the nights when Monkman stood swaying at the foot of the stairs, clinging to the banister and shouting for Earl to get himself dressed, they were going for a ride. Those nights his daughter wished him dead.

Vera did all she could to prevent him taking Earl. She offered herself in her brother's place. "Take me, Daddy," she would coax. "You don't want Earl. Take me."

He never listened. "I want my boy!" he bellowed up the stairs. "Goddamn it, Earl, get up and get yourself dressed! I want some company for a drive!"

"You'll kill him, Daddy, driving drunk. Don't," Vera pleaded. "One of these nights you'll roll that old truck and kill him."

Her father could not tell her that he took Earl because he knew that with Earl in the cab he would not permit himself to swing the wheel off the road, hard into the ditch and the racing darkness. Instead, he said, "Earl and me are different from you, Vera. We're alike. We're sad and we need each other."

"*You're* not sad. You're just sorry for yourself and drunk. That's all."

"Your daddy is as sober as a judge, Vera."

Her father carried Earl off at any possible hour – midnight, one in the morning, two. In such a state he was no respecter of anyone's sleep. All that mattered to him was the headlong rush down a country road, the old truck pressed to the limit, the speedometer needle shaking like a trembling finger. Earl sat beside him rigid and glassy-eyed as any rabbit locked in the glare of oncoming head-lights. The noise was deafening. The cab of the truck rattled and groaned and squealed. Stones spurting up against the floorboards made a crazy, ragged drumming, a drumming punctuated by the steady slap slap of the glove compartment with the broken catch flapping up and down on its hinges. The sight of the dark, flat land spinning by on either side robbed Earl of the power of speech. Even when a tire caught loose gravel and the truck lurched violently from side to side, the fields suddenly swinging towards him heavy and full of menace, he couldn't holler – only lock his knees and brace his arms against the dashboard, while in his mind's eye he imagined the truck hurtling over and over, the gas tank slopping gasoline, the windows showering glass.

It was out of fear of darkness that Alec drove. In the beginning of his crazy drives, when he was drunkest, he lost the fear, knew only abandon, release. Ever since the death of his wife the oppression and misery of night had lain heavy on him. Night work was not cure enough. When darkness fell, he grew anxious. He fidgeted, could not keep still. Everything drew in on him, shrank. It was like being squeezed and choked in a tight black suit cut for a smaller man. Monkman feared to see the world of day recede, people and buildings shut off from view. Hated the withering away – to a street, to a house, finally to one lighted room in which he sat with a ticking clock. It started him drinking, the thought of the darkness eating up the world, gnawing it smaller and smaller.

It was this which sent him out into the country. As many times as he went, as many times he was convinced this was the way to beat it. Tearing along the narrow roads helped push back what threatened him. Mile after mile he rolled up the great carpet of darkness with his headlights and proved to himself nothing had been taken away forever, the earth was still there, as it had been.

That was what he needed, wanted, when the night gathered in, to know nothing had changed. But the relief was only temporary, a drug compounded of speed and drunkenness. Lacking one or the other, it was nothing. So as he sobered, the elation drained away and the old unease filtered back. He began to see danger, to understand the durability of darkness. His hands went slick with sweat as the road tilted and swayed beyond his windshield. All went slippery and untrustworthy on him: road, tires, steering wheel.

He made himself stop the truck. When he turned off the engine and killed the lights land and sky knit solid black against him. His mind ran back over all those places on the road where a mistake might have killed them. Nothing in the world could bring him to turn his truck around and go back over those places while it was still night. In the dark, he was sure he would make that mistake.

When the truck halted, Earl knew it meant the fire. His father didn't have to say a word. Whatever they foraged out of the ditches was piled on the hard-packed surface of the road, rotten fence posts, dried Russian thistle, beer boxes. "Bigger, bigger," his father urged, as they stumbled through the dark in a frenzy, filling their arms with water-killed willow, a smashed turkey crate, a weathered fir plank fallen off a load of lumber. Some nights the flames roared and blustered ten feet high, submerging the stars in a fizz of sparks. His father stood as close to the bonfire as he could bear, so close that Earl wondered his shirt didn't begin to curl and smoke.

"There's nothing like fire," his father said, "to take the cold and darkness away. Is there, Earl?"

The sun rose on charred sticks, ashes, and Earl asleep in the truck. Only with daybreak did Monkman trust himself to start the engine and return to Connaught. In first light and the cold of dawn he wrapped his arms around himself and scattered the remains of the fire up and down the road with his boots. Then he crept home, driving painfully slow and careful so as not to disturb the sleep of his son, who, nevertheless, from time to time, spoke out in his dreams.

Monkman knew what awaited him. Vera. Vera in her mother's housecoat, looking sallow and hollow-eyed. It bothered him to see her so, in her mother's housecoat. Many a time he had almost brought himself to speak to her about her wearing of it. It wasn't respectful or right the way she had gone into her mother's closet and helped herself. To see her sashaying and promenading around in it, trailing ash and cigarette smoke like the Queen of Sheba, particularly galled him. Smoking was not a habit Martha had indulged in, or approved of.

Of course, he understood the business with the cigarettes was pure and simple defiance. Her way of saying if she must be mistress of the house she *would* be mistress of the house and do exactly as she pleased. He never said a word. The day she helped herself to his papers and tin of Black Cat tobacco and rolled a cigarette before his very eyes, he never said a word. Only watched as the cigarette came unglued and crumbled between her fingers as she puffed away.

Monkman hadn't said no to her for months. Demanding grocery money, she demanded too much – three dollars a week more than her mother had ever asked for. Vera said it was because of the war and inflation. He didn't buy that but he gave her the money anyway. He had made himself a situation and he had better learn to live with the consequences. He knew well enough where the extra money went. Into the Chinaman's pocket when she treated her former schoolmates, Mabel Tierney and Phyllis Knouch, to Cokes. They were the girls he heard so much about, the girls who were going to be secretaries in the city. Often when he drove by the Chinaman's cafe with goods from the three-twenty train, he saw the top of Vera's head bobbing above the back of one of the wooden booths. There was no mistaking her. There wasn't another head of hair like Vera's in town. She had dyed it red because of Greer Garson. He figured maybe that was the result of working in The Palladium and seeing so many picture shows. You got ideas about being different and special and decided it would be fun to be the only redhead in town. In his books she looked common, looked a tramp. Vera was taking the bit in her teeth, running away on him. There was an air of trouble about her, but what could he do? It had never been like this before; they used to be on good terms. How could she be made to listen?

The red hair was the final trial of his patience. He had deliberated taking his belt to her when he saw that. His father had always said there was two ways of raising a child: by example or by hand. Take your pick. But he had no pick. At present he was no example of much and knew it. As to doing the job by hand, it was a little late in the day for that. If you started whaling on a girl Vera's age you had no chance of mending her, only of bending her even more. He knew Vera wouldn't tolerate a whipping. She had heard her mother say often enough that any man who would strike a woman was no man at all. So naturally she had a prejudice against it.

Alec could suffer her disparaging looks and her tart tongue because what she had to say to him was mostly just and mostly the truth. What he couldn't abide was his daughter smoking hand-rolled cigarettes, dyeing her hair red, and drinking Coke in the Chinaman's on Monday, which was wash day, always had been. There was the question the old boy had never answered. If you can't appeal to example, nor raise them by hand, what in Christ do you do? He sure as hell didn't know.

———◆———

Vera hated her father. She told Phyllis and Mabel that. She was careful not to mention the smashed fence pickets, the devastated corn patch, the shattered cupboards, the night driving. Anything really peculiar in your family was better kept close to the chest because in a small town people were apt to search for the same thing in you and make sure they found what they were looking for. Besides, there were rumours. No, instead of that, Vera talked about selling tickets at the theatre with cramps from your monthlies so bad you could weep and having to stick it out because if you told him why you wanted to go home, he'd die of embarrassment. She described how he drenched his bread in gravy, ate it with a fork, and swore it was tastier than any dessert, which meant her dessert, the Nanaimo bars she had been taught to make in 4-H. And the radio. Played so loud you believed you'd lose your mind, making it impossible to escape Edgar Bergen and Charlie McCarthy and the audience laughing, so you couldn't read a book like *Gone With the Wind*, a book you really had to concentrate on.

Her friends nodded sympathetically and said, "Oh, yes," in voices flavoured slightly by alarm at the injustice of it all. Vera knew they really didn't see it. Because whenever Mabel and Phyllis got the chance they steered the conversation around to plans for the upcoming graduation and what everyone intended to do when they had finished high school. All the boys in the class, all six of them, had made a pact to enlist. Phyllis and Mabel were going to secretarial school in Regina. They mentioned that every second breath they drew.

Couldn't they see how it upset her to hear them talk of graduation glories? The only way she had to shut them up was to offer them a cigarette. That took the wind out of their sails. Neither of them dared to smoke in public yet for fear their fathers would hear of it, but they assured Vera that when they had their freedom in Regina they wouldn't think twice about it. It was one leg up on them Vera had, being able to smoke cigarettes in the Chinaman's. She might have had another advantage over Phyllis and Mabel if all the fellows already out of school weren't away in the Armed Forces. Unlike her friends, whose fathers would have forbade it, Vera could have dated an older man, perhaps even one who owned a car. Her father wouldn't have dared to try stop her. The problem was there were no older men to be had. Just shy farm boys who weren't very clean and whose mothers cut their hair.

For Vera nothing was the same anymore, it all felt wrong. She was neither fish nor fowl; neither entirely free of the old life nor begun a new one. Her dignity demanded she dismiss Phyllis's and

Mabel's concerns, concerns she desperately yearned to share. When they frightened themselves with the horror of final exams set by the Department of Education in Regina, Vera smiled as if to suggest they did not know what care and worry were until they had responsibility for a house and young boy. When they debated the respective merits and demerits of Cullen's and Creighton's, the two city secretarial schools, Vera went pale and cold with fury. "Both'll teach you to type, I'm sure," she said.

No one seemed to notice.

"They say lawyers ask for a Cullen's girl because Cullen's girls get an especially good grounding in shorthand," Mabel would say with a pensive air, bobbing her straw up and down the neck of a Coke bottle. "Shorthand is probably important taking down evidence."

"Imagine what you could hear!" Phyllis would squeal, imagining herself taking down evidence.

"On the other hand, Creighton's are supposed to be strong on bookkeeping and Dad says bookkeeping is the backbone of any business. If a girl is strong on the books he says she can rise to manage an office."

"I could never give orders!" Phyllis would sprightly confess. "Imagine me giving orders!"

Vera certainly couldn't imagine it.

Phyllis and Mabel spent all their time scheming about graduation, seeking to get their way as they always had done for as long as Vera had known them. As winter yielded to spring Vera watched them go back and forth to school in the snow and mud, their heads tilted together in excited discussion. Plotting, intriguing, endeavouring to pull wires. Vera knew one of their goals. They wanted to ensure that Bryce McConacher was made class valedictorian. "Sure," Mabel had said to Vera, "the teachers have always made the best student valedictorian. But Bryce could give an inspiring and *humorous* speech. Not some dry as dust and mopey old talk which you can bet on getting from poor old Donald Freeman. It's time for a change. We live in a democracy, don't we?"

Lying on her bed with her arms folded crushingly across her breasts, Vera had to support the knowledge that loathsome Bryce McConacher was going to usurp a place that would have been hers if her father had let her continue in school. From the day she had gripped a pencil in Grade One, Vera had waged a see-saw battle with Donald Freeman for the place of honour at the head of the class, one year Donald savouring victory by the margin of a few decimal points in the calculation of their averages, the next year Vera.

However, Vera had to agree with Mabel when she claimed that Donald was no great shakes as a public speaker. Vera had always been the speechmaker. There were four oratory medals nestled in her mother's jewellery box to prove it, emblems of consecutive victories in Grades Seven, Eight, Nine, and Ten. Vera had triumphed with the aid of her mother's coaching. "If you have stage fright don't look at the audience. Look over the tops of their heads at the back wall. Don't rush your speech, it's not a foot race with the prize going to the fastest. And remember, *gesture*!" Her mother, who was a postmaster's daughter, and who had had the advantage of music lessons, even beat time with a wooden spoon as her daughter orated in the kitchen.

Stretched out on her bed, Vera found she could still mumble to herself vast tracts of those speeches she had delivered in the Community Hall to a smiling, docile audience of parents, teachers, fellow students, and various other well-wishers. Oratory Night was an event, and its prizes hotly contested. All participants understood that what was required to win was to exploit the theme of greatness, make plain the ways of success. For several months before the big night the lives of the famous were pored over in the pages of the school's *Encyclopedia Britannica*.

Vera's first medal came when she was thirteen. Standing before a large crowd, the eyes of which she was self-consciously convinced were rivetted on her developing breasts, she was momentarily bereft of words. Then she turned her eyes to where her mother sat and caught an index finger discreetly marking tempo against a purse. That launched her. In a confident, ringing voice Vera cried: "Who was Julius Caesar? A man who always followed his star. When great Caesar crossed the Rubicon boldly in front of the legions of Gaul, he was staking everything on Rome and himself."

Vera tasted glory then, but what a pale, poor, cheating glory it was compared to the glory of graduation night, the anticipation of which could light your days for months. It was a night which had the power to transform, to raise Cinderellas out of ash pits. Vera had kept her eyes open, she had seen it happen in the past. All her old friends would be changed, none of them would be quite the same afterward. The boys would wear suits, some bought especially for the occasion, others borrowed from uncles, or brothers, or friends of the family. But all would look older, more serious.

The girls would be as no one had ever seen them before. It was rumoured that even Mary Epp would defy her parents, wear lipstick for the first time in her life and dance, if anyone asked her. Phyllis reported that Mary had already bought a tube of Heart's Scarlet and hidden it in the toe of those sensible grey stockings she wore.

Mabel and Phyllis had purchased new gowns in the city and Mabel had been promised she could wear a family heirloom graduation night, her grandmother's moonstone ring. How different they would all be! Vera knew how they would behave. After obtaining their diplomas Mabel and Phyllis would cry and hug and kiss one another and then graciously extend these favours to girls like Mary Epp (whom they had always despised), hoping to eradicate any unfavourable or harsh impressions that had rooted in such a person's mind. And perhaps they would succeed and years later Mary would remember them beautiful and generous in their dresses, think warmly of them and wonder what had ever become of her old classmates.

Vera could not change herself so simply. She saw that. If Mary ever remembered *her*, it would be with her long white legs poking out of a crinkled dress, giving some false, silly speech about

Wellington or Caesar. Vera didn't want to be remembered that way. The idea was killing. How she wanted to be remembered was as a girl different and remarkable. And she made it happen, she seized her chance.

Vera Monkman became the first girl from Connaught to enlist in the Canadian Women's Army Corps. By acting decisively she was safely settled in barracks two weeks before graduation day. Her friends were left feeling a trifle breathless and disappointingly upstaged. Vera Monkman a soldier, even before the boys! So while Phyllis Knouch and Mabel Tierney completed the grand march around the Community Hall on the arms of their escorts, Vera was being drilled in a grander march, up and down a dusty parade ground. Instead of a graduation frock she wore a sober coat whose brass buttons were embossed with the profile of helmeted Pallas Athene. Vera was officially at war. If she had been asked to explain what had led her to this she likely would have said patriotism, doing her bit to defeat Hitler, all the while knowing this wasn't true, knowing it was really her instinct for self-preservation which was responsible.

Vera had come to the end of her tether. She couldn't have listened to another moment's chatter about secretarial school, corsages, and gown lengths. She couldn't have borne seeing, one more time, her father chew with deliberate, dumb satisfaction a boiled potato and be able to stop herself from crying out accusingly, "So where's your famous grief now? Forgotten when you come face to face with a goddamn boiled potato!" She couldn't any longer stand to watch Earl waiting each night to learn if his father was off drinking supper, or would be joining them at the table. Once, when her father was twenty minutes late, and she found Earl standing tensely by the front door, listening for the sound of his truck, Vera had said, "You know, sometimes I wish he'd run that truck of his into a telephone pole and end the suspense." And Earl had flung himself at her, sobbing and flailing her with his palms. She hadn't really meant anything by it. It was queer how her brother behaved.

Vera couldn't tarry any longer. No ifs, ands, or buts about it. So she bummed a ride to Regina and enlisted. The recruiting officer gave her orders to report back in two weeks. For thirteen days she didn't breathe a word to a soul of what she had done, fearing steps could be put in motion to prevent her leaving. On the last day, with her dresser cleared and her bag packed, she put her father's dinner in front of him and announced she was leaving.

"Army?" he said in a bewildered voice. Then not another word as he slowly cut his meat and mashed his parsnips with a fork.

"Well?" said Vera.

He looked up from his plate. "You'd do this to him?" He meant Earl.

"I'm not doing this to anybody. I'm doing it *for* somebody. There's a difference."

"Who'll look after Earl?" he asked obstinately.

"He's not exactly a baby anymore. He's twelve and if he needs looking after I suppose you're the one who'll have to do it." Vera shrugged. "It's up to you."

Monkman got up from the table, walked heavily to the stove, and poured himself a cup of coffee. With his back still to her, he said, "Such a hard girl. Nothing like your mother."

Vera could read nothing of how afraid he was to be left alone to care for Earl from the rigid set of his shoulders. "Maybe," she said quickly to forestall tears that were threatening to break.

Her father went slowly back to the table, set down his coffee, took out his wallet. He counted four bills down on the table, side by side. A five and three ones. "There," he said, "it's all I have on me. This was kind of short notice."

Vera gathered it up. Money for the trip. He had placed it on the table as he had always done for her mother when she went away for a visit. Bills in a row, counted out, no mistake as to what you got.

He tried one last time. "You know what your mother would want you to do, don't you?"

"Don't you know it's my mother's dead and not me?" Vera answered quietly.

"Get out then," he said. "Get out. You know where the door is. You've been looking at it long enough."

Tramping along, swinging her arms in unison with the other women in the drill squad and listening to the rhythmic crunch of heels on gravel, imposed a cadence to Vera's thoughts. Over and over she repeated to herself that she would have stayed at home if there had been any hope of saving Earl from his father. But she knew there was no chance of that because Earl refused to show any fight.

"Stand up for yourself!" she had told him. "When the old man yells for you to come downstairs for one of those rides, don't. What's he going to do? He can hardly stagger over level ground when he's that way, so how's he going to manage stairs to get at you?"

But Earl always went to his father when he called. It was a mystery to Vera. As the saying went, God helps those who help themselves. Vera didn't see how she could be expected to go one better than God. What was there left for her to do, except save herself?

In the Army, for the first time in two years Vera felt she could breathe. The skies that summer were high, cloudless, a distracting blue across which planes of the Commonwealth Air Training Plan darted and swooped. Wheeling left and wheeling right to a drill sergeant's commands, Vera felt freer than when she had idled away her afternoons with Cokes and cigarettes and gossip. In the barracks it was interesting and exciting to talk to so many different kinds of girls, middle-class idealists full of patriotic talk and tough girls with pimples on their chins who had fled bad families for the chance to eat three square meals a day and get their teeth fixed at government expense. So many different girls with so many different reasons, an army like any other history had ever known, except that this one was female.

It was the sense of movement in the Army that Vera liked best. A short time in Regina, a month of basic at Dundurn and then she

68

was dispatched to Kitchener, Ontario, for trades training. Always new faces, new scenery, new things to learn. Because she had her Grade Ten, Vera's superiors had suggested she might train as a clerk, but when she thought of Mabel and Phyllis and secretarial school she asked to be made a cook instead.

An adventure impossible to explain or express. Eastbound, leaving behind everything she had ever known, Vera wrote her first letter home, not to her father but to Earl. Ostensibly it was written to provide information as to where she was going and how she could be reached, but in reality she was seeking a confidant, a confidant who had known the old Vera and could draw comparisons with the new. That was Earl. She wrote him everything. She told of the smart dining car with linen tablecloths and silver cutlery where she had recklessly splurged, treating herself to a meal of Winnipeg goldeye as if she had done this sort of thing every day of her life. It was the uniform, she explained. In uniform you were suitably dressed for any function, a woman could go anywhere in uniform – to a fancy dining room, to a concert. A uniform was a wonderful disguise. No one had any idea whether you were rich or poor, belonged or didn't belong. And you always looked smart. Vera proudly quoted a line to her brother from the brochure, "Women in Khaki." "C.W.A.C. uniforms have been acknowledged by leading dress designers to be the smartest in the world." There it was, from the highest authority.

Vera tried to convey, too, how she was now a traveller. She wanted to give Earl some idea of the sprawl and space and harsh grandeur of the country she was passing through. She wrote to him of what she had witnessed early one morning as her train rattled through Manitoba; wrote of a vast, distant field crawling with hundreds of minute figures. The scene would forever have remained a puzzle if the track had not curved just then, carrying her nearer and nearer. Vera had laughed aloud when the tiny figures grew larger and larger, resolving themselves into soldiers bending and straightening under the brilliant morning sun. They were stooking.

On a whim an officer had turned a day of back-breaking labour for some farmer into a few minutes of diversion on a route march for a company of men. Now the troops were larking about, ramming the butts of sheaves into the soil and tossing the heavy heads together, battle-dress drab against the sun-drenched gold of stubble. As the train rumbled by, reducing speed on the bank of the curve, the men closest to the tracks waved to the passengers who were the first witnesses to their joke, looking not at all like soldiers but like boys on an outing, and one or two threw their caps exuberantly into the air, their mouths yawning in a soundless cheer.

Vera tried very hard to get things right in her letters, to capture the strangeness of being far from home. The descriptions came so thick and fast her pen could scarcely record them. There were the prosperous farms of old rich Ontario with acres of tall corn and huge barns and sleek black and white cows with heavy udders, dreaming in the flickering shade of great trees she guessed were maples. And she described the enormous temple of Union Station in Toronto which by rights ought to have seemed empty and hollow because of its soaring roof, but which bustled and teemed with soldiers and airmen and sailors and women and children all rushing about every which way, hugging and kissing while the arrivals and departures rolled on like some awful announcement of the doom of journeys missed, chances never seized, life never lived. So hurry up! And when she came to the end of her trip, a young girl in a town in Ontario, she wanted, out of the fullness of her nineteen-year-old heart, to write a letter that said, "Tell everyone in Connaught that Vera Monkman is *alive* and *kicking*!" Both words underlined three times for emphasis. She didn't write any such words, however. Instead, she signed it, "Your loving sister, Vera," and enclosed a dollar of her pay for Earl, to show she was thinking of him and also to demonstrate to her father she was doing just fine, thank you very much, without him. Because, for as long as Vera corresponded with Earl, filing her reports on life in the Army, she never sat down to write without imagining two faces reading her letters, one Earl's, and the other, hovering just over his shoulder, her father's.

Not that everything about the Army was wonderful. By the time she was transferred to Saint Anne de Bellevue Vera was having second thoughts about being a cook. In summer the kitchens were hotter than the hubs of hell and the noise, the incessant rattle of pans and clash of pot lids, the thin steamy stench of watery veg-etable soup, the smell of raw chickens and burned food so jangled her nerves and upset her stomach that she found it next to impos-sible to eat. For days on end she could keep nothing down but weak tea, soda biscuits, and Jello. Yet never once did Vera present herself on sick parade. What if they found something really wrong and she was given a medical discharge? The last thing she wanted was to be forced to quit the Army just when she was proving herself so able. Because she was able. In six months Vera had been promoted to lance corporal in recognition of her general efficiency, precise and accurate record-keeping, and careful management of supplies. There were predictions she would make sergeant before long.

It was difficult to bring her success to Earl's and her father's attention without seeming to brag, bragging being much dispar-aged among the Monkmans. The solution proved simple in the end. Vera had a studio portrait taken of herself in uniform, taken in three-quarter profile so that the stripes on her arm were clearly visible. She was certain they would be noticed. Of other matters, which reflected less directly on her, it was not necessary to be so modest. She had the excuse that her descriptions to her brother of extended leaves taken in the fabulous cities of the U.S.A. were justified because of their educational value. If they also happened to cast Vera in a sophisticated, worldly light, maybe that couldn't be avoided.

In particular, she dwelt at great length on her one visit to New York, where she and her companions had plucked up the courage to storm the lobby of the Waldorf-Astoria looking for movie stars and from there, in a moment of insane bravado, pressed an assault on the restaurant, requesting a table for luncheon. They got one, it being an unfashionable, slack hour, and they servicewomen in the uniform of an ally. It was the uniform, Vera once again explained to her brother, which earned her the right to eat in a hotel that numbered among its guests millionaires, European nobility, and the stars of stage and screen.

Later, they took in all the city's tourist sights, saw Radio City Music Hall and the high-kicking Rockettes for whom they harboured a mild contempt as frivolous women who did not appreciate the seriousness of war and the sacrifices it demanded. They went to the top of the Empire State Building and then uptown to see Grant's Tomb.

These were the things she wrote to Earl, to mark the changes in her. There were other things of which Vera was scarcely aware and, if she had been, could not have written of to a brother.

Old friends like Phyllis and Mabel might have thought that life in the Army had led to a deterioration in her manners and turned her just a tiny bit vulgar and unladylike. They would certainly be alarmed to see the way she drank beer, straight out of the bottle rather than a glass, and how, when she was tight, she would rise unsteadily to her feet and say loudly, in mixed company, "Make way, boys, this lady's got to tinkle."

Somehow, too, the promises which Vera had made to herself to improve her mind had been neglected. She only glanced at the war news in the papers and had given up attempts to read books in the barracks during the evenings. The hubbub there was too distracting, her attention snagged on bits of camp gossip and talk of men. Most evenings she spent playing cribbage with a homesick recruit from Newfoundland who cried in the shower, believing tears couldn't be detected in the midst of all that streaming water. But as the case of that girl proved, Vera was learning it was impossible to hide anything in the Army, or hide *from* anything. Like sex. She was getting sick and tired of being importuned and bothered by soldiers. The young ones were no better than beggars, all beseeching mouths and beseeching hands. They fumbled at you on the dance floor and in ill-lit doorways. What was worse, they struck sentimental poses and talked of dying because their bragging, lying friends told them that never failed to produce the desired result. To Vera it was exasperating and wearying, fending off this desperate stroking and fondling. They were nice enough boys but fools. Couldn't they see that all this talk of death sounded ridiculous standing under a lamppost in Kitchener?

If you steered clear of the young heroes, that left only the tough rinds and peels, the vets of the Great War who had reenlisted, been judged unfit for active service, and assigned duties as drill and gunnery instructors. Vera preferred them to the boys. They were more patient and charmingly persistent. A number of times when she had drunk too much Vera had permitted them liberties. For none of these old men did she feel an individual passion but at certain times she was aroused to an impersonal excitement when a hand crept to a stocking top, or closed on her breast, muffled in its khaki tunic. Eyes pressed tightly closed, she would ask herself, Why not? Why not find out? Why not get it over with? But she didn't. Vera was put off by the element of struggle in it all, by their I win, you lose attitude, by the feeling they wanted to *take* her, to *have* her. That was the one satisfaction they would never get.

Not surprisingly, none of this found its way into her letters to Earl. The picture she drew of herself was incomplete. In reality, the correspondence of Vera and her brother was the correspondence of shadows, a record of one memory speaking to another, of two people who grew dimmer and dimmer as the months became years and the memories grew more unreliable. Their father was the wall upon which the shadows met. Because Vera knew he read her letters to Earl, she could never ask the questions that plagued her. How is he treating you, Earl? Are things better now that I'm out of his hair? Earl, are you happy? She had to rely on what she could divine from the notes written on lined pages torn from a school exercise-book, the words thick and clumsy-looking because of the heavy-handed way Earl drove his fountain-pen across the paper. The childish, immature way in which he expressed himself was never remarked by Vera. In her mind, he grew no older, was as she had left him.

> *Got better marks from the new teacher. Mr. Mackenzie joined up on the school trustees so we have a lady teacher now. She is not so strict and owly as Mackenzie. I got specs now. Catch better with them than before, but still am no great shakes at ball. Isn't in the cards I guess.*

No, Vera supposed it wasn't. Earl had sent along a photograph of himself in his baseball uniform. She was shocked to see him suddenly shot up tall and thin as a reed, his Adam's apple looking like an orange in a Christmas stocking, and his new glasses throwing sun back into the camera in a brilliant blur. It was typical of Earl to have a picture of himself taken in baseball uniform, not wearing his glove but absent-mindedly clutching it by the webbing so it hung, limp dead leather, like a trophy of the hunt, a strange beast pulled from the sea, or huge bat plucked from darkness. Oh dear, Earl, Vera thought, shaking her head.

Reading between the lines, Vera could not always piece together the actual state of things in Connaught. Much of what Earl told her was communicated offhand, by the by. In January of 1944, in a letter written to thank Vera for the present she had sent for his fifteenth birthday, Earl passed on the momentous news that his father had taken over the town garage and hired himself help.

> *Dad has taken on a man with a glass eye. Dad says men are hard to come by with the war but since this one has a glass eye he can't fight. His name is Mr. Stutz and he comes from somewhere down the line, Kimberley I think.*
>
> *We got him because Dad says he is tired of doing bullwork his time of life. From now on Dad says Mr. Stutz can*

haul freight and he will sit on his behind doing the easy stuff like showing pictures and pumping gas for a living. Dad says Mr. Stutz is a good worker but has opinions. I seen him smoking so he isn't a Jehovah's Witness although he's death on drinking. That's how he lost his eye. Somebody drunk poked it with a pencil or something.

Mr. Stutz is stronger even than Dad. Friday he carried an engine block across the shop on a dare. Was Dad ever mad when he heard. He said he could of hurt himself and been laid up and lost to him.

Mr. Stutz figured prominently in Earl's letters from that time on. He had clearly made an impression on her brother and perhaps beyond. In one of Earl's letters she came across a cryptic line. *Dad is better since Mr. Stutz came.* How exactly was this to be taken? Did he mean her father was feeling physically better now that Mr. Stutz had relieved him of heavy work, or did he mean that Mr. Stutz was exerting some kind of steadying influence on her father, discouraging his wild, erratic behaviour? She wished she knew. Vera often worried about Earl, partly out of guilt, she supposed. Her brother had always needed someone to look out for him, to take his side. Maybe Mr. Stutz was doing that. Often during lulls in the clamour of the kitchens, she thought of the man she had cast in the role of her brother's protector. However, try as hard as she might, she could only imagine him one way – as a man moving stiff-legged in a sailor's rolling walk, arms pulled straight by something heavy – a keg of nails, an anvil, an icebox which buffeted his thighs with every lurching step he took. That was Mr. Stutz to Vera.

But Vera had more to worry about than just Earl. By now she was a sergeant with a sergeant's responsibilities – that is, she had to run things in a way that allowed the officers to believe they were actually in charge. She had to manage people with an easy or heavy hand, whatever the situation required. There were times when she was all at sea. What to do about the girl who was sending gifts of chocolate and perfume to another? How to uncover a barracks room thief? There were sleepless nights enough. And then there was the final worry. With every day that passed it was becoming clearer the war was drawing to a close. There were pictures in the newspapers of Russian and American troops shaking hands and posing as comrades beside the wide, slaty waters of the Elbe.

Still, no one yet dared to think of it as finished, not with Japan holding out. On the radio sonorous voices reminded them all of the terrible price in blood which must still be paid. It was difficult to think of life outside the Army as anything but far distant. Then, very soon, Vera had to imagine it. Two bombs dropped, two unearthly flashes of light, two storms of heat and dust and it was over.

This sudden peace took her unprepared. The Army began to melt away around her. It was like waking from a dream. A week never passed that Vera wasn't down at the train station to see another of her discharged girls off home. She pressed cigarettes and bags of peppermints on them, brusquely shook their hands, and called them by their surnames before they climbed aboard. The shuddering, panting locomotives jerked forward, the carriage couplings rang, and Vera was left feeling like autumn, like those stark days when the leaves have fallen but the snow has not.

Then in 1946 it was Vera's turn. She was out on civvy street, her winter uniform carefully wrapped in brown paper, tied up in string, and laid in the bottom of a drawer in a rooming-house in Toronto. There was only one thing clear in her mind. She was not going home.

Vera would have preferred to remain in the Army if that was a thing women did, but women didn't.

7

Every night after supper Daniel walked and figured. It was his
best chance to be absolutely alone because everybody else in
Connaught was still indoors eating, he had the streets to himself. In
Alec Monkman's household supper was served earlier than in other
households because he refused to eat at six o'clock when everyone
else in Connaught did. In other houses it was the custom to seat
yourself for the evening meal when the "supper siren" blew at the
Town Hall. Three times a day a siren sounded from one end of
Connaught to the other: at noon, at six, and at nine in the evening
when it reminded children that there was a curfew for kids under
sixteen years of age. Daniel had never heard of anything so weird,
so backward. His grandfather had strong opinions about the siren,
too. He said that eating at exactly the same time as eight hundred
other people made him feel just like one more pig at the trough. All
that snuffling and chewing, he could hear it. It put him off his own
feed, he claimed. That was why at their house they ate at five.

Daniel had a route he followed on his figuring walks. Down his
grandfather's street and past the RCMP detachment he went, the
sun settling at his back, his shadow long and spidery-legged. In
the evening calm the red ensign draped limply around the police

flagpole. Mr. Stutz had been eager to tell him all about the police headquarters, had acted as if it had something directly to do with him. Daniel knew there were two cells in the basement, one of which had actually held a wife-murderer for several days before he was transferred to jail in Regina. He knew that every other month up on the second floor a judge tried minor offences, meted out fines and punishments. Whenever court was in session Mr. Stutz took a day off work and occupied a folding chair in the makeshift court-room with its picture of the Queen on the wall and the simple desk which saw duty as a judge's bench. Mr. Stutz had told Daniel that, if he cared to, he could accompany him to court next sitting.

One of the things that Daniel tried to figure as he walked was what he and his mother were doing in Connaught. There had been no warning of a move. All of a sudden she announced they were going, the furniture was sold to a second-hand dealer, and they loaded themselves onto a bus. Why? Maybe the fight with Pooch over the toenail polish had something to do with it, although he couldn't be sure. His mother had never provided a reason. Reasons were not things he expected from her. "Because I said so" was about the best you got.

He hadn't wanted to go. His mother said, "You'll make new friends. Better ones than you could here. Kids in small towns are so much friendlier." Which wasn't true. He knew he wasn't the sort to make new friends. Maybe because she had never let him get any practice at it, learn the knack of it, keeping him locked up in a dumpy apartment waiting for her to come home from work. How was he supposed to get the trick of it? Deep down maybe he was a loner like James Dean and Montgomery Clift.

Now he was passing the little shacky houses where the old foreign ladies lived, the ladies with the peach-pit faces and the ker-chiefs (babushkas, Stutz called them) knotted under their chins on even the hottest days. According to Mr. Stutz, a lot of these old women could scarcely speak more than a few words of English. English had been for their husbands. But now the husbands were dead and they had no men to interpret for them, no men to trail along after in kerchiefs, brown stockings, black dresses printed all over with tiny, dusky-red flowers. They seemed to spend all their time in their gardens. Front yards were planted with sunflowers and poppies. Back yards were full of onions, beets, dill, cabbages, cucumbers, potatoes, and the rusty tin cans they screwed into the earth to protect bedding plants. Because of the cans the back yards seemed to Daniel to be a cross between a vegetable patch and a dump.

During afternoons, if the old foreign ladies happened to be pecking in the dirt with their hoes and Daniel went by, they all straightened up and stared at him suspiciously and narrowly as if he were an alien from outer space. Which he may as well have been, his mother said sarcastically, Daniel not being native-born to Connaught.

But at present there is no sign of the foreign ladies as he passes. They are indoors, eating soup and sausage, thinking their thoughts, and remembering in some language other than English. Still, despite their strangeness, Daniel is certain that none of them could feel any more a stranger than he does himself.

The way people acted here. He couldn't get the hang of it. So different from the city. Take the other day when that man had stopped him in the street and asked, "You the one that's Alec Monkman's grandson? Vera's boy?" Asked him point-blank, right out of the blue. When he answered, Yes, that was him, the man said, "I went to school with your mother. Name's Mel Jessup." And that was all there was to it, nothing more. It seemed the man just wanted to pass on that bit of information.

It doesn't end on the street either. Two nights ago he wakes up at three in the morning in a strange bed and a strange room he isn't quite used to and gets the shock and fright of his life. This *thing* is standing in his bedroom door, watching him. He doesn't know whether to shit or go blind. It's worse than the worst horror movie he's ever seen and he's seen plenty. Everything else helps to put the chill in his blood. A moon is shining cold light through his window and the curtains are blowing around, whipping the wall with shadows. He can't move, he can't breathe. Then the thing shifts itself in the doorway enough to catch a little moonlight. He sees it's his grandfather in his gotch, hard old belly pushing out, and the thick white hair all down his chest shining in the light of the moon like frost on dead grass.

What's he up to, standing there watching him sleep?

It's a job to be able to suck enough spit up in his mouth to frame the question. "What do you want?"

The way the old boy jumps, he can tell he's returned the scare he got.

"Jesus, I thought you were asleep."

"What do you want? Is something the matter?"

No reply straight away. Finally, "I wondered if you weren't cold and needed some more covers."

That's likely. It's only about a hundred degrees here, directly under the pitch of the roof. He's cooking under a single thin cotton sheet. Sure he wants more blankets. Invent another one. But he's polite. "No," he says, "I'm fine."

The old boy knows he hasn't made a lick of sense. He fumbles to lay hands on an excuse. "It cools off worse than you think, nights. It does. You don't want to catch a cold. Summer colds are the worst." And with that he slides off, drifts out of the door, floating white in the moonlight like a sheet hung in the dark.

What a half-ass explanation that was. Of course, nobody thinks he's owed an explanation. You can do with him pretty much as you like. Drag him clear across the country, sneak into his room like some demented axe murderer or something, that's hunky-dory, that's acceptable. He doesn't need to know the why of anything.

Still, it's hard to stay mad at him. Daniel likes the old fart even though he knows he's not supposed to. His mother's not in favour of it. There's another thing for him to figure. Why'd she drag him here, on purpose, to live with somebody he's not supposed to like? Where's the sense in that? It's like some crazy test. Which he isn't passing.

Why shouldn't he like him? The old man is teaching him to drive the truck. The old man pays him to work in the garden. The old man argues baseball with him during the "Game of the Week." Not that he's all sweetness and light by a long shot, the old man. Maybe he doesn't come at you the way she does, full-bore, pointing out that this is wrong with you and that is wrong with you and when are you ever going to learn? That's not his style. He sort of crumbles up the ground under your feet and leaves you standing in thin air.

Take the other day. He's standing combing his hair in the mirror and the old man happens along, stops, hangs on the door, watches. Never said a word. It was his smile. It made him feel ridiculous, that smile. What's he laughing at? What's so funny? Then Daniel sees himself start to change in the mirror, before his own eyes. It isn't a pretty sight. He stops looking like James Dean and starts looking like a scrawny twelve year old with too much hair for his puny body with the matchstick arms that aren't big enough to lay a tattoo down on, unless it was a tattoo of a sparrow instead of an eagle. Another thing. He can't grow sideburns. So who's he kidding? What he is, is some left out in the rain, shrunken-up excuse of a James Dean.

The worst was Daniel couldn't give ground. Not while the old man was operating on him with that smile. It was like an eye-balling contest. You better not look away because that means you haven't got the nerve. So he acted like the old man was a bad smell that ought to blow away. But it was tough watching your ears turn red in the mirror and this sort of pitiful sneer edging on and off your lips because you couldn't hold it. So in the end he did lose his nerve because he couldn't take any more of that smile.

"You waiting for this mirror or something?" he asked.

"Well, I had it in mind to shave," said the old man. "But you just carry on. Beauty before age for this one time only. Besides, I never had a chance to see one of those complicated hairdos get built before."

His mother had been after him for over a year to lose the greaser look but she hadn't been able to get him to budge. Now he's considering a scalping, a brushcut, just so the old man doesn't ever google him like this again.

In this house there's no fooling yourself that being different could be like it is in the movies. In the movies, no matter what kind of shit you're taking from people up on the screen, there's always the audience that knows the truth about you, is hoping for you, even admires you. There's no audience in this house. In this house it's too hard to be a rebel.

It can be an interesting place to live, though, Daniel has to give it that. The people who are always dropping by make it so. Mostly they come to play cards and borrow money. Except for Huff Driesen, the old diabetic who can't bring himself to give himself a needle. His daughter usually does it for him but when he goes off on a toot he doesn't dare go to his daughter's because she'll read him the riot act and spoil his fun by going on about how a sick man like him shouldn't be drinking. So whenever he's been hitting the sauce he brings his needle over and Daniel's grandfather gives it to him. Daniel has seen it, right in the kitchen. Huff with his shirt pulled up, his eyes screwed tight so he doesn't see what's going to happen to him, and his mouth squinched so tight he appears to be trying to swallow his own face. And the old man taking aim at his big white belly like he's getting ready to fling a harpoon.

Mr. Stutz says the other ones, the borrowers, come to his grandfather because he's the only man of their kind who has money. The doctor and lawyer have educated money, which is a different thing all together. If you asked them for an interest-free five dollars they'd likely try to determine if it was going to a worthy cause. Your grandfather, says Stutz, isn't like that. With him it isn't necessary to humble yourself for five dollars. You just say, "Can you spare me five until I get my old-age pension cheque?"

And some five dollars, Daniel could tell, weren't loans at all but hand-outs, even though the borrowers insisted on scribbling I.O.U.'s on the backs of envelopes or cigarette boxes. "No, no," his grandfather would say, "not necessary. A man's word is his bond."

And the man might say, "But, Jesus, Alec, this is proof of my good intentions. Legal, so you'll know you'll get your money back."

His mother doesn't have a very high opinion of his grandfather's friends. She declares they're taking advantage of an old fool who's deluded himself into thinking he's lord of the manor. It's pathetic. Some lord, some manor. A manor run by the peasants, she says.

At least they're interesting peasants. In a way he's grateful to them, as grateful can be. Because if his mother wasn't worked up about them, she'd be worked up about him. He's tired of being picked on. He remembers something his mother once told him. "Don't forget," she said, "that it's the tallest tree in the forest that attracts the lightning." Well, he's been the tallest tree in his mother's forest for long enough and it's good to see somebody else catch the lightning for once. It's why he wanted a brother so badly, somebody to take a fair share of the bolts that were always jolting him. Finally, he's getting some relief. You'd have to be blind not to see who the tallest tree in the forest is now. His grandfather. He's fairly fried already. And what lightning he doesn't catch gets spread among the scroungers – for tracking in dirt, slamming the screen door, sitting on chairs with grease on their pants, and timing their visits around meal times or whenever there's anything good on TV. If the truth were known, Daniel feels as if he's on vacation.

Daniel enters Main Street. It's wide and empty, stores locked tight, blinds drawn to protect the goods in the windows from the sun. It makes him feel proud that the two biggest buildings on the street, the hotel and The Palladium theatre, are owned by his grandfather. At this hour there's not a sign of life stirring anywhere, not even any vehicles parked outside the door of the hotel beer parlour. This is because the law requires the beer parlour to close for the supper hour. Mr. Stutz says it should be supper hour all the live-long day then. He's death on drinking. The only one of his grandfather's businesses that Mr. Stutz refuses to work in is the beer parlour, because he says it goes against his principles to sell men what robs them of their senses.

At The Palladium there's no activity either. Over the summer, when the farmers are so busy, the theatre only opens for twice nightly showings on Friday and Saturday. It's one of the things that Daniel misses about the city, the choice of movies and movie houses. Connaught is so deep in the sticks the movies they show are at least a year old. This weekend they're screening *The Young Lions*, which he and his mother saw months and months ago in Toronto. His mother never misses a war movie. She has a thing about the war.

Daniel has decided that just to see Montgomery Clift again he'll spend the money he earned hoeing the old man's garden. Clift was great as the guy who everybody picked on in the barracks. Daniel could identify with that, it wasn't much different from living with his old lady.

Montgomery took it all pretty quietly until the four biggest goons in the company stole the twenty dollars he'd been saving to buy his wife a Christmas present. That severely pissed off old Montgomery. Enough was enough. It didn't matter that he was a skinny, 120-pound weakling, he challenged them to fight. Four nights in a row he took them on, one a night. Even though he always got the snot pounded out of him he was back the next night, ready to fight. Dean Martin kept telling him he was nuts but he just kept coming back. By the last night he looked like death warmed over. His lips were split and one eye was swelling out of his head, black and blue, but none of that counted against principles. Daniel wondered if he'd ever have the guts to do something like that, for honour.

The reason everybody picked on Montgomery Clift was because he read books and was a Jew. Daniel knows his father was a Jew. His mother told him. He doesn't know what that makes him.

At the end of the street he turns left. Across the road and on his right the railway track runs. The whitewashed stock pens which usually hold cattle for shipment to the slaughter houses in Winnipeg waft a stink of manure and piss-damp straw to his nostrils. This evening the pens are empty but some nights when they are full the cattle can be heard bawling clear across town, hour after hour, late into the night. Daniel passes a barbershop, a vacant lot of weeds wreathed in discarded popsicle wrappers and bits of cellophane, a lumberyard stacked with planks smelling of sawdust and resin.

When he reaches the Legion Hall he climbs the steep steps and seats himself in front of the blue double doors. From this vantage he can look out over the railway line and into open countryside. At the foot of the steps is Connaught's memorial to two World Wars, a mortar anchored in a slab of cement. The neck of a Coke bottle protrudes from its muzzle. Kids can't resist stuffing it with garbage. Daniel estimates the trajectory of the bottle if it were really a shell. He sees it launched over the rails, soaring over a mile of tired, over-grazed, beaten-down pasture and wolf willow, landing like thunder on a dun-coloured knoll outcropped with headstones and crosses. The second bomb to go off there in the last ten days.

Daniel shakes his head at the thought and reaches into his shirt pocket for the cigarette he hooked from his mother's package earlier that day. Before lighting it he casts a nervous, furtive glance up the street. He always comes to the steps of the Legion Hall for his evening smoke because from here he can see for a block in both directions up the street. He doesn't want to be taken by surprise by his mother. When it comes to her there is no such thing as being too sure. Daniel wouldn't put it past her to tail him if she noticed that her cigarettes had gone missing.

He sits, hugging his knees, smoking. When he feels lonely, as he does now, Daniel thinks of himself as Montgomery Clift. When his mother makes him mad he thinks of himself as James Dean. The thing about James Dean is the anger and pride of his apartness.

The thing about Montgomery Clift is the sadness and loneliness of his apartness. Tonight Daniel is more Montgomery Clift. He hunches himself up like Montgomery Clift and toys with and broods over his cigarette the way Montgomery Clift does. The evening is a sort of Montgomery Clift evening, too, quiet and still and slow. A kid in a Yankees baseball cap goes by, pedalling his bike so lazily that he has to crank the front wheel from side to side just to keep himself upright, steering with one hand and ringing the bell on his handlebars with the other, simply making noise to keep himself company. If he could see Daniel huddled at the top of the steps he would stop muddling along in a dream. But he doesn't. He just goes on ringing his bell the length of the street. The fainter it grows the more sweetly it chimes until it ripples so plaintive and frail that Daniel can't be sure he is hearing it or the memory of it. And then a car drives by with its windows rolled down and teenagers laughing and a radio playing and that is nearly as good as the bell.

Daniel grinds the cigarette out beneath his heel. He has one more stop to make before returning home. He wants to visit the wall.

During his first days in Connaught Daniel had come upon the back of the hardware store (what he thinks of as the wall) by accident, taking a shortcut home down the alley behind Main Street. There were two things unusual about the wall. It was all blank brick except for a single tiny window set high on the second floor and its brick was not the common, reddish variety but a brick the colour of certain kinds of raw clay, a strong yellow. Still, he might never have noticed it if it hadn't been for the little boy crouched on his haunches before it, intently scraping away at the brick with some sort of tool.

Daniel had halted in the lane and listened to the dry, persistent scratching. What's he up to? Daniel had asked himself. For several minutes curiosity kept him standing there, absolutely still, observing the child work. Then, as people will, the kid had sensed that

86

someone was watching him. He froze. Then slowly his toes began to edge around in the dust, his face twisted around over the point of his shoulder. Seeing Daniel, a big boy, and, worse, a stranger, he settled lower on his heels, trying to shrink, trying to make himself disappear against the bold, glaring, yellow backdrop of the wall. All Daniel had been able to make out were two eyes peering over the tops of knees, two dirty hands clenching shins.

"What you doing, kid?" Daniel had said, trying to make himself sound friendly. He took a step forward.

Question and step were too much for the boy. He broke for it. There was a wild, high, flickering kick of heels, a whirling and circling of arms as he swerved around the corner of the hardware and vanished.

"Hey!" Daniel had called out regretfully. "Hey!" But it had been no use, he was gone.

When Daniel had approached the wall for a closer examination, the first thing he had noticed was an old awl lying at the foundations where the boy had dropped it before he ran. It seemed he had been doing something forbidden.

Then Daniel raised his eyes up to the wall. It was a blur of scratches. To the height a man could reach and for its entire length it was written all over. Scarcely a brick was untouched. Amazed, Daniel had not been able to resist stretching out his hand and running his forefinger along the deep grooves that had been worked into the brick.

What a strange effect those words and signs, those scrawled *fucks* and sentimental, arrow-stricken hearts, those names and dates had had on Daniel who had never felt he had belonged anywhere. All those things collected there, year after year, by common consent. Everyone agreed that there was the place to leave your mark and say your say. In the very centre of the wall was the earliest date which Daniel could find, accompanied by three names: *Avery Toper, Sam Kyle & J.S. Vance*, he had read, *Enlisted Oct. 9, 1915. For King and Country.* They must have been the beginning of the tradition, the fathers of all the rest, because from that date and those names later dates and other names spiralled outward like the funnel of a tornado spinning out from the calm, unchanging eye of the storm. Daniel had counted forty-three names of men announcing enlistment between 1914 and 1918.

After the war, the custom of putting a mark on the wall had not ended but it had altered. People wrote things other than names and dates, so that the wall, like the peace itself, grew more disorderly. The brick swarmed with autograph-book rhymes (*Love many, trust few/Always paddle your own canoe*), insults (*Walter Herbert is a stock diddler*), declarations of love (*John R. & Sharon S., Eternally*).

Now once again finding himself facing the wall, as he has so many times in recent evenings past, Daniel can't explain why standing here makes him feel less lonely, less apart. Maybe it's the feeling that he is on the threshold of a room, crowded and noisy and bustling with life, a party which has been running for years.

Seeing his uncle's name up there also helps him to feel somehow part of it. It's the only name on the wall he can put a face to. He's seen his mother's snapshot of his uncle, a boy in his baseball uniform. In fact, he recently asked to look at it again to search it for some resemblance to himself. His grandfather keeps slipping and calling him Earl.

His uncle's name is high on the wall, so high Daniel has to tilt his head way back to find it. *Earl Monkman, May 2, 1946*, the wall says, *Forever and Beyond*. He had told his mother about discovering his Uncle Earl's name on the wall and asked her what Forever and Beyond might mean. She had laughed. "There must have been another name you missed," she had said. "It was something we used to write as teenagers. *Arnold and Mabel, Forever and Beyond*. It meant undying love. The next time you're there find the other name and let me know who it is. I'd be curious to know."

Daniel had checked. But there was no other name linked to his uncle's. Only *Earl Monkman, May 2, 1946, Forever and Beyond*.

8

◆

For Vera, peace proved to be a great confusion. In the months following the end of the war she began to suspect that life in the Army had cruelly unsuited her for what she now had to face. Being a sergeant had taught her that she preferred giving orders to taking them. Already it was becoming clear that women were expected to quickly lose that acquired taste.

Vera could not bring herself to look for work. It was because she found herself always tired now, an affliction so severe that it made life scarcely seem worth living. Hers was a terrifying condition; she did not know what was happening to her. Finally, when her situation grew desperate enough, Vera decided the answer was a holiday, she must have a complete rest. So she checked into a swank hotel in Toronto. To pay for this extravagance she drew on three years of savings and her $349.65 of discharge pay. For the first time in years, Vera bathed and slept in absolute privacy. She had meals sent up by room service and ate them off her lap, sitting in a chair by the window, watching the throngs flocking the sidewalks and the metal torrent of traffic roaring in the street below. It all seemed to have nothing to do with her.

Endeavouring to feel as fresh and optimistic as those people looked, she bought herself perfume, two smart expensive suits, ordered cut flowers for her room, and went to the beauty parlour downstairs for a cut and a perm. Nothing helped. After those initial bold excursions Vera did not leave her room again until her money ran out.

Not that she didn't try. Her goal was to have dinner downstairs, in the dining room, in the midst of other people. Each afternoon she began to make her preparations. She needed plenty of time to get ready because the slightest effort had become exhausting. Around three o'clock in the afternoon she started with eyebrow plucking, lipstick, and face powder. At four, stockings were rolled up what seemed like miles and miles of leg, and garters were fastened. Next, she picked every blessed speck of lint from her new skirt and jacket, bit by bit, with her fingernails. Finally, it came time to dress. But before she did that it was necessary to pause, to close her aching eyes for just a second. So Vera would stretch herself out on her bed in her bra and panties, and the voices of people passing in the corridor outside her room would come drifting through the open transom, lulling voices that murmured on and on, that pitched her into a thick tangle of dreamless sleep from which she only awoke, shivering, long after midnight, long after the dining room was closed and there was nothing else to do but crawl between the sheets and promise herself. Tomorrow, tomorrow, the dining room.

But the money disappeared, and tomorrow was Mrs. Konwicki's rooming-house. The day Vera moved in, smuggling a frying pan and second-hand hot plate in her biggest suitcase past the landlady with the flabby, baked-red arms of a domestic bully, was the day she suspended her correspondence with Earl. After all her bragging about the Waldorf-Astoria and the advantages of a uniform she was not about to confess to Earl it had all ended in a cheap rooming-house. Vera was ashamed. And to lie about her present circumstances would have meant that she didn't regard them as purely temporary. Things would soon look up. When she was back on the rails, a success again, she would resume writing to her brother and send him her address. However, things were so long in looking up that in the end she lost track of him.

With all her money gone, she had no choice but to look for work. The exhaustion that showed in her face and wilted her carriage was a disadvantage applying for jobs. So, too, were her Army discharge papers which listed her trade as cook. When she explained that she had been more of a kitchen manageress than cook, interviewers either looked indulgent or sceptical.

Once, after being turned away yet again, she had said angrily to the man who had interviewed her, "I thought veterans could be expected to be shown preference."

The man said, "Do you really consider yourself a veteran? A veteran like a man who risked his life on a battlefield? What are you a veteran of?"

Still, she continued on, applying for positions she had no hope of getting. She did this as much to escape the rooming-house as for any other reason. Vera hated it there. It smelled of dusty cocoa-matting and the Polish Princess's little shitter, Stanny. Stanislaus was Mrs. Konwicki's daughter's gift from the angels, a three year old who ran up and down the hallways persecuting his grandmother's lodgers, banging on the closed doors behind which old men coughed day and night, a dill pickle which he'd sucked white poking out of fat, rosy baby lips, and the odour of stale poop following him wherever he went.

One afternoon as Vera sat on a bench in a park it began to drizzle. Unable to bear the thought of being driven back into her musty room, she got to her feet and started to walk, walking in a rain not feeling nearly as cold, melancholy, and dispiriting as sitting in one. An hour of trudging brought her to the doors of a movie theatre. By then she was soaked, her hair hanging in strings, her shoes and stockings soggy, her teeth chattering. The price of a matinee was cheap to escape what had become an icy shower.

As she paid for her ticket, Vera read a small notice taped to the glass of the booth announcing that the theatre was seeking a presentable young man or woman to assist in seating patrons. Apply in person to Mr. A.J. Buckle, Theatre Manager. An old theatre that had once presented touring operettas, vaudeville, and melodramas before being converted into a cinema shortly before the Great War, it retained certain vestiges of opulent, crusty glory: a tracked and faded lobby carpet that had once been a lush scarlet, brass handrails on all stairs, and curtained smoking-loges whose mahogany trim was scarred with cigarette burns and jack-knife hearts and initials. In her opinion it was romantic, had style. On the spur of the moment Vera decided she would apply.

Mr. Buckle turned out to be a plump, middle-aged man, sleek as a seal, whose tiny feet transported him around the room as smoothly as if he were mounted on castors. While interviewing Vera he rolled from side to side, from one buttock to the other, and flapped his thighs together whenever he supposed he'd made a witty remark. The slapping sound helped reinforce Vera's feeling that he resembled a seal.

It soon became clear to her that Mr. Buckle was pretty full of himself. And he asked the most peculiar questions. Could she sew? When she said she could, he nodded enthusiastically. There was an inquiry about the condition of her feet. Any corns, ingrown toenails, plantar's warts? Vera assured him that the condition of her feet was excellent. That was fine, said Mr. Buckle. An usher's feet were as important as a soldier's. With that, he appeared satisfied. The motive for his question about her ability to sew became apparent when Mr. Buckle passed a large paper bag across his desk top and said, "This will be your uniform, dear. It will require alteration. Agnes was somewhat more petite than yourself."

Struggling that night to remake the uniform, Vera wondered what Mr. Buckle's definition of petite might be. Not only did the uniform look like it belonged on an organ grinder's monkey, it also looked like it would fit one. Mr. Buckle's former usherette must have been a midget. Vera couldn't see how the material could be decently stretched to cover her own long-limbed, gawky frame. Hours passed. Vera stitched madly and ripped apart what she had just stitched, made decisive chalk marks on the cloth and then indecisively rubbed them out with her thumb. She was no seamstress, just somebody who had been thimble-whacked by her mother into a modest proficiency with needle and thread. By midnight she despaired of ever putting back together what she had torn to pieces. Not only would she lose the job, she would probably have to pay Mr. Buckle for the garment she had destroyed.

All her life Vera had been a poor loser. She turned to the amputated sleeves and flopping hems with furious, tight-lipped determination. It was three-thirty in the morning when she bit off the last thread. Her task completed, she sat for a moment, massaging her aching shoulders. The thought did not occur to her that this was the first time in months that she was not the least bit tired.

She slipped into the uniform. To see herself full-length in the mirror above her dresser she clambered up on the bed and stood there unsteadily. The dusty maroon uniform consisted of a wrinkled skirt and a jacket with fringed epaulettes. Worst of all was the pillbox hat, complete with chin strap. While she balanced herself in a half-crouch, swaying on the saggy mattress, Vera examined her handiwork. The sleeves halted half an inch above her wristbones. The skirt rode above the hard ovals of her kneecaps. She looked ridiculous. Vera bowed her legs, crooked her arms, and swung them slowly in front of her from side to side, raised a hand, and scratched an armpit. Then she laughed. A real laugh, the first in ages. Laughed so long and so loud that the silence of the sleeping house was shattered. Mrs. Konwicki lodged a complaint with Vera in the morning.

Becoming the darling and champion of the theatre staff helped Vera recover her old self. It didn't matter that her admirers were a pathetic collection of oddballs and misfits who accepted Buckle's reign of terror either because they didn't have the spine to tell him to go and take a long walk on a short pier, or because they knew they weren't employable anywhere else except in another half-assed establishment run by a lunatic similar to Buckle. Their general incompetence made Vera feel protective, even motherly towards her fellow employees.

Frank the usher was fifty-five; a nancy boy with fluttery hands, wide-awake astonished eyes, and a habit of whispering conspiratorially everything he said. He sucked peppermints constantly because he worried about his breath, carried his comb stuck in his sock, and walked as if he were holding a ball-bearing between the cheeks of his ass and didn't want it to fall out. Frank was a great fan of musicals and sometimes when he watched them at the back of the theatre his feet would start to shuffle rhythmically. Once Vera saw him suddenly attempt a pirouette in the dark.

Maurice the ticket-seller was in poor health and distressed by worries about losing his job because his angina pectoris was so bad that ticket-selling was just about the only job he could do. He was Mr. Buckle's errand runner. During the summer Mr. Buckle sent him out to move the manager's Oldsmobile from parking stall to parking stall, following shade, and in the winter he dispatched him to fire the engine of the car every two hours so that when it came time to go home Mr. Buckle would have no trouble starting it.

Then there were Amelia and Doris, the weird Wilkinson sisters, who stood side by side manning the refreshment counter. They never tired of telling how since childhood they had been inseparable. Their one goal in life seemed to be to keep their destinies linked. Although Amelia was a year older than Doris, in their uniforms they appeared to be twins. Outside the theatre they dressed in identical, matching outfits so as to strengthen that impression. Doris and

Amelia liked to pretend they were twins because it made them feel out of the ordinary, special and glamorous the way the Dionne quints were special and glamorous. Their greatest fear was that the other would so anger Mr. Buckle as to get fired, leaving her sister behind, abandoned. The idea was so inconceivable, so unbearable that they had sworn a pact that if one was dismissed the other would immediately resign. However, having sworn such a rash pact, each sister began to doubt the other's judgement in dealing with Mr. Buckle. They were continually admonishing and checking up on one another. "Doris, don't you go giving Mr. Buckle one of your looks!" "Amelia, save your sauce for the goose!"

When Mr. Buckle first took over his duties as manager of the movie house, he deeply offended the Wilkinson sisters when he forbade them to take any unsold popcorn home to their mother as they had been doing for years, on the ground that it encouraged overpopping. Despite their outrage over the imputation they could ever be so irresponsible, Amelia and Doris cloaked their real sentiments and always smiled most charmingly, in unison, whenever Mr. Buckle crossed their paths or found himself in the vicinity of the refreshment counter.

The only member of the staff aside from Vera who showed no fear of the manager was Thomas the projectionist. Since projectionists did not come a dime a dozen Thomas was treated more respectfully by Mr. Buckle than the others were. He was distinguished in another important way. Because he did not come under the public eye he did not have to wear the theatre uniform and was exempt from Mr. Buckle's surprise snap inspections, occasions when all uniformed personnel would be drawn up in the lobby before the doors opened to have their turn-outs scrutinized by the manager. Nothing was more resented than this. Everyone felt Mr. Buckle's observations about their garments and personal grooming to be belittling and demeaning. Mr. Buckle seldom needed to issue a direct order about a failing in attire, a hint was enough. If, however, his hints were not acted upon, retribution was swift. The upshot could be that you found yourself detailed to pick soggy cigarette butts out of urinals for the next month.

His air when he reviewed the troops was swaggering. "Doris, I'd see to that butter spot on your jacket, if I were you. Those of us who handle food must leave an impression of immaculate cleanliness with the public. Butter spots don't look very sanitary, do they? I'd go for a thorough dry-cleaning, if I were you, not just a touch-up with cleaning fluid. You're due for a dry-cleaning. After all, Amelia had hers last week."

His praise was heartily artificial. Formerly a high school principal until certain difficulties led to his resignation, Mr. Buckle knew the value of commending the deserving. "Well, well, Maurice! Now we're certainly looking spiffy. The missus certainly got that braid back into fighting trim in short order! Good man!" And a mournful Maurice would get a cordial clap on the shoulder, the sort of warm congratulation you give a man who gets right on top of things, without a moment's hesitation.

Vera did not get right on top of things, not even after Mr. Buckle had publicly criticized her shoes. Wearing a pair of brown shoes with a maroon uniform just wouldn't do, would it? They sort of clashed, didn't they? Black would go much better with maroon, don't you think? Vera ignored Mr. Buckle and kept right on wearing her brown shoes. The next time the staff were paraded Mr. Buckle made a speech. He said that those who neglected their appearance not only let themselves down, they let down everybody else who worked at the theatre because what one employee did reflected, for good or ill, on all. There was no doubt in anyone's mind who he was talking about. Especially since he kept his eyes fixed on Vera's shoes as he spoke.

Go piss up a rope, Vera thought. She wasn't leaving the one pair of comfortable shoes she owned in the closet because some horse's patoot wanted to play Napoleon. She'd worn a real uniform in her day, one that actually stood for something, and if he thought she was going to take seriously this monkey's tuxedo, he had another think coming.

When he raised the issue again, a week later, Vera put it to him straight. "I'm wearing brown shoes because black shoes don't get picked off trees. Black shoes and my salary don't see eye to eye right at the moment."

None of the staff had ever heard anyone speak to Mr. Buckle that way. Maurice studied the toes of his shoes and nervously shunted his top plate back and forth with his tongue. Frank squeezed his lips and buttocks even more tightly together. Doris and Amelia tried to look disapproving of a woman who could be so rude.

Mr. Buckle got oilier and smoother, a sure sign in his case that he was angry. "You knew what your salary would be when you accepted your position here, Miss Monkman. You were informed."

"Sure I was. But I wasn't informed half of it would have to be ear-marked for dry-cleaning and new shoes. I didn't know I was expected to dress like a Rockefeller on what you pay me."

Mr. Buckle considered such remarks beneath reply. He simply bobbed up and down on his toes, as if he were pumping more pounds per square inch and more purple into his face. When it was sufficiently purple and swollen he turned on his heels and marched off. In retreat to his office he let fly one parting shot over his shoulder. "If shoes are beyond your budget perhaps you might manage to replace your stockings. There's a ladder in one of yours."

"Whyn't you use it to climb up and kiss my ass?" invited Vera under her breath, just loud enough so that the others could catch what she said but Buckle couldn't.

When Mr. Buckle's office door closed on that first act of defiance, Frank and Maurice, Doris and Amelia all clustered around Vera, whispering excitedly.

"Atta girl, Vera. Doesn't he know he got told!"

"What a nerve! The nerve of that man, Vera! Shoes. As if we could afford shoes! Just as easy as glass slippers!"

"The Rockefeller! Did you see his face? The Rockefeller really got to him. Boy oh boy! *The Rockefeller*!"

"Remember your heart, Maurice," cautioned Frank.

"Boy oh boy! Rockefeller right up his ass!"

"Let's not be crude, Maurice," admonished Frank. "Fair sex present."

"Well, Vera said it, didn't she? And so do I. *Rockefeller right up his ass*!"

Mr. Buckle would have fired Vera right then and there if it hadn't been for her one invaluable talent. Nobody could deal with a troublemaker the way Vera did and the theatre was situated in an area where troublemakers were not uncommon. If it wasn't for her, the kids at Saturday matinees might have pulled the building down around their ears the way Samson had the Philistines' temple. And when it came to the other insalubrious types you met running a theatre in this district – the drunks who argued with Cary Grant, the perverts who pestered unaccompanied ladies, the indecent couples who groped and writhed their way through an entire feature presentation – Mr. Buckle didn't know how these would have been dealt with if it hadn't been for that brash young woman.

Maurice certainly was of no use. The mere idea of confronting someone and ordering him to remove himself from the premises was enough to provoke chest pains so bad that the ticket-seller had to be sat down and given an Orange Crush. Frank tried but almost always made matters worse. Six trips to request some noisy chap to quieten down and the fellow grew louder with every visit. There was something about the way Frank walked and talked and breathed peppermint all over the rowdies which only whipped them up into further frenzies of misbehaviour. As for Mr. Buckle – quite early in his career he had got his nose broken when he tried out his high school principal's voice on a young soldier. He avoided running any risk of a repeat performance.

No, when it came to giving somebody the bum's rush, nobody held a candle to Vera Monkman. Mr. Buckle attributed her success to the same disagreeable qualities which disrupted his inspections and often caused him to regret the day he ever set eyes on the woman. These were cheekiness, coarseness, natural belligerence, and an outrageously inflated opinion of herself. In many respects, Mr. Buckle thought, Vera Monkman was a thoroughly hateful young woman.

At the first whiff of a disturbance Vera would swing into action, shoulders squared, mouth set, flashlight poised at the ready like a cocked pistol. Vera did not hesitate. She'd give them the high beam full in the face. As they sat blinded, shrinking behind an uplifted hand, she'd say, "Listen, pal, nobody paid good money to listen to you. They came for Clark Gable. They're having trouble hearing Clark on account of you. So button it and give us all a break. Thank you or else."

Then, snapping off her flashlight, she would wheel abruptly around and stride vigorously back up the aisle before they got a chance to answer. It was part of her tactics. Don't let them get a word back at you. Above all, never plead and never argue. Show them who's boss. If the disturbance resumed, back she went, this time to remove them. There were no second chances. She'd just reach down, grab them, and boost them out of their seats. Most rose without a whimper of protest, it was the element of surprise that did it. If they resisted, Vera quickly sketched what they could expect.

"Look, mister, you don't want to get in a scuffle with me. I don't embarrass. I've got lungs like a banshee and I hang in screaming bloody blue murder until the cops arrive. So it's that or get up quietly and leave. You've got exactly five seconds to make up your mind which it is before I start in. One, two. . . ." They usually hustled out of their seats by four.

Vera explained her method to Frank. "The most important thing is never to doubt they'll come. If you do, you're finished. They're like dogs, they can smell fear." But Frank couldn't seem to get the hang of it.

Although everyone admired Vera, no one admired her quite the way Thomas the projectionist did. Thomas was an unusual young man. Not only did he project film, he also projected wishes. He had a genius for inventing stories and telling them to people who had reason to wish they were true. For instance, he informed Maurice that Mr. Buckle suffered from a secret heart condition much more serious than Maurice's own angina pectoris. "You think you've got it bad? You'll live to be a hundred because you take care of yourself. Have you taken a good look at Buckle lately? The man looks like he's got one foot in the grave. Honest to God, he does. They don't give him much longer, Maurice. Compared to him, you're the picture of health." To Mr. Buckle he confided that both Doris and Amelia adored the manager, found him kind and sympathetic and handsome in a mature, distinguished way. "If I were you, I'd be sure not to show one favour at the expense of the other," counselled Thomas. "It doesn't do to stir up jealousy at work."

He encouraged Frank to get a hair-piece. "Why, it would take twenty years off you. Because, Frank, I have to tell you, that fresh, youthful skin of yours just doesn't jive with those scraps of old hair. Really, it doesn't."

Thomas had no stories for Vera because he could not fathom what she might like to be told. Perhaps it was the mystery that prompted and stoked his ardour. Isolated in his projectionist's booth he meditated on her constantly. Vera, for her part, hardly gave him a passing thought. If she did, it was to feel sorry for him. Sorry for his long, skinny neck perpetually inflamed with ingrown hairs, sorry that he believed wearing a bomber jacket could cover up the fact that he had been rejected for military service. (Frank laid the blame on a hernia.) Sorry that he talked so smugly and embarrassingly of his ambition to operate a small electrical appliance repair shop. "After the war is the Electrical Age. There'll be a fortune to be made in that field. For the ones with the brains to get in on the ground floor."

It never dawned on Vera that the bomber jacket and electrical shop were given such prominence for her sake. Nor that Thomas's offers to walk her home after the theatre closed were anything but a courtesy extended by a shy young man who happened to be strolling in the same direction. So it took her entirely by surprise when Thomas proposed a date. If she had smelled it in the wind she would have prepared a tactful, graceful refusal. But she hadn't and, caught without an excuse, Vera heard herself agreeing to have supper with him on Sunday, the one night they were free from work.

It was a wretched, excruciating evening, a disaster. Thomas had the taxi drop them off in front of one of the better hotels where he proposed having supper. There his courage failed. He knew he had enough money in his pocket to buy the very best, most expensive meals the dining room served, but did he know how to act in such a place? Was he well enough dressed? He ran his tie between his fingers and said, "I just remembered something. I knew a guy who worked in the kitchen here once. The stories he used to tell. I don't think we want to eat here."

So they set off walking in search of another restaurant. Thomas was in a quandary. He had boasted to Vera of the superb meal she had in store for her. "There are only three decent places to eat in town," he'd said, "and Thomas knows them all." Now he was in a dilemma: he had to deliver what he had promised but he was afraid that if he went into a really high-class restaurant he wouldn't know how to behave and would end up making a fool of himself. So he dragged Vera through a hot, humid July night, searching for a restaurant splendid enough to impress Vera but not so splendid as to bewilder him. He would lead her into a hotel, determined this was to be it, and then on the threshold of the dining room he would be assailed by doubt and would hustle her away. His explanation for these sudden retreats was that the place was clearly not up to snuff, didn't meet his demanding standards. "No," he would say, gazing with a wistful air at the waitresses ferrying food from kitchen to table, "this isn't it. I want you to enjoy something really special. I want you to have the best. Money's no object with Thomas."

There was always a better place just up the street, just around the corner. Making for it Thomas would swear to himself that this time there would be no backing down, no failure of nerve. This time he would demand a table in a firm voice, nothing would deter him. But at the last second something always did. Shamefaced he would make his excuses to Vera, invent implausible criticisms, and then bolt with her in tow. Each time his resolve collapsed he grew more desperate. He began to walk more quickly, like a man possessed, hurrying down the hot sidewalks from hotel to hotel with long, stiff-legged strides that almost jerked Vera off her high heels as she clung to his arm. "No," she heard him mumble, "not good enough."

Vera felt as if she were being asked to run a race in a steam bath. By nine o'clock she had had her fill of galloping around aimlessly in the heat with this maniac. She was starving, she had sweated clean through her girdle and was hobbled by a blister on her heel. Enough was enough. Vera made Thomas promise that they would eat in the next restaurant they happened upon, even if it was a greasy spoon. Although Thomas pretended to resist this eating house ultimatum, it came as a great relief to him. He saw to it that the next they passed was the sort of place he was comfortable and confident in, the kind that advertised working-man's specials during the week. Vera was grateful just to be able to sit down and slip her shoe off. She was going to have to stand on that stinging blister through a matinee and two screenings the next day and the sooner she got off it now, the more endurable it would be tomorrow.

The restaurant was deserted and its emptiness made Thomas's voice seem particularly strident and aggressive as he disparaged what it had to offer. After he read each dish aloud from the menu he repeated the refrain, "What a joint. You mean they've got nothing better than this?" He insisted that Vera order the T-bone steak because it was the most expensive item listed. To shut him up she did. Thomas had the Sunday supper special: vegetable soup, roast beef, creamed corn, mashed potatoes and gravy, plus a choice of either vanilla ice cream or chocolate pudding for dessert. When Vera's steak was served to her by a middle-aged waitress with powerful, spectacularly bowed legs, Thomas inquired anxiously, "Is it okay, Vera? Because if it isn't, I'll make them take it back and cook it right. You spend that kind of money – it ought to be done to your liking. Exactly so."

Vera assured him it was lovely, perfect.

"Well, if it isn't just give me the nod. I know how to handle them in clip joints like this."

To deflect Thomas before he really got humming on this topic, Vera remarked: "My, wasn't it hot today though?"

With passion Thomas agreed that it was. Damn hot. Weather like this made you awfully thirsty. Was there enough ice in her water? He could get her more if she wanted it. Boy, was he thirsty. To illustrate how thirsty he was, Thomas noisily downed a large tumblerful of water in one draught.

Never again, Vera promised herself.

Silence reigned for the remainder of the meal. When it came time for dessert Thomas pressed apple pie and ice cream on Vera. He only gave it up after she told him she was watching her figure. "I don't mind watching it myself," said Thomas coyly. Other gallantries were interrupted by the arrival of his chocolate pudding. He complained it had a skin on it.

"They all do," said the waitress implacably. "Cook made them this morning. Can't be helped."

Vera watched, fascinated, as Thomas painstakingly skinned his pudding with the blade of his knife before he mined its goodness with a teaspoon.

It was no longer intolerably hot by the time they came out of the restaurant. Thomas was relaxing now that the evening was almost over. He decided that he had handled things rather well. He sauntered along with his suit jacket slung over his shoulder and a toothpick flicking up and down between his front teeth. "That wasn't such a bad place after all," he said. "But next time, we'll go deluxe."

Vera didn't hear what he said. The softness of the warm night air had awakened memories of how her father and mother had taken her and Earl for evening drives in the country, to cool them off before they were put to bed. Earl, who was little, rode in the cab, seated between her parents, but she was allowed to ride in the open, in the box of the truck. That had been pure pleasure, her long hair whipping and streaming around her face as she leaned out against the rush of air, pretending not to hear her mother tapping on the rear window, signalling her to sit down, to be careful. And the tears springing into her slitted eyes so that the big-bellied white moon above actually seemed to be afloat and rolling in a vast black ocean.

There was longing in her voice when the thought escaped her. "It would have been a lovely evening for a drive in the country," she said.

All the next week Vera avoided bumping into Thomas and readied the explanation, the excuse she would offer when he asked her out again. On Friday, he crept down from the projectionist's booth while the first reel was running and accosted her. "I got one," he said, evidently highly pleased with himself. Vera thought he looked like the cat who had got the canary.

"Got what?"

"A second-hand Dodge so's I can take you for those rides in the country you were hoping for. What do you say Sunday we take a spin out to Niagara Falls?"

Vera was speechless. Was this misunderstanding her fault?

"My old man claims I'm crazy," said Thomas. "One minute

I'm saving every penny I earn so's I can establish myself in business and the next I blow a big chunk of it on a car when the streetcar gets me to and from work, no problem. But what Thomas says is this: If you can give a little pleasure to somebody you care about, what's money?"

Vera knew she ought to say something right then and there. But how could she? How could she spoil his fun with him looking like that, like a little boy with a new train set? She couldn't. They went to Niagara Falls. Vera and Thomas stood side by side staring at the hypnotic sheet of falling water, drenched by the fine spray diffused in the air. "Isn't this just about the most romantic place on the face of the earth?" said Thomas.

"I'm never getting married," Vera put in quickly.

For the next three Sundays in a row Vera consented to be chauffeured about southern Ontario by Thomas. Barns, cornfields, and red-brick towns slid by her dazed eyes. She was absorbed in a difficult calculation. Exactly how many outings did she owe Thomas because of the car? What it had cost him and was costing him was never long out of his mind or conversation. She wouldn't believe what oil and gas alone added up to. Then he had had to buy a new battery. "But," he added graciously, "it don't seem much when you're pleasing somebody."

When could she, in good conscience, make an end of it? And what did it mean to end with Thomas? End what? *Was* there anything to end? Everything was mixed signals, confusion, ambiguity. On one hand he seemed to assume they were sweethearts, yet he had never so much as kissed her. His behaviour towards her was always scrupulously proper, almost brotherly. The most he permitted himself was to hold her hand while he walked her to and from the Dodge. But on other occasions his talk became suggestive, even smutty. In particular, what Thomas had said about Mr. Buckle had left her feeling uneasy – not about Mr. Buckle but about Thomas. She wasn't sure she believed his story.

"You watch yourself when you're alone with Mr. Buckle," he said one golden Sunday afternoon as the Dodge whirled through a shower of autumn leaves.

Vera hadn't really been paying attention. "What's that?" she asked.

"I said," repeated Thomas with emphasis, "*watch yourself when you're alone with Mr. Buckle.*"

"I'm never alone with him."

"You will be," said Thomas, oracularly. "All the female employees are, sooner or later. It's when he gets you in his office, alone, that you've got to be on your guard."

The thought of Mr. Buckle pursuing her around his desk like some figure in a bad cartoon amused Vera. "Buckle chasing a woman would be like a dog chasing a car. Neither would know what to do with it if it caught it."

"He doesn't chase anybody. He just sits behind his desk. Ask Doris and Amelia if he ever gets out from behind his desk when he scolds them."

The significance of this was lost on her. "So he sits behind his desk. What's that supposed to mean?"

"Maybe more goes on than meets the eye."

"Thomas, if you've got something to say, spit it out." Vera was getting mightily annoyed by these riddles.

"I don't think I should say."

"Fine," said Vera. "Good. If you can't say, you can't say. The subject is closed."

It was obvious Thomas didn't want it closed. He licked his lips before proceeding. "Well, I came into his office right after he had Doris and Amelia in there about them not watching the kids stealing gum and candy and like that. When I came in he was tucking something away – if you get my drift. It seems he likes to give something an airing when he gives you women hell. Under his desk, I mean."

Vera stared.

"You get my meaning? He exhibits himself sort of. Under the desk, that's how."

"I see," said Vera. She turned her face away. A horse was standing alone in a field behind a snake fence.

"Would you say that's sick? That's pretty sick, isn't it?"

Vera didn't answer him.

"So if he ever pulls any of those tricks with you, just let me know. I'll make him sorry he was ever born. You can count on it."

It was this story and the queer sensation it left her with that prompted Vera to concoct one of her own stories. This one involved an elderly female relative whom it was necessary to visit every other Sunday. It was the first step in a plan to wean Thomas from her company. On the Sundays she supposedly spent with her female relative the phone in the rooms she had rented after leaving Mrs. Konwicki's rang all afternoon, at intervals of an hour.

Vera's feeling of uneasiness about Thomas began to grow. Nothing he had done so far was extraordinarily peculiar, but many things were slightly off, unfocussed, like a blurry film which had you wiping at your eyes as you watched it. The gifts he was constantly presenting her with were a case in point. These were small, inexpensive presents which he rather ceremoniously gave her before they embarked on their Sunday rides. His tributes, however, were strange ones, the sort of gifts given to people in hospital but not to your best girl: a bag of plums, magazines, a package of cigarettes. Never flowers, chocolates, or perfume. Not, of course, that Vera hoped for anything intimately associated with an avowal of love. Far from it. Still, his gifts were so eccentric that Vera sometimes wondered if she wasn't the butt of a subtle and devious practical joke. Were these offerings an elaborate form of sarcasm? What did he mean to say with a bag of plums?

Then on the last Sunday in October, at a time when Vera's exasperation with Thomas and his antics had reached the breaking point, she saw an opportunity to clear the air. Mixed in among five or six screen magazines he had presented her with (a case of carrying coals to Newcastle if she had ever seen one) she discovered an issue of *Vogue* devoted to bridal gowns.

What was the meaning of this? she demanded, flourishing the magazine.

"I wondered when you'd get around to it," said Thomas. He was sitting on Vera's davenport and the light coming in the window made him resemble a self-satisfied cat basking in sunshine.

"Get around to what?"

"What's on every girl's mind. Marriage. I thought I'd make it easier for you to bring it up."

"Excuse me," said Vera. She strode to the bathroom, bolted the door, and sat on the toilet. Think, she urged herself. Think. Think. But she couldn't. For five minutes, for ten minutes, she crouched on the toilet seat, her heart drumming every solution to her predicament out of her head. All she could be certain of was that she had handled all this very wrong, wrong from the start.

After twenty minutes she heard fingernails politely scratching on the door. The cat wanting to be petted, or given a saucer of cream. "Vera, are you all right?" he said forlornly.

"Yes, but I'd appreciate a little privacy all the same."

"Oh. Sorry."

Minutes later he was back. "Please come out, Vera," he said. "I know you feel embarrassed but there's no need to be. I want exactly what you do. It's natural for people our age to want to get married. You needn't hide. We both want the same thing."

"Like hell we do!" shouted Vera. No, that was not the way to handle the situation. She must control herself. Vera took a deep, calming breath and spoke very carefully. "You're wrong, Thomas. A terrible mistake has been made. You've not understood me from the beginning. I don't want to marry you, Thomas. I didn't even want to spend Sundays riding in your car. But I did and that was my mistake. But I'm not going to let this go on any longer. Do you understand? It would be easier on us and better if you left now. I'm sorry for everything. I really am."

There was a moment of terrible, hushed silence and then Thomas began to shake the bathroom door.

"I blame myself, too," said Vera, stumbling to offer an apology as the door rattled and jumped in the frame. "I ought not to have encouraged you with these Sunday rides. But I felt bad that you had bought the car. I didn't mean for you to waste your savings like that. And I wasn't sure exactly what it meant or what you were after. I kept thinking that maybe you just thought of me as a good friend, a pal. After all . . . what I mean to say, you never got overly friendly or anything, did you now?"

"I respected you, Vera."

"And I'm glad you did. I appreciate how you've always behaved as the perfect gentleman. And still will now, won't you, Thomas?"

He ceased rattling the door. All was still. Vera laid her ear to the door and listened intently. There was nothing to hear but she could feel Thomas on the other side. Then he spoke. "Who's your other Sunday man? The one you see when you won't see me?"

"Don't be ridiculous, Thomas. There is no other Sunday man. Or Monday or Tuesday man for that matter."

"Who is he?"

"I'm not talking about this. There's nothing to talk about."

"Who's your other Sunday man?" Thomas demanded, his voice rising dangerously.

"If you continue with this nonsense it's the end of our conversation. Do you understand?"

"*Who is he!*" The cry was sudden, so piercing that Vera sprang back from the door, startled. Thomas resumed his attack. The door wobbled, creaked, bulged as he flung his weight against it. Vera jerked open a drawer beneath the sink, seized a pair of scissors and retreated from the door as far as possible. This meant climbing into the bathtub. There she stood with the scissors clutched in both hands, extended at arm's length from her body and pointed at the heaving door.

"Who's your other Sunday man! Who's your other Sunday man! *Tell me!*" implored Thomas wildly.

"Stop it! Stop it this minute, Thomas!"

"Who?" It was his last question. He could not continue the interrogation because he had begun to sob.

"Thomas? Thomas?" Vera realized he had fled his station when she heard him trip over the loose tile in the hallway. Vera clambered out of the tub, rushed to the door, listened. The faint sounds of Thomas moving about in the kitchen penetrated to her. They were muffled and indistinct, unidentifiable except when she heard him blow his nose loudly. The dim noises shifted location, now they seemed to muddle about the living room. After a bit the apartment door slammed. It seemed Thomas had gone off. Vera proceeded cautiously nevertheless, scissors in hand. She did not rule out tricks. Perhaps he lay in waiting for her. She discovered his message in the living room where the word CUNT was written on the davenport in mustard, the letters a foot high.

Vera arrived for work Monday, hopping mad, determined to slap Thomas's face in front of everybody. If he thought he could get off scot-free after the disgusting thing he had done to her davenport, he had another think coming. And if anybody wanted to know why she had slapped his face, she'd tell them, word and all.

But there was no face to slap. There was no Thomas. A relief projectionist was in the booth and rumours were flying. Someone had heard that Thomas had phoned Mr. Buckle at home, on Sunday, and quit his job. No, said another, he hadn't quit, only requested sick leave because he was rundown, needed a rest. Despite the differences in the rumours all seemed to be agreed that Vera had had a hand in Thomas's disappearance. Doris and Amelia hinted to Vera that Mr. Buckle was furious with her and held her responsible for the loss of the best projectionist he had ever had, one who didn't smoke in the booth in the midst of highly inflammable film and didn't show up for work drunk. When Frank spoke to Vera he did so gently and mournfully, in a doe-eyed manner appropriate in addressing the wretched in love, the heart-broken.

Vera didn't give a tinker's fart for what they thought as long as she was rid of that geek Thomas. It looked as if she was. But shortly after she decided that, the letters began to arrive.

Dear Miss High & Mighty,

I dont expect anyone to feel sorry for me but isnt it funny. Here I am without a job and no savings because I spend my money on the Dodge all for you to make you happy. And now I cant enjoy it myself without the money to fill the tank or even buy a spark plug. Well remember lifes a funny thing and those who think there on top dont always finish that way.

People have played Thomas for a fool before like at school and whatnot. But tell your Sunday man that this fool has often fooled them and got what Thomas wants. So dont bother to laugh yet the two of you. Another thing Ive got my ways of finding out who he is.

> *Yours,*
> *Thomas*

Several days after this letter was delivered Vera came out of the theatre after it had closed for the night and spotted Thomas. He was across the street, huddled up in the dark doorway of a music store. It gave Vera quite a fright to see him there, spying on her. Her first inclination was just to walk quickly, to pretend he didn't exist. But maybe that was running away. She took three or four brisk steps, then changed her mind, swung round, and saluted him by waving to him in an exaggerated fashion, like a woman flagging down a bus from the side of a highway.

Thomas betrayed not a flicker of recognition. He remained slouched and unmoving until Vera exhausted the novelty of her performance and walked on with an angry toss of the head.

Dear Miss High Opinion of Yourself,

I suppose you figure it was a big laugh waving like that the other night. Well I wave to my freinds and I have plenty of them good ones more than you think and I dont wave to people who think waving is to make fun of somebody. I could have waved back maybe for a joke if I didnt love you Vera. But love is not a joke. It is the most serious thing there is. More serious than death is love. If you could learn that Vera you might be happier I can see you arent always so angry. Dont make jokes about me or my love. I have been awfully forgiving but it is hard when you are so miserable like me.

> *Your freind,*
> *Thomas*

Vera put a paring knife in her purse and slid a hat-pin into the sleeve of her coat where she could get to it in a hurry if she needed to. It was November. The nights came early and there were fewer people in the streets because of the cold. Vera's walk home after work seemed lonelier and longer than it had in the summer.

One night she stepped out of the lobby of the theatre and into a change of weather. There was a smell of snow in the air and a harsh wind was scurrying scraps of paper down the street and moaning through the telephone wires overhead.

Change of any sort, even the passing of autumn into winter, always had the effect of temporarily lifting Vera's spirits. Now the stinging wind which burned her cheeks braced and energized her. She went forward briskly, the rapping of her heels on the sidewalk sounding crisp and metallic in the frosty, clear night. Only the occasional late-night diner showed any signs of life. In them Vera could see cabbies arguing and drinking coffee at the counters. These were the same men who prowled their hacks back and forth in front of the theatre when the movies let out, hoping to snap up a fare. But tonight the hunting had been bad, a sparse crowd for a bad movie. So they were sitting on their duffs, trying to make up their minds whether to call it a night and go home to the little woman or to keep trying to scare up a buck against the odds. Vera might have joined them for a cup of hot chocolate if the wind hadn't felt so good in her face. It was blowing her head clean of the reek of cheap perfume, men's hair oil, and the close, hot, over-powering smell of bodies packed shoulder to shoulder so they could be entertained. She turned up her collar, hugged her coat to her bosom, lengthened her stride.

After five minutes at this determined pace, Vera turned into a narrower, quieter street of small shops over which their proprietors and families lived. For almost a year Vera had passed this way each day on her way to and from work but its strangeness had not worn off; it still seemed to her foreign and a touch romantic. Sometimes she imagined it was a street in Europe because she knew this was as close to Europe as she would ever get, and her walk home became a stroll in Vienna, Budapest, Prague. What helped this illusion was the look of the stores and the immigrant storekeepers, most of whom were Jews.

Vera always shopped on this street out of a sense of adventure, to hear the nervous, dark-suited men serve her in English accented by Polish, Russian, German, Hungarian, and Yiddish. She was secretly disappointed when she was waited on by one of the sombre, responsible children who deftly wrapped parcels and climbed onto stools to ring up sales and make change with decision. It was difficult to preserve the illusion of Vienna or Budapest when the children spoke to her in their ordinary, everyday Canadian voices. Neither the Stars of David, the Yiddish signs in the windows, nor the young boys with their beanie hats stuck on the crowns of their heads could help recapture the dream that language had shattered. No, what was more to Vera's taste was some shrunken old man bent over his counter late at night, poring over a newspaper, a single light burning in the shop for economy's sake, and the rest in shadow. That could be Russia.

There were no such sights to be seen tonight. The bad weather had long ago blown out hope of customers in even the most stubbornly optimistic. Blinds were drawn and doors were locked. The rings in the window of the shabby jewellery store were covered with a cloth, the sausages were removed from the hooks in the butcher shop; the pawnshop, the shoe store, the corner grocery were all dark.

It was on her favourite street that the absence of traffic allowed Vera to hear footsteps closing quickly on her from behind. A glance over her shoulder told her it was who she thought it was. Only one light showed on the street, a window burned on the second floor above a men's wear shop across the street. Vera fluttered toward it like a moth. She hurried across the street, coat flapping, eyes lifted to the light. Someone was up there, awake.

Behind her she heard feet break into a run, a patter of leather on asphalt.

Brought up short by the storefront, Vera jerked around, an animal at bay. When she whirled about, Thomas checked his headlong pursuit in the middle of the street. Briefly he hesitated and then came on in a stiff, self-conscious amble meant to suggest a man confident and completely at ease. Over Vera's shoulder four shadowy mannequins watched his approach, saw him snatch off his tweed cap, ball it in his fist, and stuff it in his pocket when he was just yards from her. He came on like a sleepwalker and only halted when he was so close to Vera that it was all she could do to stop herself from visibly shrinking away, backing herself up against the plate-glass window. The light from the window above revealed perspiration gleaming on Thomas's upper lip and a ghostly dab of shaving lather on the lobe of his left ear. The run had quickened his breathing. Vera saw him pant white smoke in the cold air.

"What do you want?" demanded Vera, feigning assurance. "Why are you following me, Thomas?"

Thomas did not appear to know how to reply. He started to lift his arms and then let them collapse helplessly against his sides. He shook his head, began to rock back and forth on his toes, swaying like a man overcome by vertigo on the brink of a precipice.

"What do you want?"

Thomas's answer was to lurch blindly forward, fall on his knees, fling his arms convulsively about her waist, and burrow his face into the front of her coat. The theatricality, the extravagance of this gesture, paralyzed Vera with numbing embarrassment. My God, she thought, what if someone is witnessing this performance? How ridiculous. She cast her eyes apprehensively up and down the street.

"Stop it," Vera said, her voice lowered now in such circumstances, almost a whisper. "Stop this, Thomas."

He only clung to her harder, tightening his arms around the small of her back and working his face against the cloth of her coat. The strength of this embrace almost toppled her, and she had to reach out and steady herself by placing a hand on his head, but at the touch of his hair she withdrew her hand as if it had brushed fire. The grinding of his forehead against her pubic bone was becoming painful.

"Stop it!" she cried angrily, shoving at his shoulders. "Get away!"

Which only spurred Thomas to clench her even more suffocatingly close, to crush her spine with the jutting bones of his wrists. It was the squeezing pain, the panic of being robbed of breath, that made Vera strike Thomas smack dab on the dried shaving lather plastered to his ear. Her roundhouse slap rocked him but didn't break his grip so that when she tried to tear herself free she only succeeded in losing her balance and crashing back against the plate-glass window. The store boomed hollowly, like a drum.

Vera recovered and came up fighting. She pummelled his head and shoulders with both hands, snapped her body backward in an attempt to break free. Thomas was dragged along her line of retreat, scrambling on his knees, his forehead bouncing off her pelvis and his hair shooting up in bursts of shock whenever Vera landed one of her haymakers. Whenever she missed and caught air Vera reeled and slammed against the window, striking the sound of distant thunder out of it.

Then a light burst on behind the mannequins, a lock rattled, and the door to the shop was thrown open. Vera and Thomas froze. Thomas remained on his knees, neck craned around to the door, mouth hanging open stupidly and eyes squinting against the sudden brightness. A man in a vest undershirt, trousers, and stockinged feet stood in the open doorway, a look of gentle, bemused perplexity on his face. He was middle-aged, very tall, stoop-shouldered, and had faded, reddish hair. Something about his manner made Vera think of Jimmy Stewart, her favourite actor. He had the bewildered innocence of Mr. Smith. A slow smile of amusement spread over his face as he took in the scene, Thomas down on his knees before Vera.

"I hope I haven't interrupted a proposal," was all the man said.

With that, Thomas got to his feet and began to strike ruthlessly at the dust on the knees of his trousers.

"Not likely," spat out Vera. She jabbed an accusing finger at Thomas. "He followed me. He chased me. I ran here because I saw a light was on."

The red-haired man took a step nearer, peered from one to the other, settled on Thomas. "Is that right?" he asked. "Were you following the lady? Did you chase her?"

"I only wanted to talk to her," said Thomas sullenly. "Anyway, what business is it of yours?"

The storekeeper turned to Vera. "Do you know this man?"

"Does she know me," interjected Thomas. "I'll say she does. She's my girlfriend."

The red-haired man nodded his head reflectively. "So it's like that," he said. "A lover's spat. But please, not on my window." He flattened his palm against it. "It's only glass. A really good spat could break it."

"I want you to know," said Vera, "that this man is an out and out maniac. I never was a girlfriend of his. He imagined it all. Mister, this man is crazy and I'm afraid of what he might do to me. Please tell him to go away."

"You know that isn't true, Vera. You were my girlfriend."

"And there's no lovers' spat either. He just ran up and grabbed me here on the street. What it is is a pervert attack or something."

The red-haired man was speaking to Thomas. "Please, maybe it would be better if you left the lady alone for the time being. Who knows? Maybe tomorrow she'll want to talk. But now she's upset and it's clear she doesn't want to discuss matters."

Thomas glowered at the advice. "Why don't you keep that big fucking nose of yours out of our business? Who asked you?"

"Oh, I think this is my business," the man answered calmly, "because, you see, this window the two of you were trying to crash through is my business. And if it's true that you're bothering this young woman like she says you are – well then, in all decency, that has to be my business, too."

"You'd better believe he's bothering me," chimed in Vera.

Thomas raked her with a brooding glare. "You better shut up, Vera," he warned.

Suddenly she remembered the hat-pin. She drew it out of her sleeve and held it glinting in the light. "How'd you like this rammed up your ass, buster?" she said.

"That's enough," the store owner said sharply, pushing her arm down. "Maybe everybody should calm down and stop talking such nonsense, threatening each other like children. Maybe you should go home now, son, and give her time to think about it."

"Yeah, with any more time to think about it I ought to really make myself sick to my stomach," said Vera.

The man ignored her. He continued speaking to Thomas in a soft, persuasive tone. "There's really no point, is there?" he reasoned. "This has all got out of hand. Leave her be. Sleep on it. The morning always makes a difference. Don't make yourself any more trouble."

It was the mention of trouble that seemed to agitate and incense Thomas. "There's no trouble in me standing where I choose!" he said, flying into a rage. "You can't order me off the street! You and your tribe may have bought everything on it but you don't own the road yet!" Suddenly seized by suspicion he broke off, threw Vera a cunning, measuring look. "So this is it, is it? Some dirty old Jew waiting for you in his underwear."

Vera flung her arms into the air in exasperation. "Didn't I say he was crazier than a shit-house rat?" she appealed to the storekeeper.

"Don't think I don't know who the Sunday man is now. Only light on in the street and she goes for it. Pussy bought by a kike!" he shouted. "Pussy bought by a kike!"

"Lower your voice," said the red-haired man. "There are old people who live on this street who shouldn't have their sleep disturbed by such foolish and disgusting talk. It frightens them, loud voices and such talk."

"Make me lower it," taunted Thomas, mouth twisted, bitter. "What's the old saying? Takes nine tailors to make a man. How many Jew tailors to make one? Show me. Make me lower it! But your type can't, can they?"

What astounded Vera was the composure of the red-haired man. She could detect no sign of anger in his face, only some variety of resigned melancholy. "No," he said quietly, "I suppose my type can't ever make your type do much."

"You're fucking right you can't!" crowed Thomas. "I'll make just as fucking much noise as I please. I'll, I'll . . ." and, lost without a threat, Thomas looked wildly about him, reared back, and drove his heel into what confronted him in the glass of the store window, his own desperate, unhappy reflection.

The pane exploded in fissures like the break-up of a frozen river and then the shards began to drop about them in an icy, silvery-sounding rain as the store expelled a long sigh of warm air into their astonished faces. Vera and the shop owner were still gaping when Thomas whirled about and began a panicked get-away, coat billowing out behind him as he clattered up the street. Vera, turning, wondered why the red-haired man didn't give chase. He hadn't yet lifted his eyes from the glittering wreckage strewn at his feet. So it fell to Vera to express the anger and contempt she believed Thomas had earned. "Run, you coward, you!" she shouted after him. "Run, you gutless wonder!"

The sound of her voice brought Thomas up short, looking like a man who has forgotten something. He stood facing her, indistinct, blurred by a hundred yards of night. "So, Vera," he called plaintively, "what'll it be? Whose side are you on anyway? Mine or his?" A pitiable question that only Thomas could have framed in such circumstances.

Vera squeezed her eyes tightly shut and obliterated Thomas. "His!" she shouted, shaking with fury. In the release of bottled-up tension a kind of exaltation took hold of her. "His! His! His!" she cried, eyes and fists clenched tight. A hand took her by the shoulder. "That's enough," said the man. "Quiet. He's gone now." Vera opened her eyes to lights springing on above the shops and silhouettes sliding over drawn blinds. Her gaze fell to the road. He was right. Thomas was gone. There was no trace of him. Except for the broken glass.

Vera felt a twinge of responsibility for having led misfortune to the door of a stranger. "Christ," she said, shoving a piece of glass with the toe of her shoe, "look at the mess he's made. Look at what that poor excuse for a man did to your window. If you call the police I can give them his address. I know where he lives. I'd be glad to be a witness for you."

The man shrugged, turned down the corners of his mouth expressively. "I don't think police are what that unfortunate young man needs," he said. He regarded the fragments of broken glass and the light which fell glittering upon them. "Kristallnacht," he said to himself.

Vera had not understood the foreign-sounding word. "Pardon me?"

"Nothing. Don't pay any attention to me. I was just reflecting upon the beauty of broken glass and electric light. Others have done it before me."

"There's nothing beautiful about broken glass. It only means work, sweeping it up, replacing it."

"A practical woman," he said.

"Well, maybe we should set about fixing it. If nothing else, we can tape some pieces of cardboard into the window. You must have boxes in the store."

He dismissed the suggestion with a wave of the hand. "It's much too big a hole for cardboard. Repairs can wait until morning."

"I'm not saying it would keep anybody out but what if it snows? And a window without anything in it has got to be an invitation to help yourself."

"If it snows it snows. There's nothing really worth stealing except the cash register and I can carry that upstairs with me. Besides, if there are any prowlers I'll hear them."

"You sleep that light?"

"As a matter of fact, at night I don't sleep at all." He smiled wryly at her surprise. "I'm a man of peculiar habits. I go to bed for five or six hours right after I close the store. At midnight or so I get up to read. Perfect peace and quiet. No interruptions. Except for tonight," he added. "A bachelor's freedom to do as he pleases. This is the wild use I make of my freedom."

"You read all night?"

"I also drink too much coffee. Sometimes with a little whisky in it. More bachelor wildness." He hesitated. "After such a cold and trying adventure as you've had tonight, could I interest you in a cup of coffee?"

"I believe you could."

He held out his hand. "I believe formal introductions are usually the preamble to whisky. Stanley Miller."

"Pleased to meet you, Mr. Miller," said Vera, taking his hand. "I'm Vera Monkman."

"Please, Miss Monkman," he said, indicating she should enter, courteously stooping his stooped shoulders even more.

That was how it began. Her trailing him as he puffed up the steep stairs packing an antique nickel-plated cash register in his arms. Or perhaps it didn't really begin until she stepped into his apartment and looked with amazement upon his living room, books stacked to the height of a man's head along three walls and a phonograph player spitting static because she and Thomas had interrupted his pleasure. And then he reset the needle on the record spinning there on the turntable and the music began once more at the beginning and it was classical. Pure and refined and as different from what she listened to on her radio in her rented rooms as crystal is different from everyday glass. (Kristallnacht was the word he had said.)

And the conviction took hold of her that all these books and this music were where she was headed when she was sixteen years old, reading Shakespeare and learning French, and then it got stolen from her, this dream she never quite got straight in her head because she was too young, but was nevertheless surely bound for, a true tendency of the heart's deepest ambition.

It made her feel unworthy, that room, and filled her with regret that she had never become so fine a person as to deserve sitting in such a room. And that, too, was the beginning of it.

9

Once Daniel and Alec were clear of Connaught and onto the country backroads the police seldom bothered to patrol, grandson and grandfather exchanged seats so that Daniel could drive the truck the rest of the way to the farm. Alec couldn't see any harm in this. He had given the boy plenty of practice wheeling the water-truck over the rutted trails that criss-crossed his land and tied one field and one pasture to another. He was confident Daniel could handle it. Traffic on the grid roads was always light and it was likely they would travel miles and miles without encountering another vehicle. Besides, Monkman had to admit that the kid might be less of a menace behind the wheel than he was himself. On several recent occasions Alec had caught himself just in time, at the point his truck was on the verge of careening off the road and plunging down into a ditch. There had been barely time to jerk the wheel around and recover his line in a spray of gravel.

Monkman knew it was not his eyes that were to blame; it was his mind. When it wandered the vehicle wandered with it. The young weren't prey to this particular misfortune. Look at Daniel. All attention, he was trying his damnedest to do it right, to please. Not once had his eyes left the road, his speed remained cautious and steady, both hands were quick and diligent on the wheel. He glowed with importance. Well, it never hurt to give a boy a job that puffed his chest out a little. Everybody needed to matter. That was the reason he discussed his business with the boy, just as if Daniel had a clue as to what he was talking about or owned an opinion worth listening to. Respect was not ever wasted, not even on a twelve-year-old kid. If he had finally learned anything from living, it was that.

So he had explained to Daniel at great length what they were doing today and why they were doing it the way they were. He hoped it would be a lesson in how complicated life could be, a demonstration that nothing was ever as simple and straightforward as it might look. Not even catching a thief.

For five years running the old man had been after his tenant, Marker, to break a pasture on the farm and seed it to flax. Every year Marker promised he would, but never got around to it. When he neglected again that spring to turn sod, Monkman, disgusted that land should stand idle and unproductive, bought twenty head of cattle to graze it. Now one of them was missing. Marker claimed it had been killed by lightning.

On Tuesday, when Alec and Daniel had come to pump a tank of water for the garden from the creek, Marker had been too insistent on showing them where he had supposedly disposed of the animal's carcass. He led them to the cellar hole of the original homesteader's shack. It was filled with rocks carried from a stone pile at the edge of a nearby field. Marker had asserted that the missing steer lay buried under the boulders. Alec didn't believe it for a second. First of all, there were no drag marks on the ground near the cellar hole and such marks would have been clearly visible if the steer had been pulled there with a tractor as his tenant claimed. Second, it was entirely out of character for Marker to go to all the trouble and effort of burying a dead animal, particularly one he didn't own. Over the years, to his grief, Alec had learned that Marker was as lazy as a spotted dog. He would be much more inclined to let a carcass rot and breed flies than haul boulders to cover it.

However, Alec didn't question or confront Marker with his suspicions. He held his peace. Later, when he told Daniel of his suspicions the boy had been incensed. He had said that if it were up to him, he'd make Marker *prove* that the steer was under those stones, even if that meant making him hoist every last one of those rocks out of the cellar hole, stone by stone.

"Not practical," his grandfather had said, shaking his head. "It'd be impossible to lift some of those stones out of that hole and Marker knows it. He knows I'll never know what's really under there. Remember, it's a hell of a lot easier to roll a stone into a hole than out of it. Besides, before you call a man a liar and a thief you better *know* you're right. I only suspect I am."

"What difference does it make if you're right this time or not?" Daniel had wanted to know. "You say he's been stealing from you for years. Serve him right."

Monkman had said that. Yet deep in his heart he recognized that he had some responsibility to bear for the thefts. Somehow he had allowed the line between sharp dealing and outright dishonesty to grow fuzzy in Marker's mind. He hadn't checked the man at the very beginning when it would have counted. When he had detected Marker in certain blatant fiddles – underestimating the wheat yield to reduce his landlord's share of the grain – Marker had never been shamefaced when discovered cheating. His most common reaction was to become aggrieved. By his standards his landlord was a rich man and rich men ought to expect to be taken advantage of. What was he complaining about? Caught in a lie he was apt to say disdainfully, "Well, if you say it's yours – take it. I ain't in a position to stop you. Your word's pretty close to law around here, I suppose."

Daniel thought the no-good sonofabitch should be pitched out on his ear. The young were always bloodthirsty. It was difficult for Monkman to explain why he couldn't do that. He had to think of more than one Marker, after all. There were seven other little Markers ranging in age from thirteen years to six months and a Mrs. Marker, a hard-working, long-suffering woman whom he secretly pitied. If he kicked Marker off the place a family would lose a livelihood and a house. He wasn't sure his conscience was up to that.

Whenever he thought of the Markers, Alec was reminded of rats. Alfred Marker was the very image of a rat with his slightly bucked big front teeth speckled with snuff so that he looked like he'd been chewing chop in a farmer's bin and his long, fat rat's nose keeping his dark, beady eyes from rolling up against one another. All his children took after the father in appearance and temperament.

What Alec had to accept under the circumstances was the impossibility of totally eradicating rats once they had become established as this nest had. The best he could aim at was control, at keeping their depredations within bounds. Helping themselves to a steer was definitely out of bounds. If the steer hadn't yet been disposed of – sold or butchered – Alec wanted to find it. And if he succeeded in finding it, he would give Daddy Rat such a godawful scare that for years hence he would shit yellow at the mere mention of the name Alec Monkman.

Monkman guessed that the steer might be haltered to a tree deep in bush, hidden there on the assumption that even if an old man had his suspicions he couldn't go acting on them, couldn't go beating the thickets, scrambling over deadfalls, bulling his way through willows and rose thorns looking for a steer. But what Marker had forgotten was that he had a pair of young legs to do his bidding.

The truck had come to the crest of hills which overlooked a broad, deep valley nine miles south of Connaught. Alec's farm was just the other side of this valley, situated on a plateau which drew a straight line between sky and round-shouldered, wooded slopes. From this height, Daniel and Alec could gaze out over long prospects. Above, a bleached-denim sky and flying cloud. Below, the valley bottom, the quilt of crop and summerfallow darkening and lightening with shadow and sun as the clouds streamed overhead, the turtle-backed sandbars sunning themselves in the slow pulse of a drought-starved river. Across the way, the tops of the poplars shivered in unison as the road switched back and forth like a cat's tail up the sides of the opposing hills.

Then all this was lost sight of in the descent. Hard to their left, cutbanks rose above the road, sheer clay cliffs pocked with swallows' holes and sprouting hairy tree roots which groped and fumbled in the air. To the right, at every turning, Alec could peer over the edge of the road into a gash of coulee, a dark seam down the face of the slope, choked with berry and willow bushes. The truck twisted deliberately down on to the flats, rumbled hollowly over a bridge of planks, and then began to climb, Daniel gearing down under his grandfather's direction, the sun beating on their faces through the tilted windshield whenever the trees that grew on the banks high above the road thinned and admitted a blaze of sky. Up top they rolled on for another half-mile before Daniel swung the truck into an approach, braked, and Alec got out and unhooked a barbed wire gate. They were at the farm.

The sight of the farmhouse never failed to fill Monkman with resentment and regret. It had been bought for Earl and Earl's house was still how he thought of it. It was a bitter thing for him to contemplate the state it had fallen into. The lilac hedge was dead because Marker couldn't be troubled to haul water for it. Alec couldn't remember the last time the house had been painted, although he had on several occasions bought paint for that purpose. He had no idea where it had gone to, perhaps Marker had sold it. All he knew was that it hadn't found its way onto his siding. Over the years the house had been almost completely reduced to the weary grey of weathered board, although patches of flaking paint still clung to the wood in places like stubborn lichen to rock. There was a grinning gap in the ornamental wire fence which surrounded the yard because Marker had cut it to allow the passage of his Ford tractor and cultivator to the back garden where one day he had harvested twenty hills of potatoes by tearing up the earth with cultivator shovels. Marker didn't care for potato forks and digging.

Directly outside the mangled fence, in front of the front door, Monkman's tenant had parked his farm machinery, presumably for convenience sake. However, to speak of the machinery as Marker's was not strictly correct. Many of the implements had been bought for Earl and later loaned to Marker so that he could farm more efficiently. Regardless of ownership, all the pieces of machinery were in the same state of poor repair. At the moment, a hay rake, a disker, a tractor, and a hay baler were drawn up outside the house. All the tires on the hay baler were flat and chickens were nesting in the drop chute. Several of these fluttered awkwardly up when Daniel eased the truck beside the baler and cut the motor.

Mrs. Marker bustled on to the porch, squinting. She was thin as a rake and her skinny white legs seemed to stab out of a billowing, faded housedress and into a pair of broken-down men's oxfords, as if they were trying to nail the shoes to the porch floor. Looking the way she did, she always put Monkman in mind of some stray bitch sucked too hard by too many greedy pups. He saw that they'd interrupted the setting of her hair; one half was lank, wet, and stringy, the other half, tight curls and bobby pins.

"It's you," she called out as Monkman grappled his way out of the truck. "When I heard the truck I wondered who could be company. We don't expect you except water days, Tuesday and Friday."

That's what I'm counting on, thought Monkman grimly. His salute, however, was cheerful and hearty. "Good day, missus. Is the boss around?"

The rest of the Markers, the pups who had sucked her skinny, began to show themselves. The second oldest boy crept on to the porch. When he had identified the visitors as familiar he pulled open the screen door and shouted back into the house, "It's nobody. Just Monkman."

With this reassurance the rest trooped out: the five-year-old twin boys, the two girls, the oldest with her baby brother in her arms. The twins sprang off the steps, hurled themselves onto the yard gate and began to swing ferociously back and forth on it. The remainder of the Markers aligned themselves on the porch in a fashion that suggested they were readying themselves to repulse attack.

"No, Alfred's not here," answered Mrs. Marker. "Him and Dwayne took a part to town for welding."

"Don't matter," said Monkman. "I was just going to ask him how's tricks. What about you, Etta? How you been keeping?"

"I'd keep better without the baby's eczema. I'd keep better with the electricity or if I had one of them gas washing machines. Otherwise – I got no complaints. Yourself?"

"Not bad, Etta."

"If we ain't bad, we must be good."

"If you say so, Etta," said the old man agreeably. He swept his eyes around the yard. "I was wondering if you could do something for me?" he asked. "I want to leave the truck parked here and I was wondering if you could keep the twins from crawling all over it?"

"Did you hear that, twins?" said Mrs. Marker, raising her voice. "The man wants you to stay off of his truck. You do it!"

The boys reacted to this by ducking their heads, sticking out their rear ends and swinging the gate even more violently, as if they intended to tear it off its hinges.

"I mean it!" warned Mrs. Marker. "You keep yourselves and your boots off the hood of that truck or I'll brain the both of you! No more Freshie, either," she added ominously, "if I catch you." She turned her attention back to Monkman. "What do you want to leave it here for?" she inquired. "You walking somewheres?"

"Oh, we thought we'd go scouting for saskatoons. They ought to be getting ripe by now."

"Saskatoons don't amount to much this year," offered Mrs. Marker, seizing a handful of her skirt. "And the wood ticks are awful bad. I'd stay out of the bush if I was you. I pick the kids over every night. Every night they're thick with them. For the amount of saskatoons you find the ticks don't make it pay."

"Ticks don't have a taste for bloodless old buggers like me," said Monkman, smiling. "They're for the young ones like Daniel here. The sweet ones."

"Berries don't amount to much this year. Hardly worth your while to look."

"When you're my age you find you fill your time with any kind of foolishness. I get a couple of cupfuls, I'll be happy. It passes the time."

Mrs. Marker crooked her finger at the biggest boy on the porch. "Doyle here knows all the best places to look. Doyle, you take Mr. Monkman and show him where to look. He's the wanderer," she explained. "Knows every inch of the place, Doyle does. I'd appoint him guide, if I was you."

"No, don't bother," said Monkman, holding up a hand to ward off Doyle. "Where's the fun if you don't find them yourself?"

"South," urged Mrs. Marker desperately as the old man and boy began to move off. "South's your best bet. They ripen south first," she called, pointing.

"South, my ass," muttered Monkman under his breath. "North it is." The old man led the way. A few minutes' walking brought them to four ramshackle granaries. A flock of blackbirds exploded out of the shadows cast by the buildings where they had been feeding on oats and barley leaked onto the ground. The sudden flight, the whir of wings, the indignant cries of *chek! chek!* gave Monkman a start and shook him out of an absorbing rehearsal of what exactly he would say to Alfred Marker when he confronted him with the steer that had supposedly been dispatched by a bolt from heaven. It was then it struck him what going north meant. There were only two clumps of bush big enough to hide a steer in to the north. One ran along the fence line separating quarters and the other was a five-or six-acre patch of uncleared poplar, birch, and scrub oak standing in the midst of the field.

The field. Thinking of it made him apprehensive, made him step more quickly, made his chest tighten. They were crossing summer-fallow now, heading toward the distant fence line where the tops of the poplars flickered silver in the sun and wind. The old man found it heavy going. His boots sank to the laces in the loose powdery soil as if it were new snow and the black earth radiated a fierce, dusty heat up into his reddening face. He wished he could turn back. A visit to the field was a visit to bad luck. For twelve years he had superstitiously avoided it whenever possible.

"When I reach those trees I'm going to find a spot of shade and cool myself out," he declared, trying to initiate conversation. Talking would prevent thinking.

Daniel plodded along beside him without a trace of enthusiasm. Halfway up his shins his trousers were grey with dust. "Yeah, it's pretty hot, all right," was all the response Monkman could get.

"It's hotter than the hubs of hell. A man could take a heart attack on a day like this. Plenty have."

"My Dad died from heart trouble," said Daniel. "He was forty-eight. That isn't very old."

Monkman threw the boy an appraising glance. Daniel's expression was guarded, set. "You don't remember him, do you?" asked Monkman.

The question provoked no change in the boy's face. "No," he said.

Monkman let the matter drop. They went on in silence until they reached the wood where a narrow strip of grass separated the tilled ground from the grove. Groaning theatrically, the old man shuffled over to the shade spread by the trees and lowered himself stiffly, in stages, down into the brome grass tassels. There he lay, the crushed stems prickling the skin of his back through his shirt and the pollen and dust he had disturbed settling on him. He had placed his hat squarely in the centre of his chest. Twice he sneezed violently.

"If you're too tired to walk back, I'll fetch the truck for you," the boy offered, hovering over him.

"No, I'm fine. But what you can do is take a prowl in the bush and see if that bastard's tied my steer up in there."

Daniel wasn't eager to take up the suggestion. "She said there's ticks in the bush."

The old man laughed.

"What's so funny? You think it's so funny, why don't you go look yourself?"

"Played-out, fat old men aren't built for bush. They're not built for climbing over deadfalls and squeezing through all that kind of shit."

"So why should I? What's in it for me – getting eaten alive?"

"Five dollars if you locate my steer."

"Five dollars?" Daniel was taken by surprise. For him it was a lot of money.

"Five dollars."

"And if I don't?" he demanded, suspicious of a catch.

"You'll get fifty cents for effort. The prospect of an extra four-fifty ought to encourage you to look careful. Deal?"

"Deal."

He heard the grass rustle, a dry twig crack as Daniel left him. Then he knew he was alone. Alone, it was more difficult to prevent the field beyond the curtain of trees from stealing back into his mind. To hold it out, he began to review in his mind the things he must soon tell Daniel.

It was very important to do it right. He had never said any of these things to his own son Earl. But then talking to Earl in such a fashion would have been pointless. None of it would have been any use to Earl. Earl had never been constituted to make anything out of common sense. This one was. This one weighed you while you weighed him. Earl had never weighed anybody. He had thought everyone was cut from the same cloth as he was. If you came right down to it, Earl wouldn't have been able to learn what he had to teach him. This one, he suspected, knew half of it already. A shrewd, calculating little bugger to whom five dollars made all the difference in the world. So different, the two of them, Daniel and Earl. How did it happen, the clouding and confusion of bloodlines in a family? For the life of him he had never been able to see himself in his own son and yet he believed he could in his grandson. What was the old saying? Character jumps a generation? Was there anything of Daniel's father in him? Of course, he couldn't say. He knew nothing about the boy's sire, the tailor, or whatever he had been. There must be some of that in Daniel, some tailor, although he couldn't spot it. Everything he saw in the boy struck him as pure Monkman. The last of the line. The only grandchild.

He thought of Martha, dead before she was a grandmother.

Monkman could feel his sweat drying in the folds and creases in the skin of his neck. He realized how tired he was. Not much sleep again last night on account of the dream. Now, every time his eyes closed an insect would light on his face and go for a stroll. They must take me for dead, he thought, an old man stretched flat on his back in the grass with his eyes shut.

He blinked, brushed his hand back and forth over his cheeks. The cool and damp of the earth was rising up, leaching into his flesh. How? The ground ought to be hot and dry as a fever, there hadn't been rain in weeks. He was contemplating sitting up so he didn't take a chill in his kidneys when a dragonfly came helicoptering inches above his face and pinned him to the ground with its beauty, with its ruby sheen and shimmer. Martha had owned a brooch shaped like a dragonfly. It had fragile lacquered wings. Martha died of a stroke. Vera's husband of a heart ailment. No luck in this family. The tailor had looked old in the wedding picture she sent. Too old for a wisp of a girl like her. Bride and groom standing on courthouse steps. Is that where Jewish people got married? In court? There was nobody else in the snapshot. No family, no friends. So who took the picture?

Alec's grip on his hat relaxed. It slid off his chest and dropped by his side. He was standing in a poorly lit room being fitted for a suit. The sure, deft touch of the hands running the tape over his body was lulling, soothing. The tailor was measuring him. His limbs grew heavier and heavier, his joints looser and looser.

"Hey. Hey. *Hey*!"

Monkman woke with a gasp, wincing and gaping. Daniel was kneeling in the grass beside him, his hand resting on his grandfather's shoulder.

"What?"

"You must have dropped off."

The old man reached out, seized his grandson by the elbow, and pulled himself into a sitting position. His eyes narrowed and his head wobbled, assaulted by the dazzle of sun.

"No steer," reported Daniel. His voice sounded all mumbly to Monkman because the boy had pulled out the front of his shirt and was peering down the neck of it as he spoke, searching himself closely and anxiously for ticks. "Nothing. I walked clear through and came out on crop on the other side. There's bush in the middle of that field but I didn't go on, in case you wondered why I was so long." He broke off examining himself and lifted his face. "Jeez, I feel all crawly but I can't see anything. How big are these ticks supposed to be anyway?"

Monkman was staring back the way they had come, staring out over the gently swelling and subsiding black earth. The air above the summerfallow quivered and bent, distorting the view like a pane of cheap, flawed glass.

Before he fell asleep there had been something to do with the boy. What? Then it came to him. Without preamble or introduction he simply said, "Your mother asked Mr. Stutz to have a man to man talk with you." Having delivered himself of this news he studied the boy for any sign that Daniel had been warned of his mother's arrangement. There was none. "Well," said the old man, pressing on, "were there questions you'd been asking your mother that maybe she didn't want to answer?"

Daniel shook his head.

"I guess it was her idea then? I guess she thought it was time you learned certain things it was more proper for a man to teach you."

"I guess so," said the boy apprehensively.

"Anyway, after your mother talked to Mr. Stutz he came to me because he didn't feel it was his place to talk to you. He took it for family business and thought maybe I was the one should do it." Monkman hesitated. "Seeing I'm the closest thing you have to a father." Monkman squinted up at Daniel. "So maybe you should take a seat so we can do as your mother wants."

The suggestion sounded like an order. Daniel sat with a look of extreme uneasiness. It was embarrassing to be talked to this way. Long ago he had read everything the *Reader's Digest* had to say on the impending topic and doubted there was much he could be taught. He had even been able to correct Lyle on a few points. He was satisfied that his knowledge was pretty wide-ranging. He knew you couldn't get VD from a toilet seat and he knew that husbands ought to be affectionate to their wives *after* the sex act as well as before it. Otherwise women felt used. And he knew whatever else fitted between these two bookends. With the old guy smiling that way, falser than even his teeth, he was sure he was going to be put through something horrible.

"I don't know what your mother imagines is a man to man talk," Alec began by saying, "but I'd guess it's supposed to cover what a man should know to keep himself out of trouble. To my idea, what's most troublesome for men is sex, drinking, and fighting. No particular order of importance." But the last was a lie. There was a particular order of importance and the brave thing to do would be to get the worst bit over first. He reminded himself to tell the kid only what would prove useful to him. It was likely Daniel would do exactly as everybody else before him had done. There was no percentage in ignoring that simple fact. So whatever he said should keep in mind human nature. Mr. Stutz wouldn't have kept it in mind. Mr. Stutz didn't accept human nature as an excuse for anything. He was always laying down the law as to how men ought to act, despite the impossibility of them performing any of the remarkable feats he called upon them to perform. Alec had always believed in working with what you were given, and human nature was a given. It was where he would begin.

"I don't know any polite way of saying this, and the only way I've got of saying it is straight out. A boy gets to your age, or somewhere close to it, and something happens – that thing of his starts provoking and tormenting him continual. If it hasn't happened to you yet, it will shortly. There's no getting around it, that pecker of yours isn't going to give you hardly a moment's peace. Which leads me to what I'm going to say to you now. Which is about playing with yourself. Now don't get me wrong – I'm not recommending it, I'm just saying that more than one has taken it for the solution of a predicament. There's boys your age that suffer terrible worries from that. If it's a sin, it's got to be a small one. As to whatever rumours you may have heard about the results – about going blind or mental – I can't believe it. It doesn't make any sense. How's a pecker to know the difference between a woman and a hand? A pecker doesn't have a brain, or eyes. It's just a story, like a horsehair in a water barrel turns into a worm. What I'm saying is let it alone if you can but, if you can't, remember you aren't the first and you won't be the last." Monkman paused and waited. Daniel said nothing. All his attention was fastened on a spear of grass he spun in his fingers.

"You know what we're talking about, don't you?" asked the old man sharply.

Daniel nodded his head without looking up from the stalk of grass.

At least that was over. He hoped the boy had understood. "I won't say nothing now about women," said the old man brusquely. "I'll save that one for when you're older." He took a deep breath of relief, felt himself on firmer ground. "Now drinking," he said happily. "Stutz doesn't have a single good word for it. He just goes on about how it has been the downfall of thousands. I won't argue with him. I know myself the trouble it caused me at one time. If I learned one thing from my trouble it was this: there's no point in drinking if you aren't happy. The thing about liquor is that it's an encourager. It encourages happiness in a happy man and sadness in a sad one. It encourages whatever else you happen to be feeling. The young bucks fight when they're drunk because booze adds oil to the fire young men carry around burning in their bellies. Now I'm not saying any of this to you now because I expect you to follow my advice straight off. I'm saying it so that when you come to make your own mistakes you can think back and test what's happening to you against what I said was true. It might bring you to reason sooner. There's nothing like a second pair of eyes for help. It's what Mr. Stutz did for me when he pointed out certain things about my drinking when I was bad into it. You see, I couldn't see the start of my misery because I was too deep into it. Now it's true I still take a drink – mostly when Stutz is around – but that's just to prove to him I've got my own will. I won't be a slave to it or a slave to avoiding it. Besides, if you keep company with men you're bound to keep company with liquor. Particularly around here. It won't be long before you'll be drinking beer out behind the dance hall to work up enough courage to speak to a girl inside. There's no point if the courage isn't inside you. When you're puking in the bushes, ask yourself then if what your grandfather said wasn't right."

"My friend Lyle and me drank some of the gin his mother kept hid under the kitchen sink," volunteered Daniel, encouraged by what he took to be his grandfather's tolerant attitude to drinking.

"Thief's pride is pitiable pride. I wouldn't brag on that, if I was you," said his grandfather sternly, "hooking some lady's gin the way you hook your mother's smokes." Then, noticing Daniel's obvious alarm, he added, "Don't worry. I haven't said nothing to your mother about the cigarettes. But if I was you, I'd think twice about laying hands on her property. The consequences aren't likely to be worth it. You need a cigarette that bad, lift it from my pack. Who do I have to complain to but myself?"

Daniel could feel his face flush and his ears burn. When had he seen? For a moment he considered denying the accusation but the calm, steady inspection that the old man was making of him helped Daniel recognize the futility of lying. It might, he thought, have been better to have been caught by his mother after all.

"Anybody ever teach you how to fight?" asked the old man.

The question was so unexpected, so unrelated to what had immediately gone before that Daniel was at a loss for an answer. "Pardon?"

"Can you fight?"

"Fight?"

"Yeah, fight. Anybody ever teach you to take care of yourself?"

As a matter of fact, nobody ever had. But he wasn't about to admit it. "Yeah."

"That's good. Because you better be ready to handle yourself when school starts in September. A place like this, they're not used to new boys. Anybody new is liable to catch it for a while until he teaches people to leave him alone."

"My mother says she doesn't believe in fighting. She says my father was a pacifist. So she is too."

"If your mother's a pacifist so's Field Marshal Montgomery."

"She says there's better ways of settling an argument than with your fists."

"No doubt there is – as long as you can find somebody to argue with who agrees on the procedures. I don't think you'll find many of those in Connaught." The old man gave a sharp, foxy bark of laughter. "Imagine Vera talking that way. I can't figure it. Maybe Earl but not your mother. I never came across anybody with more fight bred into them than she has. Not that she isn't right in some ways. All my life I tried to avoid settling a disagreement with my boots and fists. That's the truth. As God is my judge, I've walked away from more than one invitation to scuffle. When I was a young man I was a demon to dance and at every dance in those days there were always the cocks-of-the-walk who showed up to pick fights. They all acted as if fighting was some kind of sport, an amusement like baseball, or pool, or a game of horseshoes. Fighting was their way of attracting notice. You know how I handled them if they stepped on my toes? I took the notice away from them. I said, 'If you want to fight, you sonofabitch, I'll fight you. But a week from now, cold sober and alone. Just the two of us with nobody to watch and cheer and carry on. Just you and me, friend. Set the time and place and I'll be there.' I meant it, too. And they could see I meant it and their friends could see I meant it. You know how many takers I got?" Monkman formed a circle with his thumb and forefinger. "Zero. None. You know why? Because even the ones who pretend to like to scrap really don't. It's the cheering they like, the clap on the back, the chance to strut. Take away the crowd and you take away the guts.

"And you know how I discovered that fact?" said the old man earnestly, bending towards Daniel. "Entirely by accident is how I discovered that fact. I had this female cousin – Rose her name was, she's been dead for years now – who was the hired girl to the postmaster's wife. Now Rose was a good-natured, plain, hard-working girl but she was also a little on the simple side, not so as she couldn't do a job if it was all explained to her, she could do that, but she was still simple, what I'd call trusting-simple, and there was this young fellow who lived next door to the postmaster's who used to tease her. Now he must've been ten years older than Rose – she was about fifteen then – and he ought to have known better but he didn't. His name was Billy Atkins and he thought pretty highly of himself. I suppose people encouraged him in it. He was handsome, the kind that lounges about decorating street corners. All the girls thought he was the cat's ass and most of the boys were afraid of him because he had a reputation for being wild and one way or another he had whipped every one of them either in school or after he got kicked out of it.

"Anyway, whenever he and his friends happened to be holding up a telephone pole and Rose chanced to go by, Billy Atkins couldn't help but treat the boys to a laugh at her expense. It was an easy thing for him to do because Rose couldn't hide the fact she thought Billy Atkins was pretty wonderful. So as she went by, watching her feet, he'd call out, 'Am I on for Saturday night, Rosie?'

"And she'd stop dead in her tracks and say in her quiet voice, 'Do you really mean it this time, Mr. Atkins?'

"And he'd say of course he meant it and she'd say, 'Well then you're on,' and he'd wink at his friends and say, 'On for how long, Rose?' And one of his admirers would shout, 'For as long as it takes!' And they'd all laugh themselves sick and Rose, being slow-witted, would look from one face to another, trying to catch the joke and sometimes laughing herself, at what she didn't know, just to please Billy Atkins.

"It was getting so bad that the only decent thing to do was to try and stop it because I was a relative and Rose didn't have any brothers and her father lived out on the farm and didn't know what was going on. I didn't want to do it because I knew I was no match for Billy Atkins. He was older for one thing. Then I was about seventeen. I'd been working for almost three years on labouring jobs so I had some muscle on me, but Billy Atkins had more and knew how to use it better. Pride decided me to do it the way I did. If I was going to get my clock cleaned I preferred to have it done private rather than public.

"At the time I'm speaking of, Billy Atkins was working hauling gravel for the concrete foundations of the new Old Fellows' Hall they were putting up then. The pits were a couple of miles out of town. Haulage was all by horses then. Atkins would have to drive his team out to the pits, throw on a load, and then drive it back to town to dump. I figured the pits was one sure place to catch him alone. So one Saturday morning I walked out to find him. When I got to the gravel digs he was just topping off his wagon. He didn't see me coming because his back was to me as he worked. I was almost on him when I saw him toss his shovel up on the load, step up on the wheel, and boost himself onto the seat. He got quite a surprise when he reached for the reins and there I was, looking up at him.

" 'What the fuck brings you out here, young Monkman?' he says. 'You on a Boy Scout nature hike?'

"All the time I'd been coming on, watching him shovel, I'd held my mind blank. That's because I didn't want to have no excuses prepared and ready if my nerve failed me at the last second. There was nothing to say to him but the truth. I said it quick. I said, 'I came to tell you to leave my cousin Rose MacPherson alone. I don't want you making fun of her in the streets anymore.'

"You could have knocked him down with a feather after I said that. Billy Atkins never bargained on that sort of talk from the likes of me. He couldn't quite believe his ears, so he says, 'What did you say to me?' As if he were the King of England and somebody had asked him, 'How's your royal arse today, Your Highness?'

"Myself, I didn't see how I could draw back now. I was in the thick of it. I started pulling off my coat. 'Climb down off that wagon,' I said, 'Come off that wagon, Billy Atkins.'

"That's when he gave himself away. Billy shot a quick look all around him. He was looking for the rest of us. It was just there, for the blink of an eyelid, but I saw how he couldn't fathom I'd come alone. Where were my friends? The glance he couldn't help taking told him there was nobody else, but he could scarcely believe it. His mouth went tight on him, like he'd bit into a lemon. 'Are you in your right mind?' he says. 'Or are you as bad off in the head as that cousin of yours? If I step down off this wagon, by Christ you'll rue the day.'

" 'I'm prepared to rue it,' I said. 'Step down.' No sooner had those words left my mouth than I knew he wouldn't. It came to me that this was all too strange for his taste. He didn't want anything to do with this strange kid in an out of the way, lonely place. Maybe he took me for crazy.

" 'I'll step down when I decide to step down,' he said. 'I don't take orders from you. You can count yourself lucky I'm working. I'm not about to lose my job because I took time out to teach you your manners. I can arrange to do that some other time.'

" 'You don't have to bother to arrange nothing if you arrange to leave my cousin alone,' I told him. Didn't that frost him? Not being able to back off a young pup like me sent him white in the face. He reared up on his hind legs on that wagon and cursed me with every name he could lay his tongue to. And when he ran out of names he up with the reins and laid them down hard on his team so that they came at me with their tails flying and it was get out of the way or be run down. As he went by, wagon bouncing, he hung his face over the side and shouted, 'I'll see you in town! See if I don't!'

"And I hollered back, 'If you do, I'll be back to pay you a visit out here!' Which was obviously the right answer because he never looked me up in town and as far as I know he never bothered Rose neither. So that's how I learned about setting the price higher than anybody wants to pay. You don't have to win outright. All you have to do is make the bully boys worry more, or hurt more than they counted on. I recommend it to you. If somebody hangs a licking on you in the schoolyard with all their friends watching, make him do it again, when there's just the two of you. Catch him alone. See that you hurt him enough to spoil his fun. Teach him that picking on you isn't going to be anything but hard work. Let him understand that for every whipping he hands out before a crowd, sooner or later, he'll have to do it again, without the cheers and without the glory. There's not one in a thousand that has the stomach for that."

What made his grandfather think he had the stomach for the other? The chasing down and cornering of an enemy who had already beaten you? It seemed sick to Daniel. Why, even Montgomery Clift in *The Young Lions* hadn't been so completely on his own. He had had his friend Dean Martin there to pick him up when he was knocked down, to beg him not to go on, to tell him not to be so foolish.

"It sounds sort of stupid to me," said Daniel. "Looking to get beat up a second time."

"Not so stupid if it keeps you from getting it a third time."

Daniel thought for a moment. "Did you mean it – about them picking on me at school? Will they really?"

"Of course I can't say. But I'd be ready for it. Think the worst – then there aren't any surprises."

"I don't think I could do like you say," said Daniel.

"You could. You're your mother's son."

"She always says I take after my Dad. She says I'm nothing like her."

"Wishful thinking. You've got to be as tough as she is to have survived her twelve years. She'd have killed anybody weaker. Even as a girl she was something to watch out for. One Dominion Day she tackled a full-grown man. She couldn't have been more than ten."

"What? Mom? A man?"

"Sure. It was over her brother Earl."

"Tell me," said Daniel. "What was it about?"

"It was about Earl," Alec said. The look on his face testified to the pleasure he took in his own stories. "Earl was always shy and timid from a baby up. Vera used to tease him about it but Lord help anybody else that she caught tormenting her little brother. I remember coming home from work one night and what do I see but your mother, the one who's the pacifist, boiling down the street after Hansie Beck with a croquet mallet waving above her head like a tomahawk. She was out for blood because he'd done something or other to make Earl bawl. Your grandmother spent half her day negotiating peace with the neighbours because of the scraps Vera got herself in, sticking up for her brother.

"She got herself in a big one Dominion Day. They could have cancelled the evening fireworks because they got them early the way she went off like a Roman Candle. There was lots to see her do it, too. July First was the biggest day of the summer back then.

All the farmers came in from the country and there was crowds and crowds of people. It don't seem much for entertainment now that we got the television but then it was something, the Dominion Day Sports Day. There was a big ball tournament with prize money, a horseshoe-pitching contest, harness-racing at the track, a tug of war between the volunteer fire brigade and the Connaught hockey team – although they didn't know how to split themselves up because half of them belonged to both – and more food than you could eat in a month of Fridays. All the ladies' church groups and auxiliaries squared off to out-cook and out-sell one another. United Church ladies wanted to sell more pie than the Catholics and the Royal Purple wanted to plough the Red Cross under. Every organization had a booth with tables and benches and they sold cold pop out of tin washtubs full of crushed ice, and plates of cake and pie and potato salad and ham and cold roast beef and cabbage rolls, and mugs of coffee. It was a treat to have a seat in the booths because the husbands had roofed them for the ladies with poplar branches so it would be all green and shady and so a breeze could pass through them and stir the leaves up. On a hot day it was a cooling place to be. And all over the fairgrounds there were families, mostly country people who brought their own lunch because it seemed to them a crime to pay good money for something no better than they could get at home. They would be picnicking on blankets spread on the grass or sitting on the runningboards of their vehicles, eating. It was something. We wouldn't have missed it for the world, Earl and me and your mother. Only thing that beat a Dominion Day was Christmas.

"Now on any such day Earl stuck to me like shit to a blanket because he was so shy. He'd hook his hand in my back pocket and hang on tight, like this," said Monkman, illustrating by raising his hip from the ground and thrusting his hand into his pocket. "You couldn't have crowbarred him off me. But Vera wasn't like that at all. She preferred to go off on her own and see what trouble she could get into. Earl was more comfortable back there where he

143

could hide himself behind my legs and take a peek out around my hip now and then just to see how the world was running, then duck his head back out of sight if anybody happened to catch his eye. He was about five and should've been past that but he wasn't, so that's how we saw the Sports Day, him hanging on to my pocket for dear life as we went about our business. It was funny, he was like your own shadow, you could forget he was there he kept himself so quiet. Your mother was cut from different cloth. She couldn't be forgotten. You noticed Vera. Full of questions about this or that and if it wasn't questions she was trying to jimmy another nickel out of you for more candy. She wasn't a girl to overlook. But Earl wasn't like that. He was awful quiet, a thumb-sucker and starer.

"That day, somehow I lost him. I ran into a fellow I knew and we had ourselves a talk and then I walked off without Earl on my pocket. He must've let go for just a second, maybe to swap sucking thumbs and I was gone. He couldn't catch a hold of me because of the crowd and once he lost track of me in all that press of people, him being ass-high to the rest of the world, he couldn't spot me again.

"Soon as I realized I'd lost him I went back on the run, pushing aside anybody got in my way. Not a sign of him. So there I was running here, there, and everywhere like a chicken with its head cut off trying to find Earl before he had himself a real shit conniption. Then I came on Vera. She was crouching underneath this big cottonwood somebody had hung a set of gym rings on. A bunch of harness drivers who'd been drinking behind the stables were showing off for one another, skinning the cat and chinning themselves. Vera was squatted there watching them like a vulture. She was probably getting ready to make a grab for any loose change they flipped out of their pockets turning themselves over and then run for it.

"I said, 'Vera, your brother's lost.' It was all I needed to say. She knew what sort of state he'd be in, what that meant. She was up and gone like smoke in a wind.

"Back in those days I was a cigar smoker – White Owls – and I carried them in my back pocket because it was cut deep for a wallet. Earl must've spent a good deal of his time face to face with that white owl on the package with its big yellow eyes. Now when we got separated, naturally Earl, being Earl, panics. He gallops off this way and that way, looking. Then all of a sudden, right in the middle of all those asses what does he run up against? A White Owl package and two big old yellow eyes peeping over a back pocket. Sure enough, Earl makes a dive for it and rams his hand down in the pocket. Saved, he thinks.

"Wasn't me, though. Just another White Owls smoker with his cigars stuck in his ass pocket. Vera arrives on the scene and finds this man shaking Earl by the shoulders, yelling. Of course, he took him for a thief with his hand stuffed down to the bottom of his pocket. I arrive on the scene of the crime just as Vera flies onto this character from behind. She tackles him and clamps down hard. She's got her arms locked around his belly and her legs scissored around his shins and she's trying to sink her teeth into his back right through his jacket. She only leaves off biting long enough to holler, 'Run, Earl! Run for your life!' and then she squeezes down on the fellow and goes back to work gnawing a chunk off him.

"But Earl's too scared to run. His eyes are the size of saucers, he's sucking on his thumb so hard it's a wonder he doesn't pull the nail clean off it, and he's backing off one step at a time, slow, as this man staggers after him, Vera riding him piggyback, sticking like flypaper and bellering, 'Run for your life, Earl! Run!' "

The old man began quaking with laughter. Tears stood in his eyes. "Jesus, wasn't that something?" he asked. Suddenly, he threw back his head and roared at the sky. "*Run for your life, Earl! Run!* Jesus, what a commotion. *Run for your life, Earl! Run!*" he shouted so that his face darkened with blood and effort. "*Run! Run!*" Then, as abruptly as he had begun, he stopped. Monkman searched Daniel's face. "She had the right idea, your mother, didn't she?" he asked softly.

Daniel shifted his buttocks on the ground. He wondered if his grandfather's uncontrolled shouting had been heard up at the house. He hoped not. It had given him an odd feeling. So had his grandfather's question.

"I don't know," he said lamely.

"No, I suppose there's no reason you should. And I've gone on and on talking. I should have stopped long ago, before I got to such old stories."

"I liked them," said Daniel.

"Well, whether you did or not, they're finished with now. We'd better be getting home."

"What about the steer?"

"To hell with the steer. I don't care about the steer anymore."

"I could check the bush in the field back there."

"No."

"It wouldn't take long. No more than twenty minutes," argued Daniel. "And then you'd know."

"It doesn't matter," said Monkman irritably. "I don't care." He was picking himself off the ground the way a toddler would, braced on all fours, raising his hind end tentatively, by degrees, testing his balance. Then one final effort, an abrupt wrench up out of his stoop and he stood swaying, a little dizzy finding himself upright.

"We come all the way out here and as soon as we get here you've all of a sudden got to go. Where's the sense in that?" demanded the boy peevishly.

"It's late," said Monkman, avoiding looking at his grandson. He was angry. By arguing with him the boy made him feel foolish. Yet he knew he wasn't going to let him set one foot in that bad-luck field.

"It isn't late." Daniel glanced at his watch. "It's not even three."

"I'm the one who decides whether it's late or not. So it's late. Come along."

"What about my chance for five dollars?" the boy wanted to know. "Have you forgot that?"

"Come." The old man swung round on his heel and struck out into the summerfallow with awkward, stumbling fury. Anger jerked him like a puppet over the furrows; his boots flicked aside the hot, black, sifted earth; his shoulders see-sawed and twitched.

Daniel stood his ground. "I'm going to look," he called after him, although without much conviction.

The old man didn't bother to turn. His right hand snapped up. Pinched between forefinger and thumb something fluttered. When he saw what it was Daniel followed, resigned. The money was something.

10

———◆———

Vera stood at the kitchen sink with suds creeping up her fore-arms, remembering Bob the housepainter. Every now and then the ridiculous row about baseball going on between Daniel and her father in the living room reached such a pitch that this became difficult, but Vera did her best to disregard the noise. For the life of her, she could not fathom how nothing made the two of them happier than an idiotic squabble over something of absolutely no consequence. Of course, the old man was a great tease, always had been, and delighted in provoking Daniel. Vera had warned him not to pay his grandfather any mind, but the boy hadn't profited from her advice and rose to the bait every time. Daniel might learn yet that there was no winning with the old man. Beat him six ways to Sunday and he still would never cry uncle or allow that there was an outside chance of his ever being wrong.

It was a remark of her father's before dinner which had brought Bob to mind after all these years. Vera had just pointed out to her father that if he wanted to clean the wax out of his ears with a wooden matchstick, maybe the privacy of the bathroom was more suitable for the operation than the dinner table. He had fastened her with a look of calculated pity and said, "You ought to have considered getting married again, Vera. Then maybe you'd have learned how to live with a man."

Well, she had considered it and it was Bob the housepainter she had considered marrying. Strange to think. Since Bob, she doubted whether she'd had six dates in the past ten years and, if the truth be known, it would have been no loss to have missed any of them. Probably the business with Bob wouldn't have lasted as long as it did either, if she hadn't met him a little less than two years after Stanley died, when she still believed she was obliged to find Daniel a father and thought she couldn't raise a boy on her own. And who could say? Given the way things had worked out, maybe her thinking then had been correct.

The real mistake was going to bed with him. On the other hand, maybe she needed to make up her mind if she could live with him, day in, day out, in that department. There was nothing else to rule him out. After four months of those sedate outings of his – Saturday-night movies, picnics in the park – Vera knew he wasn't a drinker, a gambler, a ladies' man, or the sort who had a dangerous temper. Just a solid, dependable thirty-nine year old without much hair who painted houses for a living and was desperately shopping for a wife to settle down with before it was too late. That pretty well summed up Bob. And although that one trial run in the sack made up her mind, she hadn't realized it at the time. The unfortunate thing was that Bob must have come to the conclusion it was a sign, because not long after he popped the big question. Popped it standing in line at the Exhibition to buy Daniel a ticket for the merry-go-round, popped it holding her kid in his arms.

Vera didn't handle the situation very well. She should have asked him for time to think his proposal over. Anything would have been better than her flat-out no, given without a second's hesitation. It must have seemed like a fearful slap in the face coming like that, and awfully humiliating. He probably assumed he was in like Flynn after having done her the dirty. Mostly Vera blamed herself for not having an answer ready for a question she should have suspected was coming. But had she even known what her answer would be until she got taken by surprise like that and had the truth torn out of her?

Aside from turning as white as a sheet of paper and blinking his eyes a couple of times, Bob was taking it pretty well. He said he was sorry and she said she was sorry, too. Then there was a painful silence. "Look," she said finally, "maybe Daniel and I had better go home." And she stretched out her arms for the baby.

Wasn't she taken aback when Bob wouldn't hand him over? Likely he wanted to prove he could be sophisticated about this; the refusal of a proposal was no big deal to him – plenty of other fish in the ocean. The problem was he couldn't keep his voice from sounding tight and self-righteous when he said, "I don't see any reason why we should spoil the little one's fun."

Meanwhile Daniel was starting to fuss. The minute he'd seen his mother reach for him he'd held out his arms, clenched and unclenched his fists to show he wanted her to take him. Vera said, "Really, Bob, I think we should call it a day after what's happened."

"What *has* happened?" said Bob a shade belligerently. He was having a time keeping a grip on Daniel while the baby whined and twisted in his arms.

"Let's not argue about this. You're upsetting the kid. He wants to come to me. Give him over."

Bob jostled and shifted Daniel in his arms, struggling to get a better handle on him. The baby stuck out his chubby arms and whimpered. "No, Daniel," Bob said, "you can't go to your mother. It's too hot for her to lug around such a big, heavy boy."

Vera remembered the merry-go-round lurching into motion behind Bob right then, and a burst of recorded music from a speaker over the ticket booth starting up loud enough to wake the dead. And kids screaming as the ride picked up speed, and the blur of colours as it went round and round. She had felt dizzy and panicked, something inside her giving way, breaking loose, and beginning to spin and whirl heavily and slowly and then faster and faster and lighter and lighter until she thought the top of her head was about to fly off. The second she heard her voice, shrill and brittle, she knew it was all wrong, the wrong voice for a situation like that. "Bob," she said, "give Daniel to me. Give him to me right this instant." It was a school teacher's voice and Bob recognized it for that and got his back up because of the tone. He looked hurt and stubborn at one and the same time. "What? You think I'm going to do something to him? What do you think I'm going to do to him?"

"I don't think anything. I just want him," she said.

"Be sensible, Vera. To me carrying him is nothing. He's light as a feather."

Rage. When she put a name to that spinning, tearing commotion going on inside her, that was it. Rage. He was her kid. Hers. What right did Bob have to debate whether or not he'd turn him over? What's more, it was plain that Daniel, sensing a troubled atmosphere, was beginning to be frightened. He began to cry unconvincingly, without conviction, to see if it would get him what he wanted. Which was his mother.

"Hush," said Bob.

She grabbed for Daniel. Bob held on. His mouth went grim, his eyes narrowed with determination. He pulled, she pulled. Not until Daniel let loose a blood-curdling scream did she let go, throwing up her hands as if they'd been burned. She hadn't realized what they were doing to the kid. The pressure marks from her fingers stood white on the flesh of his little arms. Bob and Vera stared at each other, panting. She spoke but three words. "I'll kill you," is what she said and she meant it. If she'd have had a carving knife in her hands she'd have rammed it clean through him.

Bob had shot her a queer, ugly smile. Vera believed that the strength of what he was feeling had shaken him, just as the strength of what she was feeling had shaken her. The smile was part disgust, part injured feeling, part triumph. "Let's hear the magic word," he said. "Then I'll think of following orders."

She had been so disturbed and confused, at first she misunderstood. Vera got it into her head he was trying to blackmail her into saying yes to marrying him. But that wasn't it. All he wanted to hear her say was please. Only please. Please give me my son.

A father dictating at the dinner table, laying down the law. "No dessert until I hear the word please." Bob the housepainter was waiting for her to say it. Waiting while Daniel screamed his face purple and flopped and snapped in his arms like a fish.

He wanted her to bow down and she couldn't. Bow down to me and you can have what you want. It was her father all over again and she couldn't. "You want him so bad," Vera said, "you can keep him."

Then she had turned her back on Bob and walked away. She counted her steps while colliding with people in the crowd. "Drunk," said a woman in disgust when she bumped into her. Vera's hands trembled uncontrollably. Thirty steps, she told herself. I'll give myself thirty steps before I turn back. She couldn't walk a straight line. The tinny, shrieking carousel music behind her seemed to be tossing her from side to side. Twelve, thirteen, fourteen.

She heard someone running, a hand on her shoulder jerked her around. "Vera, what's the matter with you? Are you crazy?" cried Bob, alarmed. He set Daniel down at her feet, the baby stamped his white boots, clutched at her skirt, screamed. His face, shining with tears, looked like a wet plum. Snot was leaking onto his upper lip and slobber onto his chin. When she swept him up into her arms his body burned hers clean through her blouse.

"Lucky for you that you came after me and not me after you," was all she had said to Bob. It was all that needed to be said. She never saw him again.

"Mickey Mantle? That's your idea of a ballplayer? Mr. Showboat popping his arsehole swinging for the fence and glory every time he steps in the batter's box?" Her father's voice had built to such heights of bogus outrage that it could no longer be ignored. Vera took up the scouring pad and furiously attacked a pot.

Daniel contradicted him. "He bunts. Lots of times he bunts."

"Sure he bunts, when the count is two and two. That's when the chicken shit bunts."

"You won't say a good word about him just because he's a Yankee."

"Leaving aside he's an asshole – you're right. But it's not the Yankees I hate so much as their fans. Ever notice how everybody claims they're a Yankee fan can't name five players on the team? All they know about the Yankees is that they're winners and that's enough for them. A Yankee fan is generally ignorance tied to no convictions."

For Vera, it wasn't enough that these dumb disputes drove her crazy by endlessly running in circles like dogs snapping at their tails; what was worse was that listening to them busy themselves with their nonsense made her feel alone. Sometimes she couldn't stop herself from butting in with her shiny two bits' worth, and taking Daniel's part, even though she knew her help wasn't appreciated in the least.

"I like the Yankees!" she shouted from the kitchen.

"See?" said the old man. "What'd I say?"

It was difficult to decide what was responsible for Daniel losing his temper, the indignity of his mother intervening on his behalf, or the self-congratulatory and annoying way his grandfather had of delivering insults. "Better to cheer for the Yankees than a bunch of pitiful losers like the Red Sox!" he cried in a choked voice. "Who wants to cheer for a team of losers like them!"

"*I* do," announced the old man with some smugness. "Because me, I got a sense of loyalty. A real fan picks and sticks. A genuine fan stands by his team, win or lose, that's how you know a real fan."

"Well, you must be a real fan then. Because you've got plenty of experience sticking with losers."

This successful sally prompted his grandfather to return to safer ground. "Mickey Mantle," he said, pronouncing the name with scornful exaggeration, "isn't he the cute one, though? Cute enough for them to make a Mickey Mantle doll for little girls, I'd say. They ought to nickname him Mickey Mantle Piece because that's where he wants to be – up on some mantel where everybody can swoon at the sight of him. Up there nice and high so all the sportswriters can kiss his precious Yankee ass without the inconvenience of bending over to do it. Because you don't ever want to put a sportswriter to any trouble, he might write something bad about you."

"Oh, dear," said Daniel, sensing an advantage, "who's still mad because Mickey Mantle beat the great Ted Williams out of the '56 batting crown?"

For the first time, Vera detected the flavour of genuine anger in her father's speech. "No, I ain't mad about *that*," he said emphatically. "You know what I'm mad about, it's the MVP. One thing about the numbers, they don't lie. So what happened in '56? A young guy in the prime of life, supposed to herald the Second Coming, beats an old man, thirty-eight years old, out of the batting title by eight-points' difference in their batting averages. Oh, didn't he hand that poor old bugger a terrible eight-point whipping! If I had got licked the way Ted Williams got licked, by *eight whole points*, I don't know how I'd have been able to live with the shame. I'd have blown my brains out in the clubhouse. Yes, sir. No way else out after a crushing *eight-point defeat*," said the old man, relishing his dramatic effects. "Of course," he added, "it only makes sense that the next year when senile old Williams bats .388 and Mr. Pin-Up hits .365 that the MVP should go to Mickey. That's only fair. Why, anybody knows that an old fart like Ted Williams had to hit a lot more than twenty-three points better than Mr. Wonderful to earn a little recognition. And I won't even mention how it's the sportswriters who vote for the MVP and Williams never hid the fact he thought sportswriters were a big collection of horses' asses and wouldn't talk to them. I mean, who gave him the name Terrible Ted? You're a bright boy, you figure it out, the business of the MVP." The old man paused significantly. "So I ask you, in all fairness: Who got fucked?"

"Language!" roared Vera.

"Pardon!" His grandfather lowered his voice and leaned toward Daniel confidentially. "So, as I say, these pencil pushers gang up and fuck him. The greatest hitter for power and average the game's ever seen, fucked over by a bunch of jealous nobodies. But I ask you: What happened last year? Terrible Ted's back with a vengeance. Numbers don't lie. Hand the man another batting crown. That's his revenge on all the press boys who prefer Mr. Oklahoma because he wouldn't say shit if his mouth was full of it and Ted Williams says what he thinks. What the newspaper men can't abide in him is that he plays his game, not theirs, and his game is baseball."

"Ted Williams' game is baseball. Brilliant observation," said Daniel sarcastically. "So what's Mickey Mantle playing then? Chinese checkers?"

"Jesus, give me a chance to explain. Listen. What I mean to say is that Williams' *only* game is baseball. He doesn't play the game of pretending to be the All American Boy according to whatever some newspaper dope wakes up one morning and thinks that is. They hate him because he won't wear a tie when he goes and testifies in front of Congress. They hate him because he won't be forgiving and tip his hat to the crowd that booed him. He won't smile a shit-eating smile and kick the dirt, aw shucks. I figure what they can't stand is that he doesn't think they're important. It's baseball that's important. To my idea the man who really loved baseball would play it the same way in front of empty stands as he would in front of full ones. That's Ted Williams. He never hit a ball to hear the roar of the crowd, he hit it to prove he could. If Jesus H. Christ were to put on a glove and take the mound and everybody else dropped to their knees, Ted Williams would step into the batter's box and say, 'Okay, it's you and me. Show me the best you got.' The trouble with the fans and Ted Williams is that somehow the fans got it into their heads they ought to matter to him."

"The fans pay his salary. He owes something to them, doesn't he?"

"He doesn't owe them his character. Nobody is owed that. That's why I admire him. They boo and curse him in his own park, in Fenway. But he refuses to change to please them. He would rather be hated, even at home."

"It sounds to me," said Vera, leaning back from the sink to project her voice, "that this Mr. Williams is a big spoiled brat who wants everything his way!"

"Right now I think he'd be satisfied with a fair shake!" snapped back her father. But he knew there was no convincing Vera. He directed his efforts to Daniel. "Take all that fuss about his draft deferment. Wasn't it a crime how a healthy young man like him should get a deferment with Adolf Hitler running loose in the world? But who said boo about DiMaggio who had a deferment too? Yeah but Joe DiMaggio was a Yankee and a gentleman and everybody loves a Yankee and a gentleman. So which one sees service in *two* wars, gets called up a second time for Korea? Williams. But then nothing he ever done was right. The crap he got accused of in the papers. He wasn't at the hospital when his first baby was born. He got divorced. Then everybody wept big crocodile tears because he took a shotgun and blasted a bunch of dirty pigeons in Fenway Park so's the groundkeepers could get a break from cleaning up pigeon shit. The sonsofbitches even said he sold the furniture out from under his mother when it was his good-for-nothing brother who had stole it." His voice was growing more and more agitated, quivering with indignation. "Okay, so he didn't sell her furniture, what else could they say? Let's say he doesn't go out to California often enough to visit her. Ted Williams won't visit his poor old Salvation Army mother, the scribblers said. Who're they to say how much is enough? Who're they to say what a man feels?"

Vera, drawn from the sink by his plaintive, desperate tone, propped herself in the entrance to the living room and dried her arms with a tea-towel. "My," she said, "aren't you working yourself into a state. Who and what're we talking about anyway? I don't think it's about Williams."

"Who *else* then?" demanded her father sharply.

"Oh, I guess Earl hasn't been by in quite a time, has he? Hasn't paid a visit, I mean."

Her father didn't bother to reply, acted as if she hadn't spoken. "You know," he remarked to Daniel, "they say that even now old Ted's eyesight is so sharp he can read the label on a seventy-eight spinning on the turntable. Do you believe that?"

"I don't," challenged Vera, tossing the towel over her shoulder. "And if you do, you're even more gullible than you look."

Daniel turned himself toward his grandfather. "It isn't as if Mickey Mantle is *really* my favourite player," he said. "I like Willie Mays a lot better than I ever liked Mickey Mantle. Loads better."

There was nothing left for Vera to do but stand and stare at her son.

I I

———◆———

The station had signed off the air and now the empty, flickering screen was bleeding a numb stain of blue light into the darkness of the living room. The sound of rain on the roof, the gurgle of drain pipes discharging water from their throats masked the faint electrical buzz of the television set but did not disturb the two sleepers in the room.

Tonight was professional wrestling, scheduled after the late-night roundup of local news, sports, and weather. Daniel and his grandfather never missed it. The old man egged on the villains in their treachery and pretended to dismiss any possibility of fakery, or the fix. "You can't tell me that one of those flying leaps off a turn-buckle down onto a man lying defenceless doesn't do damage," he would argue.

Daniel, still blind to instances of his grandfather's irony, would attempt to reason with him. The old man got a kick out of seeing him so serious. "But that's exactly my point. Don't you see what I'm getting at? If it wasn't fixed, if it wasn't acting, somebody would get killed."

"Maybe an ordinary man would. But we're not dealing with ordinary men here. We're talking blond negroes. Now a blond negro has already defied one law of nature. No reason he can't do it a second time and survive somebody leaping down on him off a turnbuckle."

It was really only the sport of arguing that kept them awake, not the wrestling, and after what had happened earlier that evening neither of them had had their hearts in arguing. So they had fallen asleep. Stretched out on the chesterfield Daniel lay closest to the source of light emitted by the television screen. The wavering blue light gave him the face of a boy sunk senseless in six feet of water. Across the room his grandfather slumped in an armchair, dressed incongruously in striped grey flannel pyjamas, plaid carpet slippers, and his straw fedora.

Because he had worn the hat to the supper table there had been a dust-up with Vera. She had understood it as a provocation. That was the word she had used. He hadn't meant anything by it. He had simply forgot. He was still forgetting the hat even with them living in the house.

She had got on her high-horse, as only Vera could, and spoke of deliberate rudeness, his lack of consideration. He hadn't had the slightest clue of what she was talking about when she started in on him. "All I ask is that we eat in a semi-civilized manner. You wear that goddamn dirty hat to the table as a provocation, don't you? Admit it."

"I don't have nothing to admit."

That had started the donnybrook. Hot-tempered as she'd always been, Vera flew off the handle after a couple of exchanges and made a snatch for the offending article, tried to pull off his hat. He had thrown up his arm and knocked her hand away. It was instinct.

"Keep your hands to yourself, girl," he had warned her, with an old man's angry dignity.

"Mother may have tolerated eating with a boor in a hat," she said, "but I'll be damned if I will."

It was her daring to bring Martha into it, in the same breath with the hat. "Be damned then," he said.

Wasn't it just like her to refuse to take her meal at the table with him? And to insist the boy be her hostage in the living room, the both of them eating with plates on their laps? He knew Daniel hadn't wanted to join her. She had had to call him twice, in that certain tone of voice, before he finally got up and reluctantly went into the other room with his glass of milk and plate. He was a good boy. He had told himself that it was as much for the boy as himself that he paraded around for the rest of the evening in the hat. He had wanted to show him that everybody didn't have to wave the white flag where Vera was concerned. Where the hell did that girl get off, telling him what he could and couldn't do in his own house? She had no business grabbing things from him as if he was a sugar-tit sucking baby. Making him eat alone. He supposed she thought that was some terrible punishment being denied her company for a supper. At least he had eaten in peace.

The old man had begun to stir in his sleep. His massive head, which hung down from his neck like one of the sunflowers in his garden heavy with seed and drooping on its stalk, wobbled. His hands twitched and fumbled on the arms of his chair, opening and closing. Faster and faster the fingers curled and straightened, curled and straightened, until suddenly they shot out rigid and with a sharp, wordless cry Monkman snapped forward in his chair, eyes wide.

He stared into the screen of the television, blue, cold as the ice of the dream from which he had just surfaced. He heard the sound of water trickling in his head. Awake, he was still half-suspended in the chill, watery dark of the dream. Then he realized that the sound of water in his head was the sound of rain, the first in over a month. He passed his hand clumsily over his face and smiled for the sake of the parched garden, smiled to remember it was summer and really there was no ice.

The smile faded when he recalled what the boy had confessed to him. "Mom asked me to find out something from you," Daniel had announced after Vera had gone to bed and they were alone with their wrestling.

"What's she want to know now?"

"She wants to know where Uncle Earl is. She said you'd never tell her just to spite her, but she said you might tell me if I got around you right." The boy looked painfully guilty. "I don't know. It sounded like spying or something the way she wanted me to do it. I thought if I just came out and asked you straight – that would be better."

"I don't know where Earl is," he had answered. "Tell your mother that."

With the cold of the dream present in him, more than anything he wanted to talk, wanted to wake the boy. But that would not be fair. He has learned that dreams ought to stay dreams to the young. Nobody ought to show them different. And he cannot allow himself to become a beggar, going crawling to Vera. Having people in the house was supposed to make it easier, instead it had become harder.

Which left Stutz.

To avoid rousing the boy and questions he went as he was, turning on only the kitchen light to find a coat. He stood blinking under the unshaded bulb, wrinkled pyjama legs sagging beneath his overcoat, sockless feet sloppy in slippers, fedora tamped down until it bit his scalp. Then he stepped out into the rain. The abrupt passage from the glare of electric light to utter night left him blinded. It was only prudent to stand and wait for his eyes to adjust. Rain beat down on the stiff crown and brim of his hat, creating an unholy racket, like hail on a tin roof.

For the first time he considered what the hour might be. It had to be well past two. Stutz would be in bed. In his day Alec had knocked on his share of doors early in the morning but carrying a bottle had insured a welcome. What could he carry to Stutz who hated and despised bottles? Corn. Stutz went weak for corn on the cob. Alec had been promising him a feed of sweet corn as soon as it was ripe. Wouldn't Stutz gawk when he opened his door to a man with his arms stacked with cobs? "Get the glue on your dentures, Stutz," he'd say, "look what we got here!"

Even after his eyes started to allow for the darkness he couldn't make out much with the sky overcast, the moon and stars cloaked in cloud. The corn patch had already grown above the height of a man and in among the stalks it was black as Lazarus's tomb. He picked by feel, running his hands up the plants until they met with an ear to be pinched and measured and judged by his fingers as to plumpness and readiness for eating. Jesus wet work he swore it was, too, puddles standing between the rows and the gumbo sucking the slippers off his feet with every step he took, the long blades of the leaves laying a slash of damp on him wherever they brushed and all the while the rain pissing down for all she was worth. But at last his arms were full, his pyjama legs soddenly clinging to his legs, and he blundered out of the corn patch and into the road, bound for Stutz's house. The journey had a fugitive, furtive air. Whenever he passed under a streetlight where the rain descended in gleaming, silver lines so straight they appeared to have been drawn with a ruler's edge, Alec broke into an anxious shuffle and hunched low over his burden. What might people think if they recognized him toting corn through the streets in his sleeping costume?

Plenty of banging and hollering finally raised a light inside the house and, some time later, brought Mr. Stutz to the back door, his usual deliberate self.

"Aren't you the drowned rat?" was his only remark as he swung wide the door. "Hurry up now and get yourself out of that."

Inside, spilling water from the brim of his hat down onto a small braided rug that Stutz had steered him to, Alec pondered what it would take to rattle Mr. Stutz. It was evident from the careful way he was dressed – shirt buttoned to the collar, suspenders hooked – that he had been in no particular rush to learn the reason for all the commotion at his door so early in the morning. Everything in good time. Another thing, he hadn't acknowledged the corn piled in Alec's arms which was already scenting the kitchen with its sweet, green smell.

"This corn's for you," the old man said abruptly. "It's picked fresh."

Stutz began to scold him, ignoring the corn. "Look at you," he said, fetching a tea-towel which had been neatly hung on the door of the woodstove to dry, "you've gone and got yourself wet feet. Kick them slippers off," he ordered, going down on his knees, "and let me give those feet a rub with a warm, dry towel. An old fellow like you – why the cold can climb right up your legs and settle in your kidneys. A kidney complaint is no laughing matter your age. You catch cold in your kidneys, then where'll you be?" he asked, vigorously towelling the blue-veined feet naked on the braided rug.

"Try and leave some skin on," said Monkman, resentful at being spoken to in this way. "And don't forget I'm standing here with an armful of corn."

"You can put it in the sink when I'm finished," said Mr. Stutz, grunting like a shoeshine boy. "Right now I'm trying to work some colour into these feet of yours. They're white as snow, bless me."

While Stutz chafed his feet, Alec stared down at the creases crosshatching the back of his neck. It occurred to him that Stutz wasn't a young man anymore either. Time flies, as the man said. Yet he could remember as if it were yesterday the afternoon almost fifteen years ago that Mr. Stutz presented himself without warning at the garage and laid a claim on the job. He had acted as if it was his for the taking. It was in the week before Christmas, in the twilight of a short winter's day threatening storm, that this large man carrying a cheap suitcase had appeared in the back of the shop, his shoulders dusted with snow. Earl and he had looked up from the bucket where they were rinsing gaskets, expecting that the man was a traveller who had hit the ditch and wanted a tow. Instead, he said he had come to take the job advertised in *The Western Producer*. He could start Monday.

At first he had been leery about Mr. Stutz. Stutz was fairly young, looked fit, and wanted a job that nobody else had bothered to apply for. Immediately he had suspected a conscript on the run. Also, his last name, Stutz, sounded German. He had asked him point-blank, "You ain't by any chance dodging your call-up, are you? Because I don't want no involvement with the bulls."

"Not me," said Stutz, "I only got one eye. The left one's glass."

So he had read it as cockiness. But cocky or not he had had to hire him with a war on and a labour shortage. It took him a week or two before he changed his mind and gave it another name than cocky. Sincerity. Yes, there had been something about the bugger. He had introduced himself as Mr. Stutz and it stuck. In the back of the garage on that snowy afternoon he hadn't troubled to try and sell himself, only waited unruffled and patient for his answer, suitcase hanging on the end of his arm. Take me, or leave me, his face said.

It was Earl, always deathly shy around strangers, who had helped him decide. He spoke to the man. He said, "It was me wrote out the ad for the paper. Dad says I write a clearer hand than him." Earl had seemed to be laying a claim for some of the credit in bringing the stranger to Connaught.

Suddenly Monkman heard himself saying what he had only meant to think. "Earl's been on my mind a lot lately. I think it's because of Vera's boy."

Mr. Stutz rose, groaning, from his knees. "I can take that corn off your hands now," he said.

As the ears thudded on the sink bottom, Alec suggested, "If you got a pot of water on the boil now we could strip a few ears and have them at the pink of perfection."

Mr. Stutz was the only man capable of discomforting Alec Monkman with a single glance. He discomforted him now. "It's three o'clock," he said severely. "I eat corn at three o'clock and it'd have me up and on the toilet before six."

"Corn was intolerant of Earl the same. But he couldn't stay away from it or tomatoes. Tomatoes were the hives though. All summer long his mother used to have to watch him. He'd steal corn out of the garden; he'd sneak out with the salt shaker and eat tomatoes warm off the vines. Ate the corn raw and nearly shit himself silly. The boy never had a trace of sense."

"Now you go easy," warned Stutz, "or you'll work yourself into a state again. Remember what I told you before? You got to accept your part in it, Alec, but nobody can say how big that part is. And your part isn't all of it neither."

Monkman did not appear to notice what was being said to him. "Vera wants to know where he is. She's set the boy to spying on me."

"You know what I think. I've told my opinion before."

"And if I told her, what then? That girl's flint. I always meant to – when we settled our differences. But I can't even get forgiveness where I don't see I done any wrong. You tell me what I did that was so terrible? Asked her to stop at home and take care of her brother. Most girls would have jumped at the chance of such an easy life, keeping house for a man and a boy. She didn't have enough work to keep her busy half the day, always smoking cigarettes and drinking Cokes with her friends in the Chinaman's. That's suffering? Most girls that age would have been beside themselves to be free as a bird, a regular allowance to spend as they liked – plus what she stole from housekeeping. The way she milked me she could have been rich as a princess in a few years.

"And I wouldn't have asked her to do it but for Earl. He needed somebody after his mother passed away. Him going on about hearing Martha moving around the house when he was alone; I figured that for wishful thinking out of loneliness. So I wanted her there at home for him because he was high-strung, high-strung from a baby up. He always showed it.

"And now she wants to know where he is? Did she ever think she's got no right? Because she walked out on her brother, didn't she? I'm not just talking about the Army and the war, but after, too. Because didn't she disappear on him? After the war he never got a letter from her. You think that didn't upset him? You're god-damn right it did. No letter until the one she sent to announce she'd got married and that one was too late, he never got it. So sure he was upset. People disappearing on him left and right – his mother, his sister. No wonder he hung on my heels like a stray pup, probably afraid I was going to vanish into thin air on him, too, I suppose. You remember how that was, Stutz? We couldn't turn ourselves around without bumping into him or tripping over him. He wouldn't let us out of his sight."

"His company was no trouble. He was always a pleasant boy."

"Sure he was a pleasant boy. But you wasn't the one responsi-ble for him was you? You didn't have to get him to some point of usefulness, did you?"

"That's true. It wasn't me who was responsible."

"I mean, how long was I supposed to let him continue on that way? Isn't it natural for a boy his age to want his independence? Instead, he had to trail around after us. Christ, he could've been taken for simple. It had to stop. The boy had to make himself suit-able, had to find his place. And I tried him every place, didn't I, Stutz? I gave him his chances, didn't I?"

"Alec, nobody could ever say you didn't have his interests at heart."

"The boy graduated high school and he couldn't meet the train on time with the dray. He run the projector fine if I was there to watch him but as soon as I left he burned the film on the bulb, or didn't thread it right, or ripped it to ribbons. All he wanted to do was hang around the garage with us. The boy finished school and all he wanted to do was pass his father tools. He'd have been content to pass me tools the rest of his life if I'd have let him."

"He done a beautiful job with the garden though. He made you a beautiful garden, Alec."

Briefly, Monkman's face lit with pleasure at the praise of his son. "By Jesus, yes," he agreed. "Earl could garden. That's what gave me the idea for the farm. A grown man can't be a gardener but he can be a farmer, can't he? What's a farm but a big fuck of a garden? Make him a farmer, I thought."

He had determined to see it done. A farmer needed a farm, so Alec had bought one; the farm he still owned and Marker rented. It had been a weedy half-section the bank had foreclosed on early in the thirties and since then had installed a series of improvident tenants on. When Alec had made them an offer the bankers had been quick to accept and rid themselves of a load of care and trouble. Alec bought cheap, the way he seemed to get whatever he wanted now that his luck had changed. He had to take a mortgage on the theatre but that didn't cause him to lose any sleep. Cattle and grain prices were strong and Alec believed that the farm could pay for itself. Along with the 320 acres of land came an assortment of ramshackle, second-hand implements and a small house that was in decline but still reasonably comfortable. Only one thing more was necessary. In the spring Monkman engaged a hired man named Dover to help work the place and teach Earl farming. Nevertheless, when he proposed his plan to Earl, his son had resisted.

"I don't know if I want to be a farmer."

"Of course you don't – until you give her a whirl, give her a try. That's all I'm asking – that you try."

"What if you need me here in town?"

"What would I need you for? Stutz and I will manage. What I want to see is you managing too, on your own."

All he wanted was his son to learn self-reliance, that was what was behind the exiling of Earl. He explained it to him at length, so that the boy would know why he demanded it of him.

"The time has come for you to show you can stand on your own two feet. Dover's going to take you to the farm and see you stick to it. Don't come making your way back to town every couple of days because you're homesick, either. Maybe I'll just put it to you this way. Don't bother showing your face around here again until you've raised a crop. I mean it, Earl. If somebody has to come to town for groceries, or fuel, or parts, or whatever, let it be Dover. By September we'll have you weaned of this nonsense and a man. I think me and Mr. Stutz ought to stay clear, too. No visits until you've finished your work, done the job you've been put out there to do. But the day you've got a crop ready to cut, send us word, Earl, and we'll be there to admire what you done with bells on, me and Mr. Stutz. None gladder to offer you congratulations and shake your hand. That's going to be my dessert the end of summer, to see the crop my boy raised."

There were times when the temptation had been very great to disregard his own rules, jump in the truck, and pay Earl a visit. He missed the boy a good deal, missed his presence in the house, found himself still glancing over his shoulder to locate him when he stepped back to survey a piece of work finished in the garage. However, he curbed his desire and relied on what Dover would report when the hired man made his trips to town. The difficulty was Dover wasn't much of a talker. This was the result of having lived most of his life as a hired man in the midst of families he longed to be a part of, yet upon whom he had no right to lay any claims of affection. It had been a queer twilight sort of existence and it had taught him that what was not his to receive, was not his to give either. He grew to be a frighteningly detached and disinterested man. A lank sixty year old who became drier and sparer with every passing season that brought him nearer to the end of his working days, he volunteered nothing to anybody. An employer had once characterized him as the sort of fellow who wouldn't warn you if you were about to step backwards off a cliff because it wasn't any of his business, what you wanted to do. "Mind your own business," was Dover's practical motto. In his travels over the years, in and out of dozens of farmhouses, Dover had encountered his share of peculiar situations and peculiar types. He had learned to pretend, along with the rest of the family, that whatever was going on was perfectly normal and usual. Living alone on the farm with the boy caused him no grief. He was a quiet, polite, clean boy. If Monkman wanted to ask questions he would answer them but he wouldn't draw conclusions for him.

"So how's my boy? You turning him into a farmer?"

"Getting there, getting there," Dover would allow, sliding his eyes from one thing to another in the shop, never looking Monkman directly in the face.

"And Earl's working? He's working hard?" Laughing, "Tell him if he isn't, he'll have to dig the toe of my boot out of his arse."

"No complaints there," Dover had said slowly, "but the boy seems to have work and weather confused. Seems to think that just hard work'll allow him to take his crop off a month earlier than anybody else. I tell him it doesn't quite work that way, you can't trick the seasons. I tell him save your hurry for what can be hurried, growing can't. But he doesn't listen to me when I give him the facts."

"Oh, he just wants to prove himself," Alec had said, feeling a flutter of gratification. "Wants to show his old man what he can do."

"Pity the horses then," Dover had remarked dryly.

"How's that, 'Pity the horses'?"

If it hadn't been for the sake of the beasts, Dover wouldn't have complained. "He's been driving the horses too hard, won't give them their rest. Yesterday night he didn't come in for supper. I held it until nine and then I went out to the field to see if he'd had an accident. He was still working. I took the horses away on him, unhitched them from the harrows and took the lines out of his hands. He didn't want to give them up even though they were played-out, stumbling. I said to him, 'Work yourself as you please, but these poor dumb creatures aren't volunteers. They need rest and feed.'"

"That was the thing to do," Alec had hurriedly approved, "that was right. You got to remember he's a town boy and it's all new to him. It's just that he doesn't know horses, hasn't had the experience. Now Earl, he'd be the last boy to ever willingly mistreat an animal; he was born with a heart of gold. It was all ignorance on his part with the horses, I'm sure."

After that, Dover had kept his peace until the end of July when he suggested to his employer that Earl might benefit from a visit home. "Maybe you ought to ask your boy home for a Sunday dinner. He don't seem to care for my cooking and he can't keep working the way he's been if he don't eat. I can't seem to force hardly anything into him."

"It won't be long now," Alec had said. "In a couple of more weeks the crop'll be ready and I'll give him a dinner he won't soon forget. The boy and I had an agreement. A little rough cooking's not going to harm him. Tell him to eat what's on his plate."

In the third week of August the hired man arrived in town with the news that the crop was ready to cut. For days Alec had been anxiously awaiting the announcement, knowing the time was drawing near. He felt a great spill of relief. His gentle boy had done it. They both had weathered it. Now it was over.

Nevertheless, Alec allowed none of this relief and excitement to be betrayed to the man who stood drab and still in the garage, waiting for orders as he had all his life.

"Tell Earl that me and Mr. Stutz'll be out after work," Alec said. Already he was planning. He would take a bottle with him to the farm so that the three of them, Earl, Dover, and himself could pass it back and forth among them as they looked with satisfaction on the crop and what had been accomplished. The start of the celebration. Had Earl and he ever had a drink, man to man?

Dover shuffled his boots on the oil-stained cement. "Earl'll expect you sooner," he said apologetically. "To tell the truth, the boy is a little like the convict standing waiting for the prison gate to open. He's got it in mind I'll bring you straight back with me. He kind of made me promise."

Alec was torn. He wanted to succumb, throw up everything and go to his boy, but it would have ruined the sense of occasion. It would have felt too slapdash and hasty and undignified. Besides, Stutz wasn't in and he wanted him to share in Earl's success. The answer he gave Dover was abrupt. "I've things to do. Tell Earl we'll be out after supper."

When Stutz suggested they break off unloading a box car of coal at six o'clock because if they didn't, the light would be gone before they reached the farm, Alec balked as he had with Dover. He felt, obscurely, that to abandon the job unfinished would be admission of a weak and shameful lack of control on his part. He insisted they complete the work, sure there was time to spare.

There wasn't. Mr. Stutz was proved correct. As they pulled out of Connaught it was necessary to switch on the headlights of the truck. In the west the sky was a sheet of cold ash from which was wrung some pale colour – a few streaks of salmon and gold cloud captured between the decisive black line of the horizon and the leaden weight of sombre grey sky above. When Alec and Mr. Stutz finally bumped into the farmyard, the lights behind the clouds had gone out and night had truly fallen, dense, dark, still.

The memory of stillness awakened Alec to the stillness now in Stutz's kitchen. He realized that neither he nor Stutz had spoken for many minutes. Stutz sat with his hands on his knees, waiting patiently for him to resume speaking. Alec dredged his mind, striving to recall what his last words about Earl had been. Turning him into a farmer, he thought.

He lifted his eyes from the floor to Stutz's impassive face. "You remember the night we drove out to see Earl's wheat?" he asked. Somehow it was less of a question than a declaration of preoccupation.

"Yes," said Stutz, "I do. Same as you."

It was Dover who had greeted them swinging a kerosene lamp from side to side, sweeping back the night and lighting himself the broadest possible path.

"Where's Earl?" Alec had immediately demanded, unable any longer to restrain his eagerness.

"Earl? I believe Earl's deserted his post. Maybe you seen the kitchen chair by the farm gate when you drove up? No? Well, he carried a chair down there after I come back from town this morning and ever since he's been sitting there, waiting on you. Didn't take my word that you wouldn't be here until after supper. Just sat there with the sun beating down on him – damnedest thing. I coaxed but he wouldn't come into the house to take a meal. Was afraid he'd miss you, I guess. It's the only day he hasn't done any work since he's been here. And then, after all that waiting, he spots your lights on the approach and up he gets and makes off that way," Dover had said, indicating direction with the lantern, the light flaring yellow-white on his face as he lifted his arm, "towards his wheat."

Alec had not been able to disguise his surprise. "He's been sitting out all day? Down by the gate?"

"Down by the gate since eleven o'clock this morning. As I say, I tried to get him in but he wouldn't budge."

"And what did he have to say for himself?"

"What does he ever have to say for himself? Nothing, that's what. He didn't bother about me more than he would a fly."

"Maybe," Alec had speculated uneasily, "maybe he took off for the field and we're supposed to follow. Maybe he wants to show off the crop. Notwithstanding . . ."

"Notwithstanding it's dark," Mr. Stutz had said, completing his thought for him.

So the three of them had set off to find Earl, Dover lighting the way with his lamp, Mr. Stutz and Alec on either side of him shouting *Earl!* to the darkness and giving anxious pause for an answer. None came. Each interval of waiting was silent except for the sound of breathing, the dry whisper of dusty grass brushing boots and pants cuffs, the burble of the whisky bottle shaken in Alec's coat pocket. Each time they shouted his name and received no reply their pace quickened.

"When I first seen it, I had no idea what it was," said Mr. Stutz, shifting on his chair. "No clue at all."

"You took hold of me by the shoulder and pointed," recalled Alec. "You asked, 'What's that there?'"

"And you said, 'Fireflies.'"

"That's what I took it for. It's what it resembled to me, sparking on and off like that."

"I knew it couldn't be fireflies. Not so late in summer. Not so big and bright at a distance."

"I didn't think of the time of the year. It looked like fireflies to me. Flickering, blinking like that."

"I suppose the breeze was blowing them out. He was in the open, on higher ground, and there you always catch a breeze."

"And with us calling out, he knew we were near. He could hear us coming."

"Sure he could. And see us, too, when we came to the fence and Dover held the lamp up over his head to cast a beam far as possible."

"He'd have made us out, all three crowded underneath the lantern. Would have seen our faces, too. He wasn't more than a hundred yards off."

"A hundred yards off," echoed the old man, "striking matches in a bone-dry crop."

The small patch of brightness had taken hold so suddenly, so unexpectedly, that neither mind nor eye could comprehend it. For an instant the three of them had only been able to recognize a glow of agitation, something shuddering and vibrating like a swarm of bees in the black distance.

Mr. Stutz put the name to it. "Fire," he said.

All three men strained forward at the word, the top wire of the fence squealing and bending as they leaned upon it tensely. A wind had fluttered up behind their bowed backs and ran past them out into the field and night. It was like the long drawing of a sick, fretful breath. Alec heard the dark mass of grain rattle and shiver and sensed the heads of the wheat dipping and plunging before it, the wave rippling out to break upon the fire. It rooted him to the spot.

And when that wave dashed itself against the flames, the fire popped explosively, like a flare on a night battlefield, and there stood Earl waist-deep in the wheat, awash in a hot yellow, shaking light, smoke rising from the grain surrounding him like morning mist steaming up from a marsh.

"I never seen anything catch so fast in my life," said Mr. Stutz. "I wonder that the heat of it didn't make him run for it."

"I wonder," said Monkman.

Because Earl did not run, even though the heat caused him to flinch, to turn away his face toward the three men hanging on the fence. The boy might have been blind or deaf. He gave no sign he saw them there, beckoning desperately, or heard the two of them shouting *Run!* while the third gripped the strand of wire and stared. Earl did not move, except to draw up his shoulders against the searing heat which pounded his back and caused him to wobble as he stood his ground. Plunged to his hips in the crop, shrinking into himself, he had looked very small to Mr. Stutz and Dover, smaller still to his father. Perhaps the great flapping curtain of greasy smoke which had gone roaring up into the sky at his back had made him seem more so – a poor, lost actor without lines to speak, made to occupy and hold a stage with nothing but his face, his hands, his eloquent silence.

In scarcely a minute the curtain had risen to such a height as to overwhelm him, a drapery of grey and white smoke flecked red and orange with bits of burning awns and chaff. The three men's eyes followed it as it climbed into the night sky, swaying and billowing, blowing and sinking, its hem ragged, licked with fire. Their eyes were still on it when they felt the air tug about them as the blaze made of itself a firestorm, a whirlwind. The sudden convulsion ripped the curtain to rags and sparks, a violent updraught flung a spray of sparks higher and higher until they showered down about Earl and spattered the crop with more dark red poppies of fire.

Like his son, Monkman did not move. Did not move when the wire sagged and shrieked under his hands as Mr. Stutz flung himself over it. Did not move as in a fiery, smoky dream he watched Stutz run heavily forward, lurching as he panted through the wheat and over the hidden stones which twisted his ankles and wrung his knees, beating on to where Earl waited, face tight and gleaming, ringed by a dozen new patches of fire whose edges were running together and offering up a thin blue haze.

"I never lifted a hand to help, did I?" said Alec to Stutz. "It wasn't me that went into the fire. It was you."

"I told you before," said Mr. Stutz, "it was shock. Thinking he was going to burn put you in shock."

"He saw me stand at the fence," the old man muttered. "That's what he took away with him, me at the fence."

"He didn't take anything away with him," Mr. Stutz assured him. "Don't forget I was there. The boy had nothing in his mind. He had nothing whatsoever in his mind."

"It's not then I'm speaking of," said Monkman.

12

September was a fine month. The sun shone day after day but the air remained cool and sweet as pure well water. Alec swore he could taste the air on his tongue where it succeeded in improving the flavour of everything, even tobacco and coffee. Mornings he sat perched on his front step, a mug of coffee set steaming between his feet while he smoked the first cigarette of the day, squinting up at the sky and across the yard at the goldenrod. The goldenrod flowered bold as brass all about the garden shed but this year Alec didn't take a scythe to it. Vera had nicely requested him to spare it. "If it makes you happy to look at," was all he had said and refrained from pointing out to her that goldenrod was a weed. It did make Vera happy, too, when she saw the plants standing erect in the autumn sunshine like golden sceptres and reflected that it was she who had saved them. She also reflected that now the days were no longer so hot she might prepare creamed chicken and dumplings for her father, a favourite dish he had been hinting for all summer like a wheedling, spoiled child. It was a sign of a temporary truce.

Throughout October the weather continued remarkably mild despite the lateness of the season, although now there were undercurrents of ice in it. For days on end not a cloud curdled the soaring skies which each night's frost seemed to dye a deeper, sterner blue. In the mornings, before the sun had gained enough strength to burn it off, Alec Monkman's lawn was spread with a thick, white rime which exposed a stark trail of footprints when he crossed it to dig turnips left in his garden for the cold to sweeten in the ground. The old man loved this time of year, the chill baths of sunshine, the clearing away, the making ready, the long, lazy postponement of winter's sleep.

Late one night he flung open the kitchen door and called excitedly to Vera and Daniel to come outside, quick. At the very least, Vera had expected a house fire but the street lay dim and unremarkable as ever. "Listen!" commanded her father and she saw his face tilt up to the sky under the porch light. What they heard was the last of the migrating geese high overhead, clamouring in the limitless darkness of a fall night. Daniel and Vera and Alec stood absolutely still, tracking and straining after the wild, sad calling as it faded southward and finally dissolved into space and silence. Then, just as Vera was about to speak, a last gift. A flight of stragglers came sweeping low over the roofs of Connaught, so low that the whistle and whine of surging wings could be clearly heard, startling three hearts and lifting three faces blindly to search the sky for this mysterious passage, their common breath mingling in a golden fog under the porch light. As suddenly as they had come, the birds were gone.

The people on the porch became aware of the cold. "I wanted the boy to hear," said Alec.

"Yes," said Vera.

With no more to say, they went to bed.

———◆———

Daniel became obsessed with the Hallowe'en dance. He was pinning all his hopes on it. So far nothing at school had been as bad as he had been led to fear by his grandfather. No one had beaten him up or even bullied him. What he had been was ignored. Daniel realized that a lot of the blame was his. His pride had held him back from making overtures to anyone in case they should snub him. The mere thought of such humiliation could stick his tongue to the roof of his mouth and his feet to the floor whenever he debated with himself the advisability of approaching any of his classmates.

So he remained aloof and ran the risk of being labelled a snob, which was exactly how everyone thought of him. They knew he came from a big city in the east and they supposed he thought himself too good for the likes of Connaught. Add to that that he was the grandson of Alec Monkman who owned the delivery, the garage, the movie theatre, and the hotel, and it was not hard for them to imagine that Daniel believed he was small-town royalty. "Big shot," the other boys silently mouthed to one another when he went past them, carrying himself rigid and tense. The girls didn't care for him either because he made them wonder if they didn't seem like hicks compared to the girls he had known in the city.

At the beginning of the school year Daniel had tried to show them they were wrong about him but he only ended by making a fool of himself. It happened at the first high school football game of the season. Games were held Friday afternoons and the students of both the elementary and high schools were dismissed half an hour early so they could root for the home team, the Connaught Cougars. The football field was a raw-looking rectangle mowed out of prairie grass, lined with lime and pounded to hard pan by daily practices. Getting tackled on it was like getting tackled on a parking lot. Every September it was a school tradition to let the Grade Seven and Eight boys out of school for a day to pick the rocks off the field which the frost had popped out of the ground the previous spring, but they did a cursory job, harvesting only a portion of each year's bountiful crop, leaving behind enough stones to make a contribution to the number and severity of injuries to players. There were no bleachers, so those who had them sat on the hoods of the cars which they had bounced over the boulders and badger holes in the schoolyard to park around the field. The rest of the students formed into cliques and stood in clusters along the sidelines.

It seemed to Daniel that everyone had a group to attach themselves to except him. So that day he positioned himself five yards from the group he would have most liked to be invited to join and lingered hopefully. While he did, he made sure to cheer as loudly and enthusiastically for the Connaught Cougars as if he had spent his entire life in Connaught, lived or perished according to the team's success or failure. He did this absolutely alone, in splendid isolation. Of all the people cheering he was the only one who was aware of his own voice. Still, it seemed to him that he must be making a good impression. Surely it must mean something to them to see him rooting so wildly for their heroes.

After a bit, however, he began to suspect how foolish he must look, jumping up and down, yelling his head off like a lunatic, all utterly alone and apart. He felt exposed, ridiculous. It wouldn't take a genius to see what he was up to, what he wanted. But having once started he couldn't just quit. Quitting would be to admit that his display of loyalty and enthusiasm was insincere, false, downright sneaky. It was necessary to carry on, follow through, no matter how hard the ordeal. Face burning with shame, he shouted louder, hopped about on his patch of brown grass more grotesquely, waved his arms more frantically. "Crush 'em Cougars! Go team!" He was aware that people were starting to stare. A knot of Grade Seven girls were whispering and giggling. He pretended to be oblivious to all of this. There was no stopping now. Something was driving him to go on punishing and humiliating himself this way in front of everyone. Even during yardage measurements and lulls in play, his voice, which he had begun to lose, was the only one to be heard croaking and rasping encouragement to the team.

The crack of the starting pistol announcing half-time finally released him. He was free to slink off home. With every blundering step that hurried him across the schoolyard Daniel could feel the mortification he had repeatedly swallowed wobbling like a large stone stuck behind his breastbone. All wrong, all a mistake. Tittysucker, geek, fruit, he pronounced himself in a rage. That's what he should have written on the yellow wall which bore his Uncle Earl's name, not Daniel Miller, because Daniel Miller was too pathetic and stupid to deserve a place anywhere.

If he could only dance. Dancing you had a person all to yourself; you could have a private conversation and prove that you weren't really stuck-up, or a lunatic like you acted at a dumb football game. And being that it was a girl you danced with, that was in your favour, too, since girls were easier to persuade than boys. They were more understanding, more capable of overlooking past mistakes and bad first impressions than boys were. Girls had a knack of seeing what was really inside you. They were always doing it with James Dean and Montgomery Clift in the movies. Dancing was one way of getting a girl alone so you could talk to her. But he didn't know how to dance. Was it possible to fake knowing how? Would they be able to tell? He knew he couldn't fake jiving with all its complicated twists and turns, but waltzing didn't look so hard, a sort of walk around the floor together. And waltzing was good for conversation the way jiving wasn't. Daniel had noticed in the movies how often the most important things between a man and a woman got said while they were waltzing.

Daniel practised faking it. He closed the door to his bedroom and propped a chair under the knob so nobody could come busting in on his privacy. Positioning himself before his mirror he raised his left hand into the air, made a cradle of his right arm, and propelled himself with mincing, shuffling steps backwards, forwards, sideways, all about his bedroom.

"Well, Linda," he rehearsed, "how do you like the band? Yeah, I think they're pretty good too. Do you have a television at your house? Our reception is awfully poor, so much snow. What's your favourite program? Mine too. Yes, I like Connaught very much – everything but the teachers. Just kidding."

He went over all his invitations.

"Bernadette, would you like to dance with me?"

"Doris, might I have this dance?"

"Would you care to dance with me, Lynn?"

By the time he had completed all his dry runs he had sweated clean through his pants.

What was he going to do? There were no books in the library devoted to dancing, he'd checked. He joined his grandfather to watch Lawrence Welk but a lot of good that did him, the camera was always scooting from feet to faces so that it was impossible to follow what the dancers were up to.

Sometimes, when he was really desperate, Daniel braced himself to ask his mother's help. However, the prospect of being cross-examined as to why it was necessary for him to learn to dance would set him to writhing on the spot and drain him of resolution whenever he allowed himself to imagine the scene. Besides, he wasn't even sure his mother could dance. He had never seen her. The occasion to dance had never presented itself. His mother did not seem to be what he took to be a dancing sort of woman.

It was on October 23, with scarcely more than a week left before the Hallowe'en Dance, that Vera came face to face in the Rexall with her obligations. She really ought to volunteer to teach the boy to dance. What she faced was a rack of those record albums that old-time dance bands paid to have pressed in vanity sound studios in Winnipeg or St. Paul, Minnesota, and then peddled at the weddings they played, or twisted the arms of small-town merchants – druggists, grocers, hardware dealers – into carrying on consignment. This album was called *The Fedorovsky Family Plays For You Your All Time Favorites*, and on the jacket there was a black and white photograph of three fat middle-aged women, two of whom were seated at drums and an upright piano, the third with an accordion slung over her shoulders. The remaining two orchestra members were slightly older and more enormous men, one armed with a guitar, the other with a fiddle. Vera purchased the record, knowing for a certainty that every variety of dance Daniel would ever be called upon to dance in Connaught would be represented in the Fedorovsky Family album: waltz, polka, foxtrot, butterfly, schottische.

Vera returned home with the record at two-thirty. Her father was out so she was free to set up the phonograph, push the living-room furniture to one side, and stow away the throw rugs. That done, she sat down to wait for Daniel to come home from school. She sat with an impatient look on her face for five or ten minutes, then she got up and fetched the blazer and trousers she had hidden on the top shelf of her bedroom closet. She had ordered them from the Eaton's catalogue when Daniel first mentioned the upcoming dance. Vera laid these clothes on the chesterfield, in plain view, and smoothed them pensively with her hand.

Shortly after three-thirty she heard Daniel come into the house and called him into the living room. "You washing floors *again*?" he said, when he saw the disarranged furniture.

"I bought you some dress clothes," announced Vera. "They're there on the chesterfield. Take them upstairs and try them on and then come back down here so I can see if they fit. Wear a white shirt and tie," she added, as an afterthought.

A few minutes later Daniel presented himself as ordered. The black and white runners he had worn to school were still on his feet.

"Go and put your good shoes on, lame brain," his mother said when she saw him.

"Why?"

"Because you can't expect to learn to dance in rubber-soled shoes. They stick to the floor."

Daniel wondered if the woman really could read his mind. It was eerie.

When he was finally properly shod, Vera judged that her son was a looker in his new outfit. Of course, a navy blue blazer was a classic and never went out of style and the colour of the jacket suited his complexion and rusty hair. "My, my, what have I wrought?" teased Vera. "Could it be a genuine heartbreaker? Wait until the girls set eyes on you. You'll have to carry a big stick to beat them off, you ask me."

"Funny, funny, it is to laugh."

"Now don't get all huffy," cautioned Vera. "I was just having a little fun. Seriously, you look very nice. Very grown-up."

That he looked grown-up was not necessarily what he wanted to hear. Being told you were grown-up somehow suggested you weren't.

Vera placed the record on the turntable. The first selection was an instrumental rendering of "The Tennessee Waltz." "Now watch me," said Vera, "as I do the steps. You'll pick it up in no time. Just remember whatever I do backwards you'll do forwards and what-ever I do forwards you'll do backwards. Got that?"

Daniel was uncertain but he said he thought so. As his mother sailed over the linoleum he studied her movements with fixed con-centration. His feet twitched while he tried to commit the steps to memory. The tune ended and his mother reset the needle at the beginning of the waltz. "Now together," she said, offering herself to be held. They began to edge their way around the floor. "Don't stick your bum out like that. You look like you're afraid somebody is trying to burn a hole in the front of your pants. Stand normal. Relax." Daniel found that her criticisms seized him up even more; his joints started to lock like burned-out bearings. "Don't jerk your arm up and down that way. You're not pumping water. Hold it steady. Loosen up. Glide, don't clump. You're not walking on railway ties." She started to count time in a loud emphatic voice, even more emphatic than the pounding of the piano. It threw him off more.

Vera saw this was going nowhere and mercifully brought the curtain down on the waltz. "I think maybe we ought to start with something livelier, something that has a stronger rhythm," she suggested, "just to get the music into your feet. How about we try a polka?"

Daniel was agreeable.

"First, let's walk through it slowly," said Vera. Humming, she deliberately guided Daniel through his paces, pausing to allow him to mark each transition. He moved as if in a trance, head bowed to the floor, eyes shifting from his mother's feet to his own as she languorously stepped, turned, kicked her heels in a slow-motion dream polka. "Ready for the real music?" she inquired after they had practised for a time.

Daniel nodded.

"Now remember," said Vera, lowering the phonograph arm on the appropriate number, "this'll be a little quicker, in step with the music."

She found herself snatched into frenzy. They were off. Plunging and lunging, galloping and dizzily whirling at breakneck speed. Daniel led her in a side-long charge directly at the television and then veered sharply off at the very moment that collision seemed an inevitability and bore down on the lamp-stand, feet slithering on the slick linoleum, heels tossing high in the air as they spun into a hairpin turn. The violence of the expression on his face rather alarmed her. The speed at which he swung her, the joint-cracking centrifugal force exerted on her, made Vera wonder if this wasn't an act of revenge. But for what?

"Dear, not so . . ." she began to say, but lost the rest of her sentence when a wide, looping turn brought the coffeetable hurtling toward her legs. Only a severe, impromptu correction saved her from a kneecapping. Around and around the room they careened, flushed and gasping. Vera could feel her heart pounding like a triphammer. There was a look in Daniel's eye which she associated with runaway horses. Whenever he spun her, crane-like legs thrashing the air in the wake of a reckless change in direction, his tie streamed over his shoulder like a prize ribbon flying from the bridle of a show pony.

It hit her. This wasn't revenge. He was simply and completely in his glory, believing himself master of the polka. Daniel the Polka King. There was nothing for it but to pray they escaped a wreck and last it out.

That was what she did. The polka ended and they came to rest, bent over, panting, palms planted on their knees. Both felt oddly exhilarated for having survived an ordeal. Then the sound of clapping swivelled their heads to the doorway where Alec Monkman stood, smacking his hard palms together, laughing. "I believe I just saw a fight to the death between two dust-devils," he declared.

"We were polka-ing," explained Daniel.

"You don't need to tell me," said his grandfather. "I know them all. When I was young I used to be a dancing fool."

"I think I got the hang of that one," confided Daniel, "but that waltzing is something else."

"Nothing nicer than a waltz," stated his grandfather. "It's easier than rolling out of bed. Let me give you a few tips." He made a perfunctory, mocking bow to Vera. "May I have the honour, daughter?"

Vera didn't answer. She looked doubtful.

"We're well-matched," her father cajoled. "You're winded and I'm old."

"All right," she said.

"Find us a waltz," the old man said to Daniel.

"Turn it back to the beginning," Vera ordered. "There's one there."

Strains of "The Tennessee Waltz" once more filled the room. The old man took his daughter in his arms, stood stock still and very upright for a full count of ten, drinking in the music. Then he launched them. Very decorously, graciously, he began to dance.

Vera had the strangest feeling. He was just as her mother had always claimed, an excellent dancer, miraculously light and easy on his feet for a big man, startlingly deft and spry for his age. But that was not the strange part. The strange part was how the two of them moved together, effortlessly. Vera had no recollection of ever having danced with her father before, yet it was as if they had been partners for years. She had no sense of being led, or of following, but they danced as if they had one mind.

He was speaking over her head to Daniel. "Dancing is like swinging an axe. The man's the axe and the music is what swings him. Once you accept that and stop fighting it – battle's over. All you got to do is enjoy being swung."

Daniel nodded solemnly.

"Another pointer. You steer your partner as much with your hands as your feet. Always give her a little warning as to where you're headed. Just the least pressure on the small of her back means come this way – relax it a little means go that way. But light, Daniel, light. No pulling and shoving. Easy so they don't realize they're being steered. There's the trick to it."

Having delivered his advice the old man fell quiet. Father and daughter revolved about the room. How gentle it all was. Dusk stood at the windows and shadowed the room. When the waltz finished, Vera stepped back and curtsied ironically. Daniel, imitating the actions of his grandfather earlier, noisily clapped his hands and then threw the light switch.

13

E very year it happened. With the arrival of November, Vera felt her mood going sour.

It had taken her a long time to realize that it wasn't just the dreary, zinc-coloured skies, the listless spatters of rain, the necessity of switching on the kitchen light at four o'clock in the afternoon that was to blame for turning her temper sharp, dark, short, like the days themselves. It wasn't weather that was at the root of her irritability and heaviness of spirit.

She knew it wasn't fair to anyone around her, but she couldn't help herself. Maybe what she had was catching. Her father had gingerly risked a comment just the other day.

"You and Daniel make quite a matched pair, one as glum and cranky as the other. You two eating something I'm not?"

The old man was right about the boy and her worries over Daniel had done nothing to improve her disposition. Two months into the school year and there were still no signs that her son had made any friends. Vera had hoped that the much anticipated Hallowe'en Dance might mark some kind of breakthrough, but the way Daniel moped around the house the next day, she had gathered the occasion had not been a success. But being Daniel, he had not given much up under cross-examination.

"So did you have a nice time last night?"

A non-committal shrug of the shoulders.

"You were home early enough."

"Yeah, I guess."

"But you had fun?"

"Sure."

He hadn't had fun and Vera knew it. If Daniel had had fun he wouldn't be spending all his time with an old man, watching TV.

There was no getting around it, this was a miserable time of year. Miserable because Vera could not forget that November was the month she had set her sights on Stanley, made up her mind to have him. Miserable because, year after year, she went through it, sad and filled with longing. Longing for that room Stanley had led her to, up that steep, narrow flight of stairs the night that Thomas had smashed Stanley's window. She missed that room dreadfully, ached for it in the cold of November. She could still see it as clearly as if it were yesterday. Books stacked along three walls, still more piled on windowsills and chairs, heaped on tables. To take a seat on the chesterfield it had been necessary to disturb two dictionaries, one English, one German. In the few feet of available wall space not crammed with books, up near the ceiling, Stanley had thumbtacked portraits of important men and women. Some Vera had recognized: the Roosevelts, Franklin and Eleanor; Charlie Chaplin, Einstein. Others she had been unfamiliar with. Mixed in with the portraits were reproductions of paintings. One took Vera's fancy because it reminded her of Saskatchewan. A flock of coal-black crows floating in the sky above a yellow field of grain.

It made her sorrowful and lonesome to think of that long-ago night, Stanley busying himself with coffee in the kitchen and she moving excitedly about the living room, stopping every now and then to pick up and examine a book, to read a title or an author's name on a spine. Gorky, *Arrowsmith*, Saroyan, *An Outline of*

History, Odets. Vera had felt buoyant, intoxicated. Maybe it had been the music on the phonograph, exuberant music composed of strange clashing, jangling sounds. It had made her disdain the very thought of sleep.

When Stanley came in carrying the coffee pot, Vera had asked him about the books. The question had no sooner left her mouth than she was afraid he might consider it rude. It was obvious that he didn't. He had seemed delighted to talk about such things. Stanley had said that it was from his father he had inherited a passion for music, for reading, for collecting books. "In the old country my father was a tailor," he had explained to Vera, "and tailors and cobblers had a reputation for learning. Their work was quiet work and in the large shops they sometimes pooled their money and hired a poor student to read to them while they sewed, or they took turns reading to one another. That was how my father came to know the Torah practically by heart. Not only the Torah, but also George Sand, Hugo, Dickens, and many of the Russians, writers who were popular with the socialists in the shops. '*Toireh iz di besteh S'choireh*,' he used to say to me. It's Yiddish and it means that learning is the best commodity. I suppose I took him at his word," Stanley had said, looking around him.

Vera had not been sure what Torah or Yiddish were. All she knew was that they were Jewish. She didn't ask for fear of appearing stupid and ignorant.

The two of them talked late into the night or, more correctly, early into the morning, drinking lots of coffee sparingly anointed with whisky. Stanley seemed to naïvely regard himself as something of a devil for offering a lady whisky, and measured hers by the thimbleful. Vera liked him for that. She liked him for being softly spoken and for carefully and deliberately forming his sentences before delivering them. His thinking through them showed on his face. She liked him for the encouraging way he had of listening to what she said; a way which never suggested that this was a trade-off, part of a bargain which contracted that she was obliged to listen to him. She actually saw him brighten when she told him she was from Saskatchewan. "Tommy Douglas!" he exclaimed, as if the one name couldn't be said without the other. He questioned her about the CCF and she found herself acting as if she and her family had always been supporters, even though she knew very well that her father was a Gardiner Liberal. She did this because Stanley told her he was a socialist. "Eugene Debs," he said, pointing proudly to one of the photographs on his wall.

Vera did not ask him who Eugene Debs was. She believed she could guess what general category he fit into.

Vera found herself telling Stanley about her work at the theatre, spicing her story with anecdotes about Mr. Buckle. She liked Stanley Miller for the ironic laughter that greeted her tales about the manager. She filled him in on her woeful experiences with Thomas. She liked him for not laughing at these. Several times she interrupted herself, saying, "But you must be tired . . ." He always dismissed the suggestion. "Remember, I'm the all-night reader. The regular night owl."

Vera noted how thin he was. That he smoked too much. That he drank too much coffee. That he was at least forty-five, maybe older.

Some time after four o'clock, Stanley ran out of coffee and they switched to tea. He brewed it in a thing he called a samovar, the way his parents had. Both of them were dead. He had no brothers or sisters.

Stanley demonstrated how his father had drunk his tea, sipping it through a sugar cube clenched in his front teeth. He urged Vera to try. She was game. It wasn't the whisky either, she hadn't had enough.

Even though she kept consulting her watch and saying she must go, she didn't. It was nearly eight o'clock in the morning before she left; Stanley had to open his doors in an hour. Then came the only awkwardness of the entire night, when they shook hands and said goodbye, Vera hesitating, waiting so that he would have the opportunity to suggest they meet again. He didn't.

But Vera had no intention of letting it fizzle out and end so lamely. She reasoned that an old bachelor like Stanley probably lacked confidence with women, that's why he hadn't dared to ask her for a date. A little nudging might be required, to show him he was on safe ground. And the smashed window provided an excuse, a plausible reason, for her to make amends for bringing this misfortune down on his head.

During the course of the evening, Vera had asked Stanley who his favourite writer was. When he had told her it was someone whose name sounded like Mountain to Vera, she had nodded her head and done her best to appear knowledgeable. Setting out two days later to buy a thank-you present for Stanley, she went in search of a book by that particular author.

"Mountain?" the lady who clerked in the snooty bookstore with all the tall bookcases had said. There were four female clerks in the store and Vera could scarcely differentiate one from the other. They all appeared to have been stamped out by the same cookie cutter. Tightly waved grey hair, tweed skirts, sweaters, brown oxfords, and glasses which hung on thin chains, dangling against insignificant bosoms, were common to all four. "Mountain?" said the woman again, eyeing Vera up and down as if to suggest she had her nerve, wasting a person's time. "And what does Mr. Mountain write?"

"I'm not sure," Vera had replied tentatively, beginning to feel more and more wasteful of time and patience. "All I know is that it isn't novels."

"Not very helpful, I'm afraid," said the woman, "seeing as there are so many authors who don't write novels. Really, I'm sure we don't have it. I'm quite familiar with all our stock and for the life of me I don't recollect any Mountain."

Vera, however, was stubborn. When she wanted something, she wanted it. Besides, she didn't have much time; she was expected at the theatre where she had a matinee to work. "You have to have it!" she blurted out. "He's a famous writer!"

She had been too loud. Several patrons had turned from the study of their books to see what the commotion was about. "I'm sure I don't know what to suggest, miss," said the clerk coldly, "except that you search our shelves. All our books are arranged alphabetically by author within categories. Just possibly you may find what you are looking for."

"Thank you very much," said Vera. "I'll just do that little thing, if it doesn't inconvenience."

After forty-five minutes of hunting Vera thought she might have found what she was looking for in the section labelled Philosophy. The name wasn't Mountain but it was close. Vera opened the book. The frontispiece was an etching of a grave, sombre man bristling with a huge ruffed collar. He looked exactly like someone who might interest Stanley Miller.

Vera decided to take a chance and buy the book, gamble that she had guessed right, even though the price was steep. She held it up to her nose and smelled it. Real leather. The price alone proved it.

Vera couldn't help registering the superior smile of the old dragon who had first helped or hadn't helped her when she rang up the sale. The smirking continued while she wrapped the book in brown paper and tied it in strong cord. Passing it across the counter to Vera, she said, "Just so you know, dear. It isn't Mountain. It's *Montaigne*. In case you're ever looking again. Saying the name correctly will save you time."

At that moment it didn't matter to Vera that the old piece of starch and her biddy friends would be laughing and shaking their heads over her mistake all day long. What mattered was that as soon as she heard the name pronounced she knew she had the right one. That's what Stanley had said the other night. Montaigne, not Mountain.

She couldn't wait to see his face. Although the doors of the theatre would soon be opening to the public, Vera flew off in the opposite direction, coat open and billowing behind her as she ran down the sidewalk on her long, strong, young legs.

Stanley was alone in an empty store. He looked different dressed in a navy blue double-breasted suit. Vera judged it could do with a dry-cleaning.

"What's this?" he said, when she thrust her package into his hands.

"Open it," she said eagerly. "It's a little something to make up for the other night."

It took him forever to pick apart the knot. When the book was finally unwrapped he turned it over, examining it carefully.

Vera could not stand his silence. "Do you have it?" she inquired, doing her best not to sound overly anxious.

"Not this. Not the Florio translation."

"Then it's all right?"

"It's beautiful," he declared. "A beautiful book." Then he did exactly as she had done earlier, held the book up to his nose and sniffed the binding. Regretfully, he laid it back down on the counter. "But I can't accept it," he said.

Vera was hurt. "Why? Why can't you?"

"It's much too expensive a present. Especially for a working girl to give."

"Nowhere near as expensive as a window," she said pointing to the sheet of plywood now nailed into the window-frame. "And I can't help feeling responsible."

"Don't talk nonsense. In any case, insurance pays for the window."

"I want you to have it," Vera said. "To show my appreciation for your kindness."

"No, I couldn't," he said, picking up the book and holding it out to her. "You know you can't afford it. Return it and get your money back."

Vera refused to touch the book. Like a stubborn child she actually hid her hands behind her back and violently shook her head no when Stanley leaned across the counter and tried to prevail upon her to take it back. "Don't be foolish! Take it!"

"I won't. If you don't want it – why, throw it in the garbage."

He only relented when he realized she was becoming angry with him.

"Well, all right," he said at last, reluctantly. "Thank you." But couldn't stop himself adding, "You shouldn't have."

In the course of the next couple of weeks Vera wondered if Stanley wasn't right – she shouldn't have. After all, the gift certainly hadn't encouraged boldness on his part; he gave no indication that he was summoning up the courage to ask her out. It was true that he didn't have her address, or her telephone number, but every day a little after noon Vera walked past his store on her way to work. He might have just once come out and spoken to her instead of waving to her from behind his new window like a coward.

The whole futile performance made Vera furious, livid. Maybe she ought to have taken back the Montaigne and shown him. But then, what would have been the point? Pride would never have allowed her to return it to the bookstore where she had been treated rudely and snubbed. Of course, she reminded herself, if she *had* taken the book she wouldn't have had to go out and find her own second-hand copy of Montaigne, a book she assiduously read each morning in the hope that it would provide some clue to understanding Stanley Miller.

If there was a clue, she hadn't discovered it. Montaigne was mostly common sense and Stanley Miller mostly wasn't. Because if he had an ounce of common sense he would have recognized long ago what a good thing was sidling up to his door and purring to be let in.

It never occurred to Vera that Stanley Miller might think himself too old for her, far too ancient for such a young girl. Or that he was concerned that he was a Jew and she was a Gentile. Vera never gave a second thought to Stanley's being a Jew. In church and Sunday School Jews had been spoken of frequently and approvingly, in fact the Bible was nothing but one long story about Jews. Outside of church, when they were discussed at all, the picture was slightly different. Jews, apparently, were smarter than ordinary folk and many were prone to sharp business practices. "To jew someone" was a commonly used expression in Connaught, like "drunk as an Indian" or "don't get your Irish up," but the use was more habit than conscious, directed malice. Since she had no objections to intelligence, rather admired and hankered after it, in fact, and since neither Stanley Miller nor his business looked prosperous enough to sustain a plausible charge of sharp practice, she wasn't going to be scared off by an old characterization. Besides, the war had proved what sort of people had a prejudice against Jews, pigs like Adolf Hitler, Goebbels, and Goering. Vera believed you could judge someone by his enemies as much as his friends.

Only after they were married had Vera learned that her blindness to Stanley's Jewishness had left him confused. Did she or didn't she know? Was it possible that she hadn't picked up on his allusions to Torah, his Yiddish proverbs? In the months following the wedding, they had laughed together about how he had done everything short of pinning the yellow Star of David on his lapel and gone around proclaiming himself one of the Chosen People. Yet not a word, not a hint that she grasped what he was. Could she be really that much in the dark? Who could tell with these small-town shiksas, these country pumpkins, what they did and didn't catch? As he had been careful to explain later to Vera, all his life he had been a socialist, a passionate believer in the undifferentiated brotherhood of man. He had lived for the day when words like Gentile and Jew would lose their meaning in the word Man. As far as he was concerned, the word Jew only mattered when it mattered to someone else. After their first meeting, he asked himself, Was that the case with Vera Monkman? Without knowing the answer he was already half in love. Why else did he position himself in the window every noon when she passed on her way to work, if it wasn't to see and be seen, to wave and be waved to? Why else did he disregard the well-meaning advice an uncle had given him when he was fourteen and beginning to show interest in girls? "Don't have anything to do with shiksas," he had been warned. "Your first fight – she'll call you a dirty Jew."

One shiksa, however, hadn't been prepared to throw in the towel on the fight just yet. If Montaigne wasn't the way to a man's heart perhaps music was. Vera hadn't forgotten the classical records that had provided background music to their conversation the night they had passed talking in his apartment. It was only natural then that a poster on a notice board outside an Anglican church she passed one day should stop her dead in her tracks with its announcement of a recital of organ music. Before either pride or circumspection could make themselves felt, Vera had purchased two tickets in the church office. Offering one of these to Stanley she told a lie which involved a girlfriend unexpectedly called away by an illness in the family. Immediately Vera had thought of Stanley. Would he like her friend's ticket?

It seemed he would. Better still, he also wanted Vera's address so that he could come by and collect her for the concert in a taxi. It was beginning to feel like a proper, an official date.

In the few remaining days before the concert, she succeeded in working herself into a regular frenzy worrying about all the ways she might make a fool out of herself on this most special of occasions. What if Stanley wanted to discuss the pieces played? What in the world did she know about classical music? To be absolutely honest, nothing. Furthermore, she had to admit that the prospect of an hour and a half of continuous organ music left her feeling downright dismal. For Vera, organ music was Patricia Mackinnon, the organist at St. Andrew's United Church in Connaught, weaving back and forth on her bench and pumping pedals so desperately she left the impression that she was engaged in some hell-bent-for-leather bicycle race rather than aiming to drive a few mournful notes out of the pipes. Cripes, organ music. What she wouldn't do to please a man.

There was also the question of a hat to fret over. Vera knew that in Roman Catholic churches women were expected to cover their heads. But what about an Anglican church like the one she was going to? Where did they stand on such an issue? Vera had never set foot in an Anglican church and had no idea whether or not hat-wearing was a requirement or not. And if it was, did the rule apply just to religious services or everything else that took place under its roof, recitals included? God, the humiliation if she got turned away from the door because she didn't have a hat. Which she didn't, had never owned such an article, making it necessary to borrow a hat from Amelia, one of the weird Wilkinson sisters.

Add to all of this, she was, as usual, broke. No money for a new dress and barely enough to provide refreshments to properly entertain a guest. She blew all her ready cash on a bottle of gin, a bottle of rye, a couple of cans of smoked oysters, a jar of cocktail onions, some stuffed olives, and fancy crackers. All this on the off-chance that Stanley could be prevailed upon to drop by after the recital for a drink and a snack.

The big night, a Friday, Vera played sick, phoning in the excuse that she was laid low by the flu. Mr. Buckle was beside himself when he received the sad news. Friday was one of the busiest evenings of the week and one of the rowdiest. How was he going to cope without her? Couldn't she manage to come in, surely she wasn't as ill as all that, was she? Vera asked him how he would like it if she brought up all over a customer? That pulled the wheels off his little red wagon.

However, none of her planning and careful preparations had anticipated what she opened her door to that night. That was Stanley, looking nothing like his normal self. It was the way he was dressed, or costumed, or whatever might be the proper word for it. Stanley resembled a Ruritanian aristocrat or something along that line – Ronald Coleman stepped out of the movie *The Prisoner of Zenda*. His hat alone would have been enough to suggest that – a Homburg, Vera thought was the name for it – a smoke-grey Homburg. And more. A topcoat with a velvet collar, a tightly fitted wasp waist and flaring skirts which fell to his ankles, the sort of skirts Russian cavalry officers in historical movies spread over the rumps of their horses when they were mounted. Standing erect and tall in her doorway he looked every inch a foreign visitor holding his face clenched and composed against the strangeness of the world he was on the brink of entering. While his odd appearance surprised and dismayed her just a little, she was careful to cloak her feelings in bustle and talk as she gathered up her purse and coat, straightened Amelia's hat.

During the cab ride to the church, Stanley, for the most part, sat silent and still in his corner of the back seat, his face turned slightly to the streetlamps which intermittently lit his face in three-quarter profile. Vera didn't interpret his silence as rudeness because she sensed it was not directed towards her but turned inward on himself. He scarcely spoke at all during the short trip except to reply politely and distractedly to Vera's comments about the weather. Late that afternoon temperatures had suddenly begun to plummet and they both agreed that snow could be smelled in the air.

As she waited on the steps of the church while Stanley paid the driver, Vera was praying he wouldn't lead her to a pew in the front. Of course, this was exactly what he did. All along Vera had been concerned over the sort of figure she was going to cut in her shabby coat and out-of-fashion dress and she didn't relish the prospect of being scrutinized sashaying down the entire length of the church. Now it was even worse because she feared shaming Stanley. Some time during the cab ride it had struck Vera that she was likely mistaken about Stanley's clothes. They weren't odd at all. In fact, they were probably exactly the sort of clothes to wear to an organ recital. At the moment, she was looking at him in an entirely different light. He reminded her of a diplomat – polished, elegant, European to his very fingertips, just the man she had imagined herself walking with on the deck of an ocean liner and conversing to in French when she was a girl of thirteen in Connaught. Surely, she was too plainly ordinary a girl to be seen with such a man. Surely people would snicker when they saw him escorting her to her seat.

Once inside the church her doubts diminished. It came as something of a relief to discover that there were some women seated in the audience as shabby as she, maybe even shabbier. There were a lot of very young, very wan, very pinch-faced girls whose hair was cut like Joan of Arc's that she guessed were likely music students. Then there were the sleek, well-groomed dames huddled in their fur coats besides their bored-looking husbands. Why was it that all these women had the pointy chins and sharp, bright eyes of the small creatures trapped to furnish pelts for their coats? Vera was determined not to be their victim, not to cringe in a trap. She drew herself up to her full five feet eleven inches and sailed down the aisle.

The seats Stanley chose were in the third row, very near the front. Once they had settled themselves he lost himself in studying the program. This was fine with Vera. Having survived one ordeal she was content to recover in peace, to drink in her surroundings without the strain of making intelligent conversation. As she ran her eyes over the scenes from the Bible depicted on the stained glass windows she could sense the church filling behind her and the atmosphere thickening and tensing with anticipation. It must be almost time. She checked her watch. A few minutes before the hour.

Vera directed her gaze to the choir screen. There stood the four apostles carved in stone, granite eyes staring blankly out at the restless flock. Vera recalled a childish blasphemy. Matthew, Mark, Luke, and John, hold the horse while I get on. As she smiled to herself, a paunchy little man (nothing like the sinewy stone apostles) mounted the steps leading upwards to the altar, turned, and launched into a description of the evening's program. Vera, her mind wandering, soon lost interest in what he was saying. The unfamiliar words, toccata and fugue, were often repeated and she was dimly aware of his fat white hands flogging the air as he talked.

A hush fell. Vera realized that the man had disappeared. For the first time that evening, she asked herself where the organ was and searched the front of the church for it. She couldn't find it.

Then, just as her eyes passed over the reader's desk with the great eagle carved in relief, the eagle of St. John the Divine, the opening notes of Bach's Toccata and Fugue in D Minor tumbled down from the organ loft above and behind her, from where she had least expected them to come, as if rolling thunderously down from heaven itself.

She was stunned. The eagle with the outspread wings, each feather distinct and bristling, neck ruffled, curved beak agape, took wing on the stately wind of soaring music. It filled Vera with yearning. She, too, wanted to whirl up, free. What was lost did not need to be lost forever. Couldn't Stanley teach her? Couldn't he tell her the wise books to read? Couldn't he play her the music that fine, educated people listened to? Couldn't he explain to her the pictures he hung on his wall, teach her the names of their painters? There was no need to remain forever ignorant and common. People could rise. She would rise.

Instinctively, she turned to Stanley and found him sitting hunched on the edge of the pew, elbows propped on his knees, chin jacked on his palms, face rapt. He appeared to be a man leaning forward into the warmth cast by a fire. Watching him, Vera felt that she, too, had a share in the comfort it shed. Already the music had melted the deep lines in his forehead and to Vera he looked ten years younger than when they had stepped into the church.

At the end of the recital Stanley and Vera rose from their seats, reluctant but happy. Outside, the snow which they had both predicted earlier was falling. It was a heavy, wet snow which blurred the darkness and swirled a mysterious code of white dots and dashes through the arcs of the streetlamps. Among the last to exit from the church, Stanley and Vera found themselves virtually alone in the street, the rest of the crowd having hastily dispersed in the snowstorm. There was not a taxi in sight.

"Should we start out walking?" suggested Stanley. "Just until we find a cab, or a streetcar comes along?"

Vera agreed that was a good idea. The big, drowsy flakes surrounded them in a curtain which cut Stanley and her off, isolated and screened them from the rest of the world. If this sense of privacy did not lend Vera the courage to take his arm, at least it made her feel easier in his company. The two of them went down the long, empty prospect of a tree-flanked street, wrapped in snow and their own thoughts, frequently halting so that Stanley could remove the Homburg and dust it with the sleeve of his coat before the snow melted and left water stains. That done, he would press the hat firmly back down on his head and travel another block before it was necessary once again to pause and sweep the hat clean.

Stanley and Vera were forced to wait for a light to change on a busy road. The snow streamed down brightly in the light of windows, the light of streetlamps, the beams of car headlights. Traffic had churned the snow into slush on the pavement. Without daring to look her in the face, Stanley reached out and shyly rested his arm across her shoulders. Before they crossed the road she slipped her arm around his waist.

Two months later they were married.

14

In the weeks before Christmas, *wild* and *frantic* were the words Vera most often employed. "That old man is driving me absolutely *wild*," she could be heard muttering under her breath. Or, "They are goddamn driving me *frantic*," they meaning the scabby crew of buzzards who tracked in and out of the house morning, noon, and night, eating and drinking them out of house and home. What really irked Vera was that her father assumed it was *her* duty to feed and water these old hogs. "Vera, could you make another plate of ham sandwiches for the boys?" he was always asking. "Is there another pan of date squares?" The last time her father had ordered up sandwiches she had told him where the bear shit in the buckwheat. "You want sandwiches, make them yourself. I don't see any piano tied to your ass."

She was surprised when that was what he did. He hadn't made a scrap of fuss, just meekly left his rummy game and started slicing up a loaf of bread crooked as a dog's hind leg, so crooked she couldn't bear to watch and finally took the knife away from him and tackled the job herself.

This was supposed to be Christmas? A collection of derelict old farts cluttering up her kitchen, tracking in snow and leaving puddles on the floor wherever they stood or sat, the door swinging open every five seconds so that the day was one long continual draught, all of them eating as if it were their last meal and drinking up the rye and beer as if it were their last chance for a drink. The house getting dim and blue with cigarette smoke and loud with accusations of cheating and arguments over who played what card in the games of poker and rummy that went on most of the day and night. Daniel and she having *their* home (in fairness it was theirs, too) disrupted by a bunch of dirty old men, who shouted in their deaf-men's voices, laughed wet, gargly laughs that rumbled into coughing fits, hawking and spitting, and generally conducted themselves in a pleasant and attractive fashion.

And the feeble excuse her father offered for this holiday invasion was that every merchant in Connaught is obliged to dispense Christmas cheer to his customers. Yes, yes, said Vera, she knew that. But every other merchant in town invites his best customers to step into the storeroom for a quick nip out of the bottle kept there for that purpose. None of the other businessmen turns the family residence into a Sally Ann or Harbour Light where every moocher feels free to camp out for as long as the fancy takes him.

Well, countered her father, he couldn't really offer drinks out of the businesses because Mr. Stutz doesn't approve of alcohol and won't have any part in distributing it. And he can't be expected to be everywhere, can he? One minute pouring drinks at the garage, the next at the hotel? So really the most sensible arrangement is to have the boys drop by the house.

It suits him but not Vera. As the lady of the house she's responsible for keeping it cleaned and the larder stocked, tasks which are endless when you're faced with guests the likes of them. As she's pointed out to her father any number of times, there might be some reason for tolerating these nuisances if any of them had ever spent a nickel in any of his enterprises but she is willing to bet dollars to doughnuts they never had. They couldn't rustle up a nickel among them if they went shares. So what was the percentage?

Besides, they were a rebuke and an insult to family pride. Of the half dozen or so regulars which were underfoot, not one of them would have been permitted to darken the door of any of Connaught's respectable citizens. They were taking advantage of the Monkmans, turning them into laughing-stocks.

All scrubs and good for nothings of one description or other. A couple of serious drunks, a suspected dog poisoner, a pair of shiftless bachelor brothers, aged sixty-five and sixty-seven, who've whiled away the decades telling each other smutty stories and signing social assistance cheques until they shifted to signing old-age pension cheques. The leading light of this peerless band was Huff Driesen, the man with the sugar diabetes who comes to her father to get his needle whenever he's been drinking and doesn't dare show up at his daughter's for his injection. Of all the renegades and reprobates it's Driesen that Vera dislikes the most. He fancies himself God's gift to women, a lady-slayer. Whenever he finds himself in Vera's vicinity he makes calf eyes and says, "I care for nobody, not I/If no one cares for me." This is supposed to be witty or charming, or something. Vera would like to play a tune on him with the cast-iron frying pan.

Whenever she draws the dreadful behaviour of his guests to her father's attention he just shrugs and says, "I don't see the harm." "They only get a chance to have a good time but once a year. I can hardly begrudge them that."

Vera can.

There's more. Daniel, now that he's on Christmas holidays, spends all his time playing cards with this sorry testament to humanity. That began when they were short a player for rummy and his grandfather staked him in the game. He soon got the hang of it and proved himself a natural, instinctive player, quick-witted, attentive to the cards, blessed with more than his share of luck, patient as Job. In the course of that first afternoon he won more money than was good for him. He was hooked on cards.

Vera doesn't like him to gamble. It's not that she worries about the money he might lose, or even win. It's the way he behaves when he plays, cold-blooded, like a reptile. Most kids his age are restless and impulsive playing for stakes. The young are optimists inclined to trust that luck, fortune, is principally concerned about them and unlikely to let them down. So they lose. Not Daniel. He is a twelve-year-old crocodile who is content to lie disguised as a log until one of the old boys forgets himself and splashes down into the shallows during a poker game. Then the jaws snap shut. Vera's seen it. Watching him gamble she can't help thinking that he's years and years older than twelve. How did he get so old? The old fellows he plays with sense this unnaturalness also and it shows in the way they treat him – sometimes like a boy, sometimes like a man. They're not entirely sure which he is, or what is due him. They get mad as hell when Vera hauls him away from the table and sends him upstairs to bed at a decent hour. Winners don't walk away from a table, the old men grumble and complain.

Another thing, Vera knows they've been giving Daniel whisky to drink. She's smelled it on his breath. And she doesn't care if it's mixed nine-tenths water to one-tenth whisky, which was her father's justification when she cornered him on it. "He's not getting enough to hurt," he said, "and it's Christmas. Anyway, getting it at home spoils the novelty and takes the curiosity out of a boy his age." Whatever he says, it's just plain wrong to give a kid Daniel's age whisky. Of any amount.

What a shit of a Christmas it's turning out to be. And her father hasn't done one single, solitary thing to make it better, as Christmas ought to be. The other day she asked him when he was going to pick up a tree and he acted as if the thought of a tree hadn't even occurred to him. "Christmas tree?" he said. "What do we want bothering with a Christmas tree? I mean to say there's no little kids here who believes in Santa Claus, is there? And they're nothing but a goddamn fire hazard. You weren't really wanting a Christmas tree were you, Vera?"

No, not really.

Learning that he was intending to give Daniel money for a Christmas present was the last straw.

"Well, why not?" he wanted to know. "I'll just pop ten or twenty bucks into an envelope. Thirty, if you think that would be better. What's wrong with that?"

What was wrong was that that was the sort of Christmas present cleaning ladies got at Christmas, bills in an envelope. She had no doubt that he planned the same for her.

"It's not very personal is all," she said. "It doesn't show much care and consideration, much thought, you ask me. Money stuck in an envelope."

"That way he can get what he wants," said her father. "How the hell am I supposed to guess what a kid his age wants for Christmas? I got no idea. If I give him thirty bucks, forty bucks, he can buy himself whatever he wants. Something real nice." He hesitated. "You think forty bucks is enough, Vera?"

"Maybe," said Vera, her voice laced with sarcasm, "you don't have time to shop for your grandson what with entertaining your charming friends full time. You'd rather throw a lot of money at him, it's easier."

This is Christmas? A twelve-year-old boy playing cards on a kitchen table covered in a ratty tablecloth, drinking whisky, watered or not. A houseful of vultures diving onto whatever appears to eat and drink, squabbling and farting and picking their teeth with matchbook covers, if they've got any teeth to pick. No tree. Money in envelopes. And roast pork for Christmas dinner. When she asked him what he'd like for Christmas dinner, meaning what sort of trimmings to accompany the bird, her father had squinted up sideways at the ceiling and allowed that a roast pork would be nice. He hadn't had a roast pork for a while. Suffering Jesus. How could you get into the spirit of the thing when people requested roast pork for Christmas dinner?

If nobody else knows what Christmas is supposed to be, Vera knows. She sees it everywhere, mocking her. Sees it on the television, in the magazines, even the pictures in the Eaton's and Simpsons-Sears catalogues. There's a wreath of holly nailed to the door, a sprig of mistletoe, a tree decorated with strings of popcorn, and an angel perched on its tip. There's oranges and nuts in a bowl on a sideboard and a punch bowl full of eggnog and nutmeg. There are plenty of presents done up in silver paper and big red bows and the men relax in white shirts, ties, and their favourite comfortable sweaters as the women pass around Christmas cake and mince pie. Everybody laughs and conducts themselves properly, in a Christmas spirit.

What she would like to say to her father is this: My husband made me a Christmas a thousand times better than this is and he was a Jew. She hadn't asked him to either. Their first Christmas together he'd gone out and bought a tree, along with the decorations which, quite naturally, he didn't have. Christmas was her right, Stanley explained.

But what, Vera had wanted to know, about him? How had he felt carrying a tree home past all the shops of his Jewish neighbours?

"I had an answer prepared in case anyone said anything," Stanley told her with a wry smile.

"And what was that?"

"That the star on the top of the tree would be the Star of David."

Nevertheless, despite his jokes, Vera knew it had not been an easy thing for Stanley to do. What made the gesture even grander for her in retrospect was that there had been only one Christmas tree and one Christmas for them to share. It was the year Vera was pregnant with Daniel, already six months gone when December rolled around. By then the episodes of morning sickness had passed and although she was as big as a house, Vera had never felt better. Or looked better, according to Stanley, who appreciated his wife big-breasted and moon-faced with new, healthy flesh. Each morning Stanley served her her favourite breakfast in bed, a large glass of milk and two peach jam and bacon sandwiches.

This weight'll come off nursing the baby, she told herself, licking her fingers.

Most of Vera's days in the weeks preceding Christmas were given over to preparations – making cranberry sauce, candy, short-bread, mincemeat pies and tarts, light and dark fruit cake, puddings. When she wasn't cleaning the apartment and polishing the silver which had belonged to her mother-in-law, she sat in a kitchen full of the warm, spicy smells of baking and the sharp, tart smells of grated orange and lemon rinds, studying recipes, and rubbing the bowl of the expensive English pipe she had bought Stanley for Christmas against the side of her nose. The proprietor of the smokeshop had said there was nothing better to shine and condition a good brier than nose oil.

Whenever she felt lonesome and needed to hear the faint, comforting sounds of life below in the shop – the murmur of voices, the front door swinging shut – she turned down the Christmas music on the radio and listened intently, keeping absolutely still. Then, smiling enigmatically, she turned Bing back up and returned to thinking.

In some fashion, Vera felt herself to be a pioneer, a trailblazer. Stanley brought no Christmas baggage with him, so it fell to her, the one with experience, to invent a family tradition, to set the tone for all the Christmases that they and their children would celebrate in all the years to come. Santa Claus but no Jesus, Vera decided, turning over the pages of the cookbook. A bowl of eggnog standing near to hand when the tree was trimmed. Gifts opened Christmas Eve, not Christmas morning, so everybody could get a decent night's sleep. Turkey for dinner, not goose, because Stanley preferred white meat.

In the end, Christmas turned out perfectly, exactly as Vera had planned. The candlelight flickered on her mother-in-law's pieces of crystal and silver, Stanley praised every bite he took, her cheeks flushed warmly with wine and pride.

After the steamed pudding, at Stanley's suggestion they went into the living room to listen to music as he liked to, in a completely darkened room. He even unplugged the Christmas tree lights.

The record he chose was Mahler's Symphony No. 4. Stanley settled in his armchair, the special blend of Irish tobacco Vera had bought him glowing red in the bowl of his new pipe and wafting its aroma to where she sat on the sofa holding the pearl earrings he had given her, one in each hand. Stanley hadn't realized her ears weren't pierced.

When the haunting music commenced, Vera felt the child stir within her. With each measure, these movements grew stronger and stronger until the ferocity of them came near to frightening her. Of course, the baby had kicked before, but never like this.

Before she knew it, Vera had called out to Stanley. "Come here," she said.

He crossed the room to the sofa. At once Vera felt foolish. Really, it was nothing after all.

"What do you think of this?" she asked, fumbling for his hand in the dark, pressing it to her belly.

For a time neither of them spoke.

"I believe he's conducting," said Stanley, breaking their silence.

"What?" Vera had not caught his meaning.

"Conducting." In the meagre light she could just make him out, illustrating what he meant, flailing his arm about more or less in time with the music.

At that moment she could not stop herself from reaching out and seizing the hand moulding and carving the dim, shadowy air, carrying it to her mouth and kissing it passionately.

"Why, Vera," said Stanley, surprised. She was not given to such displays, even in darkness.

"Never mind," said Vera, recovering. "Go on back to your music."

That, she told herself, had been a proper Christmas. Not this. This was Hallowe'en, a Grey Cup drunk, an all-night poker game rolled into one, but it sure as hell wasn't Christmas. Where had decency, gentleness, kindness gone? Sometimes she doubted she could stop here any longer in this desert, in this absence of love.

———◆———

It was December 22, nine-thirty in the morning, and Vera was struggling to raise the tree she had bought and carted home herself the day before. Flushed and tight-lipped with determination she battled to hold the spruce upright while attempting to tighten the screws in the stand to lock it into position. In the kitchen her father was hosting the day's first arrivals, Huff Driesen, the McIlwraith brothers, Adolf Romanski. Daniel was finishing his breakfast, lounging against the kitchen counter with his plate under his chin. The visitors had begun the morning with coffee and rummy, a warm-up for beer and poker by eleven o'clock. Right at the moment, the first argument of the day was in full spate. Whose turn was it to deal?

The tree swayed, toppled. Vera sprang off her haunches, caught it with a jerk, shaking loose a shower of dry needles into her hair and down onto the floor. The evidence of earlier crashes lay thickly all about her, crackling under the soles of her shoes, and making her feet skid with every step she took. She had been wrestling the tree unassisted for the past half-hour but had no intention of planting the suggestion that she needed help.

Just then her father eased into the living room and, blind to her difficulties, inquired whether she had noticed his spectacles lying around.

"No," said Vera, teeth clenched as she shoved the tree upright in the stand again.

"I can't think where they could've got to," he said helplessly, looking about vaguely. When it became clear she had no intention of joining the search he wandered off, with a forlorn, neglected air.

Five minutes later he was back. The tree was now standing, or rather leaning, in the corner of the room, and Vera was asking herself why she hadn't thought to attach the star to its tip before she got it completely vertical. Now she was going to have to risk her neck standing on a chair, fending off branches as she leaned out precariously to fix the star.

The missing glasses had made Monkman as peevish and frustrated as his daughter. "I've lost my reading glasses," he announced in a loud, slightly belligerent voice. "I can't find them anywhere."

Vera kept her eyes fastened on the top of the tree, like a bird judging a perch. "So what've you got to read that can't wait?" she said. "Maybe you haven't noticed, but I'm busy here."

"It's not reading. It's for Huff. He wants his sugar diabetes shot and I can't do it without my glasses. It's close work."

"It's just about time you stopped babying Huff Driesen. He's a big boy. Let him do it himself."

"Vera, you know he can't. He's squeamish about needles."

"So let one of his other bosom buddies in the kitchen do it. If he hurries he can get one while they're still sober."

"He don't trust *them*," said her father, dropping his voice.

"Neither do *I*," Vera whispered back theatrically.

Her sarcasm appeared to be lost on her father, who hesitated before revealing his proposal. Still speaking in an undertone, he said: "As a matter of fact, Huff was wondering if I didn't find my glasses . . . could you maybe do it, Vera?"

Vera laughed in his face. "Driesen's got to be out of his mind. Not a chance."

"It isn't hard," said her father. "Really it isn't. Huff'll load the needle for you. All you got to do is stick it in and push down the plunger."

"Dream on. Push down the plunger. You make it sound like the French Resistance blowing up bridges in the movies. If I could blow that old sonofabitch sky high, then I'd press down the plunger."

"Now don't make jokes, Vera. This is serious business. He's got to have his shot. And if you won't do it, I'll have to get Daniel to."

Vera was aghast. "Don't be ridiculous. You can't ask Daniel to give him a needle."

"I did already. He says, 'If Mom can't do it – I will.' "

"Use your head. Where's your sense? Nobody lets twelve-year-old kids give old men needles. It's just not proper."

"Well, maybe it isn't," said Alec, feeling she was ready to give ground, "but if there's nobody else to do it, what can I do?"

"Oh, Christ!" cried Vera. "All right, all right, I'll give him his bloody needle. Get him in here and let's get it over with. Jesus."

Moments later her father returned, escorting a shuffling, grinning Huff. For the sake of privacy, Vera led him off to her bedroom. The notion of administering a needle made her feel slightly queasy and she was afraid that an audience might cause her to botch the job completely.

Once inside the bedroom Huff sniffed the air appreciatively. "Smells all perfumy," he remarked. "Smells like a garden."

Vera had no time for pleasantries. She wanted this done with, before she lost any more of her nerve. "Okay, okay," she said brusquely, "let's get this show on the road. That thing loaded?" she asked, pointing to the syringe in Driesen's left hand. In his right he clutched a bottle of alcohol and some cotton balls.

"Loaded and ready to fire," said Huff agreeably. "Loaded and ready to fire."

"Fine," said Vera, betraying gathering apprehension as she gnawed her bottom lip. "Get your sleeve rolled up."

"Oh, not in my arm," said Huff smoothly. "I don't take my needle in my arm, Vera."

"Where do you take it then?"

"Here," said Driesen, striking his flank with his palm. "Here, where I got some meat."

Vera looked doubtful. On the other hand, she didn't want to prolong the ordeal with argument and questions. "All right," she said, "what do I do?"

"You wipe me down with alcohol, pinch up some skin and fat, shove in the needle, and push down the plunger. You do it right, Vera, you got yourself a full-time job as my nurse."

"Don't tempt me to injury, Driesen."

"Oh, don't give me none of that, Vera. You wouldn't hurt a fly."

"I don't hurt flies," said Vera. "I kill them."

Driesen chuckled. "'I kill them,'" he repeated to himself. "'I kill them.'"

"Come on," said Vera, "I haven't got all day. Get your pants down."

Huff was eager to comply. He turned his back on her, unbuckled his belt, and dragged down trousers and underpants all at once, exposing saggy, creased buttocks to view.

Vera swore to herself she wouldn't get rattled. Concentrating, she gingerly swabbed down a patch of skin, then pinched up a roll of flesh and skin. It felt queer and rubbery to the touch and left her with a distasteful sensation.

"My," said Huff, "aren't your fingers cool? But you know what they say. Cool hands, warm heart. That's what they say. Is that true, Vera?"

"Shut up and hold still," ordered Vera, taking aim with the syringe. It wasn't easy because Driesen seemed to be fumbling and fidgeting with something in front, shirt buttons perhaps.

"You know," he said, his voice suddenly grown harsh, "it's what you want at a time like this – a woman's gentle touch. I could get used to this. How about it? Would Vera like to be Huff's private nurse?"

Vera's answer was to stick him. The sight of the needle buried in the old man's tensed buttock came as such a shock to her that she lost all recollection of what the next step was. Several seconds ticked by before she recovered, eased down the plunger with shaking fingers, and snatched out the syringe. There, it was done.

Huff turned and faced her. He smiled as he lifted up his shirt. "Look what Vera done. Pretty good for an old fellow, eh?" He smirked proudly, displaying a mangy nest of pubic hair from which a limply swollen member dangled, making fitful attempts to lift a head drooling a drop of liquid the colour and consistency of egg white.

"Oh yes," he said, looking down at himself approvingly as he began to roughly pull and stretch his penis, "just give the old fellows half a chance and they're sure to satisfy."

It was with the broom near to hand in the corner that Vera knocked him down. The jars of face cream and hand lotion which he dragged down from the dresser as he fell were still rattling like hail on the floor when she burst out of the bedroom, across the living room, and blew wild-eyed and raving into the kitchen.

"*Out!*"

Driesen's cronies had time only to pop open their mouths before the broom slashed the tabletop and sent cards and money flying, glasses skittering, and beer spraying into the air.

"*Out!*"

Chairs were overturned in the scramble to escape her, cries of consternation and alarm arose as Vera's broom descended on heads and upraised hands, left, right, and centre. A panicked Huff, hands clutching his waistband, bolted past her and flung himself out the door. They all followed, one of them trailing the tablecloth knotted in his fist. Vera landed her final blow cleanly between a pair of shoulder blades and heard the handle snap with a pistol-shot crack. It made her feel wonderful.

"And don't come back!" she shouted, pitching coats and over-shoes into the snow after them, disregarding her father's beseeching cries of "Vera! Vera!" from the open door behind her.

◆

The last of their belongings were finally loaded and they were ready to leave. Daniel clutched the tow rope of a sleigh piled high with suitcases and cardboard boxes and, like a dog straining on a leash, leaned abruptly into the thickening darkness of five o'clock on a winter's afternoon. One sharp tug, two sharp tugs. The sleigh jerked stickily under its load, then relaxed into a smooth, flowing glide, its runners squeaking over the dry snow gone pewter in the failing light. Vera hoisted the handles of the wheelbarrow and rattled her cargo of dishes into the icy, rutted road.

Her father called out to her one last time from the doorway where he stood coatless in the cold. "If you have to go – all right. But it doesn't have to be like this. Let me put your things in the truck and take you there. Please, Vera, listen to me. Will you listen to me? Vera!"

Vera pushed on, shoulders bouncing as the wheel of the barrow jumped in the ruts and tire tracks. She knew this was how she must go – with a sleigh and wheelbarrow borrowed from a neighbour, striking out across town for a three-room shack on the other side of Connaught, the only house to be rented on such short notice just before Christmas. The owner, who had inherited the house from his mother when she had died six months before, had been delighted to get a tenant. Nobody was willing to rent such places any more. It was too small, the thin, uninsulated walls made it impossible to heat, and it lacked running water. Mindful of its disadvantages, he had struck a deal with Vera, selling her whatever of his mother's furniture remained in the house for next to nothing. For fifty bucks she got a woodstove in good condition, two cots, a table and four chairs, and a woodpile of seasoned poplar out back to boot.

Her father had made the last two days hell, pestering her with questions. What was wrong? Why was she leaving?

"What exactly did Huff do?" The big question.

"I told you I don't want to talk about it. It doesn't matter now what he did. What's done is done. Let's just say I don't want any more of this atmosphere for Daniel and leave it at that."

"I'll be sorry ten times over as soon as you tell me what I'm supposed to be sorry for. But how do you expect me to apologize until then? And, Vera, forget all this foolishness about moving out. It's crazy. What did I do that you've got to move out?"

"Isn't this typical? Isn't this typical you'd have to ask?"

What had worried Vera most was that Daniel might mutiny. So far he had only sulked and applied the cold shoulder. At present he was stepping out so briskly that she couldn't keep pace pushing the wheelbarrow. A show of anger, she supposed. Yesterday they had fought.

He'd been upset about the move. "*Why* do we have to go? We just moved this summer. Why again so soon?"

"It's not a big move, Daniel. It's just across town, and it's not as if you have to change schools or anything like that. That's why I ruled out leaving Connaught right now, so you can finish the year in the same school. When school's over then we'll see what we'll do."

"I hate that new house. It's a shit hole."

"It's no palace, I grant you. But it'll do until we can find better."

"Three crappy little rooms. An outdoor toilet. It doesn't even have a TV."

"Woe is Daniel, no TV. Tragedy of tragedies. Aren't you hard done by? Maybe a weekend in India would teach you what hardship is. It's not missing TV."

"You better be prepared to miss me, then," Daniel announced. "Because I'm going to be over here with him – watching TV."

"If I were you I'd be careful of declarations about what 'I am and I am not going to do,' including where you're going to watch television. All your decisions aren't yours to make until you're twenty-one and that's some time off yet, sunshine. For your information what you don't do is watch TV over here with him. I don't want to catch you hanging around here – *ever*." Her rage was the weak, jealous, tainted rage of a child and it often drove her into thoughtless, shameful declarations. She consoled herself that Daniel knew better than to take seriously, literally, what was said in the heat of the moment. Nobody ever meant *exactly* what they said, did they?

"Why not? Why shouldn't I?" Vera could see he was fighting back tears. She could only guess at their meaning. Anger?

"Don't trot that tone of voice out with me, young man. Understand?" Mother and son stared challengingly into one another's eyes. Daniel was the first to look away. His yielding allowed her to speak more softly to him. "I think it's time we both had a break from your grandfather, and the company he keeps. He and his cronies are having a bad effect on you – I see it more and more every day. Those old men aren't company for a boy your age. It's unhealthy, you ask me."

"If that's what it is – he already said you don't want them coming around he'll keep them away. He already promised you that – I heard him!"

"When you get to be as old as I am, maybe then you'll have learned what your grandfather's promises are worth."

"Well, so what? Those guys won't be coming around again anyway. Not after what you did. So who's going to corrupt me?"

"You're wasting your breath," she said grimly. "It's decided."

Yet saying it was decided didn't make it so. That was the sudden lurch of hot anger speaking, not really her. Vera knew better than to bank on anything ever being decided.

Snow had begun to fall. Vera felt flakes tickling and melting on her hot face. Pushing a wheelbarrow was hard, awkward work. She halted, set down the wheelbarrow, and took a breather, lifting her eyes to the blue corona of the streetlight. It resembled a fishbowl, the flying snow tiny darting creatures which flashed briefly and brightly before settling, extinguished, dead-white and numb on roofs and roads, empty yards, and stripped gardens. It settled on Vera, too, on her coat, her scarf, the moon of her uplifted face. She was looking back in the midst of flight, back to that night so many years ago, the night of the snow, the night of the recital, the night of their unspoken understanding.

She started, wiped the moisture from her face, coming back to Daniel. There he was, far ahead of her, at the very end of the street. The snow was falling thicker and faster with every passing minute, but still not so thick as to rub out the distinctive stoop to his shoulders and the peculiar toed-out walk he had been bequeathed by his father. At this distance, and in the midst of a blizzard, one could easily have been mistaken for the other.

15

The day after Christmas, temperatures plummeted to −40°F, and every chimney in Connaught ran a plumb-line of smoke against the windless, blue sky. These columns of white smoke shone in the intense sunshine, temporary pillars of marble erected by stoves and furnaces all over the town. Around two o'clock when Vera discovered the woodbox was getting dangerously low she sent Daniel out to split some wood. The clumsy thunking of his axe outside kept her company as she sat at the kitchen table, smoking, drinking coffee, and pondering her future. When a knock came at the door she supposed it was Daniel, kicking at it with his arms filled with wood, summoning her to open it and let him in. Instead, she found Mr. Stutz, red-faced, nostrils steaming in the bitter cold, and his broad chest stacked with parcels done up in Christmas paper.

"Come in, come in," Vera urged, and Stutz did, ricocheting through the door-frame, stamping his feet noisily to shed the snow from his heavy, felt-lined boots. Once across the threshold he stalled, searching for a mat on which to remove his overshoes. There was none. As he looked around him, the bareness of the place impressed itself upon him. There were no curtains on the windows

of the cramped kitchen, and Mr. Stutz could gaze out onto the out-
skirts of Connaught, a glacial sweep of frozen prairie broken only
by a line of telephone poles rambling west. The austerity, the
vacancy of the house, was extreme. However, compared to what he
could see of the rest of the rooms, the kitchen verged on clutter. It
held a table and two chairs, and the cast-iron range filled one wall
with its squat solidity and stove-pipe angles. Stutz wondered when
the pipes had last been cleaned. There were brown scorch marks on
the beaverboard indicating they were given to overheating. To his
left he could look through a narrow door that gave onto an equally
narrow living room, empty except for one of the cots that made up
the dead lady's estate and a forlorn display of Christmas presents set
out in the middle of the scuffed linoleum floor – a bottle of perfume,
a boy's sweater, a box of Black Magic chocolates, a number of
books. Gifts that Vera and Daniel had exchanged. Beyond this,
another door stood open on Vera's bedroom and Stutz could make
out a cardboard box filled with clothes and the corner of another
cot, twin to the first. There was nothing more to be seen.

"Just kick them off where you stand," said Vera, noting Mr.
Stutz's indecision as to what to do with his boots, "and come and
take a seat by the stove."

Mr. Stutz carefully placed the presents on the table. "We're late
with these," he apologized, "but the old gentleman thought that
yesterday being Christmas you might have dropped by with the
boy. When you didn't, he asked me to deliver them."

Vera was clearly annoyed at the presumption. "He had no
reason to expect any visits from us. You can tell him I said as much.
And you can take these back where they came from," she said,
indicating the parcels.

"They're not all from him," said Mr. Stutz quietly. "I put one
or two in myself."

This news embarrassed Vera. "I never," she said. "What am I
going to do? I – Daniel and I – never thought to get you a thing."

"What's to get the man who's got everything?" He laughed artificially to signal he was making a joke. There was an awkwardness in his manner that Vera hadn't seen before. As a way of offering him some relief she began to sort through the presents.

"This is from you then?" she said, smiling and holding up a package.

"What does it say?" Mr. Stutz wanted to hear her read the tag aloud.

" 'To Mrs. Vera Miller from H. Stutz.' "

"That's me all right."

"H. Stutz," said Vera, trying to peel away the Scotch tape with her fingernail so as not to rip the paper. "Isn't that strange? I don't know your first name. What's the H stand for?"

"Herman. Herman is my Christian name."

Wouldn't you suspect? thought Vera. What she said was, "A sensible name. It suits you, Mr. Stutz, Herman does. Take a chair, Herman, and as soon as I've got this present unwrapped we'll have us a cup of coffee."

When the paper decorated with jolly Santa Clauses was finally removed, a carton of cigarettes was disclosed. "Isn't this nice," said Vera. "My brand, too. Millbank. Thank you, Mr. Stutz."

"I made a point of watching what you smoked," said Mr. Stutz.

"I appreciate it," Vera assured him, pouring coffee. "I just feel awful we didn't shop for you."

The topic of presents and purchases exhausted, conversation lapsed. In the silence, Daniel's axe could be heard ringing in the frozen air. Looking ill at ease, Mr. Stutz blew energetically into his coffee mug. Vera noticed that in the warmth of the kitchen his nose had begun to run, a drop hung trembling on its tip, prompting her to turn her eyes away. When she did, Mr. Stutz cleared his throat and launched into what he had come to say. "You know, Mrs. Miller, your father can't understand what all this is about – this packing up and leaving him."

"I'm not surprised," said Vera, struggling to appear calm, reasonable. "I must say that doesn't surprise me in the least. The only thing my father's ever been able to understand is what matters to him. Did you ever notice that about him, Mr. Stutz? Nothing exists unless it's of some use to him. Do you know when I figured that out? I must have been sixteen, just after my mother died. He seemed to think that my brother and I were there just to make him feel better about the situation. One servant and one pet, you might say. He couldn't think of anyone but himself. My father's a very selfish man, Mr. Stutz."

"He's always treated me fair," observed Mr. Stutz.

"And why should he have any trouble treating you fair?" challenged Vera. "When were the two of you ever at cross purposes? Never."

Mr. Stutz frowned. "I wouldn't know about that. I wouldn't go that far."

"I would," said Vera, breaking open her carton of Millbanks and lighting herself a cigarette. "I know all about my father and cross purposes. We wrote the book on that. It was because he always assumed the choices were his to make. Back then, when I was sixteen, I wanted to be somebody. Maybe it's true I wasn't exactly sure what – what kid of sixteen does? But *something*, a teacher, a nurse, something." Vera held up the burning match, blew it out with an angry puff of breath. "That's how he put me out," she said to Stutz, "like that. He blew out my fine ideas because *he* knew what was best for me. Best for me was to stick at home and relieve him of the trouble of looking after my brother Earl. I believe he would be surprised if anyone was to point out the difference between good for him and good for me. He thought they were always the same thing." Vera leaned forward tensely in her chair. "And he hasn't lost the habit. Do you know what the latest is? He won't tell me where my brother is. And do you know why he won't?"

At the mention of Earl Mr. Stutz cast his eyes down to the floor. He shook his head in reply to her question.

"I'll tell you why," said Vera with quiet, measured vehemence. "Because he doesn't think I deserve to know. I lost the *right* to know because I didn't stay behind to raise Earl the way he thought I should. I wasn't noble, I didn't sacrifice, I disappointed. Instead, I went off and joined the Army." Vera fell back against her chair, smiled ironically. "Desertion, Mr. Stutz. Vera Monkman stands accused of deserting her post, charged by the commanding officer. That's why I have no claim on my brother. No difference between me and the bad girl who gives up a bastard baby for adoption. *Bad girls lose their rights, didn't you know?* My father has made up his mind I have no right to Earl because I ran out on him. But I never ran out on Earl. It's not my brother I was running out on, it was him, the miserable old bugger. Sixteen years old and already I was a housewife. A *housewife*!" Vera burst out indignantly.

For several moments she sat rigid and motionless; then her shoulders relaxed and she resumed speaking in a controlled way. "This is how I thought then, Mr. Stutz. I figured the one he loved had the best chance of surviving him. That was Earl. I think he loved Earl almost as much as he loved himself. All I knew for sure was that Vera wasn't going to survive him. I had to get out – and I got. But he's not one to forgive. That's why he's keeping me and my brother apart – to punish me."

Mr. Stutz raised his eyes from the floor. There was a heaviness in his face that suggested a man with a desire for confession. But all he said was, "Your father doesn't want to punish you."

"You're wrong there."

"No. He wants you and Daniel to come back to his house. On your terms. Everything agreed. He wants to look after the two of you."

"Not a chance. We'll never go back to him."

"Never is a long time, Mrs. Miller."

"If there was a word longer than never, that's the word I'd use."

"If you don't go back, what will you do?"

"I'll find a job."

"For a woman, there are no jobs in Connaught. At least none that aren't taken. Maybe you could work at the hotel as a waitress, a cook, a barmaid, a chambermaid – but your father owns the hotel."

"I'll find something."

"Maybe you could clean houses. There isn't very much money in it but it's something a woman can do. You could clean the lawyer lady's house, the doctor lady's house, the druggist lady's house. Would you like that? Cleaning houses and those ladies being so good as to point out to you the spots you missed?"

"I don't miss spots."

Mr. Stutz smiled knowingly. "Mrs. Miller mightn't miss spots – the cleaning lady always does. It's a fact of life. You ought to consider that."

"I'm past considering."

"Then you better be past pride, too."

Vera didn't respond. She was listening to the axe thud on the chopping block.

After a time Mr. Stutz sighed and said, "The old Bluebird Cafe has been empty now for two years. No one could seem to make a go of it after the Chinaman died."

"And?"

"And did you ever think of going into business for yourself? Two thousand dollars, more or less, would get it operating again. You're a good cook. You could manage a cafe, I'm sure. Your father claims you're clever, at any rate."

"My father never claimed any such thing."

"You don't know everything about your father. Your father claims you're clever. I heard him," repeated Stutz with emphasis.

"All right, so I'm a genius without two thousand dollars. A lot of good it does me, brains without money."

"Your father will give you the money if you ask him."

"What? Give me money to set up in competition with him? The Bluebird's directly across the street from the hotel and its restaurant."

"Do you think he cares about competition? When's the last time he gave a thought to his businesses? He leaves the running of them to me, or they run themselves. Alec's got enough. If you ask, he'll set you up."

"Haven't you heard a word that I've said? You've got to be crazy if you think I'd ask. Especially after you've sat at this table and heard me say exactly what I think of him. Don't mistake me for a hypocrite, Mr. Stutz."

Mr. Stutz took a deep breath, shifted himself on his chair seat. "All right," he said, "then I'll lend you the money."

Vera was so taken aback that she doubted she had heard him correctly. "What's that? What did you say?" she demanded rudely.

"I'll lend you two thousand dollars to give The Bluebird a whirl. If you want," said Mr. Stutz, twisting his neck uncomfortably in his shirt collar.

She was incredulous. "And why in the world would you do that, Mr. Stutz?"

This question only increased Mr. Stutz's discomfort. "Well, Mrs. Miller," he said, "you've got the boy to look after and I know you're an honest woman and . . ." here he broke off, cast around desperately for a conclusion to his speech, and blurted out, "and if Christ was in my shoes, I think he'd give you the money!"

Vera could not restrain a smile. "I never thought of Christ as a money-lender," she said. "It was the money-lenders he whipped out of the temple, wasn't it?"

"He wouldn't have done it if they were doing good," replied Stutz with a stubborn look.

"So you want to do some good, do you?" Vera teased.

Stutz, deaf to her frivolous tone, nodded his head soberly. "Yes."

"And what if it gets you in trouble with my father?"

"Why would doing good get me in trouble with Alec?"

"It might seem to him like you were switching sides."

"There are no such things as sides for me, Mrs. Miller."

"Come, come, Mr. Stutz, you're not that innocent."

"You don't hurt a man by helping his daughter."

Vera gave him an appraising look. "The question is: Why do you want to do this, Mr. Stutz? For whose sake are you offering help? His or mine?"

"For everyone's sake I would like to do good," said Stutz.

"And that's it?"

Stutz chose not to answer. The monotonous chop chop chop of the axe striking wood penetrated the kitchen. Mr. Stutz seized the opportunity it presented. "What's that?" he asked.

Vera did not renounce her suspicions but she allowed them to relax. Stutz could be a deep one, perhaps too deep for her ever to see clear to the bottom of. "It's Daniel splitting wood," she said. "He's been out there forty-five minutes already, but by the sound of it he doesn't seem to be making much headway."

"Oh, I thought maybe . . . you know . . . we were alone, that Daniel was out with friends."

Vera said nothing, watched her fingers fiddle with the charred matchstick in the ashtray.

"It's a chance to be independent," said Mr. Stutz encouragingly.

"The reason he's still out there chopping," said Vera, "is that he doesn't know how to go about it. Plenty of wasted effort when you don't have the knack."

"He must be getting cold. What if I send him in and finish up for him?" suggested Mr. Stutz. "I could split you a woodbox full in no time at all."

"Yes, maybe he should come in. It wouldn't do to have him freeze his face."

Mr. Stutz got up from the table. "Think about it, Mrs. Miller," he urged, stooping over and pulling on his overshoes.

"And what if I lost your money, Mr. Stutz?" she said playfully, attempting to make light of his proposal so it need not be faced.

Stutz straightened up and considered her question. His deliberation, his grave manner of answering, denied Vera a flippant escape.

In his dumb, fumbling way he made it impossible for her to avoid taking him seriously.

"It's only money," he said, "and I've got nobody to hurt by losing it. I've nobody to leave it to. No wife or anything."

"But there's always family. You must have some family."

"No family," he said, shaking his head.

"None?"

"None."

So much for that. Vera struck a match and lit one of Stutz's Millbanks while she collected and marshalled her thoughts. She couldn't help being both excited and afraid. The old christer, the old do-gooder meant every word he said. It could be read plainly in his smooth, innocent face. The money was hers for the asking. The only difficulty was that Vera was not much good at asking; she lacked the talent. And the way he had presented it to her, implying that she had no choice but to take his money because it was the only way out for someone in her position, wouldn't make asking any easier. What Stutz had suggested to her might be God's unvarnished truth, but Vera didn't welcome having it brought to her attention. Besides, she knew there was always a choice, even if it was only choosing not to choose. She still had that left to her.

Vera bit at a speck of tobacco clinging to her bottom lip. Stutz stood patiently by the door, waiting. The last word she could recall him saying was "None." A barren, lonely word. Poor devil, Vera thought. Poor kind devil.

"Do you need kindling?" he asked, resting his hand on the doorknob.

"Pardon?"

"Do you need kindling for the stove?"

"Do I need . . . yes. Please."

He nodded and went out.

So what was she going to do? The truth was she didn't know. Her mouth was dry with the desiring of it and dry with the fearing of it. Over the years she had let the lie of confidence carry her through most situations. She wasn't sure she could make that work for her anymore. Too much strength had been used up. Worn down as she was, could she survive disappointment and failure if they came?

Jesus, Vera thought, I don't need this now, a temptation at this late date. Or maybe she did. Her father had fallen into the accident of success, why couldn't she? Why not? There had always been more to her than her father had ever guessed at, or that she had had the opportunity to show.

She got to her feet and circled the kitchen. Twice around the room and she resumed her seat, laid down her hands side by side on the tabletop as if they were gloves. Then she took a deep breath and pressed down with her palms as hard as she could. Time passed. Her fingers went white.

Vera had made her decision.

16

When he was finally persuaded they were gone for good, Alec was torn by loneliness for his grandson and daughter. Loneliness led to a discovery. It was this: alone in his empty house he heard a voice. So loud, emphatic, and inescapable a voice that in the beginning it frightened him, even though most of what it announced was commonplace enough. *Time for a cup of tea*, it said. Or, *Looks like snow*. Of course, it was not so troubling after he recognized the voice as somehow his own, that it did not come from outside him. This did not happen at once. For a long time he was undecided. It sounded and did not sound like him. His disbelief was of the order of a man hearing, for the first time, a recording of himself speaking. Could that awful voice really belong to him?

To start with, he wondered if he might not simply be hearing himself talking to himself. He could have fallen into the habit, he supposed. It wasn't so. Even with his lips firmly pressed together he could still hear the voice. Besides, what he was listening to was not the ordinary, familiar voice which had been his all his life – this voice was different. Not only did it fall strangely on his ears; it said strange, surprising things without warning. One day, out of the blue, it said: *Did I have a hand in it.*

Is this the sort of thing which Earl had complained of?

The night of the fire, Alec and Mr. Stutz rushed Earl back to town, leaving the hired man Dover to keep an eye on the progress of the destruction. From the first, it had been obvious that there was nothing they could do to save the crop. It was an outright loss. Fortunately, the burning field was bordered on all sides by summerfallow, either Alec's or a neighbour's, so the men were confident that the bare, tilled earth would contain the flames on Alec's property and prevent them spreading. Nevertheless, when they reached Connaught Mr. Stutz was to call out the town's fire brigade, chiefly so that the neighbours couldn't accuse them of not having done all that was humanly possible if the fire carried, although they all knew that a single pump truck would be next to useless in such a situation. As Dover had said, "If that happens we may as well all sling out our dinks and piss – for all the good it'll do."

That night, however, Alec was less concerned with the fire than he was with Earl. On the way to Connaught he bombarded him with questions. "Are you hurt?" "What the hell happened back there?" His son made no response, merely sat pale and silent, watching the beams of the headlights bouncing on the rough road.

After a while, Stutz suggested there might not be any point to more questions. Perhaps Earl wasn't speaking because he was in shock. Alec drove even faster and more recklessly when he heard this. Couldn't people die from shock?

When he reached Connaught and saw a light showing in Dr. Dowler's house he braked the truck, ran up the steps, banged on the door with his big, hard fist, and shouted unceremoniously up at the porch light. Mr. Stutz followed, leading Earl, who moved like a sleepwalker, by the hand. An unfamiliar young man came to the door and explained that Dr. Dowler was away on his annual two-week fishing trip up north to Lac La Ronge and he, Dr. Evans, was relieving him.

Mr. Stutz, seeing that matters were being taken in hand, sprang off the porch and hurried to raise the fire brigade as the young doctor directed Earl and Alec to the office at the back of the house. Because of the nuisance Alec made of himself on the walk through the house, talking of shock, pointing excitedly to the blisters forming on Earl's neck and hands, and rushing through a garbled story of a fire, the doctor discouraged him from accompanying Earl into the examining room. "Wait here, please," he said and shut the door in his face.

For a half an hour Alec sat and watched the closed door, rubbing his hands together and stretching his face in grimaces. Then Stutz came in and took the chair beside him. "The fire truck's off," he said.

Alec nodded, although he had scarcely heard what he had been told.

"They still in there?"

"Yes," said Alec. It was obvious they were. The murmur of voices could be heard behind the closed door. Alec didn't like it. The longer it went on, the more certain he was the news would be bad. Ten minutes more, fifteen. The door handle turned and Alec was on his feet, drying his hands on his pants legs before the door swung fully open. Dr. Evans ushered Earl out. Alec saw that one of his son's hands was swathed in gauze and that dabs of greasy ointment glistened under the electric light nearly as much as his eyes, which appeared to be filled with tears.

"Have a seat with your friend," Dr. Evans said softly to Earl, indicating that he meant Mr. Stutz. Earl betrayed no sign that he had heard or understood the doctor, but remained where he stood, arms hanging slack at his sides. Stutz rose from his chair and guided Earl across the room by the elbow. "Here," he whispered earnestly to the boy, "doctor means over here, Earl. Right here. See?"

Dr. Evans turned to Monkman. "Could I have a word with you?" Alec followed him into the examining room and the doctor closed the door carefully after them, leaning against it until he heard it click shut. The room was small and crowded, because of the examining table there was hardly space left over for a couple of chairs. The two men were forced to sit face to face, their knees almost touching. The doctor breathed peppermint into Alec's face. Alec didn't wait for him to begin. "What's wrong? Is Earl hurt bad somehow?" he demanded.

The doctor was relieved to find he could begin on a note of reassurance. "No, from what I can gather your son was very lucky," he said. "Most of his injuries are pretty superficial, a few first-and second-degree burns. He'll be all right on that score."

"What about this shock business? That doesn't look too hot to me."

"In pathological terms he's not suffering from shock at all – not shock as a result of physical trauma at any rate. I've checked his blood pressure for instance and it's not depressed, all other vital signs are normal." The young doctor realized he had lost his listener. He hadn't been long out of medical school and medical school clung to him still. He tried again. "We don't have to worry about shock – not that kind at any rate," he said.

"Why don't he talk then?" Alec asked. "Why does he look so Jesus awful then?"

"He talked to me," said Dr. Evans.

"Earl never said a word to me or Stutz on the way in – you can ask Stutz."

"I don't doubt he didn't," said the doctor. He paused before taking the next step. "Mr. Monkman," he asked, "has your son ever mentioned anything to you about hearing voices?"

Monkman gave the doctor an uncomprehending stare. It was clear he didn't grasp the question. "How do you mean – voices?"

"Voices which aren't there. Voices with nobody speaking them. Voices that urge him to do things. Things like happened tonight."

"Christ." There was no place for Alec to turn his eyes. The doctor was too close to him to avoid looking at.

"No signs of anything like this before? No auditory hallucinations?" He rephrased the question. "I mean to say, he's never heard things that weren't there, or seen things that didn't exist?"

"No." No sooner had he said that than Alec recollected Earl's complaining of his mother banging cupboard doors and walking through the house after she was buried. Still, he was just a child at the time. It was nothing more than imagination and shouldn't count. Yet the memory made him compromise. Guiltily he retreated, but only so far. "I'm not sure. Maybe. I haven't seen much of him this summer."

"Let me ask you something else then. Has Earl ever tried to harm himself before tonight?"

"Who says he tried to harm himself tonight?"

Dr. Evans disregarded the challenge. "I know this isn't a pleasant discussion – but I want you to tell me if he's ever tried to hurt himself. He's never burned himself with matches, or stuck himself with pins, has he? Nothing like that? Any exhibition of self-destructive behaviour before?"

"On purpose, you mean?" asked Alec, astounded.

"Yes, on purpose."

"If I had, I'd have self-destructed him. I'd have kicked his arse until he barked like a bloody fox," asserted Monkman, shaken by outrage at the very idea. Imagine Earl, his gentle boy, ever doing such a thing!

Dr. Evans tapped his jaw with the barrel of a fountain-pen. "It's not, as you say, a question of 'kicking him in the arse,'" he said severely. "That's not how sick people are made better." He paused to let his statement sink in. "And after what your boy has told me, I have no doubt he's sick."

"He's worn out with all the work he done this summer. He needs building up."

"He needs more than building up to get better."

"Whatever he needs, give it to him."

"It's beyond me what he needs. I'm not equipped to give it to him. Neither is Dr. Dowler. No G.P. is. But there is a place he can go for treatment."

"What you're talking about is the Mental, isn't it?" said Monkman.

"If you mean the Provincial Mental Hospital – yes, that's exactly what I'm talking about."

"Fuck that noise. My Earl's not going anywhere near that place."

Young Dr. Evans had expected as much. They had been warned at medical school to expect such reactions from families. "Listen," he said, choosing his words carefully so that the man sitting across from him could comprehend, "there's nothing to be ashamed of. Mental illness is an illness like any other, like pneumonia or appendicitis, say. If your boy had appendicitis you wouldn't deny him treatment, would you? No, you'd say, 'Do whatever needs to be done to make him well.' That's what you'd say, wouldn't you? And another thing. It's not the way it used to be there. Forget the old stories you may have heard. Most of them weren't true anyway. There are new treatments now. Patients get well. They come back to their families and homes. You must understand. There's nothing to be ashamed of."

Alec wasn't ashamed. How to explain to the doctor? He clenched and unclenched his fists. "I couldn't do it to him," he said. "I couldn't put him in a place like that, full of strangers, without a face he knows. He's too shy. He isn't capable. Ever since he was a little one, all he wanted was to be with his own, his family. Know what his sister called him? 'Home-sticker.' Because he wouldn't play any place but his own yard. He was that timid, you see? All he wanted was home."

Alec hoped that what he said would make the doctor understand. He searched for some change in his manner, for some sign that he was no longer so sure. Monkman knew that otherwise he would have to give way. A simple, uneducated man like him could not, in the end, resist medical arguments, medical authority.

The doctor's face was implacable.

It was Stutz and Alec who delivered Earl with the necessary papers. A long, exhausting drive with stretches of indescribably bad road. The men commented on the progress of the harvest to distract their minds from what they were doing.

At one point in the trip Alec said to Stutz, "If anybody asks where Earl's at – he went east to visit his sister and maybe to look for work. When he comes back better, he won't need this as common knowledge." Earl's complete and unbroken silence had already caused his father to fall into the habit of talking about him as if he wasn't present.

Stutz pursed his lips disapprovingly. "That's a lie."

Alec lost his temper, something he seldom did with Stutz. "If you're too goddamn pure to tell a lie – then refer them to me. I can tell enough lies for the both of us if I need to. Just promise me to keep quiet. Can you do that much?"

Quiet they both kept.

17

─────◆─────

Although Vera had come to a decision, for nearly two weeks she held her cards close to her vest and gave no hint of what she was thinking, even when Stutz went fishing by reminding her that his offer still stood. She was behaving exactly as she had done years before when she joined the Army without taking anyone into her confidence. There's many a slip betwixt cup and lip, Vera was fond of telling herself.

That was part of it, but not all. She didn't want to leave the impression of being desperate by grabbing at the money too quickly. It was undignified. A respectable delay between offer and cautious acceptance gave the whole transaction more of a business-like air and made it feel less like charity. There were reasons of pleasure, too. Vera liked the tease of anticipation, the slow boil of excitement that came with knowing she was going to shake and throw the dice. Last of all, she was not inclined to rush headlong into this because she half-expected to one day soon find her father on her doorstep, prepared to apologize. The great man himself, not Stutz.

Sitting in the bare, rented shack without so much as a radio to distract her, pictures would form in her mind. There she stood with her father having a real conversation, all the pieces of the puzzle that was their lives falling into place and locking solid in exactly the way they never had before.

And then suddenly she would be furious with herself for making the same stupid mistake she had been making since the first day she had set foot back in Connaught. Hoping for the miracle to occur, hoping that honesty, if nothing else, would force him to settle the score. How many times was she going to imagine him humbly saying it? "I was wrong to take you out of school, Vera. It was just that I couldn't see what you had it in you to become." Her saner self knew that hell would freeze over before she heard that. Twelve days passed, her moods swinging like the bob of a pendulum, and then her instincts directed her to put an end to it. There came a time even a man like Stutz lost patience. Besides, the edge was coming off the anticipation, the doubts multiplying and whispering too loudly.

It was flattering to see how grateful Stutz was to her for taking his money. Once she had it safely transferred to her account Vera moved to make up for any time she had lost. Within two days of the transfer she had, with Stutz's assistance, negotiated and signed a lease for The Bluebird Cafe, scratching her signature in a headlong scrawl that was the only sign she gave of how wild and impetuous she felt at that moment. There had been nothing like it since the Army.

Having allowed herself that one self-dramatizing flourish, henceforth Vera went doggedly forward. Almost immediately she felt her spirits dip, felt worry and fear crowd round her shoulders. Over and over she had to remind herself that if success depended on hard work then she would triumph. Yet just in case she didn't, she wished all this was happening someplace else, someplace her father wasn't present, scrutinizing her every move, ready to pounce on every miscalculation and foolishness.

The only effective antidote to the poison of such thoughts was to fling herself into work and, if nothing else, The Bluebird provided an unlimited supply of that. Vera asked herself whether the cafe had ever had a thorough cleaning since the days she had sat in its booths, drinking Coke and gossiping with her old chums Mabel Tierney and Phyllis Knouch. Now these girls she had believed she had left trapped in Connaught were long departed, married to men in the city who had freed them from a short servitude as secretaries, while she, adventurous Vera, was back home standing in the midst of the mouse dirt and cobwebs of the past.

But cobwebs could be brushed away. For a week, commencing a little after seven each morning and continuing until midnight, Vera scrubbed away years of neglect. Layer after layer of wax rolled up under the blade of her putty knife, saharas of dust and the haphazard sprinklings of mouse and rat shit scattered before her diligent broom, twenty years of smoke and grease caking the walls dissolved in pail upon pail of hot water, turning it the colour of strong tea. An entire afternoon was spent attacking the old yellow pee tracks in the toilet bowl in the men's washroom, bleaching and brushing, brushing and bleaching, until the stains had subsided into acceptable pale ivory water marks. Vera had not slaved like this in years. It was for her, for Daniel. Her arms and shoulders ached and trembled, her eyes smarted and her nose ran in the fumes of powerful disinfectant as she winced, lowering knuckles (that had been scraped scouring corner grime) into a bucket of Lysol and scalding water. Muscle spasms in her lower back caused her to limp and list but not to cease her war on filth. She ate standing because she had difficulty raising herself from a chair if she sat for any length of time.

Daniel helped after school. He polished windows with newspaper, buffed the paste wax his mother laid down on the floors, mended tears in the upholstery of the counter stools with electrician's tape, removed rodents from traps and disposed of the bodies.

When Vera collapsed on her bed some time after one o'clock in the morning, after she had thrown together Daniel's school lunch for the next day, she seldom slept more than an hour or two before snapping awake. Did she lock the front door of the cafe? Did she turn the grill off after frying up supper for herself and Daniel? On a number of occasions she went so far as to steal out of the house and hurry across town in the cold and dark to lay her palm on the top of the grill and rattle the lock on the front door one last time.

She left it to Mr. Stutz to order whatever she would need from a restaurant supplier in Regina. He knew what was necessary because for years he had performed that service for her father's restaurant in the hotel. Still, Mr. Stutz did not really presume. He made a list and went over it with her, item by item, explaining. The shipments soon began to arrive. Vera unpacked plates and cups, gigantic roasting pans and pots, cutlery. It was all vaguely familiar from the Army kitchens she had known. There were serviette dispensers, a coffee-maker, a milkshake mixer, banana-split boats, and sundae dishes that resembled vases. One day she became the owner of an ice cream freezer and an electric cash register.

According to Vera's calculations, Mr. Stutz had dispersed the two-thousand-dollar loan and still he continued buying, ignoring her protests. He ordered a meat saw, arguing that if they bought whole carcasses of beef and pork and he cut them up into steaks and roasts, ribs and chops, the savings would be enormous. One more thing. Vera ought to have an electric meat grinder to grind her own hamburger on the premises, fresh. Whenever Vera pointed out the mounting cost Mr. Stutz said, "You have to spend money to make money," and wrote another cheque. Vera wasn't exactly convinced by his reasoning. All she could think of was the money flying away, disappearing. It was like standing in a whirlwind, money torn out of her fingers and scurried off to the four points of the compass.

On the eve of her opening the food was delivered. Butter stacked like bars of gold in a sturdy wooden box, sacks of sugar and flour, burlap bags of potatoes and carrots, string bags of onions, cans of coffee and tea, gallon jars of pickles, crates of eggs, salt and pepper, herbs and spices, slabs of bacon, a pink carcass of beef stamped with the government inspector's blue ink, fryers, cardboard cartons of canned goods, drums of ice cream surrounded her in raw profusion.

Her father's watchful eye had been trained on all this. It was no coincidence that he had taken to hanging around the hotel across the way more frequently than had been his habit. And whenever a delivery truck drew up in front of The Bluebird Cafe he just happened to step out onto the front steps of the hotel lobby to salute a passerby and delay him with his observations about sports, or politics, or the weather, all the while throwing glances over the man's head to the goods being hauled through his daughter's doors. At other times when he did not realize he was being watched himself his nosiness was rude and undisguised. Then he would roost on the top step of the hotel like a cock on its favourite fence post, thrusting out his neck, a rooster preparing to crow, eyes darting an angry bird-like stare at the windows of the cafe. When Vera saw him like this, naked in his disquiet, feathers ruffled up and bristling, she had an inkling of how deeply she had gotten under his skin.

The day the poster went up in her window announcing the Grand Opening, free coffee and doughnuts, he telephoned. His abruptness spoke of a long struggle to suppress emotion. "Vera, this is your father," he announced in a rush. His voice sounded thick, hoarse. "What's this I hear about you borrowing money from Stutz. Is it true?"

"You know it's true – since you heard it from Stutz," Vera answered.

"I don't like it. You're in no position to borrow money. You've got no collateral. Who do you expect to bail you out if you go belly up? Me?"

"Expect a call when hell freezes over."

"You might as well have come to me in the first place. I know who's going to get stuck with paying up. I'd feel it was my responsibility to Stutz. He works for his money, you know. What he has didn't grow on trees."

"Ever think you might have jumped the gun with this mean-minded speculation about Vera's impending failure? The money isn't lost yet."

"It will be. You'll find out just how easy it is. Soon enough you'll find out." He paused. "Anyway, what business did you have going to him for money? Why didn't you come to me? What's the matter with my money?"

"Nothing. Aside from the fact it's yours."

"What kind of answer is that?"

"The best answer because it's the most obvious."

"Let me give you some advice, girl. You'd do well to forget your high and mighty style if you intend to serve the public. The public isn't looking to have their coffee poured by the Queen of Sheba – which you sometimes seem to mistake yourself for."

"No," said Vera, "the public would rather have its coffee poured and its eggs fried by a woman who doesn't wash her hands after she's been to the washroom to pee – which is the case with that jewel you've employed across the way."

That took the wind out of his sails. The best reply he could manage was, "Rita is a good worker and loyal."

Vera refused to miss an opportunity. "Loyal like Stutz?" she asked.

Her father went silent. She could hear him breathing into the mouthpiece of the receiver. "You think you're so clever," he said at last. "But did you ever stop to ask yourself what Stutz is up to?"

As a matter of fact she hadn't, not really. But one thing she could be sure of – if Stutz was up to anything it wouldn't be crooked. Vera's voice was confident and cocky. "So tell me, what do you think he's up to?"

"You figure a careful man like Stutz hands over his savings like that without he has a view to something in particular?"

Vera found her father's tone annoying. "A view to something else. What?"

"You really ought to dig a little deeper into your business partners," said the old man. "Of course, how were you to know all the lengths Stutz went to over the last fifteen years trying to land himself a wife? Went to each of the three Protestant churches in turn – Anglican, United, and Lutheran – in search of the girl of his dreams. The only man in town to have sung in all three choirs. Offered to tie himself to anything available for the three-legged races at the church picnics. No takers though, no one willing to lend him a leg. Maybe it was his honesty worked against him, his talk of tithing and his glass eye. They found it very off-putting, virgins and widows alike, the tithing and the glass eye – not to mention the man is as homely as a mud fence. But despite his setbacks Stutz doesn't lose hope. Seems he's still in there pitching. Has he referred to the glass eye yet? They say it's a foolproof sign of serious intentions once Stutz gets around to confessing the glass eye. Mr. Stutz doesn't want any of his prospective brides to be buying a pig in a poke, so he's always perfectly honest about that glass eye of his. Try and act surprised when he tells you."

Vera slammed down the receiver on the mocking voice, hard.

—◇—

The day of The Bluebird's official opening Vera hosted a crowd of respectable size lured by free coffee and doughnuts and rumours of a falling-out between Alec Monkman and his daughter. Visitors were quick to note that there was no sign of the old man about the place, just the boy passing around a plate of sugar doughnuts and Vera smiling in a new apron as she poured the coffee. The puzzling element was Mr. Stutz nodding to everyone with a proprietorial air from a back table. No one was sure how to read the significance of that, Mr. Stutz, Alec Monkman's right-hand man, conspicuously seated at a back table in The Bluebird.

Despite the modest but encouraging success of the Grand

Opening, in the days and weeks immediately following, business was slack. There was no give in the market. Alec Monkman kept his regulars because his regulars were creatures of habit. The local storekeepers and clerks still migrated twice a day to the hotel and seated themselves at their customary tables during coffee breaks. They were like dumb horses plodding to familiar stalls, thought Vera. That way get-togethers remained cozy and unchanging, as unchanging as arguments about Saturday night's hockey game, or the time-honoured ritual of matching for the coffee bill. Each morning and each afternoon the jokes made at the loser's expense would be repeated and the laughter would be just as loud and appreciative as if it was all happening fresh and for the first time. What Vera couldn't understand was that the old jokes were better *because* they were predictable and comfortable. It seemed that people in Connaught didn't like surprises.

Her father had close to twenty regulars upon whom he could depend. Vera had one, an admirer of her raisin pie, the jeweller Wiens, a German immigrant and resolutely solitary man who appeared punctually at ten-fifteen each morning and three-fifteen each afternoon for a glass of chocolate milk and slice of raisin pie which he consumed in sad silence. After scraping his plate with his fork he rose, paid his bill, and left, having scarcely uttered a word.

A business, Vera had to remind herself, could not be supported on the back of a Mr. Wiens, no matter how faithful he was to her cooking. It was discouraging but true that the only times when The Bluebird held more than a single customer was when the quota opened at the elevator and grain trucks backed up for more than a block waiting to deliver their wheat to the Pool. Then the farmers who couldn't find a seat at the hotel crossed the street to Vera's so they could nurse a cup of coffee and not have to wait in the bitter cold to unload.

With so few demands on her time Vera could often be seen standing in the large front window of The Bluebird, arms folded over her breasts as she meditated on the snow blowing and shuddering like smoke on the roofs across the way. There were afternoons she didn't speak to a soul until Mr. Stutz dropped in to have his supper after work. Regardless of her objections, Mr. Stutz always insisted on paying for his evening meal, which only made Vera feel even more of a charity case. Many nights he sat at the back table as late as eight o'clock, toying with his coffee cup and being sickeningly cheerful, advising her not to worry, she'd soon turn the corner. By mid-February, Vera was convinced there wasn't any corner to turn, no corner existed. Her sole concern was now endeavouring to desperately pry a nickel loose here and there. That was what it had come to, a scramble for nickels. She hoped that by staying open two hours later than her father's restaurant she might capture a few dregs of business, but what she got was scarcely enough to pay for the extra electric light she burned. The Bluebird had rapidly become a losing proposition. Night after night while Daniel worked on his homework in one of the booths, Vera perched on a stool at the deserted counter, crossed her right leg over her left and flicked her foot up and down like a cat does its tail as it watches the mouse's hole. Her anxious eyes seldom left the door of The Bluebird as she waited in a misery of anticipation, an ashtray overflowing at her elbow. If the door did swing open it was sure to be a teenager wanting a package of Old Dutch potato chips, or a Coke, or a young father asking if he could buy a bottle of milk from her because his wife had forgotten to go to the store that day and now they were out and the baby was crying for a bottle. Slim profits in a bag of chips or a quart of milk.

It was a relief, when midnight finally crawled round, to check the grill, draw the blinds, and lock the door. In seven short hours Vera would be obliged to start the slow water-torture all over again. Until then there was sleep, an exhausted reprieve from worrying how to meet the rent in March or thoughts of the $3100 she now owed Mr. Stutz. That was how winter stumbled on. Vera barely noticed the sun gaining strength, the icicles hanging from the eaves suddenly one day releasing a rain of pattering drops on the sidewalk outside The Bluebird's window, the children running home from school with their coats unbuttoned, their toques clutched in their hands, the puddles in the shining gravel of Main Street reflecting blue sky.

The change of seasons also seemed to bring a change of luck. Vera had the Portuguese to thank for that. The motives behind the arrival of the Portuguese in Connaught were by no means straightforward or simple. For more than a year there had been vague but persistent rumours circulating that an American mining company was considering establishing a potash mine somewhere in the vicinity of Connaught. The rumours could not be dismissed as far-fetched since a mine had opened in the province only five or six years before. Nevertheless, for months no one could really believe such a stroke of good fortune could smite their particular sleepy backwater. Yet, if it did, the stakes would be enormous. If the mine did go ahead, the American company would need to choose a town for their headquarters, a town in which to settle office staff and miners. That would mean prosperity and unprecedented growth, a spectacular, heady boom in business. Anyone with a head on his shoulders could see that if a mine were to be established in the district there were only three possible choices for a headquarters, the three towns which stood within twenty miles of one another – Hildebrook, Czar, and Connaught. Of course, it was all a gamble, a gamble that the mine would go ahead at all, a gamble as to which town would claim the glittering prize if it did. But it was Connaught's town council which acted first, having weighed the odds, then hesitated and see-sawed for months before taking a deep breath and casting the dice. The stakes were too high, too tempting to stand aside. Besides, all of the councillors were also businessmen and stood the most to gain from risking the tax-payers' money. They reasoned that if the mine was to proceed, the Americans would select the most progressive, the most go-ahead town as centre of their operations. As Councillor Stevenson, who owned a plumbing business, put it, "No American is going to pick some backward shit hole to live." This was the argument that clinched the decision to pave Connaught's dirt roads and lay new cement sidewalks as an enticement to the Americans and a way of gaining a march on Connaught's unpaved rivals. A contract was hurriedly signed with an Edmonton company and, on May 1, the Portuguese arrived to lay asphalt and pour cement.

Vera could almost have believed that the angels sent them. New to town, strangers, they took their meals where they were made to feel most welcome, at Vera's. In a single stroke her fortunes were reversed. Suddenly she found herself serving breakfast, lunch, and supper to thirty men, seven days a week. It didn't matter that Daniel was run off his feet serving tables and herself cooking in the kitchen. What counted was the money she found in the cash register at the end of the first day of the Portuguese invasion. The total astounded her. Vera made up her mind that no one, but no one, was going to take her Portuguese away from her. In a matter of days she was on the friendliest of terms with the short, dark men who smiled so brilliantly and laughed so easily. Soon they were teasing her in fractured English, proudly displaying to her snapshots of wives and children, and teaching her to twist her tongue around their names. Soon they were at ease enough with Vera for their foreman Domingo to approach her with a request. "Please, can you make a party Portuguese for them? To help the homesick?" Diffidently he held out to her several sheets of wrinkled paper covered with awkward, misspelled translations of recipes. "Please, these foods?"

Vera agreed to help if Domingo would assist and guide her. Lacking certain ingredients it was necessary for her to improvise, Domingo at her side, sampling and judging. "Like this, Domingo? More or less?" And he nodded or shook his head, smacked his lips in theatrical appreciation or curled them in distaste.

The party was set for eight o'clock Saturday night. As the hour drew near Vera hung a sign on the door of the cafe which announced "Closed for Private Function," and stood guard, ready to turn back anyone who wasn't Portuguese. Vera had never seen any of her guests in anything but work clothes and now they struck her as a tiny bit comical, solemnly and identically dressed in tieless white shirts buttoned to the throat and sombre black suits whose pockets bulged with bottles of home-made wine. She hadn't counted on the wine and it made Vera nervous that some Nosy Parker would report her to the police for serving liquor in an unlicenced establishment. So the Portuguese were unceremoniously scooted through the door and, once the flock was all safely inside, she practically nailed the blinds to the window-ledge so no snoop could steal a peek in. The last thing she needed now that she was finally turning a buck was to get her business licence pulled.

It was a memorable party. They ate, they drank, and after they had done enough of both they began to sing and even dance. Elaborately courteous, they offered Vera ecstatic compliments in barely comprehensible English which grew less comprehensible the drunker they got. Vera understood that their grandiose praises bore little relation to the quality of her Portuguese cooking which could be, at best, only passable. Rather, they were expressions of gratitude for her willingness to attempt to please them and make them feel at home.

"Missus, is good dinner," one after another of them reported gravely to her. Domingo, drunk by midnight and unhinged by the nostalgia evoked by the taste of boiled potatoes served with olive oil and wine vinegar instead of butter or gravy, sat by himself, surveying the scene. Suddenly he lifted a glass of wine high above his head and shouted, "You are Queen, Vera! Queen of the Portuguese!" The toast was taken up with a roar of drunken enthusiasm. "You are Queen of the Portuguese, Vera! Queen!"

The proclamation was true. After that night Vera was Queen of the Portuguese, treated with the respect owed a queen and given unswerving loyalty. From the time of the party Portuguese Vera knew these customers were hers, no one was going to entice them away from her.

Something else became plain after the party. Vera could see it was impossible for her to carry on in the fashion she had for the past few weeks. It was too much to ask Daniel to serve breakfast before school, rush back to The Bluebird during lunch hour to wait tables, and then return after school to work the supper shift. At first she had been leery of hiring staff because she could not believe that this unanticipated burst of busyness could continue, but now it seemed certain that it would, that The Bluebird really did have some sort of future. So Vera became an employer, engaging two high school dropouts as waitresses and a middle-aged woman with a history of alcohol problems as dishwasher. Daniel was relegated to lighter duties, manning the till at supper, clearing tables, mopping up the floor once the supper rush was over.

Her new employees didn't know what to make of Vera. She expected them to match her frantic pace and when they didn't they caught hell. Mad, Vera could strip the paint off an outhouse wall with her tongue. Irene, one of the waitresses, burst into tears several times during her first week of work. On the other hand, Vera's workers earned more money at The Bluebird than they could anywhere else in Connaught. They started at better than the minimum wage, Vera explaining that she didn't expect minimum work out of them so they ought to get paid better than minimum pay. As boss, she stressed one thing to her waitresses. It was their job to get the Portuguese fed and out the door as quickly as it was humanly possible. The men had to be at work by seven in the morning and back on the shovel after lunch by one o'clock. She promised her waitresses that every day they got the crew clear of the restaurant by starting time, morning and noon, they would each get a three dollar bonus, paid straight out of the till at the end of the day.

Stutz had warned her against paying higher than average wages, as if her decision was simply a bid for popularity. Yet despite paying higher salaries, despite performance bonuses for hustle, the sums of money she banked at the end of each week slowly and steadily mounted. Soon she was writing weekly cheques of fifty dollars against Stutz's loan. Within the year she hoped her debt to him would be paid in full.

On June 1, with great fanfare, the provincial government and an American mining company had announced that a potash mine would be developed six miles south of Connaught. The choice news was that the town council's gamble had appeared to have paid off; Connaught was chosen as company headquarters. A surge of activity followed hard on the heels of this announcement. Overnight things began to change. Strangers appeared on the streets. The entire second floor of Alec Monkman's hotel became temporary offices for geologists, engineers, planners, while the third floor became their living and sleeping quarters.

A three-shift crew of shaft sinkers arrived. No one in Connaught had ever seen their like before. To the citizens of Connaught they were a different breed of man, grey-skinned from lack of sun, hard, wild, desperate in the pursuit of their pleasures. Drawn from all over North America, they spoke with every accent, lured by the big money which goes hand in hand with work that demands you risk your life hourly. Their hard-earned wages ran between their fingers like water and they wanted the best that life had to offer and money could buy. They ordered steak and eggs for breakfast, drank Crown Royal. Their cars were big, flashy, expensive, and neglected – Buicks and Chryslers and Oldsmobiles caked in mud or floured in dust. The dangers of the job had made them addicts to excitement so when their shifts were over they made trouble drinking and fighting. There seemed to be no let-up to the noise, the confusion, the disorderliness. Day and night, semis rolled through town bearing huge pieces of earth-moving equipment lashed to their trailers with chains, shaking people in their chairs and in their beds, making the dishes jingle in the cupboard and spoiling television reception. The town council hurriedly passed a by-law outlawing the big trucks from travel on the newly paved streets. Sometimes the drivers heeded the ordinance, sometimes they didn't. When they did, the air was filled with rumble and clouds of yellow dust, and when they didn't, the fresh pavement had to be patched and repaired by the crews of Portuguese.

At the hotel the mining company had started to hire. Men the locals did not recognize caused resentment when they stood in a line that stretched the length of the corridor and slithered down the stairs, each man waiting his turn to step up to the desk and state his occupation – electrician, carpenter, welder, pipe-fitter, labourer. Miners would not be needed for a long time yet. On site a chain-link fence was being raised around the property, an army of men were throwing up temporary offices, warehouses, bunkhouses, cook shacks, tool sheds. To make themselves heard above the roar of graders, Euclids, and bulldozers which wheeled and plunged and bucked all over the grounds, everyone shouted.

The people of Connaught stood by like witnesses to a catastrophic accident. In the blink of an eye, everything had changed and they weren't sure how it had happened. On the east side of town a disorganized, ramshackle trailer court had sprung up, by day populated with frowsy women screeching at slummy kids, and by night the scene of all-night drinking parties from which husbands stumbled out in the morning, bound for work. There were rumours that there was another kind of woman out in the trailer court, the kind that lived by herself and entertained men at any hour.

On the west side of town a different kind of development was taking place. It was marked by newly excavated basements surrounded by heaps of earth and the skeletal frames of the split levels the Americans were building to house their families. Rumours mushroomed like the houses themselves. The town was making a fortune selling lots to the Yankees at inflated prices, so much money there would be a moratorium on taxes next year. You wait and see, others said, the taxes we'll all be paying when we start laying water and sewer lines for the Americans and building them their hardtop roads. This was the viewpoint which suited the old-timers – that the mine meant nothing but heartbreak and disappointment. Wasn't the school board already worrying where they were going to put all those unplanned-for kids when classes started in the fall? Some said there was no avoiding it, a school would have to be built next year. Then taxes would go through the roof. And prices were going up in the grocery store, going up everywhere you looked. There was too much drinking and fighting and general carrying on, nobody could deny that either. These newcomers were a bad lot and their kids were worse, shifty-eyed little buggers you couldn't trust as far as you could pitch one of them. Wait and see what Hallowe'en is like this year. Wait and see. Your eyes'll pop.

The feeling took root in the ordinary citizen that whatever benefits this hullabaloo brought weren't worth it. Vera did not share this opinion. To her, life seemed to have made an unexpected detour through Connaught, stirring it up, waking it up. The sudden flush of raw, uncouth energy, the jump and bustle, the easy come and easy go of it, reminded Vera of what it had been like during the war.

It didn't hurt either that her business had taken another upswing, nearly doubling, with the start of mine operations. A sudden flood of men, many of them single, meant she could barely meet the demand for meals. There might be cook shacks out on the mine site but when the day shift ended the first thing on every man's mind was to drive into town for a couple of cool ones. Usually they didn't bother to return to camp for supper. "Let's eat at Vera's," someone would suggest, and it was decided. Besides, if they remained in town for their meal they could get back to the beer parlour with scarcely an interruption.

Circumstances had reversed themselves. Now it was her father's restaurant which was the second choice and received the overflow, not The Bluebird. Men were willing to wait for a place at Vera's. Vera had Mr. Stutz hammer together a long sturdy bench which she set outside, against the front wall of her cafe. There her customers could wait in comparative comfort when the weather was fine. Townspeople strolling by during the supper hour never counted fewer than ten men sitting there side by side, waiting their turn and considering what it would be tonight – a half-chicken crisp and golden and savoury, a T-bone smothered in buttered mushrooms, a thick slab of pink roast beef, or maybe Vera's pork chops and sauerkraut. Then dessert. Deep-dish apple pie, hot, with two scoops of ice cream melting into the pastry. Or a maple walnut sundae. They would sit, dog-tired, smoking cigarettes and drinking the complimentary coffee which Daniel brought out to them, the evening sun spreading its still bronze light over them so that it would have been easy to mistake them for statues representing some quiet virtue such as patience or fortitude.

Inside, however, it was bedlam itself. Vera had installed a juke box, and if the men weren't feeding it quarters she'd toss in a few herself, just to keep the mood cheerful. She'd also taken on another cook so that no matter how busy it got she could always take a few minutes to have a word with her patrons. Floury-armed and red-faced, the Queen of the Portuguese went on her walkabouts, distributing the regal smile and nod, chaffing this one, dropping a joke here, exhibiting the common touch. The men loved it.

"Hi, good-looking. What's cooking?"

"Not your supper, John. You talk to me that way yours goes on the back burner."

"Hey, Vera, Tony wants a date!"

"So does his wife. They ought to get together."

Roars of laughter, forks ringing on water-glasses in applause, and Vera would glide through the swinging doors of the kitchen, buoyant on a wave of popularity.

"That Vera, isn't she something?" they'd declare, shaking their heads.

For the first time in a good many years Vera was inclined to agree with them. Yes, she *was* something. Damn right she was. People were beginning to sit up and take notice. "That one is a goer," Connaught's old-timers would say. Even her father couldn't overlook her now. She couldn't suppress a small smile of triumph when Mr. Stutz reported that Alec had crossed out the prices of all the meals on the hotel menu and reduced them all by twenty-five cents. When she learned that, Vera also crossed out her prices, but instead of cutting them, she increased them all by a dime. It wasn't greed which prompted this; she merely wanted to demonstrate that the success of The Bluebird had nothing to do with cheapness, nothing to do with money was at the heart of it.

The daily take continued to grow. Working seven days a week, fifteen hours a day, there was little opportunity to spend her money. The best she could manage were daydreams while rolling piecrust or scraping carrots, daydreams of the things she could afford to buy herself now: tailored suits, a good cloth coat, smart wool skirts. Clothes that didn't go in and out of fashion on a whim, clothes that bespoke quality. Katharine Hepburn clothes. It was good enough to know that she could have them if she wanted them; the money would stay in the bank, earning interest for the day Daniel would need it.

Vera had made a strange discovery. Money was like a telescope, extending the range of vision. In the bad old days, when she had been a checkout girl in the supermarket, Vera had seldom allowed herself to look beyond payday, the end of the month, further than thirty-one days. There seemed no point to it. Now things were different. Letting her imagination run free she could see him through six or seven years of university, or however long was required to make him something really fine, a doctor or a lawyer perhaps. Contemplating that made clothes unnecessary. Anticipation was sweeter than any showy glad rags, so were feelings of sacrifice. She thought of how proud Stanley would be – of her, of their son.

Each night, regular as clockwork, Mr. Stutz slipped into The Bluebird minutes before it closed. While Vera counted the day's receipts and transferred them to a heavy canvas deposit bag, Stutz stood in the window, scanning the street. When the money was safely stowed in the bag, the two of them went out together. For weeks Mr. Stutz had insisted on walking Vera to the bank's night deposit chute to protect her from attack and robbery. "Connaught's changed," he would say, "there's bad characters around who wouldn't give it a second thought."

Mr. Stutz was a sternly chivalrous man and he could not be persuaded that she was in no danger on her short walk to the bank. Only when the cash was safely deposited could he be made to say goodbye in his reluctant, formal manner. There had been arguments when he first began to escort her because he had wanted to see Vera all the way home, to her doorstep, but after strong protests he had relented. Mr. Stutz suspected what made her so uneasy. A single woman seen home each and every night of the week by a man might be running risks with her reputation. He could see her point, he supposed.

Of course, it had never entered Vera's head that her good name was in any sort of peril. She simply wanted to avoid stimulating his hopes, if he had any. She didn't know whether to believe her father or not. Besides, the walk home was the only time she had to herself, completely alone. It was pleasant to feel the summer night like a shawl, warm and soft about her shoulders. The streets occupied by natives of Connaught, unlike those of recent immigrants, were silent and dark, except for the occasional glow of a porch light haloed in a swarm of moths. Vera liked to remove the shoes from her aching feet and pad along the sidewalks the Portuguese had laid, the coarse texture of the concrete prickling the soles of her naked feet.

Going barefoot she remembered how it used to be, headed for home in the dark as a girl of ten, every nerve alive and quivering, a stealthy, wary animal. Vera, "the big show-off," always made a point of walking home from the movies alone. It was a way of attracting attention; everybody else travelled in a giggling pack, or at least in pairs, because they were scared of the dark and their own shadows.

"How can you!" Phyllis and Mabel used to exclaim, causing a half-smile to briefly flit across their friend's lips. Phyllis and Mabel walked hand in hand, took turns delivering each other home first, the lucky one standing on her doorstep to watch her friend sprint the yawning black distance of two doors down, the yawning black distance which separated the Knouch and Tierney verandas, populated with God knew what – the Lindbergh baby kidnappers, mad dogs, crazy tramps.

Vera refused to let her own fear master her. She made herself walk purposefully slow under the big white moon smoky behind a smear of cloud, her heart pattering fast as it tried to climb up her throat, her feet dragging as if they were in chains. She wasn't going to permit herself to run no matter how strong the impulse grew to scamper for the lighted kitchen where her mother and father sat. "Sissy!" she hissed at herself under her breath. "Pissy-pants!"

Between Vera and safety was the weird rustling of caragana and lilac hedges crowding the wooden walk, the slap of an unlatched gate in the wind, the shadows which shifted like premonitions across her path, the big boys who crouched in the limbs of the trees that grew by the funeral parlour, ready to spring howling and whooping down out of the trees which bore berries bright as blood, the ones every kid in Connaught called undertaker berries and believed were poison and red because the undertaker poured the buckets of blood he drained from corpses onto their roots at midnight.

If you didn't run screaming when the big boys dropped out of the trees screeching like baboons their dignity was offended. They crowded threateningly close and tried to make you cry with lurid suggestions as to what they might do with you. "Let's tie her up and leave her for the night in the back of Michaelson's hearse, right on the spot where the stiffs ride!"

There was very little satisfaction to be got trying to terrify Vera. One night when they threatened to make her eat a poisonous undertaker berry she said, "I don't believe they're poisonous anyway. Anybody with a brain knows that."

"So eat one then," a big boy dared her.

She didn't hesitate but stared him straight in the face, reached up with her eyes still on him, fumbled with the branch, plucked a single berry, popped it in her mouth, and swallowed it at once, like a pill, before she realized exactly what she was doing. A second later she had spun round and was running for all she was worth to her house because if she *was* going to die it had to be at home. She found her father alone in the kitchen, playing solitaire. Her mother had been tired and had gone to bed early. Vera dragged a chair up as close to him as she could get and sat down to wait for whatever was going to happen to her. Her knees were jammed so tightly together that her legs shook.

"Are you cold?" her father said, looking up from his cards. "You shouldn't be out at night dressed like that."

Vera wanted to tell him she had eaten an undertaker berry to show it wasn't poisoned and she wasn't afraid. She thought it would please her father more than straight A's, more than getting the lead in the Grade Four play, to know this because he had always told her that the most important thing in life was "to have the courage of your convictions." Well, she had had them. She'd swallowed that awful berry to prove she was right. But if she had come right out and told him that it would be bragging, and bragging had nothing to do with the courage of your convictions. Convictions were just convictions.

So there was nothing to do but sit close to him and think about what that berry might be up to in her stomach.

Yet the next morning when she woke and found herself alive, Vera knew that she would have eaten a whole pie made from undertaker berries, eaten it all, just to please him.

18

During the spring, what with chores at The Bluebird, school, and difficulties in out-manoeuvring his mother, Daniel had found it possible only to make hurried, furtive visits to his grandfather. Strictly speaking, his mother had never actually forbidden him to call on his grandfather, but Daniel had never had a moment's doubt as to what she preferred him to do. The visits Daniel made to his grandfather's felt furtive. He and his mother had chosen to pretend that he no longer had any interest in seeing the old man. It didn't matter that this was a lie. What was important was that it made life simpler and safer for all concerned. His mother could ignore his disloyalty as long as he didn't rub her nose in it and Daniel could play the game of the good and obliging son. In this situation he couldn't help feeling devious and insincere and the promoter of injured feelings. If two weeks passed without his dropping by Alec's, his conscience was clear with his mother but unsettled and guilty in regard to his grandfather.

It was bad news when the old man punished him by sulking, but some relief could be had from that, he could look away from the long face and concentrate his attention on the television. What was in his grandfather's favour was that he never had a harsh word to say about her, while she was constantly going on about him, hammer and tongs, harping and nattering on his faults and failings and downright black nature. Sometimes Daniel wanted to ask her who she was trying to convince. Although she didn't know it, it had been one of these rants shortly before Valentine's Day that finally drove Daniel over the edge. For the six weeks following the breach that occurred at Christmas, he had not been able to summon up the courage to seek his grandfather out. But her going on like a maniac, yammer, yammer, had finally driven him to it. Fuck that noise, he said to himself, and went out and bought Alec the biggest, dopiest, most sentimental valentine he could find and delivered it by hand to his grandfather's house. The old boy was tickled pink, there was no hiding it. Never handy with words, he tried to slip his grandson a five-dollar bill. Ordinarily, Daniel would have snatched it up, but that day, under the circumstances, he felt it would be like taking a bribe or kickback or something. So he said no, so as not to spoil the mood of the occasion.

It really did gripe his ass the way his mother went on about his grandfather. He wished she'd shut her mouth. "He was giving you cigarettes and whisky when I was living right in the house," she was fond of saying. "God alone knows what he'd feel free to introduce you to with me nowhere in sight."

In May, Daniel took the risk of playing hooky for an entire day to help his grandfather plant the garden. His mother would have had him by the short and curlies if she'd got wind of that. Daniel understood how stupid it was to take the chance, but the old man's continual fretting and fussing over whether or not he would get his garden seeded by Victoria Day struck Daniel as so pathetic that he thought he had better pitch in and help finish the job or the old man would never enjoy a moment's peace that spring. Daniel was pretty sure the worry over such a stupid thing was actually preventing his grandfather from sleeping.

As Victoria Day drew nearer, Daniel heard Alec say a hundred times if he heard him say it once: "There isn't a year in the last twenty I missed having the garden in by the Queen's birthday – and look where I'm at now."

Daniel sensed that lately his grandfather wasn't quite the same. He would brood about silly things like the garden and was prone to hair-trigger explosions of temper. When Daniel asked him what difference it made if the garden wasn't planted by Victoria Day but instead went in a few days later, the question seemed to confuse and confound the old man. But from confusion he quickly passed over into anger and began to shout menacingly that if Daniel didn't know what difference it made, that only proved what an ignorant snip he was. There were other changes Daniel had noticed since Christmas. His grandfather struck him as generally less alert and certainly much more forgetful than before.

To put an end to all the bitching and moaning about the approach of Victoria Day, the boy promised the old man that he would give him a hand with the planting on the Friday before the long weekend. On the weekends his mother would monopolize his time at The Bluebird. Daniel lied and told his grandfather that he would have the Friday off because of a teachers' convention. When his grandfather saw all the kids trooping past the house with books stacked in their arms on the day of the "holiday," Daniel supposed the old boy would give him a sly wink and call him a rascal. But when Friday arrived and all the kids went streaming by the house at eight forty-five in the morning, obviously on their way to classes, Alec didn't give them a second glance as he turned the earth in his garden with a potato fork. Nor did he say a word to Daniel. Why? Daniel asked himself. Didn't he see them? Or was it that he couldn't put two and two together? Or was he so obsessed with his Victoria Day deadline that he was prepared to overlook anything, so long as it helped him to meet it?

As to why his grandfather had fallen so far behind in his planting schedule – that was no mystery to Daniel once he had seen him at work. There were moments, standing in the midst of his plot, that Alec looked positively bewildered, a man who had lost his bearings and had no inkling of where he was. He would barely begin one task when he was distracted by another. No sooner did he pick up a rake than he laid it down with a bemused look on his face and wandered off to the tool shed to hunt up stakes and twine to lay out rows. With his hands full of stakes and twine it would suddenly strike him that there wasn't much sense in stringing out guides over unraked ground. The stakes and ball of twine would be tossed in the tall, unmowed grass at the edge of the garden where they would be lost. Meanwhile, Alec would take up a rake and scratch furiously back and forth in the dirt until another notion seized him. By mid-morning Daniel was so exasperated he could have screamed. Everything was taking twice as long as it should have, the old man misplaced everything he touched, he blundered into the taut twine Daniel stretched, stumbling and wrenching the stakes from the earth; he sowed the first half of a row with peas and the last half absentmindedly with beans.

Somewhere around four o'clock, after nearly seven hours of uninterrupted labour, the garden was finished. The old man surveyed their work and his face visibly relaxed as he announced that a small celebration was in order. While Daniel stowed the tools away in the shed, he would go into the house and crack them a couple of beers.

Five minutes later, Daniel found the dusty, sweaty old man asleep on the chesterfield. The boy hunted up a blanket and covered him so he wouldn't take a chill when the perspiration dried on him. Then he went into the kitchen and opened the fridge, found a beer, and settled on a chair to drink it. Promises were made to be kept. Alec owed him this. Before leaving, he turned on the kitchen light, so that if his grandfather woke in the middle of the night he wouldn't be confused about where he was, the light would act as beacon to help him find his way up the stairs and to his bed.

Now, with the start of summer vacation, Daniel is able to visit the old man nearly every day. He reaches an agreement with his mother that if he works for her half-days, the other half of the day is his own. Either he takes the morning shift, clearing tables, scraping, rinsing, and stacking breakfast dishes, and doing other odd jobs that have to be completed before preparations are begun for making dinner, or he can take the supper shift which begins at four and lasts until nine when the last man belches and farts his way out the door of the restaurant. The choice is up to him. All his old lady asks is that each Monday he mark his schedule on the calendar which hangs by the stove so that she can allot the remainder of her staff their hours. As long as he is punctual and sticks to the allotted shifts, she doesn't poke her nose into his comings and goings too closely, although every once in a while in the midst of the clamour of the kitchen she remembers she is a mother and brushes up on the old Spanish Inquisition. It keeps them both in practice.

"So where were you all afternoon?"

"Around."

"Around where?"

Being as there is not much around in a turd town like Connaught, it is not always easy to manufacture a plausible and satisfactory lie just like that, at the drop of a hat. He tries on the library for size. His mother favours libraries as suitable haunts.

"I went to the library and looked at books."

"Find anything interesting? What did you read?"

"I don't know. Just books."

"I can check you know. One phone call is all it takes. I can ask that woman at the library if you were there all afternoon. Should I phone her?"

"Do what you like." He can say this because he knows the library closes at five. Now it is six. Tomorrow his mother will be too busy to remember to check his alibi.

The question is, how much does she know for sure? There are days when he thinks it's all a guess and others when he's convinced she knows everything. Whenever she drills him with that flat, steady stare of hers, the one that makes him feel like a bug in a bottle, Daniel asks himself, What experiment is she running on me now? There are times when it would be a relief to confess and end the awful suspense. But turning gutless wonder, breaking down and offering some snivelly, grovelly confession to clear the books with her, would be stupid if she didn't know, *really* know. It would be like sticking his neck out for the axe and he didn't fancy that at all.

So he kept on doing as he had been, but uneasily. Nearly always he signed himself on for the morning shift so that he was free to watch television with Alec in the afternoon. In the summer, during the afternoons, the local station ran pretty decent old movies, Abbott and Costello comedies, Errol Flynn swashbucklers, dusters. And on Saturdays there were the baseball games which both he and the old man loved.

Despite his grandfather's rash of new oddities Daniel still found him easier to deal with than his mother. He hated to think what she would have to say about Alec if she could see him now, sitting in the house in a bulky knit Siwash sweater with two pairs of heavy wool socks on his feet while the mercury stood in the thermometer at 85°F. It was little wonder that his head didn't work one hundred per cent, he was probably suffering from heat stroke, boiled brains. Whenever Daniel gave him the gears about overdressing, the old man grew sulky and grouchy. "Laugh now you little bastard," he warned, "your turn'll come to feel the cold."

Although he got hostile any time Daniel teased him, it was the only way Daniel had of snapping him out of his moods. If he was sunk up to his ass in his thoughts he didn't trouble to answer simple questions. He had to be ragged or needled into saying something. Daniel not only found the old man's withdrawals into blankness upsetting, he also regarded them as insulting. What business had he switching off his own personal control switch to the outside world, shutting Daniel out and falling into a trance? Most often it happened when he watched television. It annoyed and aggravated

Daniel to no end because when the old man came out of his reveries he demanded explanations as to how the runner came to be advanced to third base, or how Miss Kitty came to be tied to a chair in her own saloon and where the hell was Matt Dillon anyway?

Daniel would have liked to tell him to take a flying fuck at the moon if he couldn't bother to watch the television himself. But he didn't. He just sourly let things take their course, the old man staring glassy-eyed off into space, one hand laid like a brick on the crown of his fedora as if he feared a windstorm might erupt in his living room and tear it from his head, the barely discernible twitching of his lips signalling some hunt of the mind the way shivers and tremors in a sleeping dog's limbs betray pursuit in a dream.

The famous hat. There was a time when his grandfather had merely forgotten to remove it indoors, now it was clear that he refused to. Daniel thinks that only a crowbar could get between the two of them and effect a separation. He remembers the day late in July he let himself into the house and discovered his grandfather dripping onto sheets of newspaper spread on the floor in front of the kitchen sink. A froth of soap suds bubbled on the mat of his thick, grizzled chest hairs and there were smears of white lather caking his flanks and thighs. He was scrubbing himself with a scrap of washcloth so hard that his private parts were flapping energetically up and down and making the occasional sideways squiggle left and right. He was absolutely naked if you didn't count the straw hat stuck to his head. Daniel was struck dumb in the beginning. It was embarrassing to be looking at an old person, a senior citizen, without his clothes on, and it got even more unnerving when his grandfather tried to engage him in a conversation as he skidded a soap-slippery washcloth over his belly. Daniel couldn't stop his eyes from veering back and forth between the hat and the bobbling parts, between all that limber action down below and the rock solid steadiness of the hat riding up top. With every passing second his embarrassment grew more and more acute, finally transforming itself into hysteria and nervous giggles which sent him scrambling for the living room. There he hunkered in the easy-chair, gasping out choked answers to the questions his grandfather flung at him from the kitchen, biting down hard on his knuckles to control himself during pauses in the conversation. Soon, however, the old man was roaring that he couldn't hear him, what was he doing in there, come out and make himself understood. It was like trying to listen to a boy with a mouthful of marbles.

Somehow Daniel pulled himself together and returned to the kitchen. What he now saw didn't strike him as funny any longer, just a sorry sight, vaguely disgusting, the white body bloated and sagging underneath a ridiculous hat. Before he could censor himself, Daniel heard himself saying, "Jesus, Alec, if you want to wash all over, whyn't you do it like normal people and take a bath?"

And Alec said stonily, "Because I'm so goddamn old and so goddamn stiff and so goddamn fat I can hardly jack myself up out of a tub anymore. That's why."

Although there were sometimes awkward moments such as that, by and large the two of them got along well enough in the touchy, complaining, grudging fashion usually associated with long-married couples. Lacking any other companions their peculiar partnership had become the centre of their lives. Alec had summarily ordered his old friends, Huff and colleagues, to keep clear of his property following the uproar at Christmas and they had sulkily done so, even when they learned Vera had moved out. Also, Alec's relations with Mr. Stutz were not quite as they once had been. The old man held himself very cool and aloof in Stutz's presence for fear that a heated word might betray how hurt he had been by his friend and employee going behind his back to lend money to his daughter. Now all Alec's natural mischievousness, his desire to get sober Stutz's goat, were suppressed in case his teasing might be interpreted as bitterness or injured pride. He bit his tongue and didn't say, "What's this Stutz? You set on a promotion? Interested in moving from general manager to son-in-law? Interested in buying into the business?" No, following the opening of The

Bluebird the two men treated each other with business-like rectitude. Nor did Mr. Stutz receive any more late-night phone calls from his employer.

Daniel was similarly isolated. Kids might say hello to him on the street but they never bothered to stop and talk. Dancing lessons had not saved him from loneliness; no girl had looked at him and imagined Montgomery Clift. On the other hand, he knew that whatever qualities he owned were not ones to endear him to the boys. He was hopeless at sports, no joker, and too proud to play Tonto to anybody's Lone Ranger.

So that summer Daniel and Alec had their routines and each other. An hour each afternoon was spent pottering in the crazy garden which had sprouted chaotically, rows sown half with one vegetable, half with another, rows sown twice with different vegetables, a thicket of dill bristling in the potato patch because the old man had accidentally spilled a packet of seed there in the spring. Alec wouldn't let Daniel pull it up. He said it never hurt to be reminded of your mistakes. Daniel didn't argue. The garden was his grandfather's business. He directed the boy in weeding, thinning, and hilling, while reserving watering rights for himself. He was never happier than when he plodded about the garden in black, high-topped rubber boots, a hose snaking after him as he sprayed the sweet peas entwined in the chicken-wire fence, doused the bald green heads of the cabbages, shook a shower over the potatoes, or sprinkled the marigolds.

Growth that summer was abundant, lush. There was really no reason to water at all except that it gave the old man pleasure. Rain was plentiful, unlike the previous year when it had been necessary to haul tanks of water from the farm. Spectacular storms often broke late on hot afternoons, black and purple thunderheads swelling on the horizon like bruises, lightning breaking open the sky in jagged, bluish-yellow cracks that spilled down a blur of wild rain and wind. Then stillness, the garden awash in water, the rain barrels foaming and swirling under the drain spouts.

The storms frequently interfered with television signals and the reception of the movie matinee. While the lightning clashed apocalyptically overhead there were arguments about unplugging the set.

"Yeah, if we unplug the set now I'll never find out what happens. Just wait a minute. The movie's almost over."

"It's over now. That goddamn aerial on the roof is no better than a lightning rod, it'll suck the juice right out of the sky and down into the set. That's an RCA there and I don't want the sonofabitch fried. Unplug it."

"What if the aerial gets hit while I'm unplugging the set? Who gets fried then?"

"If you're worried, wear my rubber boots. Come on, quit stalling. Just unplug the sonofabitch."

Staring intently at the screen, doggedly delaying. "You unplug it."

"You want me to shut that set down for the Olympics? That what you want?"

"No."

"Then unplug it. *Now.*"

Daniel slouched sullenly to the TV. "Jesus."

It was a potent threat. For weeks Daniel had been anticipating the Games. Growing more and more excited as publicity and news coverage built, he was given to lecturing his grandfather, passing on with an air of sublime self-importance whatever information he had managed to glean from studies of *Sport* and *Sports Illustrated* in the magazine rack of the drugstore. It was a premeditated attempt to arouse interest in his grandfather so he wouldn't balk at watching a bunch of foreigners competing in sports he didn't understand and probably hadn't even heard of. Perhaps it worked because when the Olympics finally began the old man proved to be a quick sell. He was easily as enthusiastic as his grandson, maybe more so.

For the duration of the Games their routine altered and their days rearranged themselves around the broadcast of Olympic reports. Alec greedily immersed himself in the spectacle, even insisting on watching events that Daniel had trouble considering sports at all: dressage, field hockey, European handball, race-walking, to name a few. The sorts of activities which communists excelled at, but which no self-respecting North American athlete would be caught dead doing. Daniel thought that any sport which required a man to wear tights wasn't a sport at all and as for race-walking, that was a comedy routine.

To make matters worse, his grandfather liked to enliven their viewing by cheering for the Iron Curtain countries. Daniel knew what he was up to, but being a Russian-hater he couldn't help getting hot under the collar when the East bloc won and was applauded by the old man. Just once he wanted to get under his skin the way his grandfather got under his. He tried. Rome was not the only scene of fierce Olympic competition. Daniel had something disparaging to say about every Soviet success.

"There goes another Ivan to get his medal for being best at some pukey sport played by about four people in the whole world. And of the other three who play the dumb sport, likely two of them are Russian anyway."

"Magnificent athletes, the Russians," said his grandfather.

"Whoever heard of this stuff? European *handball*, for chris-sakes. That's a game? And why do we have to play their sports and they don't have to play ours? How come no baseball or football? I'd like to see how they'd do having to play a real game like base-ball or football. Then we'd see."

"Oh," said his grandfather with maddening calmness, "give them a year or two of practice and they'd master that the way they've mastered everything else. Magnificent athletes, the Russians."

They only struck a truce when it came to cheering for the Italians and Canadians; then they found themselves temporarily in the same camp. Both were downcast when Harry Jerome of Canada cramped in the semi-finals of the one hundred metres and had to hobble pitifully off the track. After that happened, despite

268

his protestations of admiration for the Russians, the old man only really cared about the Italians. He liked the way Italians wore their hearts on their sleeves, without excuses, like kids, weeping at a loss, exulting in a victory. He even forgot his fellow-traveller pose in the welter-weight boxing final, cheering Giovanni Benvenuti's win over the Russian Radonyak. When Berruti won the two hundred metres, stylishly insolent in sunglasses, Alec was delighted by the sight of the ecstatic Roman crowd lighting newspapers in the stands and waving them aloft to salute their hero. "Look at those crazy Italian buggers," he said, shaking his head at the carnival, "having themselves a time like a bunch of kids."

Today they are watching Olympic officials in white suits and white fedoras sort and organize runners for the marathon. Alec has never heard of a marathon and Daniel is passing on to him whatever he has learned from his reading of *Sports Illustrated*. He speaks reverently of Emil Zátopek, most famous previous winner of the 26 mile, 385 yard race. At first his grandfather refuses to believe it possible, that human beings could, or would, run such a distance, but Daniel keeps assuring him that it is true, that the spare, sinewy men with hollowed cheeks who are nervously shuffling their feet and prancing on the spot are prepared to race each other over all those punishing miles.

"This I've got to see," says Alec in disbelief. "Why, that's further than Hyacinth," he remarks, naming a town down the line. "And why 26 miles and 385 yards? Why those extra yards? Is it because somebody once survived the 26 miles and they needed those 385 yards to finish him off? If you wanted to race horses that far the SPCA would have you up on cruelty to animal charges."

The announcer seems to view the race in a similar light. His preamble is full of words like pain, courage, suffering, endurance. He speaks of a marathoner arriving at that stage in a race when the body's resources are utterly depleted and the runner's muscles, sapped, function on will alone. As he talks, the cameras sweep over the drawn, anxious faces of the race favourites, pausing briefly for a moment to dwell on an oddity, a slight, grave black man who, it is announced, has inexplicably chosen to run the marathon in bare feet. The announcer states his opinion that no matter how unaccustomed to footwear this primitive African might be – an Ethiopian in Emperor Haile Selassie's bodyguard named Abebe Bikila – he is making a serious miscalculation choosing to run barefoot. The cobble-stoned streets of Rome that make up part of the route will be considerably less forgiving to his feet than the highland meadows around Addis Ababa where he is accustomed to train.

Yet at the six and a half mile mark of the race the Ethiopian can be found in the leading group of runners. Monkman can't believe their pace and predicts they'll never maintain it. "They'll never hold it," he says, "never." Six miles further on Rhadi the Moroccan and the barefoot Ethiopian surge away from the pack, Rhadi in front and Bikila poised at his shoulder, running relentlessly and mechanically like a wind-up toy, bringing Daniel and his grandfather to the edge of their seats, leaning forward toward the screen. The elapsed time is announced as sixty-two minutes, thirty-nine seconds and his grandfather excitedly urges Daniel to find a pencil and paper and compute exactly how fast the two leaders are running. Daniel has never seen him this excited, crouched in his chair, hands rubbing his kneecaps, eyes welded to the television and its fleeting figures, the old man is utterly enthralled by the drama. Before Daniel completes his calculation the television reports that Rhadi and Bikila are covering one mile approximately every five minutes.

"That can't be right. Is that right?" his grandfather demands without shifting his eyes from the TV.

Daniel gives a flick of the pencil on the sheet of paper and confirms it. "Yes," he says, "that's about right."

"How do they keep going?" asks the old man softly.

At the twenty-two-mile mark Bikila spurts past the Moroccan bringing Alec out of his chair and onto his feet. Alec jabs a forefinger at the figure on the television, pumps his shoulder, *"Run you black bastard!"* he exults. *"Run!"* Stabbing his finger at the runner on the screen as if it were a prod. Daniel glances up at his grandfather and feels a slight alarm. Alec, swaying, has to reach out and steady himself with the chair back. The old man's eyes are burning.

Now the Ethiopian is in first place and Rhadi pursuing. The camera fixes on the rigid, determined mask of Bikila's face, sweeps down for a shot of naked feet skimming above and whispering on the pavement. Twilight lowers on the city and the little man forges on through the waning light, seemingly blind to the cheering crowds thickening along the race route. He looks to neither side, refuses blueberry juice and glucose offered from a refreshment station, simply runs on. The old man knows this is proper, this is how it must be. Bare feet and unslaked thirst.

Alec wishes he could watch the black man run forever. But Abebe crosses the finish line and the spell is broken. Then it is over for both of them. Bikila waves away the blanket race officials press on him. This too seems correct to Alec. As the tension drains from his body Bikila begins to laugh, then suddenly his laughter becomes tears and he weeps like a broken man. Monkman feels his own eyes filling. The winning time, two hours, fifteen minutes, sixteen and two-tenths seconds, is announced. The old man asks Daniel to write it down for him, carefully folds the paper the boy gives him, and slips it into his wallet, declaring to Daniel that he ought to remember this moment, they've just seen the toughest man in all the Olympics.

Daniel, desiring to get his own back for the Russians, says that is ridiculous. Come on, tougher than the boxers?

But the old man doesn't trouble to answer his challenge. He seems to have slipped off in one of his trances again, wallet lying open in his lap.

In September the Games ended, leaving behind a legacy. Daniel got the idea he would turn himself into a distance runner. He had never been much good at sports but distance running appeared to him mostly a matter of training and will. All that was necessary was to harden his body until it was capable of stubbornly doing its duty. Maybe he couldn't run fast but he might learn to run hard and long, harder and longer than the talented ones who hit and caught balls effortlessly. Best of all, he could learn to do this in secret, on his own. He took a grim, sweet delight pushing his body until it hurt and thinking of spring and track season and the surprise he would have in store for them all then. It was like a story in a boys' book, he imagined the end of the race and Biff or Todd, somebody with that kind of name, somebody who hadn't thought him much at all, coming up to congratulate him, saying "I didn't think you had it in you. But say, Danny, you're all right!"

Daniel had no real idea how to train. He simply laid out a course and, each time he ran it, tried to run it faster than the last time. Afraid of being seen and laughed at, he waited until dusk to train and took an added precaution. He ran in blue jeans rather than shorts, so if anyone noticed him he would not be a runner – only a boy happening to run.

Alec became his timer. Each night when twilight fell his grandfather packed his captain's chair out onto the front lawn and settled himself into it with his wristwatch nestled in his palm. Daniel had asked him if it was necessary to make himself so conspicuous but the old man said, Yes, it was. If Daniel wanted an accurate timing the timer had to be exactly flush with the finish line which was the north corner of the house. He needn't think he was going to wait on him standing, not with his legs. Consider his age.

They estimated the route to be approximately three miles. The highway which led west out of Connaught made the first side of the loop and if Daniel encountered a car approaching there, he slowed to a walk as soon as the headlights picked him up. When the car passed, he resumed running. At first he hadn't bothered to slacken his pace when he met a vehicle but this had caused people to stop their cars and ask, Did he need assistance, had there been an accident? Answering such inquiries had been embarrassing so now he went along at a jerky, impatient walk until the coast was clear again.

A mile outside of town a grid road crossed the highway and Daniel turned left onto it. His passage down this deserted stretch of road launched a flock of mallards from a slough and flung them in relief against the sky, stroking their way across the cool, impassive disc of the risen moon. Ahead he could see the railway crossing sign standing stark before a pale horizon floating above darker, settled earth. Daniel always returned home on the railway embankment. Cinders made for a difficult footing. Panting, he slipped and lurched, torturing ankles and shins, but on the embankment there was no traffic to contend with and at this point in his run he knew that if he was forced to walk he would never be able to pick up the pace again. So he slogged on resolutely to the beads of glowing lights which spelled Connaught, and when he reached the first streetlight swerved abruptly down from the embankment, plunged recklessly down the slope in a rattle of cinders, and sped across the brightly illuminated street into the shielding darkness of the alley running behind the main street.

It was full dark at present, the shade had come down upon the window. His breath sawed rustily in his chest, his sneakers slapped noisily in the narrow passage. He ran unheeding past where the yellow brick wall carved with his uncle's name stood obscured in darkness.

Bursting out of the throat of the alley into his grandfather's street he knew he had only two more blocks to go. Nothing must be held back, kept in reserve now. His mouth hung slack and loose, rhythmically gasping with each jolt of his legs.

The old man waits for his grandson in the chair. He holds a flash-light on the face of the wristwatch. While waiting he thinks about the black man and the endless race. He remembers best when the black man ran entirely alone. It grew dark and soldiers lit his way, holding flaming torches in upraised hands, high above their heads. The black man went deaf past the cheering crowds, sightless past the Roman ruins, the ancient broken walls, the carved gravestones, the headless, armless statues. The torches flickered and smoked, the flames nodded and bent in his draught as he went past, blind or indifferent to the women in dark, shapeless clothes who knelt and crossed themselves to ward off suffering as it crossed their path.

19

What's the point? Vera sometimes asks herself when she feels most discouraged and neglected. Why not just stop in bed, pull the covers over my head, and let the damn kid have his wish and roll into hell on a handcart. Because without me watching him he'll betray all that is finest in him, all that he inherited of Stanley's nature. Let him slap me in the face if he cares to, but not his father. Not Stanley.

You tell yourself it's just a stage he's in and not really personal. After twelve or thirteen years of living something happens in a kid's head – all of a sudden there's not another soul in the universe to consider but himself. Might be I was the same, although I can't remember it was so long ago.

What would he miss first, me or dinner? Didn't Stutz look the other day when I said, "If I was lying dead on the floor between him and the TV I swear he'd vault over the corpse to switch it on and never turn a hair." "Now Vera," said Stutz.

That goddamn television. It's all I heard about all blessed summer. TV, TV, TV. Always with the complaining how he was so hard done by to have to go without. Again the only soul in the universe. Quite the performance seeing as he wasn't missing much of it sitting over at the old fellow's every afternoon, staring at the screen. I'm proud of myself that I never so much as dropped a hint I knew – which wasn't an easy thing to do with him giving himself away every time he opened his mouth. Right under my nose arguing with Stutz as to which was the better program, Tennessee Ernie's or "Peter Gunn." Wasn't I sorely tempted to put him the question: "How is it you're the big expert on Peter Gunn when we don't own a television to watch it on?" But I didn't.

And I didn't buy the television to compete with anybody either. That wasn't it at all. In any case, trying to keep him away from that old bugger is like trying to keep a wasp out of jam. Try too hard and you're liable to get stung.

A sensible person would have given the television money to Stutz against the loan, but you think, What the hell have I been able to give the kid in the last ten years? Food and clothes and me, which strictly speaking doesn't add up to entertainment. And figuring we practically live in The Bluebird, where else would I put it except here? Naturally, Daniel would prefer to have it at home. Now why's that? Because if he claims to be watching television at home, how am I to know if he is or not, with him there and me here? He and the old charmer could be sitting thick as thieves and me without a clue, an inkling. Not on your life, Mother Brown.

What I'd like to say to Daniel is this: Don't go making the mistake of thinking you're something special to him. Everybody's had their turn at that – me, Earl – and what did it ever come to? He's old and there's nobody else for him but you because the rest of us ran away to save whatever we could before he'd used us all up. I wouldn't wish that feeling on my worst enemy, let alone you. So don't flatter yourself when you're no more than a convenience.

The trouble with truth is it's cruel. That's why nobody can bring themselves to tell it and I can't neither. He's never heard the word convenience out of my mouth.

And then he has the gall to tell me I never bought the television for him anyway. No, I bought it for myself and for the customers.

"We wouldn't have got a TV," he says, "if Kennedy wasn't running for president. And the reason you set it up in The Bluebird was so you could see him every night on the six o'clock news. And now those dumb Portuguese couldn't live without watching 'The Roy Rogers Show' five nights a week while they wait for their supper. If you moved it out now, they'd riot."

The resentment in his voice when he said that, where'd it come from? Patience is supposed to be the cure for what ails them, so I was patient. Didn't I explain how, this being an election year in the U.S., a person could learn a lot about world affairs watching the news and hearing the candidates discuss the issues? Kind of a practical education. "You're getting to an age where you ought to be paying attention to these sorts of things. They're talking about your future," I told him.

All he said was, "I like Nixon."

I gave up and went to scrub potatoes in the kitchen then. Retreat so's you live to fight another day. It's hard to blame the kid when Stutz is as bad, an encouragement to him really. He hasn't got a good word to say about the Senator either. Of course, Stutz being the sort of religious he is, the Senator's being Catholic is no incentive. Tolerance was always a watchword with Stanley, and I tried to show Stutz that he had a prejudice but he couldn't bring himself to agree. Never mind that after the first debate he as much as said that if you elect the Senator you're mailing America parcel post to the Pope. "Change all the menus, it's fish on Fridays for everybody," he says. Considers it the height of wit to call the Pope "Big John" and the Senator "Little John." It gets on your nerves after a while, a person with one joke.

The problem is that the Senator's got too much class for the likes of Connaught to appreciate. I said as much to Stutz. "Yes," he shoots back. "Class spelled M-O-N-E-Y." You know exactly what kind of individual you're dealing with when they confuse the two. Stanley always knew the difference. Say with Roosevelt, who wasn't exactly a rag-picker. I looked Stutz straight in the eye and said, "Don't talk to me about class. Class around Connaught is when a man doesn't wear brown shoes with a blue suit."

How's Stutz expect to win an argument with me when he doesn't have the facts? Me, I've got them cold. "Look," I told him, "Senator Kennedy's been to Harvard and Princeton, the best colleges in America – ask anybody, it's public knowledge they are – and one in England besides, the name of which I don't recall offhand. He's a war hero and he reads 1,200 words a minute – about a thousand more than you do in a year. He's visited thirty-seven countries and wrote a book that won the Pulitzer Prize. And look, just look at that wife of his. They say she speaks five languages and buys her clothes in Paris. It isn't any ordinary dope that attracts a wife such as that. Like attracts like."

When I was Daniel's age I was going to speak French. Now there's nothing left but *Je ne sais quoi. Quelle heure est-il?* Not enough for a conversation with Jacqueline Bouvier Kennedy. Not enough for a conversation with a dark, sophisticated man on the deck of an ocean liner.

She's a beauty, that Jackie Kennedy. Even pregnant she's beautiful, which is a feat. It's how you can judge if a woman is *really* beautiful, if she can hold onto her beauty six months gone. Then the good bones and breeding shine through. Me, I was never happier in my life than I was six months pregnant, my feet disappearing underneath me, ankles like an elephant's. But beautiful I wasn't. Now I'm sorry I wouldn't let Stanley take my picture. "Next time, next baby," I said. "I'll improve with practice."

What gets to me is nobody around here is smart enough to recognize what's truly beautiful. In particular the men. Big tits is their idea of beautiful. Ask a man in this dismal hole to name a beautiful woman and nine times out of ten you'll get Marilyn Monroe. A person shudders to think that their kid will grow up no different. Not that I expect Daniel to marry a Jackie Kennedy. I'm not that far gone. Just so's it isn't some doll who wears too much make-up, tight skirts, and owns a pair of pointy boobs that look like they're trying to drill their way out of a pink angora sweater. All I ask is for her to be good enough for him and not so good that she doesn't want to have anything to do with me. Amen.

Still, the rumour is that Papa Joe Kennedy isn't cut from the finest glass himself. You have to hand it to the old Paddy sonofabitch, he saw to it that his boys were an improvement on him. Which is all I aim for. I take heart when I see what can be done when you put your mind to it. Love conquers all. Not one of those Kennedy boys can't pass for the finest Irish crystal – Waterford, no less.

Which must make it kind of disheartening for a father when he sees those brainless women carrying on over his boy, misjudging the Senator for a movie star instead of a future president. Old Joe didn't raise him to be Errol Flynn, did he? The reporters have a name for them – jumpers. The double-jumpers are the ones holding the babies. They ought to have their heads examined, bouncing up and down on tiptoes, jiggling, squealing. It's enough to give us all a bad name. Worst of all, men like to see it. A certain kind of smile will pass over Stutz's face when he sees them hopping all over the TV. Deep down, he has it figured for sex, even in my case. Let him suppose what he supposes. Nobody imagines a person like me can believe in the higher, finer things. My friend Pooch certainly didn't. That time I made the mistake of letting down my guard and talking of Stanley, what did she say? "Rub your eyes, Vera. Nothing could ever have been like you say, that good. How long were you married? Less than two years, right? Trust Pooch, who knows whereof she speaks, two years is as long as the warranty lasts and then something is sure to break. Money troubles, he starts running around, something. Seems to me that what you've been admiring all these years isn't a husband but a character out of a book. Either way, he's dead or never was. A ghost."

She had no notion whereof she spoke. She never even met Stanley.

I've lived most of my life with the feeling that I missed the important things by a breath, an inch. Daniel isn't going to. That's why I try to point him in the right direction every chance I get. "The Senator is a man you can look up to and admire," I said to him. "A man like your father was. A scholar and a gentleman. The type of man who can be an inspiration to you."

And he laughs at me and says, "Let him be your inspiration, Nixon's my man."

You can lead a horse to water but you can't make him drink. Of course, if nobody shows him the trough then he's done for. He didn't want to sit through that first debate with me but I made him, the two of us side by side in the restaurant on counter stools. You can't tell me he didn't see Nixon all shifty-eyed like a door-to-door salesman asked to show his business licence. Yet when it's all over and I ask him what he thought, he says, "Couple of times it looked to me like Kennedy was lying."

He can't fool me. Deep down inside he's his father through and through.

Old Joe Kennedy says he never interferes with what the Senator thinks. Regardless, I don't doubt he gets the Senator to where the Senator doesn't know he's going. That's love, too, in a good cause.

20

———◆———

A cheerless Saturday morning in October found Daniel standing beside his grandfather's pickup in a windy street, waiting for the old man to come out of his house. With each new gust the wind seemed to gather strength, setting all the naked elms which lined Monkman's street swaying and creaking faintly. By nightfall their broken branches would litter the road. On Main Street, the tin store signs flapped and clanged as clouds of grit were driven down its length with the force of buckshot, pinging softly wherever they struck glass. Overhead the sky was streaked like a river heavy with silt, murky with the dust swept up from farmers' fields and scurried into the heavens. A blanched, fuzzy sun tried to break out from behind this dirty grey curtain.

Daniel, shivering, leaned his back into the wind, wobbling indecisively on his heels when he lost his balance in its violent fluctuations. Every now and then he blew on his numb red fingers and then drew them up inside the sleeves of his jacket. Underneath the jacket he was wearing a white shirt and tie as his grandfather had requested.

He wondered if maybe being so nervous made him feel the cold more. There were times – if he was really nervous – that he shivered in a perfectly warm room. Now he trembled like a leaf thinking about how he was going to tell Alec it was out of the question, there was no way he was going to do what he wanted. It wasn't so very long ago that he had stepped out of his grandfather's house and into the windy street in the hope that he would find there the courage to say what had to be said. He hadn't though.

Now he repeatedly and impatiently glanced at the front door, wanting his grandfather to make an appearance so he would be forced to settle it. When Daniel had left him over a quarter of an hour ago, his grandfather had promised to be right out. So where the hell was he? Dawdling and pottering, most likely. Checking all the lights and the burners on the stove for the tenth time, looking for the cigarettes or matches he had mislaid. He was getting to be a proper pain in the ass to get moving, apt to lose track of time and things, speedy as a drugged snail. Hurry up for chrissakes, don't you know it's cold enough to freeze the balls off a brass monkey out here?

Daniel had debated climbing into the cab of the truck where he would be warmer out of the wind, but he worried he would feel trapped again, like he had in the house. He was still convinced it was wiser to break the news to his grandfather out in the street, rather than inside the house, or inside the truck where the old man had a chance to corner him. Inside anywhere Alec might be tough to escape. But out in the street if the old boy started to argue and kick up a fuss all Daniel had to do was turn away and walk off in any direction. That was his right, wasn't it? There was nothing that said he had to go along with every crazy idea the old bugger dreamed up, was there?

When his grandfather had raised the matter nine or ten days ago, Daniel had naturally assumed he was speaking of some time in the far distant future, not thinking in terms of weeks or even days. He remembered how and when Alec had broached the topic because it was at an historic moment, only minutes after Bill Mazeroski had homered in the last half of the ninth inning to give the Pirates a ten-nine win and the World Series. Daniel was still crowing in triumph over the two dollars his grandfather had handed him to settle their World Series bet when Alec suddenly said: "I been thinking – some time you and me ought to take a trip."

"Why not?" Daniel, vindicated, grinned delightedly. It wasn't just the two dollars which had put him in a good mood, it was also coming out on top for once. He had finally got the better of him. The old bugger's jaw muscles had locked when he saw that rocket from Mazeroski's bat go sailing over the fence. For a second he looked like a man pissing ground glass. Tough titty.

"A long trip," his grandfather qualified.

"The longer the better," said Daniel.

"Of course, with my eyes the way they are lately," said Alec, "you'd have to do the driving. Be my chauffeur."

His pronunciation made Daniel smile. Chuffer, he'd said. Be my chuffer. "I'm your man," Daniel agreed. "The two of us'll see the world together. You and me."

"Good," said Alec, nodding his head. "Good."

Nothing more had been mentioned until several days later when Alec began to think aloud in Daniel's presence. "I guess it would have to be on a Saturday," he mused, "when you don't have school?"

Daniel didn't have a clue to what he was referring. "What would have to be on a Saturday?"

"The day we take our trip – it would have to be on a Saturday, wouldn't it?" asked the old man earnestly. It was his earnest air which led Daniel to suspect a joke. His grandfather was always particularly, devoutly earnest when he argued that pro wrestling was on the up and up.

"For sure a Saturday," said Daniel, assuming an equally serious manner. "Even a globe trotter like me can't afford to miss school."

In the next few days Daniel watched his grandfather's prank grow more elaborate and detailed. Alec related his plans to make the truck roadworthy for a long trip. It needed an oil change and wheel alignment and while it was in the garage he might as well put new tires on all around, didn't Daniel think? Daniel soberly thought and agreed. Two could play this game. Yes, by all means, tires all around. And his grandfather went off, pretending to order it done.

On Thursday, however, when his grandfather had set their departure for eight o'clock Saturday morning, and issued directions as to how Daniel was to dress for the trip, the boy experienced a pang of uncertainty. But reason urged him to dismiss it and he did. In the past his grandfather might have allowed him to pilot the truck on country backroads where cops never patrolled and traffic was virtually non-existent, but he had more sense than to encourage an unlicenced thirteen year old to venture out on the highways. Daniel's height alone would make him conspicuous behind the wheel. The RCMP would stop and charge them before they made fifty miles.

Daniel, with spiralling anxiety, wished his grandfather would give up his practical joke. But there were no signs he was ready to relent, not even when Daniel provided him with opportunities to make a clean breast of it. When Daniel had asked: "So where are we going Saturday, on this big trip of ours?" his grandfather had replied: "Saturday's soon enough to know. Marching orders issued Saturday." Then, with hesitation. "You haven't said a word to *her* now, have you?"

Daniel had sworn he hadn't.

Putting on a white shirt and tie this morning, as his grandfather had told him he must, was part of Daniel's attempt to turn the tables on Alec. Hoist him with his own petard, as Mr. Gibson who taught Shakespeare was fond of saying. If that old fart thought he was going to have a good laugh at Daniel's expense, tricking him into a white shirt, a tie, and expectations of a trip, he'd better think again. Because how would Alec feel if, rather than going all foolish and sheepish at falling for a practical joke, instead Daniel went all downcast and heart-broken?

Alec might learn that there was more than one actor in this

family. *Oh, how could you play such a mean trick when you knew how I was looking forward to this? he'd accuse him mournfully. It's a pretty raw deal, if you ask me, to raise a person's hopes way up and then crush them.*

He'd feel King Shit of Turd Island then, wouldn't he?

And the bonus would be beating the old bugger twice in less than ten days. First the World Series, then giving him a dose of his own brand of mischief. He who laughs last, laughs best.

Yet this morning it had only taken Daniel a minute to realize the mistake was his. His grandfather really *did* expect them to leave on a trip within the hour. For Alec it was no joke, but a certainty, real. There he was, all in a fuss in his Sunday best, a wrinkled, dark blue suit. "There's something else," he kept muttering to himself as he quick-shuffled his feet from room to room. "Just hold your horses. It won't take me but a second to find it once I think of it." Daniel couldn't take his eyes from the huge black oxfords which Alec dragged back and forth on the linoleum. He could see his grandfather had made a disastrous attempt at polishing the shoes. His eyesight must be as bad as he claimed because there were thick dabs and crumbs of polish stuck like mud to the oxfords, which left a dull, streaky finish.

Suddenly the old man brought himself up short, frozen in the effort to recollect what was nagging at him. Grandfather and grandson stood face to face. The boy glimpsed a series of black smudges all down Alec's white shirt front, fingerprints left behind when he did up his buttons with shoe polish sticking to his fingers.

He's dotty, thought Daniel.

A surge of blood chased this unbidden thought and heated his face. It was then he rushed off outside, to wait in the street and consider what he must do.

There was no longer any question that Alec meant what he said. The truck was the clincher. In all the time Daniel had known him his grandfather had never once washed or cleaned the truck. This morning it gleamed, even under the muddy sky. Months, maybe years, of mud and dust had been hosed and scrubbed from fenders and door panels. His grandfather would never have carried any joke that far. Never.

Every few seconds Daniel cast an apprehensive eye at the house. What in Christ was keeping him? It had been almost twenty minutes. Then the door opened and Daniel could guess the reason for the delay.

His grandfather forged his way down the walk, swerving unsteadily from side to side as he was buffeted by the wind, his suit jacket tail whipping and flickering out behind him, his left hand grimly pinning his hat to his head. Held tightly in his right fist an enormous bouquet of artificial flowers he had spent the last quarter of an hour turning the house upside down for wildly fluttered and flaunted their blooms in the gale. Mrs. Harding, the beautician famous for her useful hobbies, whom he had appealed to when he realized that all his own flowers were brown and withered in the garden, was much celebrated for her skill at manufacturing paper flowers to decorate wedding cars, high school graduation exercises, and anniversary parties. The bouquet Alec bore was testimony to her floral artistry. For him she had created three dozen red crêpe-paper poppies tastefully set off by contrasting Kleenex carnations in pink, yellow, and white. Each of Mrs. Harding's flowers was furnished with wire coat-hanger stems wrapped in green tape.

Daniel's need to purge himself of his bad news made him rude and abrupt. No sooner had his grandfather reached the truck than Daniel lunged forward at him, desperately shouting, "I can't go. Forget it. There's no way I can go. Just forget this trip, okay?" But his words were drowned in the roar of the wind, scattered harmless down the street.

"What?" shouted back Alec. "What?" He went to cup his hand behind his ear but when it came up full of artificial flowers, confounded he had to let it fall back down to his side. He leaned forward and tried to tip his head to better catch what his grandson had to say. When he did, the wind curled up his hat brim and the fedora shuddered, threatening to take flight.

"I can't go on any trip with you!" cried Daniel, going up on tiptoe so that he was shouting directly into his grandfather's face. Still, his grandfather couldn't grasp what he said. The old man shook his head and gestured impatiently toward the truck, waving the bouquet. "You'll have to get out of this wind! I can't make out a goddamn thing you say!" he bellowed, jerking open the passenger door and clambering into the cab. Daniel was left no alternative except to crawl in on the driver's side, where he didn't want to be. He slammed the door and sat clenching the steering wheel while the old man fussily arranged the gaudy, showy abundance of the bouquet on the seat beside him. What was he doing with pretend flowers? Could it be that the old fart was angling to pay a visit to some woman? Daniel found the notion pretty disgusting. Yet he knew it was possible. One of Pooch Gardiner's admirers had been nearly as old as his grandfather. Old Softy was Lyle's nickname for him.

It seemed to have slipped his grandfather's mind that Daniel had something to say to him. He was lost in sorting through his flowers, examining them for damage and carefully setting aside any whose petals had been torn by the wind.

"I can't go on any trip with you," said Daniel. His voice, pitched to overcome wind, was much too loud for the small space and quiet of the cab. "I just can't," he added, dropping his voice.

Monkman did not lift his eyes from the flowers. Only a pause in the sorting signalled he had heard his grandson. A white carnation hung still in his fingers. He twirled the stem and the bloom spun. "We aren't going too far," he said.

Daniel, his eyes fastened on the dizzy blur of spinning white, was tempted to say, *We* aren't going anywhere. Instead, he asked, "How far is not too far?"

"A hundred and ten, maybe a hundred and twenty miles one way."

"On the highway?"

"On the highway," confirmed Alec quietly. He glanced up at the boy for the first time.

The undisguised, naked eagerness Daniel encountered in his grandfather's face caused him to lower his eyes. "I can't drive on the highway without a licence," he said. "The police would arrest us."

His grandfather's failure to agree, his silence, condemned Daniel. Guiltily, the boy could feel Alec's eyes crawling up the back of his neck. He struck out angrily. "Where do you get such a god-damn stupid idea! Expecting I could drive you so far! I couldn't manage it. I'd likely kill us and somebody else too! You've got no business asking me to do it! What got into you? You ought to know better. You want to get us both into serious trouble?"

The only reply to this outburst was the dry stirring and rustling of paper. Daniel threw a furtive, sidelong look in the old man's direction and discovered that he was gathering all the artificial flowers into his lap. They lay in a profuse, tangled heap across his thighs, a drift of blossoms banked against the bulge of his belly.

Alec, when he detected Daniel spying on him, said with dignity, "You promised."

"I thought it was a joke. Honest I did."

"You promised, and I got nobody else to take me."

"There's always Stutz," suggested the boy.

"Stutz," said his grandfather, scorn surfacing in his voice. "Stutz's kept busy acting as banker and handyman to your mother. He's got no time for me. No, I'll leave Stutz to the kind of company he prefers."

His stubbornness only succeeded in exasperating Daniel. "I don't get it," he said sharply "Where is it that you've got to go all of a sudden? What is it you've got to see? And what're you doing with those stupid-looking flowers? Who are they for? You got a ladyfriend or something?"

"Earl," said Alec. "The flowers are for Earl."

Daniel's surprise at this answer drove any other questions out of his head for the moment. In the ensuing silence he became aware of the ferocity of the wind's assault upon the truck – he could feel it rocking and jarring beneath him. The sloppy swaying of the chassis and the intense, fixed gaze of his grandfather through the windshield produced a queer sensation in the boy; he fell prey to the illusion that the truck was actually travelling down a road he could not see, a road hidden from him but clear and plain to his grandfather's staring eyes.

Unable to understand what he had been told, Daniel asked, doubtfully, "Earl? Do you mean to say you want to take these flowers to Earl?"

"Yes," said Alec. His eyes remained trained down the long, straight street. "That's right. To Earl."

Daniel was confused. He tried to remember how his grandfather had answered his last questions as to Uncle Earl's whereabouts. Finding his Uncle Earl's name scratched on the yellow wall had made Daniel curious about him. He had wondered if it wasn't possible that the two of them, uncle and nephew, might not share some profound family resemblance. Daniel could recognize little of himself in either his mother or grandfather, and the desire to find himself in another was strong. For a time he had been full of questions about Earl, questions that his grandfather seemed to wish to avoid answering. The last thing he had learned about Earl was that he was in the States, working on an oil-drilling rig. That was what his grandfather had told him.

"So Earl's back?" Daniel inquired innocently. "Back in Canada?"

The old man's head snapped furiously around.

"Back?" His voice was grating, harsh. "What the fuck are you talking about? What the fuck are you talking about – back? Earl's dead. He's dead."

It sounded like an accusation. As if his grandfather was accusing *him*, Daniel, of murdering Earl. But what he was saying had to be wrong. "Dead?" said Daniel. "He can't be dead." Then a possibility struck him. "Has there been an accident? Tell me, did Uncle Earl have an accident on his drilling rig?"

"He's been dead since July 21, 1948," said the old man in a dull voice, spent now of its earlier fury, earlier passion.

"What're you talking about, dead since then?" demanded Daniel fearfully. Was his grandfather really crazy? "Not Earl. You don't mean Earl. You've mixed him up with somebody else. Maybe somebody whose name sounds like his. Talk sense. Think. Just a couple of months ago you said he was working in the States. That's what you told me, didn't you? Well, didn't you?"

"It was July 21, 1948 Earl died," said his grandfather wearily. "Died in that goddamn hospital full of nurses and doctors and not one of them – not one – ever did him an ounce of good. I should have kept him at home for all the good was ever done him there."

"But that can't be!" Daniel objected, incredulous. "That was twelve years ago. Twelve years? I mean –" he fumbled, attempting to express himself, "I mean people aren't dead twelve years and nobody knows."

"Stutz knows. I know. Now you do, too."

But Daniel didn't want to know. Not this. "It's crazy what you're saying. How could Mom not know? His own sister. His own sister would have to know. She'd *have* to know."

"I don't quite understand how it happened myself," said his grandfather quietly. "I didn't plan it. One thing led to another and somehow it got away on me, I couldn't turn back. It started the summer – it was the summer Earl came down with his nervous trouble – I mean to say, well, his nerves got bad and they said he'd have to go away to the hospital. Stutz and me figured at most he'd be gone a couple of weeks, no more, that they'd get him rested up and we'd have him home again in no time. So I didn't see any point in upsetting your mother with that kind of news. Especially as we looked on it as . . . as temporary, I didn't think she'd ever need to hear about it. Anyway, well," he said, stumbling as he explained himself, "if she heard how it was with Earl she was likely to put the blame on me for it. Your mother and I weren't on the best of terms at any rate, so I didn't think there was any percentage in stirring things up. Let sleeping dogs lie, I thought to myself.

"The problem with all my figuring was that Earl was gone a long time longer than I had counted on. The thing was – he'd stopped talking. The doctors in that place were determined to get him talking, but no dice, he wouldn't. Mostly he just sat. He sat through the fall and he sat through the winter and he sat through the spring and not a word out of him. The fucking doctors couldn't fix him. Then come summer in that place he came down with the other – the spinal meningitis. How was it he caught a disease in a hospital where nobody was really sick? They couldn't explain that one to me. Had an explanation for everything else wrong with him but not for that.

"Then he talked – with the spinal meningitis he talked. The doctors couldn't make him talk but the meningitis could. Fever had him talking the whole of the day before he died. It isn't something I care to remember . . . him talking in this stuffy little room with the flies buzzing and dancing against the window screen and the meningitis curling him up on the sheet. He just curled and curled like something drying up maybe, a leaf or something. And there was a smell in the room, I remember this smell – and somebody shouting down the hallway and Earl curling up."

He stopped, rubbed his forehead slowly and deliberately with his fingertips. "Stutz had to take me out when he died. It was me shouting then. By Christ, yes. I was telling those doctor bastards what I thought. Shouting how come it was that you went into their hospital with one thing and went out in a box with another." He laughed bitterly. "Oh yes, I had plenty to tell *them*. It was different when it came to your mother. I had nothing to say to her. How was it going to look me not notifying her of how things had stood with her brother for eleven months and then suddenly writing that he was dead, all the how and when and where of it? All of that which has to be explained at such a time. Because people are full of questions then, it's natural. I knew she'd never forgive me, that it would finish it with us. I kept thinking that if I could get face to face with her then I could explain it the way I couldn't in a letter, make her see that I meant the best for him, did my best for him – that it wasn't my fault.

"Because I *did* do my best for him," said Alec, beginning to speak more emphatically. "It's God's truth that I did. I visited him once a week over bad roads in every kind of weather – a hundred and twenty miles there and a hundred and twenty miles back. I made sure they kept him nice in there. Every visit I brought him a new shirt, or pants, or sweater, or shoes. Something so he'd know. And I kept bringing them until the doctors and nurses said I should stop. That's why I quit it. They said it was making the other patients jealous how he was dressed. It was causing trouble. They had started stealing his things, or maybe he was giving them away. Two of them dividing up his clothes had got in a fight. I seen the doctors' point. What they said was true, I suppose. I seen it myself, a fellow walking around on the ward bold as brass in a shirt I'd bought for Earl. Earl's shirt he was walking around in.

"But the thing is . . . the thing is I never got a chance to explain to your mother how it was because she never came home. So there I was, lying. And the longer the lying went on, the harder I knew it was going to be to tell her. For all those years I carried it, and then the two of you came home to me and when I finally came face to face with your mother I could see it was no good. I saw there was no explanation she would accept after all that time. Whatever I said would only push us farther apart." He dropped his voice. "So I didn't say nothing. I kept quiet."

Daniel shifted on the truck seat, cleared his throat. "So if Earl's dead, where is he?"

The old man roused himself, blinked his eyes. "Beg pardon?"

"So where is he – Earl?"

"There's a graveyard on the hospital grounds," said the old

man matter-of-factly. "He's buried there." Monkman knew how that must sound to the boy, hard, unfeeling. He also knew it was beyond his power to explain why he had done what he had done. There could be no putting into words what had prompted his decision not to bring Earl home for burial. Part of it had been not knowing whether he possessed the strength to see the boy lying beside his mother, beside Martha. Seeing that would have made his losses somehow crueller, unbearable. But there was more to it than even that reluctance. There was the trick, the game he had already started to play with himself. If Earl's grave was not in Connaught, reminding him, it might be possible to imagine him some place far away like Vera was, not forever lost but capable of someday finding his way home like Vera could.

If the old man could not entirely correct the impression his bald statement about Earl's burial had left with the boy, at least he could try to soften it. "That's what I had in mind for you today," he continued, "to show you where Earl is. It's been a while since I was there. . . ." Faltering, he broke off and tried another tack. "I had these flowers made special for him," he declared, staring down at his lap. "Flowers for winter," he explained, "they don't freeze." Alec lifted his eyes to the dirty dishwater sky. "It won't be long now before the snow flies. I ought to get my garden cleared. . . ." He lost the thought, the sentence trailed away. He began again. Daniel sensed his effort to concentrate, to speak firmly. "I thought you would take me," he said, "and that I could show you where he is, so when the time comes you can tell your mother."

"What do you mean when the time comes?"

His grandfather tried to smile but only succeeded in baring his false teeth in a disturbing grimace. "Maybe you haven't noticed but I'm no spring chicken. I'm getting on. While I'm still alive I don't want your mother to know any of this, but after – well, she has to finally know, doesn't she? And another thing, I've been thinking Earl ought to be brought home. You can tell her that for me, can't you? Tell her to bring Earl home. She's been left most everything I got so she can afford it. Tell her to bring him home, won't you?"

Hearing him beg made Daniel uncomfortable. "Stutz knows all this stuff," he said uneasily. "Let Stutz tell her. Why do you want to get me involved in all of this? I've got enough trouble of my own with her. I don't need any of this shit."

His grandfather went on doggedly pressuring him. "No," he said. "This is family. It's for the three of us to settle. I want you to settle it for me, Daniel. Would you do that? I want you to promise me you'll tell her – but not before time. Remember, not before time. I've got to know in my mind it's taken care of. Promise."

The way he was carrying on, Daniel didn't see he had any choice but to promise. Seeing the old man in such a helpless state was upsetting. Yet it made him angry, too, because this was not a kid's business. What right did he have foisting it off on him? It felt like blackmail. "All right," Daniel snapped, only wanting to shut him up, "so I promise."

"Good, good," breathed the old man. But the relief Daniel's pledge gave Alec was only temporary. He started in again. "Don't you think we could go?" he wheedled. "It's not really so far and nobody's going to stop us. If you're worried about looking small behind the wheel we can set you up on a cushion so you sit every bit as tall as me. That would do it, don't you think?"

What Daniel thought could be surmised. He was pointedly ignoring the old man, looking away from him, across the road and into a neighbour's yard where the storm-shattered limb of an austere and venerable elm dangled, hanging from a pliable shred of the tree's tough inner bark and twisting in the wind.

"Look at all these flowers made special for Earl," implored Alec. "Mrs. Harding put a drop of perfume on each of the paper heads so they'd be as near real flowers as can be. What's the use of these flowers if we don't go? It'd be a terrible waste. Just smell them," he coaxed, holding out a few to the boy.

Daniel knocked them aside with the back of his hand. "Look," he said angrily, "why don't you just leave me alone? I can't take you. Why do you keep at me? How many times do you need to be told? Do you want to get me in trouble? Do you believe she won't find out if I take you? She always finds out!" he cried.

"Daniel –"

But Daniel had finished with him. The boy flung himself out of the truck, slamming the door on the startled face of an old man awash in artificial flowers.

It was shame that drove Daniel to run down the bare, windy road, shame at disappointing someone he had only just that minute realized he loved.

2 1

◆

The following Wednesday morning Alec Monkman began to clean his garden. When he started the job the air was keen and thin, so keen and thin that the only smell it could float was the itchy, prickly one of tomato bushes and even that smell drifted in and out like radio reception from a distant station – despite his carrying armfuls of frost-blackened tomato plants directly under his nose.

By nine o'clock the sun was shining with a cold, untempered brightness and the sky was the palest blue, an exact match for the colour of Monkman's eyes, which seemed intent on reflecting the season. However, Monkman paid no notice of the sky. He was too busy pulling up tomato plants, wrenching stakes out of the obstinate earth and throwing them in a pile in the middle of the garden. In no time at all even this easy work made him grow flushed and warm. It was because he had let himself run to fat, he told himself, prodding his middle. When he turned to the corn patch he was already slowing, visibly tiring. He cleared it as a child might, uprooting each stalk and bearing each singly to the rubbish heap upright in his fist like a withered staff of office, its roots dribbling earth onto his shuffling boots and the drab leaves rustling alongside his ruddy, sweaty, dirt-streaked face. Having deposited a stalk with the rest, he turned mechanically on his heel and trudged back to pull up another. The corn on the rubbish heap stood stacked higher than his head before the plot was eventually cleared and at the close of that task he was sweating so freely that he removed his jacket and, without thinking, tossed it up on the pile, repeating the same motion that had disposed of the last of the corn. The jacket was soon covered by his next load, pea vines, and forgotten.

Clearing was nothing like planting had been. He had gotten confused planting. He hadn't remembered certain things. But clearing was easy, there was nothing to be confused about. You just took everything up. You worked until all was bare, empty.

Alec worked blindly on. At mid-afternoon, as he approached the last of it, what was left of the cucumbers and beans, the pain in the small of his back grew so sharp that he was obliged to breathe quickly and shallowly through his mouth. Something else. There was a loud, windy roar in his ears whenever he bent over. But he disregarded the pain and the roaring and stumbled about his garden with his nose to the ground like a dog, swinging his head from side to side, suddenly stooping to seize a single parched leaf, a broken twig, the smallest scrap of waste he had earlier over-looked. Back and forth he went, racing the approaching dusk, his breath coming faster and faster, stiff fingers pecking at the dirt, pinching up this or that.

The supper siren wailed from Connaught's town hall, the dim light was failing. It was time to give up. He could no longer spot the last tiny shreds of refuse and his hands trembled so violently that the only way he could control them was to stuff them in his trouser pockets. The garden was as clean as he could make it. He went into the house and closed the door.

22

It was a little past noon when Daniel let himself into his grand-father's house, unannounced, without bothering to knock. Having once lived there, he was inclined to treat it as his own and never give a second thought to the old man's privacy. Making amends was uppermost in the boy's mind, not respecting his privacy. He had come to tell his grandfather he was sorry for what had happened and how he had treated him. For a week he had avoided him because he knew, no matter what excuses he made to himself, that he had been afraid and disloyal. Over and over he had asked himself how Montgomery Clift or James Dean would have behaved in his place. The answers always came out the same. Montgomery Clift would have driven the old man wherever he wanted to go, to the ends of the earth. If need be, James Dean would have stolen a car to transport him.

He was a coward.

Because the television wasn't blaring, at first Daniel assumed the old man must be out. Alec never missed the farm report and markets which were broadcast over the noon hour. Yet despite the utter quiet and stillness of the house Daniel had the sense it wasn't empty. An unsettling feeling arose in him that he was being watched or listened to.

"Anybody home?" He paused, shouted again. "Anybody home?" He felt a mixture of uneasiness and relief that no one answered and he was free to leave. But as he turned to do so he got his answer, a vague confusion of sounds that came from the direction of the living room, muffled, deliberate thumps; a gritty scrabbling which sounded like a dog's nails slithering on a polished floor. Then as abruptly as they had begun the sounds ceased. Either that or they had been overwhelmed by the loud, frantic drumming of his heart. Daniel strained to catch them again, face drawn and rigid.

"Who's there?" he called out.

No reply. The rooms thrummed vacantly. "Alec?"

Nothing.

With reluctance Daniel stole to the entrance of the living room and eased his way through the door for a look. It came as a great relief to him when he saw it was only the old man after all, the old man standing in the middle of the living room with his back to him, leaning on one of the kitchen chairs.

"Alec?"

He did not answer, did not move a muscle.

The boy wondered if this was a display of sulking, a bit of the cold shoulder because he hadn't got his way last Saturday. Daniel decided to ignore it. "You gave me a scare," he said brightly to the hunched, brooding shoulders. "Didn't you hear me call?"

No reply. And there was something in the manner his grandfather held himself, a stubborn, secretive dignity, which rooted Daniel just inside the doorway, which prevented him as surely as a hand thrust in his chest from taking one more step into the living room and trespassing. He was convinced his grandfather had heard him, knew he was there. The awkwardness of the situation kept him nervously talking.

"I suppose you're pissed off at me about last Saturday. Okay, I get the message then – I know you're pissed off. I'm sorry. But I've been pissed off at you, too, lots of times – about baseball, about all kinds of things. But that didn't mean I wouldn't talk to you. So what do you say? You going to talk to me?"

His grandfather stood leaning on the back of the kitchen chair, monumental in his silence. A doubt crossed Daniel's mind. What's wrong with this picture? Something was. The doubt carried him two steps further into the room. "Alec, what's the matter?" he asked. His voice was louder than he had intended.

The bowed shoulders heaved, the chair scraped and shifted on the floor. His grandfather used the chair to support himself as he fought to turn around; it was his prop, a four-legged crutch which he savagely jerked and shoved so that its abrupt, violent hopping on the floor made it seem alive, something struggling to tear itself free from his grip. Between the sudden, desperate leaps of the chair on the floor the old man adjusted his balance, scuffling his feet into a new position while the chair that kept him upright trembled and quivered under the burden of his weight, threatening to tip. A brief pause, the room swelling with the rasp of his laboured breathing, and then once again the dull, heavy load of flesh tried to turn itself to the boy. The chair rocked, its feet scratched, it gave a startled jump. A few inches closer. And with each painful step, with each convulsion, the understanding grew in Daniel that something terrible was striving to show itself to him.

At last he was face to face with it and only wanted to look away. His grandfather was not right. One side of his face had melted and run like hot wax, the muscles were all loose and hanging. His mouth sagged open and his left eyelid drooped, obscuring half the staring blue of the pupil.

"What happened?" Daniel whispered. "Why are you like this?"

The old man's right hand rose slowly from where it rested on the back of the chair. Up, up it came and laid a forefinger like a bar across the slack lips and fallen mouth. The child's sign for secrecy.

He tried to shush but the sound he made bubbled instead, loose, sloppy, full of spit.

"Oh God, oh God," Daniel muttered, stepping from foot to foot in his apprehension. "Oh God, oh God. Somebody. Please."

A word was floundering in his grandfather's mouth. His tongue could be glimpsed fluttering rapidly between the barricade of false teeth. "*Fro'en!*" he blurted suddenly.

"I don't understand. I don't understand what you're trying to tell me. I don't know what to do for you. Tell me what to do," whispered Daniel, hopping lightly from foot to foot like a small boy needing a pee.

"*Fro'en!*" cried the old man, banging the chair on the floor, shaking it, shaking his head violently from side to side. "*Fro'en! Fro'en! Fro'en!*"

Daniel started to cry. "Don't you see?" he asked. "I can't understand you. I can't understand you, Alec. Don't you see?"

Maybe he did. The rage died. The old man stood staring and panting. Then once more his right hand lifted to his face; awkwardly he stabbed three of his fingers into the cheekbone beneath the partially veiled eye and drew them deliberately and brutally down to his jaw. The white pressure marks showed on his skin like frost.

"*Fro'en,*" he said, speaking softly now but with urgency. "*Fro'en.*"

At last Daniel understood. His grandfather was telling him he was frozen.

Panicked by the emergency, Daniel turned to his mother, spilling into the telephone the story of how he had discovered the old man clinging to a chair back for dear life. "He's sick or something," he kept repeating. "Real sick."

"All right, Daniel," said Vera calmly, once she had judged the seriousness of the situation. "I want you to stay there with him.

Don't leave him and see that he doesn't fall. Don't try and move him yourself, he's too heavy for you. Just wait. Someone will be there right away. It won't be long. Just stay calm and collected. I know you can. I know you can be brave for me. Will you do that for me, dear?"

Daniel promised he would.

Vera made a quick decision not to call for the ambulance. It was stationed at the mine site twenty-four hours a day in readiness for serious accidents and in the time it would take the ambulance to cover the distance to town, Stutz could be at her father's with minutes to spare. When she rang Stutz at the garage she was cool and terse. "Listen, Daniel just called to say something has happened to Dad at the house. The kid says he's sick and he's plenty upset so I think he must be. You better get over there, fast. By the sounds of it he probably needs the hospital."

Mr. Stutz burst into the house and upon Monkman swaying behind a chair in the living room, his face scarcely recognizable. Daniel stood beside him, his grandfather's sleeve knotted in his fist to help anchor him. When the boy saw Stutz he began to clumsily pat the old man on the back. "Here's Mr. Stutz," he said encouragingly. "You're okay now. Mr. Stutz is here."

Mr. Stutz came very close and peered into Monkman's collapsed face with disconcerting directness. Then he took a step backward and asked, "What's the trouble, Alec?"

Daniel hastened to answer for his grandfather. "He can't talk very well. He's hard to understand."

Stutz nodded, absorbing this news. "All right then," he said, addressing Daniel, "we better see he gets to the hospital." He turned to Monkman and spoke very slowly and deliberately. "Not to worry. We're going to see Doctor now."

He hadn't expected to prompt a rebellion. Shaking his head vehemently no, Monkman tightened his grip on the chair. Mr.

Stutz was a practical man not given to hopeless coaxing and cajoling. After several attempts at persuasion failed, he simply pried Monkman's fingers one by one from the chair back. Daniel supported the unsteady old man from behind while he did this, his arms wrapped around his waist. Then as Monkman frantically pawed and dog-paddled the air, straining to reattach himself to the chair, Stutz kicked it out of his reach and slung one of the old man's arms over his shoulder. "Now," he said grimly to Daniel, "if you take his other arm maybe we can get this show on the road."

They half-led, half-carried the old man to the truck, and as they did Daniel lapsed into tears again, tears which Mr. Stutz discreetly overlooked and allowed to pass unremarked. Daniel was crying again because this felt like a second act of treachery, helping to compel Alec to go to the hospital against his wishes. It didn't matter that Daniel recognized the necessity of what they were doing; what they were doing seemed to be adding to the old man's suffering. He moaned and twisted fitfully in their grip, flapping his hands and slurring protests. It upset Daniel dreadfully when Stutz made him hold his grandfather back against the seat as they drove to St. Anthony's Hospital and the old man struck feebly at him with his hands. But all of this was nothing beside the moment before the door to his grandfather's room was swung shut and Daniel saw him sitting blank-faced and defeated on the edge of his bed while a chattering nurse eased him out of his shirt. At that moment a wilderness of loneliness opened up before the boy.

The doctor told them that Monkman had had a stroke. He said it was too early to make predictions about an outcome. Sometimes elderly gentlemen recovered from such blows, sometimes they didn't. For the time being, it was important to get the patient settled and quiet. Perhaps it was better that he have no visitors until tomorrow.

After Stutz phoned Vera with this news, he and Daniel returned to the house to collect the personal effects Alec would require – razor, underwear, slippers. Going from room to room, hunting up these articles, something came to Mr. Stutz's attention. It was in the living room that he first noticed deep scratches in the floor. Monkman's standards of housekeeping had declined badly since Vera had left last Christmas and he seldom bothered sweeping up the dirt and even sand he was constantly tracking into the house from the garden. Daniel had once told him that walking across his floor sounded like scrunching your way over spilled sugar. When a chair bearing all of Monkman's two hundred and twenty pounds had been skidded over this dirt it had acted like sandpaper, producing deep scratches and gouges in the surface of the linoleum. What surprised Stutz was that this damage was not confined to the living room where the old man had been found, but was spread throughout the house – in the kitchen, in the bathroom, in the downstairs bedroom. He studied the intersecting trails of many laborious journeys in a doorway, a welter of cuts and tears, one overlapping another. They resembled the angry scribbles of a child and had come close to obliterating the pattern of flowers on the linoleum.

How many trips back and forth? Stutz asked himself. How many days?

"Daniel, when did you last see your grandfather?"

"Last Saturday."

Stutz had briefly talked to him Tuesday. Today was Friday. One thing was certain. All this hadn't happened today. All these marks hadn't been made in a single day. He had a vision of Alec alone, staggering from room to room behind the chair, blundering desperately through a vacant house.

They were leaving when Daniel spotted the straw fedora on the hook by the door. He took it down and set it on top of the bundle of his grandfather's things.

"You better leave that here," suggested Mr. Stutz quietly. "He isn't going to have any call for a hat in a hospital."

"But he'll want it to come home in," said Daniel.

Stutz left it at that. Daniel and he went out together. Halfway to the truck Stutz remembered. He turned back and locked the door on the puzzle of scars. Nobody would be coming back to the house tonight.

23

Four hours after he was admitted to St. Anthony's Hospital, Alec Monkman was stricken by another, much more severe stroke. From that moment on he swung between coma and brief explosions of agitation when he tried to escape his bed and clawed, whimpering and bewildered, at the I.V. tube inserted in a vein in the back of his hand.

Circumstances, it seemed to Vera, dictated she take charge. Despite the differences which existed between her and her father, she was not going to have it said his daughter let him die like a dog in a ditch. To see he did not harm himself during one of his "spells" – Stutz's description – she decreed he would be watched around the clock and she drew up a schedule of shifts. From eight A.M. to four P.M. Mr. Stutz would keep him company. After school let out, Daniel would sit with him until his mother closed up The Bluebird at eleven. Vera's shift was what the shaft sinkers called the grave-yard shift, midnight to morning.

Vera only desired to get through her father's last days as people would expect her to, without giving rise to comment, or worse, scandal. She purchased an expensive winter coat, matching scarf and gloves, matching shoes and handbag so when she paid her visits to the hospital she would be presentable, respectably dressed. It had been a long time since she had bought herself any good clothes. The importance of dressing well was linked to a feeling of anticipation, a feeling that she was standing on the brink of an important event for which it was necessary to prepare – like running away to join the Army, or choosing Stanley – an event the consequences of which it was impossible to foresee.

Because of the hours of his shift it was Mr. Stutz who most often received visitors as Monkman's proxy. He took deep satisfaction in their numbers. Old customers and neighbours paid their respects, employees dropped by to inquire as to his condition and left, shaking their heads, quiet, subdued. Mr. Stutz accepted their offerings – the get-well cards, the home-made squares, the boxes of Black Magic chocolate – with ceremonious dignity. "Alec thanks you," he said to each.

Among the first visitors to make an appearance at St. Anthony's were the old men who played cards at Alec's house and borrowed money from him before Vera put the run on them. On their arrival they displayed a reluctance to be drawn too far into the sickroom despite Stutz peremptorily beckoning them from his chair beside the bed. They remained huddled a step or two inside the door, milling about, craning their necks at the patient and blinking owlishly.

"It's a shame," someone in the back of the group volunteered. "Life's a bugger," observed another. There seemed to be nothing further to venture on that topic. The old men uneasily eyed the medical rigmarole, the bottle of I.V. fluid, the transparent plastic tubing, the oxygen tank. They appeared on the verge of stampeding at any moment. Huff Driesen, who led the delegation, said, "If he comes around . . . you'll tell him we came to ask after him?"

Mr. Stutz solemnly nodded.

"He was a prince of a fellow," declared one of them with fervour. That seemed to sum up, exhaust all that there was to say.

Murmuring agreement they filed out, stumbling hard upon one another's heels in their haste to quit the room.

Mr. Stutz was sadly, dutifully resigned to this business of dying. When Alec was both conscious and quiet, Stutz would draw back the blankets on his bed, hike up his hospital gown, take his penis delicately between thumb and forefinger, aim it into the neck of a plastic flask, and patiently wait for the trickle. If he wasn't given the opportunity to frequently relieve himself, the old man would wet the bed. During his "spells," when he tore at the I.V. tube, jerked his head from side to side, kicked and tangled the sheets about his legs, and cried out unintelligibly, Mr. Stutz pinned him to the mattress, leaned his face close to the old man's ear, and advised him in a whisper, "Don't you fight it now, Alec. Let it be. Let it come," until he grew quiet again.

In the course of Vera's and Daniel's vigils these upsets were uncommon, and, if they did occur, were much milder. Stutz told them they were lucky the old man kept banking hours. Daniel dreaded having to sit with the old man, feared his "spells," feared even more that it would be his bad luck to have him die when they were alone together. He had never seen anyone die and didn't intend to if he could help it. Once, when he was offering lame excuses as to why he couldn't take his shift – something about decorating the gym for a dance – Vera nearly told him he needn't worry, most people didn't die in the evening. She had read that somewhere, or heard it, she couldn't recall. Something made people hold out through the dark hours. It was in the morning they gave up the ghost, in the light, at the end of their strength. But Vera caught herself in time and didn't make the observation.

No one had come right out and said it yet, that her father was dying, and she didn't know how Daniel would take to hearing it, especially coming from her. When he said, "I thought it was the nurses' job to look after sick people," Vera replied, "It is. But they can't be with him every minute. I know it's not easy for you but it has to be done and there's no one else to do it but us, the family. This is part of being a family. Take your school books and study. If he gets bad, call a nurse. If you occupy your mind you won't think of it, you won't feel so bad."

This was Vera's tactic. She wasn't sure she had anything to feel, but if she had, she didn't want to turn it loose now, let it run wild when it might interfere with what needed to be done. At present she had to be cool and calm. But it wasn't easy. She was finding how much turned on the smallest, most insignificant things. Take teeth. The nurses had removed her father's dentures and now she didn't quite feel the same about him as she had before. His sunken mouth made him look weak, frail, pitiable. Not much of an enemy. Robbed of those big, white, aggressive teeth he was a less domineering figure. It seemed the wall she had been pushing against all her life was giving way, collapsing before her very eyes.

Vera was out of his hands and he was into hers. He would be sure to hate that if he knew. If he had to be in anybody's hands he would have wished to rest in Earl's. Earl was the one he trusted, loved. Earl was who he had turned to for comfort when their mother died. It was Earl he went riding with through the night. Earl the weakling. There, she had put a name to him. Her brother was a weakling and because of his weakness it had fallen to her to try and stop it. There was another reason that had led her to interfere. Jealousy. Why was Earl his choice to ride with? Didn't he realize it was she who was capable of riding through anything? The two of them could have swept through the darkness at any speed, invincible. Faster? You're goddamn right faster. As fast as you like.

It was ironic that the punishment which was intended for her had become her father's. If he hadn't refused to give her Earl's address, her brother could be summoned home now. And Earl *ought* to be home because death in Connaught was a family business. It was what people always said with hushed voices: *They* had a death in the family.

Mr. Stutz wanted to pick Vera up each night at The Bluebird and deliver her to the hospital but she preferred to walk. Vera said if he wished to make himself useful he could see Daniel safely home and ease her mind that way. Which Mr. Stutz was only too willing to do. Anything to oblige. Each night she could see his vehicle in the deserted parking lot, waiting to carry Daniel home when she relieved him at half-past eleven. Vera never crossed the lot to say hello. The best Stutz got was a casual wave from under the fan light above the main entrance to the hospital. Vera had concluded that any and all encouragement of Mr. Stutz was to be devoutly avoided.

It wasn't just to prevent finding herself alone with him that Vera refused a nightly ride, the walk provided her with a rare opportunity to think. She had plenty to think about. Vera pondered what she might say to Daniel in his present obvious misery, what words might help him to accept what was happening to the old man, happening to them all. But she dismissed every possibility. Her own hard experience had taught her there was nothing to say. The few people who had tried to speak to her after Stanley died had not succeeded in comforting her. Their words were inadequate. Now what they had had to say seemed merely clumsy. The same words, but perspective had changed their meaning. Something like that was happening to her at the moment. The whole story of her life was rearranging itself.

The wind of the previous Saturday had recently returned, a little less savage but more persistent and enduring, and for several nights Vera had had to brave it on her way to the hospital. A cold, stinging wind, it brought winter if not snow. Each night froze harder than the last. The dirt of the roadways thudded under her heels; even the dust seemed to have turned hard as iron filings. Vera stepped in a puddle in the dark and the ice crackled so explosively she nearly jumped clean out of her skin.

By the fourth day of her father's hospitalization the constant wind had swept every trace of cloud beyond the horizon and the night skies appeared black and infinite, tiny distant stars showing like a scattering of salt grains. After a fifteen-minute walk Vera's cheeks were burning and her eyes red and streaming with tears so that she looked as if she had been weeping for days. The matronly nurse on the desk noted all this when Vera checked in and shot her a sympathetic smile.

As usual, before sending Daniel home, Vera cautioned him to be sure to lock the door and go straight to bed. However, unlike other nights, he seemed in no hurry to quit the hospital. He hung in the doorway of his grandfather's sickroom, tracing and retracing the shape of a floor tile with the toe of his runner.

"Stutz is waiting," Vera reminded him.

Daniel drew in the last side of the square tile with the tip of his shoe, closing it, and lifted his face to his mother. "I was wondering . . ." he said hesitantly. "Do you think he can hear us talking when he's like that?"

"You mean when he's unconscious?"

Daniel returned his eyes to the tile. "Yeah, unconscious." He took a deep breath. "Do you think maybe he can hear us?"

"I doubt it," said Vera. "Why do you ask?"

"I was just wondering."

"Why were you wondering?"

Daniel did not reply.

"Did you say something around him you wouldn't want him to hear?"

Daniel glanced up at her. "No," he said definitely.

Another possibility came to mind. "Is there something maybe you wanted him to hear you saying? Is that it?"

Daniel bit down hard on his lower lip, shifted his weight back and forth uneasily. When he felt he could trust himself, he began. "There was something he asked me to do for him. Something he thought was pretty important. I needed to tell him I would do it, just like he asked –" Daniel broke off, shrugging his shoulders.

A moment later he straightened himself up and gave his mother an uncertain look. "So I did it this afternoon. I promised. Promised him I'd do it, just like he wanted."

"Then it's all right, isn't it?" said Vera gently. "You took care of it. You did all you could, right?"

"If you'd like," he said, "I could stay on tonight. Then there'd be two of us. It can't be any fun sitting here by yourself all night."

"And what about school tomorrow morning?" said Vera, struggling to hide how his offer had touched her.

"I missed school for him once," Daniel confessed abruptly. "We did the garden."

"It was very nice of you to volunteer to stay with me," said Vera, "but I think you've had enough of this place for one day. And you need your rest."

"I just thought maybe you'd want the company. It can't be any fun sitting here by yourself all night," he repeated lamely.

"I want the company," Vera assured him, "but I want you home in bed more." She put her arm around his shoulders and walked him to the hospital entrance where she stood watching as he hurried across the parking lot and sprang into Stutz's pickup.

The interior light flashed on and Stutz seemed to be pointing to something on the seat. Vera thought she could recall some previous mention made of Daniel spilling a Coke. They talked on for several minutes. Vera guessed Stutz was quizzing Daniel on her father and his condition, and at one point Stutz laid a big brown hand briefly on the boy's shoulder. Then the interior light went off and she lost sight of her son. The truck crawled stiffly away, wreathed in clouds of exhaust that the wind was folding up into the truck bed. The brake lights stuttered at the parking lot exit and then Daniel and Stutz were gone.

It wasn't wrong to bring him, Vera found herself thinking. I'm sure it's done him good.

She turned around briskly and went back down the hallway to a stores room where she helped herself to a basin, soap, and towels, just as she had done every night for the past three. In the sickroom her father still lay unconscious, his skin gleaming with a film of clammy sweat. Vera wiped that away in the fashion she might dust a sideboard. Then she went to work. He did not stir while she roughly scrubbed his feet, hands, face, and neck. In her opinion, the hospital staff was not keeping her father as clean as they might. She took her time washing him because she had plenty of time to kill. A long night faced her. She dried each finger separately. It was surprising how heavy even one thick, swollen-knuckled finger of a man who had worked all his life with his hands could be. Lying across her palm she could feel the weight of it.

With the washing and towelling done, Vera had nothing left to do but sit and wait. She considered shaving her father, but the prospect of working a razor over that deeply seamed face with its loose, folded skin scared her off. Instead, she patted some skin bracer into his crop of stiff, white bristles to keep him smelling fresh.

She sat back down in the chair. The need to be busy made her wish for other chores. If only he had a different sort of illness, one that required her to feed him, if only he had wounds to dress and clean, bandages to change. The night before she had occupied herself trimming his fingernails so he wouldn't scratch himself during one of his spells. For good measure she had cut his toenails, too, holding a one-sided conversation with the unmoving body which had the blankets and sheets turned back over the ankles so that she could attack with the scissors. "Jesus, these are thick toenails. What have you got growing here? Three-quarter-inch plywood?"

The sobbing, nagging wind made waiting harder. Of course, the wind was all she had to listen to, the only company she had. Sudden gusts battering the windowpane like hands, shaking the glass in the sash so ferociously that she half-expected everything else in the room to set to jumping and the night-light on her father's headboard to flickering. Then the startling lull, the moan of withdrawal, the long recovery of breath sucking at the window, a calm in which the smells of the hospital crept back into the room.

Ether, disinfectant, antiseptics that were the odours of unreality. The gap of silence magnified every sound that had been blunted by the clamour of the wind, the ticking of her watch, the stealthy, squeaky tread of rubber-soled shoes, the drifting, interminable call of the old woman two doors down who cried, "Nursie, nursie, nursie," all night long in a voice inflected neither with urgency nor hope. And then it was back, beating the building like a drum.

So Vera waited, sleepless in the clash of the wind. Waited for her father to open his eyes, recognize and acknowledge her. It wasn't gratitude she was seeking. He didn't owe her gratitude for being there any more than she believed she owed him gratitude for harbouring her and Daniel sixteen months ago when she had come to the end of her strength and had nowhere else to turn. Vera thought in terms of debt rather than gratitude. It was easier to calculate. She simply wanted him to know that she was doing what she could, settling up. Decency for decency. It was the reason she never closed her eyes; so she could make plain to him who it was that waited with him if he came out of the coma.

Tonight, after nights of waiting, it happened. Her father opened his eyes and spoke. "Cold," was what she thought he said. The wind was banging on the wall behind her, it was past four and she was dizzy from lack of sleep. So it was impossible to be certain exactly what he had said. But he had said something. Vera rose awkwardly from her chair – one leg had gone to sleep – and she hobbled to the bed. Her father hadn't shifted so much as an inch, nor stirred a limb as far as she could see, but his eyes followed her to the side of the bed. As soon as she was close enough she noticed something else about his eyes, about the way they looked in the direct light of the lamp clipped to the headboard. They had undergone a transformation, turned cloudy, milky, the eyes of a man hardening into the eyes of a marble statue. They were practically white. And his face, too, and the pillowcase, the sheet tucked up under his chin, the stubble of his beard, all white as snow.

Vera bent low over the bed, determined that the milky eyes would know who she was. "Dad, it's Vera," she announced in a voice designed to penetrate. "Vera, your daughter. Can you hear me? Do you know me?"

"Cold." This time she heard him clearly, the word surprisingly distinct in his toothless mouth.

Vera wasn't absolutely certain what her father meant to say. "Are you cold, Dad? Do you want another blanket?"

He made no attempt to answer. His eyes tracked her as she stepped to the foot of the bed, wriggled her hands under the blankets, and pressed one of his feet between her palms. It felt like a block of ice. "Jesus," she said, "you are cold, aren't you? We better see what we can do about that, hadn't we?" She went to the wardrobe, rummaged about noisily in it, and reappeared holding up the socks he had been wearing the day he was admitted to hospital. It was a trial to get them on him. He was unwilling or unable to cooperate, his feet remained stiff as boards, each toe as unyielding as a picket in a fence. The elasticized nylon socks kept snagging on calluses and corns, making tearing, rasping sounds as she tugged at them.

"There." Finally she had got them on him.

"Cold."

Now she had something to do besides sit and wait. She talked to him as she bustled around the bed. "Yes, yes, I know you're cold, Dad. Just be patient. There's an extra blanket up on the shelf in the wardrobe. Wait until I get you tucked up in that."

When she had, he said it again. "Cold."

"I understand. I know you're cold. But just give yourself a minute to see if you don't get warmer with the blanket. It's a nice wool blanket. See?"

Poor circulation, Vera supposed. She laid her hands on his calves. As cool to the touch as spoons in a drawer on a summer day. She flew about the room emptying whatever the wardrobe contained onto his bed – two more wool blankets, a counterpane; last of all, an extra sheet. "Not any better yet? Jesus, you can't still be cold. You just want to see me run, that's it, isn't it?" She flapped out the sheet and let it float down upon him.

"Dad, Dad?" she cried anxiously. "Is that any better? Can you hear me, Dad? Do you know who it is, Dad? It's Vera. I'm Vera."

"Cold."

She worked on with steady, angry determination, unwilling to give up. She found more towels in the bathroom and wrapped them like puttees around his legs. Still he grew colder. When she touched him she could feel it; her hands came away chilled and damp. Nervously she tried to blot away, wipe away, the sensation on the bedclothes.

"Cold."

"Goddamn it, I know you're cold. I'm trying. Don't you see me trying? You try, too. Move your legs a little, rub them up and down on the sheets. Do you understand? Can you hear me? *Rub your legs on the sheets!*"

Nothing stirred, responded, but his eyes.

Vera wouldn't quit on him. Somehow she wrestled her father into his shirt. He was all dead-weight and it took all the strength in her to pull him upright and prop him there while she manoeuvred him into the shirt. His hospital gown kept getting in the way and she managed to stab only one of his arms into a sleeve, the one that didn't have the tube in it. She was trembling and panting breathlessly by the time she finished. Cold and again cold and cold once more. Over and over cold.

Vera muffled him up in the last bit of clothing she had, her coat, even though she knew it was hopeless. At last there was nothing to place between her father and the cold but herself. Vera pressed him close. He fell silent. She looked into his eyes until, an hour later, she saw them finally overcome, the last of him to be possessed.

Adrian Ewins

Guy Vanderhaeghe was born in Esterhazy, Saskatchewan in 1951. He is the author of six books of fiction. His first two books were collections of short stories: *Man Descending* (1982), which won the Governor General's Award, and the Faber Prize in the U.K., and *The Trouble With Heroes* (1983). *My Present Age*, a novel, was published in 1984. That novel was followed by *Homesick* in 1989, which was a co-winner of the City of Toronto Book Award. His third book of short stories was the highly praised *Things As They Are?* (1992). *The Englishman's Boy* (1996) was a long-time national bestseller and won the Governor General's Award for Fiction, the Saskatchewan Book Award for Fiction and for Best Book of the Year, and was shortlisted for The Giller Prize, and the prestigious International IMPAC Dublin Literary Award, the world's largest monetary award for a single book.

Acclaimed for his fiction, Vanderhaeghe has also written plays. *I Had a Job I Liked. Once.* was first produced in 1991, and won the Canadian Authors Association Award for Drama. His second play, *Dancock's Dance*, was produced in 1995. He is currently completing a screenplay for *The Englishman's Boy*.

Guy Vanderhaeghe lives in Saskatoon, where he is a Visiting Professor of English at S.T.M. College.

W9-BMF-616

French
Phrases
FOR
DUMMIES®

by Dodi-Katrin Schmidt,
Michelle M. Williams,
Dominique Wenzel

WILEY

Wiley Publishing, Inc.

French Phrases For Dummies®

Published by
Wiley Publishing, Inc.
111 River St.
Hoboken, NJ 07030-5774
www.wiley.com

WILEY

About the Authors

Dodi-Katrin Schmidt has been a writer, a translator, and an editor for almost ten years. Aside from translating German, French, and English text of various kinds, including linguistic handbooks, film reviews, travel guides, and children's books, she has also been involved in developing language textbooks, language courses, teachers' handbooks, and grammar companions for video language courses. Dodi has been teaching for more than two decades at high school, adult education, and college levels in Europe as well as the United States. She also writes test items for various national language tests and recorded textbook and test material. Together with her husband, she travels a great deal, and they continually house and entertain foreign students and former students in their home in Princeton, NJ.

Michelle Williams is an editor at a major educational publisher. A former French teacher, she has taught students ranging from two years old to adults, in both the public and private sectors. She is currently a private French tutor to a young Olympic-hopeful figure skater. She is a firm believer in making language fun and accessible to all who want to learn. Her most rewarding experience, however, is in watching and listening to her son, Nathaniel, learn to speak and sing in French.

Dominique Wenzel has been a freelance teacher of French and translator for 15 years. Born and raised in France, she received a Master's degree from the University of Paris-Sorbonne and studied at the University of Chicago on a postgraduate Fulbright scholarship. Her students include business professionals, children, and adults of all levels and interests. She travels regularly to France. Dominique raised two bicultural, bilingual children who are both active in the international field.

Publisher's Acknowledgments

We're proud of this book; please send us your comments through our Dummies online registration form located at www.dummies. com/register/.

Some of the people who helped bring this book to market include the following:

Acquisitions, Editorial, and Media Development

Compiler: Laura Peterson

Senior Project Editor: Tim Gallan

Acquisitions Editor: Stacy Kennedy

Copy Editors: Laura K. Miller, E. Neil Johnson

Assistant Editor: Holly Gastineau-Grimes

Technical Editor: Language Training Center

Editorial Manager: Christine Meloy Beck

Editorial Assistants: Courtney Allen, Melissa S. Bennett

Cartoons: Rich Tennant, www.the5thwave.com

Composition

Project Coordinator: Nancee Reeves

Layout and Graphics: Andrea Dahl, Michael Kruzil, Jacque Schneider, Julie Trippetti

Proofreaders: Laura Albert, Susan Moritz

Indexer: Becky Hornyak

Publishing and Editorial for Consumer Dummies

Diane Graves Steele, Vice President and Publisher, Consumer Dummies

Joyce Pepple, Acquisitions Director, Consumer Dummies

Kristin A. Cocks, Product Development Director, Consumer Dummies

Michael Spring, Vice President and Publisher, Travel

Brice Gosnell, Associate Publisher, Travel

Kelly Regan, Editorial Director, Travel

Publishing for Technology Dummies

Andy Cummings, Vice President and Publisher, Dummies Technology/General User

Composition Services

Gerry Fahey, Vice President of Production Services

Debbie Stailey, Director of Composition Services

Table of Contents

● ●

Introduction

● ●

*A*s society becomes more and more international in nature, knowing how to say at least a few words in other languages becomes more and more useful. Inexpensive airfares make travel abroad a realistic option. Global business environments necessitate overseas travel. You may just have friends and neighbors who speak other languages, or you may want to get in touch with your heritage by learning a little bit of the language that your ancestors spoke.

Whatever your reason for wanting to learn some French, this book can help. We're not promising fluency here, but if you need to greet someone, purchase a ticket, or order off a menu in French, you need look no further than *French Phrases For Dummies.*

About This Book

This book isn't like a class that you have to drag yourself to twice a week for a specified period of time. You can use this book however you want to, whether your goal is to learn some words and phrases to help you get around when you visit France, or you just want to be able to say "Hello, how are you?" to your French-speaking neighbor. Go through this book at your own pace, reading as much or as little at a time as you like. You don't have to trudge through the chapters in any particular order, either; just read the sections that interest you.

If you've never studied French before, you may want to read Chapters 1 and 2 before you tackle the later ones. These chapters give you some of the basics that you need to know about the language, such as how to pronounce the various sounds.

Conventions Used in This Book

To make this book easy to navigate, we've set up
some conventions:

- ✔ French terms are set in **boldface** to make them
  stand out.

- ✔ Pronunciations set in *italics* follow the French
  terms.

  The nasal sound (see Chapter 1) is indicated by
  a capital *N* in the pronunciations.

- ✔ Memorizing key words and phrases is important
  in language learning, so we collect the important words in a chapter or section into a list
  with the heading "Words to Know." French
  nouns have genders, which determines which
  article each noun takes. In the Words to Know
  lists, we include the article for each noun so
  that you can memorize it at the same time as
  the noun.

You may notice that the pronunciation guides don't
tell you which syllable to stress. French doesn't place
significant stress on one syllable over another. One
less thing to memorize!

Also note that because each language has its own
ways of expressing ideas, the English translations that
we provide for the French terms may not be exactly
literal. We want you to know the gist of what you're
saying or hearing, not just the words that are being
said. For example, the phrase **C'est normal** *(say nohr-
mal)* can be translated literally as "It's normal," but
the phrase really means "It's no big deal." This book
gives the "It's no big deal" translation.

Foolish Assumptions

To write this book, we had to make some assumptions about who you are and what you want. Here are
the assumptions that we've made about you:

✔ You know no French — or if you took French back in school, you don't remember a word of it.

✔ You're not looking for a book that will make you fluent in French; you just want to know some words, phrases, and sentence constructions so that you can communicate basic information in French.

✔ You don't want to have to memorize long lists of vocabulary words or a bunch of boring grammar rules.

✔ You want to have fun and learn a little bit of French at the same time.

If these statements apply to you, you've found the right book!

Icons Used in This Book

You may be looking for particular information while reading this book. To make certain information easier to find, we've placed the following icons in the margins throughout the book:

 This icon highlights tips that can make picking up French words and phrases easier.

 To ensure that you don't forget important stuff, this icon serves as a reminder, like a string tied around your finger.

 Languages are full of quirks that may trip you up if you aren't prepared for them. This icon points to discussions of weird grammar rules.

 If you're looking for information about French-speaking culture, look for this icon. It draws your attention to interesting tidbits about the countries in which French is spoken.

Where to Go from Here

Learning a language is all about jumping in and giving it a try (no matter how bad your pronunciation is at first). So make the leap! Start at the beginning or pick a chapter that interests you. Before long, you'll be able to respond, **"Oui!"** when people ask, **"Parlez-vous français?"**

Chapter 1

I Say It How? Speaking French

. . . .

In This Chapter
▶ Recognizing the French you already know
▶ Figuring out basic pronunciation
▶ Using popular expressions

. . . .

*T*his chapter lets you get your feet wet. Well, actually, we kind of throw you right into the pond. We start by showing you how French and English are similar; then we present some French expressions that you probably already know and understand; and then we talk about pronunciation.

The French You Know

People tend to forget that French was the English court language for a very long time. Today, about 45 percent of English vocabulary is of French origin. That being the case, you already know an impressive amount of French, whether you realize it or not. That's what you are going to find out in this chapter. The only pitfall you have to watch for is that sometimes these English words have different meanings from their French counterparts, and they almost certainly have different pronunciations.

Friendly allies — bons alliés (bohN-zah-lyay)

The following list shows words that are spelled the same — and have the same meaning — in French and English. The only thing that may be different is the pronunciation.

- **art** *(ahr)*
- **brave** *(brahv)*
- **bureau** *(bew-ro)*
- **client** *(klee-yahN)*
- **concert** *(kohN-sehr)*
- **condition** *(kohN-dee-syohN)*
- **content** *(cohN-tahN)*
- **courage** *(koo-razh)*
- **cousin** *(koo-zaN)*
- **culture** *(kewl-tewr)*
- **différent** *(dee-fay-rahN)*
- **excellent** *(ayk-say-lahN)*
- **garage** *(gah-razh)*
- **guide** *(geed)*
- **important** *(aN-pohr-tahN)*
- **journal** *(zhoor-nahl)*
- **machine** *(mah-sheen)*
- **moment** *(moh-mahN)*
- **nation** *(nah-syohN)*
- **orange** *(oh-rahNzh)*
- **parent** *(pah-rahN)*
- **possible** *(poh-seebl)*
- **principal** *(praN-see-pahl)*
- **probable** *(pro-bahbl)*

- ✓ **question** *(kehs-tyohN)*
- ✓ **radio** *(rah-dyo)*
- ✓ **répétition** *(ray-pay-tee-syohN)*
- ✓ **restaurant** *(rehs-to-rahN)*
- ✓ **rose** *(roz)*
- ✓ **rouge** *(roozh)*
- ✓ **route** *(root)*
- ✓ **science** *(syahNs)*
- ✓ **secret** *(suh-kreh)*
- ✓ **service** *(sehr-vees)*
- ✓ **signal** *(see-nyahl)*
- ✓ **silence** *(see-lahNs)*
- ✓ **solitude** *(soh-lee-tewd)*
- ✓ **sport** *(spohr)*
- ✓ **station** *(stah-syohN)*
- ✓ **statue** *(stah-tew)*
- ✓ **suggestion** *(sewg-zhehs-syohN)*
- ✓ **surprise** *(sewr-preez)*
- ✓ **table** *(tahbl)*
- ✓ **taxi** *(tahk-see)*
- ✓ **tennis** *(tay-nees)*
- ✓ **train** *(traN)*
- ✓ **urgent** *(ewr-zhahN)*
- ✓ **violet** *(vyo-leh)*
- ✓ **voyage** *(vwah-yahzh)*

Kissing cousins

Table 1-1 shows words that are spelled almost the same in French and English and have similar meanings.

Table 1-1 Words Similar in Meaning, Slightly Different in Spelling

French	English
acteur (ahk-tuhr)	actor
adresse (ah-drehs)	address
âge (ahzh)	age
allée (ah-lay)	alley
américain (ah-may-ree-kaN)	American
artiste (ahr-teest)	artist
auteur (o-tuhr)	author
banque (bahNk)	bank
chambre (shaNbr)	chamber (or bedroom)
chèque (shehk)	check
classe (klahs)	class
comédie (koh-may-dee)	comedy
congrès (kohN-greh)	congress
démocratie (day-moh-krah-see)	democracy
développement (day-vlohp-mahN)	development
gouvernement (goo-vehr-nuh-mahN)	government
hôtel (o-tehl)	hotel
leçon (luh-sohN)	lesson
lettre (lehtr)	letter
mémoire (may-mwahr)	memory
musique (mew-zeek)	music
nationalité (nah-syo-nah-lee-tay)	nationality

French	*English*
nécessaire (nay-say-sehr)	necessary
ordinaire (ohr-dee-nehr)	ordinary
papier (pah-pyay)	paper
poème (poh-ehm)	poem
potentiel (po-tahN-syehl)	potential
problème (proh-blehm)	problem
saison (seh-zohN)	season
sénateur (say-nah-tuhr)	senator
tragédie (trah-zhay-dee)	tragedy
visite (vee-zeet)	visit

False friends — faux amis

The words that follow look similar to English words, but they don't have the same meanings:

- ✔ **actuellement** *(ak-tew-ehl-mahN)*: This word means "now," not "actually." The French word for "actually" is **en fait** *(ahN feht)*.

- ✔ **assister** *(ah-sees-tay)*: This word means "to attend," not "to assist." The French word for "to assist" is **aider** *(ay-day)*.

- ✔ **attendre** *(ah-tahNdr)*: This word means "to wait for," not "to attend." The French word for "to attend" is **assister à** *(ah-sees-tay ah)*.

- ✔ **bague** *(bahg)*: This word means "ring," not "bag." The French word for "bag" is **sac** *(sahk)*.

- ✔ **librairie** *(lee-breh-ree)*: This word means "bookstore," not "library." The French word for "library" is **bibliothèque** *(bee-blee-oh-tehk)*.

✔ **place** *(plahs):* This word means "square or seat at the theater or on the bus," not "place." The French word for "place" is **lieu** or **endroit.**

✔ **rester** *(rehs-tay):* This word means "to stay or remain," not "to rest." The French word for "to rest" is **se reposer** *(suh-ruh-po-zay).*

Lenders and borrowers

Quite a few English words have been borrowed from French, thus retaining their French meanings with different pronunciations.

However, French has also borrowed many words from English and continues to do so in spite of the loud protests by purists who condemn this trend as a sign of cultural contamination and name it **franglais** *(frahN-gleh):*

✔ **cool**

✔ **le budget**

✔ **le business**

✔ **le fast food**

✔ **le jet set**

✔ **le job (la job** in Québec)

✔ **le manager**

✔ **le marketing**

✔ **le parking**

✔ **le rock**

✔ **le shopping**

✔ **le steak**

✔ **le tunnel**

✔ **le weekend**

Mouthing Off: Basic Pronunciation

The hardest part of pronunciation is overcoming your fear of not sounding French when you speak the language. You're probably afraid that you'll never be able to reproduce the sounds that you hear in French songs or movies. Remember, though, that any time anyone hears any foreign language spoken or sung at a normal speed, the words — which don't make sense to begin with — create a muddle of sounds impossible to reproduce. After you overcome your fear of sounding funny, everything else is fun and easy. Hopefully, our reassurance helps reduce your fear.

Before you can enjoy watching or playing a game, you have to understand its basic rules. Acquiring another language is no different. After you master these pronunciation rules, you need to practice whenever you have a moment to do so, just as you had to practice the piano as a child. (Aim for short but frequent practice sessions.) Your best bet is simply to repeat over and over again, no matter how boring that sounds.

The French alphabet

The French alphabet has the same number of letters as the English alphabet — 26. As you already know, many of the letters are pronounced differently. Table 1-2 lists the letters and their pronunciations, which you may find useful to refer to, if, for instance, you have to spell your name on the phone or write down an address. Whenever possible, the table refers to sound-alike English words so that you can have a pretty good idea of the way the letters are pronounced. Such helpful hints aren't always possible, of course, because even though many sounds are roughly the same in French and in English, some French sounds don't exist in the

English language. The fact that these sounds are unfamiliar doesn't mean that you can't pronounce them.
Just read the next few sections for some help and tips.

Table 1-2	The French Alphabet	
Letter	*Sound*	*As in English*
a	ah	card
b	bay	baby
c	say	say
d	day	date
e	uh	but
f	ehf	effort
g	zhay	
h	ahsh	ash
i	ee	igloo
j	zhee	
k	kah	car
l	ehl	elegant
m	ehm	employee
n	ehn	end
o	o	rose
p	pay	paper
q	kew	
r	ehr	ersatz
s	ehs	estimate
t	tay	take
u	ew	

Letter	Sound	As in English
v	vay	vague
w	doobluhvay	
x	eeks	
y	eegrehk	
z	zehd	

Vowel sounds

Vowel sounds are the most difficult to pronounce in French. They're shorter than in English and usually end syllables. Almost all of them have an equivalent in English. Take a look at Table 1-3.

Table 1-3		French Vowel Sounds	
Sound	Spelled	As In English	French Word
ah	a, â	card	la tasse (lah tahs) (the cup)
uh	e, eu	but	le petit (luh puh-tee) (the little one)
ay	é, ez, er, et	take	les cafés (lay kah-fay) (coffee houses)
eh	è, ê	bear	la mère (lah mehr) (the mother)
ee	i, y	feet	vite (veet) (quickly)
o	o, ô, au, eau	boat	l'eau (lo) (water)
oh	o	love	la pomme (lah pohm) (the apple)

(continued)

Table 1-3 *(continued)*

Sound	Spelled	As In English	French Word
oo	ou	you	l'amour (lah-moor) (love)
wah	oi, oy	watch	la soie (lah swah) (silk)
ew*	*		salut (sah-lew) (hello)

The ew sound, represented in French by the letter u, doesn't exist in English, but it's not difficult to pronounce. Here's a little trick to help you: Say ee; the tip of your tongue is against your front bottom teeth. Keeping this position, you then round your lips and the sound coming out of your mouth is . . . the French ew (u).

The accent

The accent over a vowel in French doesn't indicate that a syllable is stressed. It only affects the letter on which it stands and doesn't even change the pronunciation of that letter unless it's an *e* (see Table 1-3).

The mute e

At the end of a word or between two consonants, the *e* isn't usually pronounced; it's called mute. For example, you don't pronounce the *e* at the end of **grande** *(grahNd)* (tall) or in the middle of **samedi** *(sahm-dee)* (Saturday). (See also the section "The elision" later in this chapter for more about final *e*.)

The nasal sounds

The nasal sound is very common in French and doesn't exist in English. It's also fairly easy to pronounce. Imagine that you have a cold and pronounce the sounds *ah, ee, oh* through your nose. They come out nasalized. Be sure not to pronounce the consonant *n* afterward.

Table 1-4 lists the nasal sounds.

Table 1-4	Nasal Sounds	
Sound	*Spelled*	*French Word*
ah -> ahN	an, en	grand (grahN) (large)
ee -> aN	ain, in, un, aim, im	pain (paN) (bread)
oh -> ohN	on	bon (bohN) (good)

Consonants

French consonants are pronounced almost like in English, except that you don't linger on them; let them explode and move on to the vowel that follows. You can't pronounce French with a lazy mouth. Remember to articulate.

Another few words of caution: In French, the consonants at the end of a word are not usually pronounced, except for *c, f, r,* and *l* (the consonants in the word *careful*).

Table 1-5 lists French consonant sounds that may puzzle you either because they come in different spellings or because you think they don't exist in English.

Table 1-5		Tricky French Consonants	
Sound	*Spelled*	*As In English*	*French Word*
s	ss (between two vowels)	sole	poisson (pwah-sohN) (fish)
	c (in front of e and i)		ciel (see-ehl) (sky)
	ç (in front of a, o, u)		garçon (gar-sohN) (boy)
g	g (in front of a, o, u)	greed	gâteau (gah-to) (cake)
	gu (in front of e and i)		guerre (gehr) (war)
zh	j, g (in front of e and i)	azure	jour (zhoor) (day)
			genou (zhuh-noo) (knee)
sh	ch	ship	chapeau (shah-po) (hat)
ny	gn	canyon	montagne (mohN-tany) (mountain)

Two extra consonants to mention:

> ✔ The letter *h* is always silent in French. Just ignore it.
>
> ✔ The French *r* often scares foreigners. Don't be afraid. You have to pronounce it with your throat, but make it as soft and gentle as you can, and you're in business.

The liaison

Have you ever thought, when listening to a French conversation, that it sounded like a great big, long word? Probably. That is because of a French phenomenon called the liaison. **Faire la liaison** *(fehr lah lyay-zohN)* (to make a liaison) means that the last consonant of a word is linked with the vowel that begins the following word. Check out these examples:

> ✔ **C'est_un petit_appartement.** *(seh-tahN puh-tee-tah-pahr-tuh-mahN)* (It's a small apartment.)

> ✔ **Vous_êtes mon_ami depuis six_ans.** *(voo-zeht-moh-nah-mee duh-pwee see-zahN)* (You have been my friend for six years.)

But the French language being full of exceptions, you have to be careful each time that you learn a new grouping of words: The liaison isn't systematic. One important exception is for words following the word **et** *(ay)*, which means "and."

> **un livre et // un crayon** *(aN leev-ray // aN kray-yohN)* (a book and a pencil)

The elision

When a word ending with an *e* or an *a* (usually an article or a pronoun) is followed by a word starting with a vowel, the first *e* or *a* disappears and is replaced by an apostrophe. This rule, like the liaison, contributes to the easy flow of the French language. Here are some examples:

> ✔ **la + école -> l'école** *(lay-kohl)* (the school)

> ✔ **je + aime -> j'aime** *(jehm)* (I like)

> ✔ **le + enfant -> l'enfant** *(lahN-fahN)* (the child)

Stress

Don't stress! In French, every syllable is of equal importance in volume and stress. The emphasis in French words of two or more syllables is on the last syllable — but that stress is moderate. For instance, the stress — very slight — in the French word **pho-tographie** *(fo-to-grah-fee)* (photography) is on the last syllable of the word.

Remembering to unstress the syllable that you're used to pronouncing in those words that have similar spellings in French and in English may take quite a bit of practice. It's like ironing the pleat out of a pair of trousers over and over again.

Idioms and Popular Expressions

French, like English, has many *idioms* (unusual ways of expressing feelings and ideas). You may find the meanings of these expressions puzzling if you try to translate them word for word.

These fixed forms of expression — you should recognize and use them as such — belong specifically to the language in question. If you walked up to a French man and said, **"Il pleut des chats et des chiens"** *(eel plew day shah ay day shy-aN)* (It's raining cats and dogs), he'd question your sanity. You may find yourself wondering what a Frenchman means when using one of his language's idioms, such as **"Il tombe des cordes"** *(eel tohNb day kohrd),* literally "ropes are falling," the French expression corresponding to "it's raining cats and dogs."

Apart from those idioms, which take a long time to recognize and belong specifically to a culture, you find many expressions and phrases that you can't translate word for word but which you can easily learn and use.

Here are a few useful expressions you frequently hear in French:

- **Allez! Un petit effort!** *(ah-lay uhn puh-tee-teh-for)* (Come on! Try a little!)
- **à mon avis** *(ah mohN-nah-vee)* (in my opinion)
- **bien sûr** *(byaN sewr)* (of course)
- **de rien** *(duh ryaN)* (don't mention it)
- **d'accord** *(dah-kohr)* (okay)
- **jamais de la vie!** *(zhah-meh dlah vee)* or **pas question!** *(pah kes-tyohN)* (no way)
- **tant mieux** *(tahN my-uh)* (so much the better)
- **tant pis** *(tahN pee)* (too bad)
- **tout à fait** *(too-tah feh)* (quite)

Here are other miscellaneous expressions that use the word **faire** *(fehr)* (to do; to make):

- **faire une promenade** *(feh-rewn pro-muh-nahd)* (to take a walk)
- **faire le plein** *(fehr luh plaN)* (to fill up)
- **faire attention** *(feh-rah-tahN-syohN)* (to pay attention)
- **faire partie de** *(fehr pahr-tee duh)* (to be part of)
- **faire ses valises** *(fehr say vah-leez)* (to pack)

Here are some other expressions with **avoir** *(ah-vwahr)* (to have):

- **avoir besoin de** *(ah-vwahr buh-zwaN duh)* (to need something)
- **avoir peur de** *(ah-vwahr puhr duh)* (to fear)
- **avoir envie de** *(ah-vwah-rahN-vee duh)* (to feel like)
- **avoir mal à la tête** *(ah-vwahr-mah-lah-lah teht)* (to have a headache)

- ✔ **avoir chaud** *(ah-vwahr sho)* (to be hot)
- ✔ **avoir froid** *(ah-vwahr frwah)* (to be cold)
- ✔ **avoir faim** *(ah-vwahr faN)* (to be hungry)
- ✔ **avoir soif** *(ah-vwahr swahf)* (to be thirsty)
- ✔ **avoir raison** *(ah-vwahr reh-zohN)* (to be right)
- ✔ **avoir tort** *(ah-vwahr tohr)* (to be wrong)
- ✔ **en avoir assez** *(ahN-nah-vwah-rah-say),* literally to have enough; in Québec, **être tanné** *(eh-truh tah-nay)* (to be fed up)

Chapter 2

Grammar on a Diet:
Just the Basics

. . . .

In This Chapter

▶ Constructing simple sentences

▶ Forming questions the easy way

▶ Conjugating past, present, and future tenses

▶ Solving the gender debate

▶ Getting to know "you": the tu/vous issue

. . . .

Although the word "grammar" may make you as nervous now as it did when you were in grammar school, you can relax your grip on that number 2 pencil: Grammar is merely the school glue that holds your French sentences together. In fact, grammar is simply a word for ways of combining nouns (to name things), adjectives (to qualify these nouns), verbs (to show action or a state of being), and adverbs (to describe verbs, adjectives, or other adverbs). This combination of words makes possible the expression of our needs, desires, likes, and dislikes; our present, past, and future actions; and the ways and means of these actions.

Constructing Simple Sentences

A simple sentence construction (in French or in English) consists of a noun, an adjective, a verb, and, possibly an adverb.

Nouns

All French nouns have a sex instead of being just neutral like nouns in English: They are either masculine or feminine. But, instead of calling it sex, grammarian types talk about the gender of a noun (perhaps to avoid giggling too much).

Also in French, as in English, nouns are either singular or plural. The French say they have a number.

French nouns are almost always preceded by articles — small words like "the" or "a/an" in English — that mark the gender and number of nouns. The best way to get used to knowing the right gender of a noun in French is to try to remember the article with the noun. In other words, never memorize a noun without its marker. Instead of **table** *(tahbl)* (table), say to yourself **la table** *(lah tahbl)* (the table) or **une table** *(ewn tahbl)* (a table). Instead of **livre** *(leevr)* (book), think **le livre** *(luh leevr)* (the book) or **un livre** *(aN leevr)* (a book). This chapter looks at this gender issue in more detail later on.

Whereas in English the plural of a noun is not always marked by an article, for example, "a table" becomes plural "tables," in French the masculine article for "the," **le** *(luh),* and the feminine **la** *(lah)* both become **les** *(lay)* in the plural. The masculine article for "a," **un** (aN), and the feminine **une** *(ewn)* both become **des** *(day).* **Le livre** *(luh leevr)* (the book) becomes **les livres** *(lay leevr)* (the books), and **une table** *(ewn tahbl)* (a table) becomes **des tables** *(day tahbl)* (tables).

Adjectives

Adjectives describe nouns. Because French nouns have gender and number, any adjectives have to match the nouns they qualify in gender and number. Remember, too, that in French, some adjectives are placed before the noun while others follow the noun. For example:

> ✔ **le papier blanc** *(luh pah-pyay blahN)* (the white paper)

- **la grande maison** *(lah grahNd meh-zohN)* (the big house)
- **les feuilles vertes** *(lay fewy vehrt)* (the green leaves)
- **les petits oiseaux** *(lay puh-tee-zwah-zo)* (the little birds)

As a rule, adjectives that precede the noun usually relate to

- Beauty: **beau/belle** *(boh/behl)* (beautiful), **joli** *(zhoh-lee)* (pretty), and so on
- Age: **jeune** *(zhuhn)* (young), **vieux/vieille** *(vyuh/vyehy)* (old), and so on
- Goodness, or lack of it: **bon/bonne** *(bohN/bon)* (good), **mauvais** *(moh-vay)* (bad), and so on
- Size: **grand** *(grahN)* big, **petit** *(puh-tee)* (small), and so on

Remember that an adjective varies in gender (and number) according to the noun it qualifies. Said more simply, if a noun is feminine, you usually add an *e* at the end of the adjective that goes along with it. For example:

- **un petit appartement** *(aN puh-tee-tah-pahr-tuh-mahN)* (a small apartment)
- **une grande maison** *(ewn grahNd meh-zohN)* (a big house)

But this does not always work! In French, there is a saying that **l'exception confirme la règle** *(layk-sayp-syohN kohN-feerm lah rehgl)* (the exception confirms the rule). Thus, the feminine of **beau** *(bo)* is **belle** *(behl)* (beautiful). This is just one example of several exceptions.

Verbs

A verb expresses an action or a state of being. This action has a subject (such as the person who acts or the thing or idea that exists). This subject may be a noun (as in "the leaf falls") or a pronoun (as in "they sing").

Just as in English, you make the verb match the subject (you don't say, of course, "the leaf fall"), so, in French, the verb has a special ending for each subject (I, you, we, she, and so on).

Here's what a simple sentence looks like:

Les petits oiseaux chantent.

lay puh-tee zwah-zo shahNt

The little birds sing (or are singing).

Check out the section "The Simple Tenses: Past, Present, and Future" for more details about how to conjugate verbs — that is, make the verb match the subject.

Adverbs

An adverb is a word that modifies (describes) a verb, an adjective, or another adverb. In English, most adverbs end with -ly, as in, "Please, speak slowly." In French, the adverbs end in **-ment.** So the same sentence would be: "**Parlez lentement, s'il vous plaît**" _(pahr-lay lahNt-mahN seel-voo-pleh)._

The sample sentence is now complete and reads like this:

Les petits oiseaux chantent joyeusement.

lay puh-tee-zwah-zo shahNt zhwah-yewz-mahN

The little birds sing happily.

Asking Questions

Believe it or not, some grammar issues in French are easier than in English. A good example of this is the way you can form questions.

✔ The easiest way, of course, is to use intonation by raising your voice at the end of your statement.

Vous avez un ticket? *(voo-zah-vay-zaN tee-keh)* (Do you have a ticket?)

✔ Another easy way is to add **est-ce que** *(ehs-kuh)* at the beginning of your phrase.

Est-ce que vous avez un ticket? *(ehs-kuh voo-zah-vay-zaN tee-keh)* (Do you have a ticket?)

Note that these easy forms of questioning are valid no matter what the tense of the verb is: present, past, or future.

But take note of the fact that if a word beginning with a vowel follows **est-ce que** *(ehs-kuh)*, it becomes **est-ce qu'** *(ehs-k)*. For example:

✔ **Est-ce qu'elle a un ticket?** *(ehs-keh-lah aN tee-keh)* Does she have a ticket?

✔ **Est-ce qu'il fait chaud?** *(ehs-keel feh sho)* Is it warm?

Or you can move on to a third option that is still pretty simple: Making "inverted" questions, just as in English (have you? are you? can you? must you? will you?), by simply turning around (inverting) the subject and the verb.

✔ **Avez-vous une chambre libre?** *(ah-vay voo/ewn shahNbr leebr)* (Do you have a vacancy?)

✔ **Êtes-vous/Es-tu français?** *(eht voo/eh tew frahN-seh)* (Are you French?)

✔ **Pouvez-vous/Voulez-vous remplir ça?** *(poo-vay voo/voo-lay voo rahN-pleer sah)* or

Peux-tu/Veux-tu remplir ça? *(puh tew/vuh tew rahN-pleer sah)* (Can you/do you want to fill this out?)

You hear this kind of question mostly for the **tu** and **vous** forms. It is easiest for you if you don't invert any other forms.

Commanding Your Subjects

The imperative, or command, form of a verb may be used only with the **tu** (you, informal/singular), **vous** (you, formal/plural), and **nous** (we) forms of the verb. You cannot give yourself a command, nor can you give he, she, or they one either. The subject of the verb is not used, only implied. Table 2-1 shows some examples. Note that the last two examples show that the imperative may be used with all verbs, not just -**er** verbs.

Table 2-1 Using the Imperative Form of Verbs

Phrase	Pronunciation	Meaning
Tu restes ici.	tew rehst ee-see	You stay here.
Reste ici! (drop the final s with -er verbs)	rehst ee-see	Stay here!
Vous ne parlez pas.	voo nuh pahrlay pah	You don't talk.
Ne parlez pas!	nuh pahrlay pah	Don't talk!
Nous mangeons des frites.	noo mahN-zhoN day freet	We are eating some fries.
Mangeons des frites!	mahN-zhoN day freet	Let's eat some fries!
Allons-y!	ahl-ohNz-ee	Let's go (there)!
Finis ton lait!	fee-nee tohN lay	Finish your milk!

For negative commands you need to "wrap" the **ne . . . pas** *(nuh pah)* (not) that you use for straightforward negations around the verb, including any pronoun, such as **vous,** that goes with the verb. Check out these examples:

> ✔ **N'attendez pas Paul.** *(nah-tahn-day pah pohl)* (Don't wait for Paul.)
>
> ✔ **Ne vous inquiétez pas.** *(nuh voo-zaN-kee-ay-tay pah)* (Don't worry.)

And just like in English, never use a subject in a command, be it negative or positive.

Regular and Irregular Verbs

In French, as in English, the verb form that has no marking to indicate a subject or a tense (past, present, future) for the action is called the infinitive form. For example, English infinitives begin with **to**, as in "to go" or "to speak." In French, infinitives have special endings, such as **-er, -ir,** or **-re: aller** *(ah-lay)* (to go), **parler** *(pahr-lay)* (to speak), **finir** *(fee-neer)* (to finish), **être ou ne pas être** *(eht-roo nuh pah-zehtr)* (to be or not to be).

The conjugation (adding the markers for subject and tense) of verbs is based on the infinitive form. In English and in French, verbs are either regular or irregular in their conjugations.

Regular verbs follow a common pattern. For example, in English, the verb **to love** is spelled the same way whoever the subject is except for the third person (he, she or it):

I love, you love, he/she loves, we love, you love, they love.

To love is a regular English verb because many English verbs follow this same conjugation.

But **to be** is irregular. The form of the verb depends on the subject:

I am, you are, he/she is, we are, you are, they are.

Regular verbs

In French, regular verbs belong to three large groups that are determined by the endings of their infinitives:

- ✔ The largest group, whose infinitive ends with **-er**, such as: **acheter** *(ah-shuh-tay)* (to buy), **chanter** *(shahN-tay)* (to sing), **parler** *(pahr-lay)* (to speak), and **donner** *(doh-nay)* (to give).

  But **aller** *(ah-lay)* (to go) is irregular.

- ✔ The group whose infinitive ends in **-ir**, such as: **finir** *(fee-neer)* (to finish) and **choisir** *(shwah-zeer)* (to choose).

- ✔ The group whose infinitive ends in **-re**, such as: **attendre** *(ah-tahNdr)* (to wait) and **vendre** *(vahNdr)* (to sell).

All these verbs are regular in French in the sense that they follow a definite pattern belonging to each family, and within that family, are conjugated in the same manner with the same ending, depending on the subject and the tenses. The section "The Simple Tenses: Past, Present, and Future" shows you how to conjugate these regular verbs.

Irregular verbs

An irregular verb means that the forms of the verb do not follow the regular pattern for verbs with that ending. You have to make a special effort to memorize the conjugations of these verbs by heart.

The most important ones are the following:

- ✔ **être** *(eh-truh)* (to be)
- ✔ **avoir** *(ah-vwahr)* (to have)

Not only are they used in many expressions, but they also serve as helping verbs — in making up past tenses.

Other common irregular helping verbs are **pouvoir** *(poovwahr)* (to be able to), **vouloir** *(vool-wahr)* (to want), or **doir** *(dwahr)* (to need). They require a verb after them in the infinitive form, as in these examples:

✔ **Tu peux traduire.** *(tew puh trah-dew-eer)* (You can translate.)

✔ **Vous pouvez choisir.** *(voo poo-vay shwah-zeer)* (You can choose.)

✔ **Pouvez-vous signer ici?** *(poo-vay voo see-nyay ee-see)* (Can you sign here?)

✔ **Je veux changer de l'argent.** *(zhuh vuh shahN-zhay duh lar-zhahN)* (I want to change money.)

✔ **Il doit attendre un peu.** *(eel dwah-tah-tahN-draN puh)* (He has to wait a little.)

Check out the section "The Simple Tenses: Past, Present, and Future" for the conjugations of these irregular verbs.

The Simple Tenses: Past, Present, and Future

"Tense" simply means "time." So if you want to express an action or a state of being taking place in the present, you use the present tense. If it hasn't happened yet, you use the future tense. And if it took place in the past, you use a past tense.

In French, you can express the past tense in several ways, but the simplest and the most common is **le passé composé** *(luh pah-say kohN-po-zay)*. The word **composé** (complex) means that it is made up of more than one component. So for this tense, you use two parts: an auxiliary verb (such as **avoir** or **être**) and the past participle of the action verb (the form that in English often ends with -ed.)

Examples:

J'ai chanté. *(zheh shahN-tay)* (I sang.)

Il est parti. *(ee-leh pahr-tee)* (He left.)

If the action is going to take place in the future, the French use a form similar to the English "to be going to" with the verb **aller** *(ah-lay)* (to go).

Example:

> **Demain Sylvie va voyager.** *(duh-maN seel-vee vah vwah-yah-zhay)* (Tomorrow Sylvie is going to travel.)

To give you an idea of what a regular verb looks like in these three simple tenses, the following list shows how to conjugate the verb **parler** *(pahr-lay)* (to speak) with the subject pronouns I, you, and he/she.

Présent *(pray-zahN)*

Je parle *(zhuh pahrl)*

Vous parlez *(voo pahr-lay)*

Il/elle parle *(eel/ehl pahrl)*

Passé composé *(pah-say kohN-po-zay)*

J'ai parlé *(zheh pahr-lay)*

Vous avez parlé *(voo-zah-vay pahr-lay)*

Il a parlé/elle a parlé *(ee-lah pahr-lay/eh-lah pahr-lay)*

Futur *(few-tewr)*

Je vais parler *(zhuh veh pahr-lay)*

Vous allez parler *(voo-zah-lay pahr-lay)*

Il/elle va parler *(eel/ehl vah pahr-lay)*

Now you can proudly say: **Bientôt, je vais parler français** *(byaN-to zhuh veh pahr-lay frahN-seh)* (Soon, I am going to speak French).

Using the past tense with avoir

Now to dig just a bit deeper into the past tense: In French, the past tense is formed by using a helping verb, either **avoir** *(ahv-wahr)* (to have) or **être** *(eh-truh)* (to be) and a past participle. Most past participles use **avoir** (see the next section for verbs that use

être in past tense). Review the conjugation of **avoir** (to have) in Table 2-2 before continuing.

Table 2-2	The Conjugation of the Verb Avoir
Conjugation	*Pronunciation*
j'ai	zhay
tu as	tew ah
il/elle a	eel/ehl ah
nous avons	noo zavohN
vous avez	voo zahvay
ils/elles ont	eel/ehl zohN

You make regular past participles by dropping the stem of the infinitive and adding the following endings:

✔ The past participle for **-er** verbs ends in **é**:

téléphoner *(tay-lay-foh-nay)* (to telephone or call):

J'ai téléphoné à Monique. *(zhay tay-lay-foh-nay ah moh-neek)* (I called [have called] Monique.)

regarder *(reh-gahr-day)* (to watch)

Nous avons regardé un film. *(noo zahvohN reh-gahr-day aN feelm)* (We watched [have watched] a movie.)

✔ The past participle for **-ir** verbs ends in **i**:

choisir *(shwah-zeer)* (to choose):

Il a choisi une banane. *(eel ah chwahzee ewn bahn-ahn)* (He chose [has chosen] a banana.)

finir *(fee-neer)* (to finish):

Elles ont fini leur conversation. *(ehl zohN fee-nee luhr kohN-vehr-sah-see-ohN)* (They finished [have finished] their conversation.)

✔ The past participle for **-re** verbs ends in **u**:

attendre *(ah-tehn-druh)* (to wait):

Tu as attendu le bus. *(too ah ah-tehn-doo luh boos)* (You waited [have waited] for the bus.)

répondre *(ray-pohN-druh)* (to answer):

Vous avez répondu à la question. *(voo zahvay ray-pohN-doo ah la kehs-tee-ohN)* (You answered [have answered] the question.)

French also has several irregular past participles. The irregular verbs don't have a set pattern like the regular verbs do, so you just have to memorize them. Table 2-3 lists the most common irregular past participles.

Table 2-3	Common Irregular Past Participles	
Infinitive	**Past Participle**	**Translation**
être *(eh-truh)* (to be)	été *(ay-tay)*	been
avoir *(ahv-wahr)* (to have)	eu *(ew)*	had
faire *(fehr)* (to do/make)	fait *(fay)*	done/made
pouvoir *(poov-wahr)* (to be able to)	pu *(pew)*	could have
vouloir *(vool-wahr)* (to wish/want)	voulu *(voo-loo)*	wished/wanted

The following list gives some examples of how you use the past participles of irregular verbs in a sentence:

✔ **Nous avons été en retard.** *(nooz ahv-ohN ay-tay ehn reh-tahr)* (We were late.)

✔ **Il a eu un message.** *(eel ah euh uhn may-sazh)* (He had a message.)

✔ **Qu'est-ce que tu as fait?** *(kes kuh too ah fay)* (What did you do?)

✔ **Vous avez pu téléphoner à votre bureau.** *(vooz ahv-ay poo tay-lay-foh-nay vohtruh byoo-roh)* (You were able to call your office.)

✔ **J'ai voulu un sandwich.** *(zhay voo-loo uhn sahNd-veech)* (I wanted a sandwich.)

Using the past tense with être

Sixteen irregular verbs are conjugated with the helping verb **être** instead of **avoir**. Most of these verbs are verbs of motion. Table 2-4 presents the conjugation of **être**.

Table 2-4	The Conjugation of the Verb Être
Conjugation	*Pronunciation*
Je suis	zhuh swee
tu es	tew eh
il/elle est	eel/ehl eh
nous sommes	noo sohm
vous êtes	voo zeht
ils/elles sont	eel/ehl sohN

The main difference with these 16 verbs is that the past participle must agree in number and gender with the subject. Luckily, most of the time the pronunciation doesn't change.

We can show you what we mean using the past participle of **aller** *(ah-lay)* (to go):

✔ Suppose Janine, a girl, said that she'd gone to the post office. She would say:

Je suis allée à la poste. *(zhuh sweez ah-lay ah lah pohst)*

However, if John, a boy, said the same thing, it would sound the same but be spelled differently:

Je suis allé à la poste. *(zhuh sweez ah-lay ah lah pohst)*

✔ Here's a mother telling her son, "You went to the post office": **Tu es allé à la poste.** *(tew ay ah-lay ah lah pohst)*

Now she tells her daughter the same thing:

Tu es allée à la poste. *(tew ay ah-lay ah lah pohst)*

Do you see the difference in spelling with the past participle? Here are some more:

✔ **Elle est allée à la poste.** *(ehl ayt ah-lay ah lah pohst)* (She [feminine singular] went to the post office.)

✔ **Nous sommes allés à la poste.** *(noo sohmz ah-lay ah lah pohst)* (We [masculine plural] went to the post office.)

✔ **Vous êtes allées à la poste.** *(vooz eht ah-lay ah lah pohst)* (You [feminine plural] went to the post office.)

✔ **Ils sont allés à la poste.** *(eel sohNt ah-lay ah lah pohst)* (They [masculine plural] went to the post office.)

The rules for making past participles agree with the number and gender of the subject are as follows:

✔ If the subject is masculine, singular, the past participle does not change. It will end in **é, i,** or **u** accordingly. The past participle changes spelling only in the following cases:

✔ If the subject is feminine singular, the past participle ends in **-e.**

✔ If the subject is masculine plural, the past participle ends in **-s.**

✔ If the subject is feminine plural, the past participle ends in **-es.**

Table 2-5 shows the 16 participles that make their past tense with **être**:

Table 2-5   **Participles That Make Their Past Tense with Être**

Participle	Pronunciation	Infinitive	Translation
Verbs of coming			
allé	ah-lay	aller	to go
arrivé	ah-ree-vay	arriver	to arrive
entré	ahN-tray	entrer	to enter
venu	vuh-new	venir	to come
Up and down verbs			
descendu	deh-sahN-dew	descendre	to go down
monté	mohN-tay	monter	to go up
resté	rehs-tay	rester	to stay
tombé	tohN-bay	tomber	to fall
Verbs of leaving			
parti	pahr-tee	partir	to leave
passé	pah-say	passer	to pass by
rentré	rahN-tray	rentrer	to come back home
sorti	sohr-tee	sortir	to go out
Verbs for in and out of life			
né	nay	naître	to be born
mort	mohr	mourir	to die
décédé	day-say-day	décéder	to decease
devenu	duh-vuh-new	devenir	to become

Doing the future with aller

One way to form the future tense is to use the helping verb **aller** *(ah-lay)* (to go) and an infinitive verb. In this respect, the future tense in French is similar to that in English: I'm going to read tomorrow, He's going to get married. Table 2-6 shows the conjugation of the verb **aller,** which is a bit sneaky because it hides as an **-er** verb but actually is extremely irregular.

Table 2-6	The Conjugation of the Verb Aller
Conjugation	*Pronunciation*
je vais	zhuh veh
tu vas	tew vah
il/elle va	eel/ehl vah
nous allons	noo-zah-lohN
vous allez	voo-zah-lay
ils/elles vont	eel/ehl vohN

Future tense is pretty easy because you don't have to remember any past participles. Take a look at these examples:

- ✔ **Tu vas nager demain.** *(tew vah nah-zhay duh-maN).* (You will swim tomorrow.)

- ✔ **Nous allons aller à Paris.** *(noo zah-loN alay ah pah-ree)* (We will go to Paris.)

Conjugating the tenses

This section shows you how to conjugate all three tenses of several common verbs. Remember, all regular verbs conjugate the same way, so you can flip back to this section when you want to know how to conjugate a new regular verb.

Table 2-7 conjugates **parler** *(pahr-lay)* (to speak), a regular verb ending with **-er.** The past participle is **parlé** *(pahr-lay)* (spoken):

Table 2-7	Regular -Er: Parler (To Speak)		
	Present	*Past*	*Future*
je/j' (I)	parle	ai parlé	vais parler
tu (you, inf.)	parles	as parlé	vas parler
il/elle (he/she)	parle	a parlé	va parler
nous (we)	parlons	avons parlé	allons parler
vous (you, form.)	parlez	avez parlé	allez parler
ils/elles (they)	parlent	ont parlé	vont parler

Table 2-8 conjugates **finir** *(fee-neer)* (to finish), a regular verb ending with **-ir.** The past participle is **fini** *(fee-nee)* (finished):

Table 2-8	Regular -Ir: Finir (To Finish)		
	Present	*Past*	*Future*
je/j' (I)	finis	ai fini	vais finir
tu (you, inf.)	finis	as fini	vas finir
il/elle (he/she)	finit	a fini	va finir
nous (we)	finissons	avons fini	allons finir
vous (you, form.)	finissez	avez fini	allez finir
ils/elles (they)	finissent	ont fini	vont finir

Table 2-9 conjugates **vendre** *(vahN-druh)* (to sell), a regular verb ending with **-re.** The past participle is **vendu** *(vahN-doo)* (sold):

Table 2-9	Regular -Re: Vendre (To Sell)		
	Present	*Past*	*Future*
je/j' (I)	vends	ai vendu	vais vendre
tu (you, inf.)	vends	as vendu	vas vendre
il/elle (he/she)	vend	a vendu	va vendre
nous (we)	vendons	avons vendu	allons vendre
vous (you, form.)	vendez	avez vendu	allez vendre
ils/elles (they)	vendent	ont vendu	vont vendre

Table 2-10 conjugates the irregular verb **avoir** *(ahv-wahr)* (to have). The past participle is **eu** *(ew)* (had):

Table 2-10	Irregular Avoir (To Have)		
	Present	*Past*	*Future*
je/j' (I)	ai	ai eu	vais avoir
tu (you, inf.)	as	as eu	vas avoir
il/elle (he/she)	a	a eu	va avoir
nous (we)	avons	avons eu	allons avoir
vous (you, form.)	avez	avez eu	allez avoir
ils/elles (they)	ont	ont eu	vont avoir

Table 2-11 conjugates the irregular verb **être** *(eh-truh)* (to be). The past participle is **été** *(ay-tay)* (been):

Table 2-11	Irregular Être (To Be)		
	Present	*Past*	*Future*
je/j' (I)	suis	ai été/e	vais être
tu (you, inf.)	es	as été/e	vas être
il/elle (he/she)	est	a été/e	va être
nous (we)	sommes	avons été	allons être
vous (you, form.)	êtes	avez été	allez être
ils/elles (they)	sont	ont été	vont être

Probing Pronouns

Pronouns are handy little words that you can use to avoid repetition. Instead of repeating "Jane did this. Jane did that," you can say "Jane this this. She did that." This section gives you some of the different uses of pronouns.

Subject pronouns

Subject pronous are the I, he/she, and we of English and replace the subject of a sentence. Table 2-12 gives them to you:

Table 2-12	Subject Pronouns	
Pronoun	*Pronunciation*	*English*
je/j'	zhuh/zh	I
tu	tew	you, inf.

(continued)

Table 2-12 *(continued)*

Pronoun	Pronunciation	English
il/elle	eel/ehl	he/she
nous	noo	we
vous	voo	you, form.
ils/elles	ell/ehl	they

Here is an example:

Janine et Marie parlent.	**Elles parlent.**
(Janine ay Marie pahr-leN)	*(Ehl pahr-leN)*
(Janine and Marie speak.	(They speak.)

Direct object pronouns

In a conversation, you wouldn't sound very natural if you kept repeating the same words: "I would like <u>a room</u>. Can I see <u>the room</u>? Let's go and see <u>the room</u>."

Saying "I would like <u>a room</u>. Can I see <u>it</u>? Let's go and see <u>it</u>" sounds a lot better, doesn't it?

So, drop your object and replace it with **le, la, l'**, or **les,** depending on whether it's feminine or masculine, singular or plural, but be careful: You must put it in front of the verb. Check out the examples:

Il voit le guide/l'hôtel.	**Il le voit.**
(eel vwah luh geed/ lo-tehl)	*(eel luh vwah)*
He sees the guide/ the hotel.	He sees it.

Nous suivons la réceptionniste.	**Nous la suivons.**
(noo swee-vohN lah ray-sehp-syoh-neest)	*(noo lah swee-vohN)*
We are following the receptionist.	We are following her.
Elle vérifie les dates.	**Elle les vérifie.**
(ehl vay-ree-fee leh daht)	*(ehl leh vay-ree-fee)*
She is checking the dates.	She's checking them.

The other object pronouns are even easier because there is only one form for masculine and feminine. Here are a few examples:

- **Elle me regarde.** *(ehl muh ruh-gahrd)* (She looks at me.)
- **Je te vois.** *(zhuh tuh vwah)* (I see you.)
- **Il nous suit.** *(eel noo swee)* (He follows us.)
- **La réceptionniste vous écoute.** *(lah ray-sehp-syho-neest voo zay koot)* The receptionist listens to you.

Naturally, there is an exception to the preceding rule: When you have a helping verb plus the infinitive in your sentence you need to put the object pronoun in front of the infinitive form.

Il veut voir la chambre.	**Il veut la voir.**
(eel vuh vwahr lah shahNbr)	*(eel vuh lah vwahr)*
He wants to see the room.	He wants to see it.

Objects of prepositions

After a preposition such as for, with, without, and so on, the pronouns me, you, him, us, you (plural), or them becomes **moi, toi, lui/elle, nous, vous,** or **eux/elles** *(mwah, twah, lew-ee/ehl, noo, voo, uh/ehl).* Here are the personal pronouns after prepositions:

- ✔ **pour moi** *(poor mwah)* (for me)
- ✔ **avec moi** *(ah-vek mwah)* (with me)
- ✔ **sans toi** *(sahN twah)* (without you)
- ✔ **pour lui/elle** *(poor lew-ee/ehl)* (for him/her)
- ✔ **avec nous** *(ah-vek noo)* (with us)
- ✔ **sans vous** *(sahN voo)* (without you)
- ✔ **pour eux/elles** *(poor uh/ehl)* (for them)

Indirect pronouns

In the phrase **Ça convient à Mme Paulet** *(sa kohN-vyaN ah mahdahm poh-leh)* (It suits Mrs. Paulet), **à Mme Paulet** is the indirect object of the sentence. You can replace the indirect object with an indirect object pronoun: **Ça lui convient** *(sah lwee kohN-vyaN)* (It suits her). Here are the other pronouns:

- ✔ **Ça me convient.** *(sa muh kohN-vyaN)* (That suits me.)
- ✔ **Ça te convient.** *(sa tuh kohN-vyaN)* (That suits you.)
- ✔ **Ça lui convient.** *(sa lwee kohN-vyaN)* (That suits him/her.)
- ✔ **Ça nous convient.** *(sa noo kohN-vyaN)* (That suits us.)
- ✔ **Ça vous convient.** *(sa voo kohN-vyaN)* (That suit you.)
- ✔ **Ça leur convient.** *(sa luhr kohN-vyaN)* (That suits them.)

By the way, only **lui** and **leur** differ from the direct object pronouns (which are **le, la, les**); the others coincide.

All the Little Words: Gender, Articles, and Adjectives

All the little words and endings of words may seem trivial when you're first tackling a language, but incorporating them while you learn vocabulary makes your life much easier in the long run. This section covers gender endings, articles, and adjectives.

Gender bending

Remembering the gender of nouns may at first seem to be an almost impossible obstacle to speaking French. But don't worry! In this section, we give you some guidelines that make it easier to know right away the gender of many words.

With a few exceptions, the ending of a noun is a rather good indication of its gender. The following list shows some common endings of masculine nouns:

- ✔ **-age** *(ahzh)*

    le fromage *(luh froh-mahzh)* (cheese)

    l'étage *(lay-tazh)* (a story, a floor)

- ✔ **-eur** (uhr)

    l'auteur *(lo-tuhr)* (author)

    le bonheur *(luh boh-nuhr)* (happiness)

- ✔ **-isme** *(eesm)*

    le capitalisme *(luh kah-pee-tah-leesm)* (capitalism)

    le féminisme *(luh fay-mee-neesm)* (feminism)

- ✔ **-ment** *(mahN)*

    l'appartement *(lah-pahr-tuh-mahN)* (apartment)

- ✔ vowels other than **-e**

    le cinéma *(luh see-nay-mah)* (movies)

    le bureau *(luh bew-ro)* (office or desk)

And here are some common endings for feminine nouns:

> ✔ **-ade** *(ahd)*
>
> **la promenade** *(lah proh-muh-nahd)* (walk)
>
> **la limonade** *(lah lee-moh-nahd)* (lemonade)
>
> ✔ **-ance/-ence** *(ahNs)*
>
> **la naissance** *(lah neh-sahNs)* (birth)
>
> **la différence** *(lah dee-fay-rahNs)* (difference)
>
> ✔ **-oire** *(wahr)*
>
> **la mémoire** *(lah may-mwahr)* (memory)
>
> **la victoire** *(lah veek-twahr)* (victory)
>
> ✔ **-sion/tion** *(syohN)*
>
> **l'impression** *(laN-pray-sy-ohN)* (impression)
>
> **la condition** *(lah kohn-dee-sy-ohN)* (condition)
>
> ✔ **-son** *(zohN)*
>
> **la saison** *(lah seh-zohN)* (season)
>
> **la maison** *(lah meh-zohN)* (house)
>
> ✔ **-é/ée** *(ay)*
>
> **la liberté** *(lah lee-behr-tay)* (freedom)
>
> **l'idée** *(lee-day)* (idea)

Now instead of memorizing every single noun's gender, you can make a good guess based on these endings. When you can readily recognize a noun's gender, then you instantly know which third person subject pronoun to use:

> ✔ **Il** (masculine)
>
> ✔ **Elle** (feminine)

An article on articles

A noun is almost always preceded by a little word called an article that tells you whether the noun is masculine, feminine, singular, or plural. **Le** *(luh)*, **la**

(lah), l' *(ehl ah-pohs-trohf),* and **les** *(leh)* are called definite articles because they refer to an object or a person already mentioned, like "the" does in English. **Le**
refers to a masculine object, **la** to a feminine object,
and **l'** to an object starting with a vowel, which can be
masculine or feminine. **Les** is the common plural form.

Un *(aN),* **une** *(ewn),* and **des** *(deh)* refer to undeter-
mined objects, just like "a" does in English. These
words are called indefinite articles. In the singular,
French has, of course, a masculine form **(un)**, a feminine form **(une),** and a plural common form **(des).**
Following are some examples of how French speakers
use indefinite articles:

- ✔ **Paris est une grande ville. La ville est belle.**
  (pah-ree eh-tewn grahnd veel lah vee-leh behl)
  (Paris is a big city. The city is beautiful.)

- ✔ **Je voudrais un café. Le café est bon.** *(zhuh voo-
  dreh-zaN kah-fay luh kah-fay eh bohn)* (I would
  like a cup of coffee. The coffee is good.)

Dealing with possessive adjectives

Possessive adjectives — my, your, his, and so on —
change to "agree" with the gender and number (singular or plural) of the noun, just as the articles **(le, la,
les)** *(luh, lah, leh)* do. Here's the lowdown — quick:

Masculine noun in the singular:

- ✔ **mon, ton, son chèque** *(mohN, tohN, sohN shek):*
  my, your, his/her check

- ✔ **notre, votre, leur chèque** *(nohtr, vohtr, lewr
  shek):* our, your, their check

Feminine noun in the singular:

- ✔ **ma, ta, sa carte** *(mah, tah, sah kart):* my, your,
  his/her card

- ✔ **notre, votre, leur carte** *(nohtr, vohtr, lewr
  kahrt):* our, your, their card

Masculine or feminine noun in the plural:

- ✔ **mes, tes, ses dollars** *(meh, teh, ses dohlahr):* my, your, his/her dollars

- ✔ **nos, vos, leurs dollars** *(no, vo, lewr dohlar):* our, your, their dollars

The Formal/Informal Debate

How you address someone in French depends on how well you know the person. Someone you meet for the first time (unless it is a child) will expect you to address him or her using the more formal **vous** — a polite and respectful form of the English you.

So start practicing your greetings using **vous** and the corresponding verb form (ending **-ez**) in all circumstances, whether you are addressing one person or more, because **vous** is both singular and plural.

Do not use at first the informal, friendly **tu,** and you will avoid making etiquette mistakes.

Soon you will become more familiar with French ways and the French language, and then being able to choose between **tu** and **vous** will become an indication of your degree of integration with French customs.

Remember: In France, you would sound strange at best and impolite at worst using **tu** to address a stranger or a new acquaintance. However, if you go to Quebec, you may soon discover that the familiar **tu** is much more liberally used at all times.

For more on when and where to use **tu** or **vous,** refer to Chapter 4.

Chapter 3

Numerical Gumbo: Counting of All Kinds

In This Chapter

▶ Watching your cardinals and ordinals

▶ Telling time

▶ Saying the days of the week, months of the year, and seasons

▶ Talking about spending money

*N*umbers make the world go round — or is that money? Well, it's probably both, so this chapter gives you the number and money phrases that you need to get around your world. It also shows you how to tell time and navigate the months of the year.

1, 2, 3: Cardinal Numbers

Knowing the plain old cardinal numbers from 0 to around 100 enables you to express, for example, how much money you have in your wallet, how many sheep you have to count before you fall asleep, how many hours you'll have to wait before your plane takes off, and, of course, to tell time. Check out the numbers in Table 3-1.

Watch out for the numbers begining with 70. They follow a little different pattern than you're used to.

Table 3-1	Cardinal Numbers	
French	*Pronounciation*	*Number*
un	aN	1
deux	duh	2
trois	trwah	3
quatre	kahtr	4
cinq	sank	5
six	sees	6
sept	seht	7
huit	weet	8
neuf	nuhf	9
dix	dees	10
onze	ohNz	11
douze	dooz	12
treize	trehz	13
quatorze	kah-tohrz	14
quinze	kaNz	15
seize	sehz	16
dix-sept	dees seht	17
dix-huit	dee zweet	18
dix-neuf	deez nuhf	19
vingt	vaN	20
vingt et un	vaNt ay aN	21
vingt-deux	vaNt duh	22
vingt-trois	vaNt trwah	23
vingt-quatre	vaNt kahtr	24

French	Pronounciation	Number
vingt-cinq	vaNt saNk	25
vingt-six	vaNt sees	26
vingt-sept	vaNt seht	27
vingt-huit	vaNt weet	28
vingt-neuf	vaNt nuhf	29
trente	trahNt	30
quarante	kar-ahNt	40
cinquante	saNk-ahNt	50
soixante	swah-zahNt	60
soixante-dix	swah-zahNt dees	70
soixante onze	swah-zahNt ohNz	71
soixante-douze	swahzahNt dooz	72
quatre-vingt	kahtr vaN	80
quatre-vingt-un	kahtr vaNt aN	81
quatre-vingt-deux	kahtr vaN duh	82
quatre-vingt-dix	kahtr vaN dees	90
quatre-vingt-onze	kahtr vaNt ohNz	91
quatre-vingt-douze	kahtr vaN dooz	92
cent	seN	100
cent un	seNt aN	101
cent deux	seN duh	102

Switzerland and Belgium often use the easier forms of **septante** *(sehp-tahNt)* (70) and **nonante** *(noh-naNt)* (90). In some remote parts of Switzerland, they use the form **hui-tante** *(ew-ee-tahNt)* or **octante** *(ohk-tahNt)* (80).

Discovering Ordinal Numbers

Ordinal numbers are pretty important to conversation, especially if you're going to follow or give directions. A couple of simple rules can help you recognize ordinal numbers:

- ✔ Except for **premier** *(pruhm-yay)* (first), they all have **-ième** after the number (just like the -th ending in English).

- ✔ If the cardinal number ends in an **-e,** the **-e** is dropped: For example, **quatre** *(kahtr)* (four) becomes **quatrième** *(kat-ree-ehm)* (fourth).

Un *(aN)* (one), **cinq** *(saNk)* (five), and **neuf** *(nuhf)* (nine) have special forms, as you can see in Table 3-2.

Table 3-2	Ordinal Numbers	
Word (Numeral)	*Pronunciation*	*English*
premier (1e)	pruhm-yeh	first
deuxième (2e)	duh-zyehm	second
troisième (3e)	trwah-zyehm	third
quatrième (4e)	kah-tryehm	fourth
cinquième (5e)	sahN-kyehm	fifth
sixième (6e)	see-zyehm	sixth
septième (7e)	seh-tyehm	seventh
huitième (8e)	wee-tyehm	eighth
neuvième (9e)	nuh-vyehm	ninth
dixième (10e)	dee-zyehm	tenth

Word (Numeral)	Pronunciation	English
onzième (11e)	ohN-zyehm	eleventh
douzième (12e)	doo-zyehm	twelfth
treizième (13e)	treh-zyehm	thirteenth
quatorzième (14e)	kah-tohr-zyehm	fourteenth
quinzième (15e)	kahN-zyehm	fifteenth
seizième (16e)	seh-zyehm	sixteenth
dix-septième (17e)	dee-seh-tyehm	seventeenth
dix-huitième (18e)	dee-zweet-yehm	eighteenth
dix-neuvième (19e)	deez nuh vyehm	nineteenth
vingtième (20e)	vahN-tyehm	twentieth
vingt et unième (21e)	vahN-teh-ewn-yehm	twenty-first
vingt-deuxième (22e)	vahN-duh-zyehm	twenty-second
trentième (30e)	trahN-tyehm	thirtieth
quatre-vingtième (80e)	kahtr vahN-tyehm	eightieth
quatre-vingt-deuxième (82e)	katr-vahN duh-zyehm	eighty-second
centième (100e)	sahN-tyehm	one-hundreth
deux centième (200e)	duh sahN-tyehm	two-hundreth

Here are some common phrases using ordinal numbers:

> ✔ **L'appartement est au troisième.** *(lah-pahr-tuh-mahN eh to trwah-zyehm)* (The apartment is on the third floor.)
>
> Two things about ordinals and floors: You can use an ordinal number by itself, without saying

étage *(ay-tahzh)* (floor) after it. Also, because the ground floor is called **le rez-de-chaussée** *(luh reht-shoh-say)* (street level), the first floor **(le premier)** is what Americans consider to be the second floor.

✔ **Dans quel arrondissement est le restaurant?** *(dahn kehl ah-rohN-dees-mahN eh luh reh-stoh-rahN)* (In which district is the restaurant?)

✔ **Il est dans le deuxième.** *(eel eh dahN luh duh-zyehm)* (It is in the second district.)

✔ **Prenez la troisième rue à droite, et c'est tout droit.** *(pruhnay lah trwah-zyehm rew ah drwaht ay seh too drwah)* (Take the third street on the right, and it's straight ahead.)

Telling Time

You wouldn't want to miss your plane or a great concert because you don't know how to ask the time. This section tells you how.

Counting the hours

Both Europe and French-speaking Canada use the 24-hour clock (military time), so you don't need to distinguish between a.m. or p.m. One less thing to worry about is always good, right? To say what time it is, simply add the number of minutes to the hour, using a lowercase *h* to separate the hour from the minutes rather than a colon. Here are some examples:

✔ **Il est 11h (onze heures).** *(eel ay ohNz uhr)* (It's 11:00 (a.m.).)

✔ **Il est 11h30 (onze heures trente).** *(eel ay ohNz uhr trahNt)* (It's 11:30 (a.m.).)

✔ **Il est 16h (seize heures).** *(eel ay sehz uhr)* (It's 4:00 (p.m.).)

✔ **Il est 16h10 (seize heures dix).** *(eel ay sehz uhr dees)* (It's 4:10 (p.m.).)

To express time before the hour ("It's 10 minutes to 2"), the French use **moins** *(mwahN),* which means "minus":

> ✔ **Il est huit heures moins dix.** *(eel eh weet uhr mwahN dees)* (It's 7:50 (a.m.).)

> ✔ **Il est dix heures moins vingt-cinq.** *(eel eh deez uhr mwahN vahN sayNk)* (It's 9:35 (a.m.).)

As in English, the French also use quarter after, **et quart** *(ay kahr);* half past, **et demi** *(ay duh-mee);* and quarter till, **moins le quart** *(mwahN luh kahr).* Here are some examples:

> ✔ **Il est 9h15 (neuf heures et quart).** *(eel eh nuhv uhr ay kahr)* (It's 9:15 (a.m.).)

> ✔ **Il est une heures moins le quart.** *(eel eh ewn uhr mwahN luh kahr.)* (It's 12:45 (a.m.).)

Words to Know

Quel heure est-il?	kehl uhr ayt-eel	What time is it?
Il y a 10 (dix)	ill ee ah dees	10 minutes ago (minutes pronounced *mee-newt*)
Dans 20 (vingt)	dahN vahN	in 20 minutes (minutes pronounced *mee-newt*)
Et quart	ay kahr	quarter past
Et demi(e)	ay duh-mee	half past
Moins vingt	mwahN vahN	twenty (minutes) to
Moins le quart	mwahN luh kahr	quarter to

Being on time

Here are some timing phrases that may come in handy when making travel plans, meeting friends, making appointments, and more:

- **demain matin** *(duh-maN mah-taN)* (tomorrow morning)

- **tôt le matin** *(toh luh mah-taN)* (early in the morning)

- **demain après-midi** *(duh-maN ah-preh mee-dee)* (tomorrow afternoon)

- **Il est trop tôt.** *(eel eh tro to)* (It is too early.)

- **Il est trop tard.** *(eel eh tro tahr)* (It is too late.)

- **À quelle heure commence l'excursion?** *(ah kehl uhr kohm-ahNs lehks-kewr-zee-ohN)* (What time does the tour begin?)

- **à quelle heure?** *(ah kehl uhr)* (at what time?)

- **un moment/un instant** *(aN moh-mahN aN naN-stahN)* (one moment)

- **Nous sommes en retard.** *(noo sohmz ehN ruh-tahr)* (We're late.)

- **Oh non! Allons-y! Dépêchons-nous!** *(oh nohN ahl-onz ee day-pesh-ohN nu)* (Oh no! Let's go! Hurry up!)

The little word **tout (toute, tous, toutes)** is used in many different combinations. It adjusts its ending to the noun it gets connected with. It means "every" when it's connected with a time definition in the plural, such as:

- **tous les quarts d'heure** *(too leh kahr duhr)* (every quarter of an hour)

- **tous les jours** *(too leh zhoor)* (every day)

- **toutes les vingt minutes** *(toot leh vahN mee-newt)* (every twenty minutes)

However, when it's connected with time definitions in the singular, it takes on a different meaning:

> ✔ **toute la matinée** *(toot lah mah-tee-nay)* (all morning long)
>
> ✔ **toute la journée** *(toot lah zhoor-nay)* (all day long)
>
> ✔ **toute la vie** *(toot lah vee)* (the entire life)

Days, Months, and Seasons

Okay, so days and months aren't really numbers, but they're a way of measuring time. The following sections give you what you need to know.

What day is it?

Table 3-3 has the days of the week.

Table 3-3	Days of the Week	
French	*Pronunciation*	*English*
lundi	luhn-dee	Monday
mardi	mahr-dee	Tuesday
mercredi	mehr-kreh-dee	Wednesday
jeudi	zhuh-dee	Thursday
vendredi	veN-dreh-di	Friday
samedi	sah-meh-dee	Saturday
dimanche	dee-mahNsh	Sunday

If you want to be more general, you can say:

> ✔ **après-demain** *(ah-preh duh-maN)* (the day after tomorrow)
>
> ✔ **samedi prochain** *(sahm-dee proh-shaN)* (next Saturday)
>
> ✔ **la semaine prochaine** *(lah suh-mehn proh-shehn)* (next week)

Month by month

You may need to know the months of the year in French. Check out Table 3-4.

Table 3-4	The Months	
French	*Pronunciation*	*English*
janvier	zhan-vyay	January
février	fay-vree-ay	February
mars	mahrs	March
avril	ah-vreel	April
mai	meh	May
juin	zhwaN	June
juillet	zhwee-yeh	July
août	oot	August
septembre	sehp-tahNbr	September
octobre	ok-tohbr	October
novembre	noh-vahNbr	November
décembre	day-sahNbr	December

Specific dates

When expressing a more specific date, you use the following construction:

Le + cardinal number + month + year

Here is an example.

> ✔ **C'est + le + six + avril + 2000.**
>
> *(seh luh see zah-vreel duh meel)*
>
> (It's the sixth of April 2000.)

Use this formula to express all dates, except for the first of the month:

C'est le premier mai. *(seh luh pruhm-yay meh)*
(It's the first of May.)

Less specific dates

Use **en** *(ahN)* with months to express "in":

> ✔ **En janvier, je pars pour la Martinique.** *(ahN zhaN-vyay zhuh pahr poor lah mahr-tee-neek)* (In January, I leave for Martinique.)
>
> ✔ **Je reviens en avril.** *(zhuh ruh-vyaN ahN nah-vreel)* (I am coming back in April.)

Here are a few question-and-answer sequences using this scheduling vocabulary:

> ✔ **Quel jour est-ce aujourd'hui?** *(kehl zhoor ehs oh-zhoor-dwee)* (What day is today?)
>
> **Aujourd'hui, c'est lundi.** *(oh-zhoor-dwee seh laN-dee)* (Today is Monday.)
>
> ✔ **Quelle est la date?** *(kehl eh lah daht)* (What is the date?)
>
> **C'est le onze juillet.** *(seh luh ohNz zhwee-yeh)* (It's the 11th of July.)
>
> ✔ **Quand voulez-vous partir?** *(kahN voo-lay voo pahr-teer)* (When do you want to leave?)

Le quinze mai. *(luh kaNz meh)* (On the 15th of May.)

✔ **J'aime voyager au printemps.** *(zhehm vwah-yah-zhay o praN-tahN)* (I like to travel in the spring.)

Moi aussi: en avril ou en mai. *(mwah oh-see ahN ah-vreel oo ahN meh)* (Me too: in April or in May.)

✔ **Mon ami arrive en septembre.** *(moh nah-mee ah-reev ahN sehp-tahNbr)* (My friend arrives in September.)

Il reste jusqu'à la fin du mois? *(eel rehst zhews-kah lah faN dew mwah)* (Does he stay until the end of the month?)

Meet the four seasons

Here's an introduction to what the French call each of the four seasons:

✔ **au printemps** *(oh praN-tahN)* (in the spring)

✔ **en été** *(ahN nay-tay)* (in the summer)

✔ **en automne** *(ahN noh-tohn)* (in the fall)

✔ **en hiver** *(ahN nee-vehr)* (in the winter)

With seasons, to express "in the," use **au** before a consonant sound and use **en** before a vowel sound.

How about some phrases with those seasons?

✔ **Qu'est-ce que vous préférez en hiver? La plage ou le ski?** *(kes-kuh voo pray-fay-ray ahN nee-vehr lah plahzh oo luh skee)* (What do you prefer in the winter? The beach or skiing?)

✔ **Et en été? La mer ou la montagne?** *(ay ahN nay-tay lah mehr oo lah mohN-tah-nyuh)* (And in the summer? The ocean or the mountains?)

✔ **Au printemps? La campagne ou les grandes villes?** *(o praN-tahN lah kahN-pan-yuh oo lay grahNd veel)* (In the spring? The country or the cities?)

> ✔ **En automne? Les musées ou les monuments?**
> *(ahN noh-tohn lay mew-say oo lay moh-new-mahN)* (In the fall? Museums or monuments?)

Money

Most of Europe uses the euro, which means only one exchange rate for most European countries. However, Switzerland, Great Britain, Sweden, Denmark, and Norway are keeping (at least for a while) their own currencies.

When you travel to French-speaking Canada, you pay with Canadian dollars. No sweat — they're worth a little less than the U.S. dollar, so you have nothing much to figure. Although the math of traveling is quite stress-free, the language is another matter! But don't worry, the following sections explain how to conduct your business at a bank or a currency exchange smoothly.

Exchanging your dollars at a bank

One of the first places you may need to locate when you travel is a place to exchange your currency for the local currency. Following are the three convenient places to exchange money at a reasonable rate:

> ✔ **les banques** *(lay bahNk)* (banks)
> ✔ **un bureau de change** *(aN bew-ro duh shahN-zh)* (a currency exchange)
> ✔ **la poste** *(lah pohst)* (the post office)

Although you may find places other than those listed here to change money, you're most likely to get the best deal if you change money at a bank.

When you enter a bank, you may hear one of these phrases, which both mean "Can I help you?":

✔ **Vous désirez?** *(voo day-zee-ray)*

✔ **Je peux vous aider?** *(zhuh puh vooz ehday)*

But even if nobody asks you, just walk up to an employee and state what you want. The two most common things you want to accomplish in a French bank are changing money from one currency to another and cashing a check of some kind.

Start your request with

Je voudrais . . . *(zhuh voo-dray)* (I would like . . .)

and then add the specifics:

✔ **. . . changer des dollars en euros.** *(shan-zhay day doh-lahr ahN yuhr-oh)* (to change dollars into euros.)

✔ **. . . encaisser un chèque.** *(ahN-kehs-say aN shehk)* (to cash a check.)

Of course, because banks charge an additional fee (the rate may vary from bank to bank), you usually want to know the exchange rate first, so simply ask for it very straightforwardly:

Quel est votre taux de change? *(kehl eh voh-tr toh duh shahN-zh)* (What is your exchange rate?)

Words to Know

changer	shahN-zay	to exchange
ça fait	sah-feh	it is (it makes)
une carte de crédit	ewn kahrt duh kray-dee	credit card
un chèque de voyage	aN shehk duh vwah-yah-zh	traveler's check

le guichet (de change)	luh gee-sheh duh shahN-zh	cashier's window
une devise (étrangère)	ewn duh-veez ay-trahN-zhehr	foreign money
un distributeur (de billets)	uhn dees-tree-bew-tuhr	ATM (automated teller machine)
en argent liquide	ahN nahr-zahN lee-keed	in cash
le reçu	luh ruh-sew	receipt
la signature	lah seen-ya-tewr	signature

Using credit cards and ATMs

Credit cards are widely accepted in French-speaking countries. However, you can't necessarily count on being able to use them outside big cities, and if you can, you may just happen to be carrying the wrong kind. Also, places that take credit cards are sometimes pricier than the ones that don't.

ATMs have become quite the rage ever since they appeared. You find them in big and small towns, usually at a bank, in a shopping area, at train stations, at post offices. You can access them all day and night . . . unless, of course, they're temporarily out of order. But nothing's perfect, right?

Machines basically work the same way they do at home. Usually, you can choose that your prompts be in English; if not, here are the French phrases that you need to know to use an ATM:

> ✔ **Insérez votre carte svp.** *(aN-seh-ray vohtr kahrt seel voo play)* (Insert your card, please.)

> ✔ **Tapez votre code svp.** *(tah-pay vohtr kohd seel voo play)* (Type your PIN, please.)

✔ **Retrait d'espèces.** *(ruh-tray dehs-pehs)* (Cash withdrawal.)

✔ **Voulez-vous un reçu?** *(voo-lay-voo aN ruh-sew)* (Would you like a receipt?)

✔ **Carte en cours de vérification.** *(kahrt ahN koor duh veh-ree-fee-ka-syohN)* (Checking your balance.)

✔ **Patientez svp.** *(pa-syahN-tay seel voo play)* (Wait, please.)

✔ **Reprenez votre carte svp.** *(ruh-pruh-nay vohtr kahrt seel voo play)* (Take your card, please.)

✔ **Prenez votre argent.** *(pruh-nay votr ahr zhahN seel voo play)* (Take your money, please.)

✔ **N'oubliez pas votre reçu.** *(noo-blee-ay pah vohtr ruh-sew)* (Don't forget your receipt.)

✔ **Au revoir.** *(ohr-vwahr)* (Good-bye.)

Chapter 4

Making New Friends and Enjoying Small Talk

*G*reetings are the first steps in establishing contact with someone, whatever the language. Then comes the small talk. Small talk allows you to remain vague, if you so desire, and exchange simple questions and answers. Of course, it can lead to a more serious conversation, but it generally deals with innocuous subjects, such as the weather, family, or work. In other words, it's a wonderful way to acquaint yourself with someone else and enables you, as you're sitting in your airplane seat, to decide whether you want to pursue the conversation with the stranger next to you or go back to the great book you're reading.

French refers to small talk in several ways. One of them is **parler de tout et de rien** *(pahr-lay duh too ay duh ryahN)* (talk about everything and nothing).

Hello! Greetings and Introductions

The following sections present plenty of very simple French greetings that you may use on different occasions to help you meet people.

Saying hello and good-bye

When you're visiting a foreign country, the locals usually appreciate your effort to speak the language, and nothing's easier than saying hello. Actually, the French language has a saying, when referring to something that is really a cinch: **C'est simple comme bonjour** *(seh saNpluh kohm bohN-zhoor)* (It's as easy as saying hello). So go ahead, practice these few greetings:

- ✔ **Bonjour!** *(bohN-zhoor):* This phrase literally means "Good day," but you can use it when first greeting someone, morning or afternoon, roughly as long as the sun is shining.

  In Québec, people also say **Bonjour** when leaving, which mirrors the custom in English of saying "Good day" when parting.

- ✔ **Bonsoir!** *(bohN-swahr)* (Good evening!)

  You can use this greeting in the late afternoon and the evening to say hello or good-bye.

- ✔ **Salut!** *(sah-lew)* (Hi!)

  This is the most informal of all hellos and is also a way of saying good-bye; you can use it at any time of day but not with just anybody. Check out Chapter 2 to understand better when to say **"Salut."**

Now try a few good-byes:

- ✔ **Au revoir!** *(o-ruh-vwahr* or *ohr-vwahr)* (Good-bye!)

  Like its English counterpart, it applies to any time of day or night.

✔ **Bonne nuit!** *(bohn new-ee)* (Good night!)

You say this farewell only when retiring (or when someone retires) for the night, or when putting a child to bed. It's sort of like saying "Sleep well."

✔ **A bientôt!** *(ah-byaN-to)* (See you soon!)

That means anytime soon.

✔ **A tout à l'heure**! *(ah too tah-luhr)* (See you later!)

Use this expression only when you will see the person the same day.

✔ **A demain!** *(ah duh-maN)* (See you tomorrow!)

✔ **Bonne journée!** *(bohn zhoor-nay)* (Have a nice day!)

Asking "How are you?"

Most of the time, you follow your greeting with the question "How are you?" In French, you have several different ways of asking the question, depending on the level of formality between the two speakers.

This way of asking is very formal:

Comment allez-vous? *(koh-mahN-tah-lay voo)* (How are you?)

This way is also very polite:

Vous allez bien? *(voo-zah-lay byaN)* (Are you well?)

A more informal approach is to ask:

Comment vas-tu? *(koh-mahN vah-tew)* (How are you?)

This is the familiar version of the preceding one, using the **tu** form rather than the **vous.**

Rather informal but usable with both **tu** and **vous** are the following:

✔ **Comment ça va?** *(koh-mahN sah vah)* (How are you?)

✔ **Ça va?** *(sah vah)* (How are you?)

Replying to "How are you?"

Naturally, others expect you to reply to the question (probably without going into lengthy details about your health, your work, or your private life). A short phrase will do, such as:

✔ **Ça va!** *(sah vah)* (I'm okay.)

✔ **Ça va bien!/Ça va très bien!** *(sah vah byaN/sah vah treh byaN)* (I'm fine!/I'm very well!)

✔ **Bien, merci!/Très bien, merci!** *(byaN mehr-see/ treh byaN mehr-see)* (Fine, thank you!/Very well, thank you!)

If you are less enthusiastic, you may say:

Pas mal! *(pah mahl)* (Not bad!)

Even if you feel really bad, no one expects you to answer a simple greeting by saying how things really are for you. Introductions and greetings are for politeness and not for sharing feelings.

Whenever you answer a "How are you?" question, the least you can do is inquire about the well-being of the person you are talking to. You then follow your answer with "And you?":

✔ **Et vous?** *(ay voo),* which is the formal way,

✔ **Et toi?** *(ay twah),* a variation of the informal **tu.**

Introducing yourself and others

Greeting people and asking how they are isn't enough; you also need to introduce yourself and find out what their names are. You may use either of these phrases:

✔ **Je m'appelle . . .** *(zhuh mah-pehl)* (My name is . . .)

✔ **Je suis . . .** *(zhuh sew-ee)* (I am . . .)

✔ **Facile, non?** *(fah-seel nohN)* (Easy, isn't it?)

Now, that takes care of you. But you may want to know who that person over there is. So you ask:

Qui est-ce? *(Kee ehs?)* (Who is that?)

and you receive the following answer:

C'est . . . *(seh)* (That is . . .)

Now, suppose you want to introduce someone. You say:

Je vous présente . . . *(zhe voo pray-zehNt)* (Let me introduce . . . to you)

or with the informal variation on **tu:**

Je te présente . . . *(zhe tuh pray-zehNt)* (Let me introduce . . . to you)

or else:

Voici . . ./Voilà . . . *(vwah-see/vwah-lah)* (Here is . . . /There is . . .)

and the other person then says:

Enchanté! (if the speaker is a man)/**Enchantée!** (if the speaker is a woman) *(ahN-shahN-tay)* (Delighted!)

Here's how you may introduce yourself to a colleague for the first time:

✔ **Marc: Bonjour, madame. Je m'appelle Marc Sauval.** *(bohN-zhoor mah-dahm zhuh mah-pehl mahrk so-vahl)* (Hello, ma'am. My name is Marc Sauval.)

✔ **Claire: Ah, monsieur Sauval. Je suis Claire Rivet. Enchantée! Comment allez-vous?** *(ah muh-syuh so-vahl zhe sew-ee klehr ree-vay ko-mahN-tah-lay voo)* (Ah, Mr. Sauval. I am Claire Rivet. Delighted to meet you! How are you?)

✔ **Marc: Très bien, merci.** *(treh byaN mehr-see)* (Very well. Thank you.)

Later on, you may want to introduce someone else to your new colleague:

✔ **Marc: Madame Rivet, je vous présente ma femme, Christine.** *(mah-dahm ree-vay zhe voo pray-zahNt mah fahm krees-teen)* (Mrs. Rivet, let me introduce you to my wife, Christine.)

✔ **Claire: Enchantée, madame!** *(ahN-shahN-tay mah-dahm)* (Delighted, ma'am!)

✔ **Christine: Enchantée!** *(ahN-shahN-tay)* (Delighted!)

Of course, on the playground or at a gathering of young people, it's a different story, and you may hear:

✔ **Comment tu t'appelles?** *(ko-mahN tew tah-pehl)* (What's your name?) [informal]

✔ **Et lui, qui est-ce?/Et elle, qui est-ce?** *(ay lew-ee kee ehs/ay ehl kee ehs)* (And who is he?/And who is she?)

When you say in English "I introduced myself," you're using a reflexive form of the verb "introduce." In French, when you want to say "My name is," you use a reflexive form of the verb **appeler** *(ah-puh-lay)* (to call). Thus, **je m'appelle** *(zhuh mah-pehl)* means literally, "I call myself."

For reference, Table 4-1 shows all the forms of **appeler** in the present tense. (Refer to Chapter 2 for general statements on French verbs.)

Table 4-1	Appeler
Conjugation	*Pronunciation*
je m'appelle	zhuh mah-pehl
tu t'appelles	tew tah-pehl
il/elle s'appelle	eel/ehl sah-pehl
nous nous appelons	noo noo zah-puh-lohN
vous vous appelez	voo voo zah-puh-lay
ils s'appellent	eel sah-pehl
elles s'appellent	ehl sah-pehl

Grand Inquisitor: Questions

To start a conversation in any language, you have to know how to ask basic questions.

Question words

Here are the basic French question words — the Five W's plus some:

- ✔ **Qui?** *(kee)* (Who?)
- ✔ **Qu'est-ce que?** *(kes-kuh)* (What?)
- ✔ **Où?** *(oo)* (Where?)
- ✔ **Quand?** *(kahN)* (When?)
- ✔ **Pourquoi?** *(poor-kwa)* (Why?)
- ✔ **Comment?** *(ko-mahN)* (How?)
- ✔ **Combien?** *(kohN-byaN)* (How much?)
- ✔ **Quel/Quelle?** (masculine and feminine) *(kehl)* (Which?)

Here are a few examples of how to use these French question words in simple sentences — you can also use some of them on their own occasionally — just like in English:

- **Qui est-ce?** *(kee ehs)* (Who is it?)

- **Qu'est-ce que tu fais?** *(kehs-kuh tew feh)* (What are you doing?) [informal]

- **Où habitez-vous?** *(oo ah-bee-tay-voo)* (Where do you live?) [formal or plural]

- **Quand part l'avion?** *(kahN pahr lah-vyohN)* (When does the airplane leave?)

- **Pourquoi allez-vous à Paris?** *(poor-kwa ah-lay-voo ah pah-ree)* (Why are you going to Paris?)

- **Comment s'appelle la petite fille?** *(koh-mahN sah-pehl lah puh-teet fee-y)* (What is the little girl's name?)

- **Comment s'appelle . . .?** *(koh-mahN sah-pehl)* (What's . . . name?)

- **Quel est son prénom?** *(keh-leh sohN pray-nohN)* (What's his/her first name?)

- **Combien coûte le billet?** *(kohN-byaN coot luh bee-yeh)* (How much is the ticket?)

- **Quel hôtel préférez-vous?** *(kehl oh-tehl pray-fay-ray-voo)* (Which hotel do you prefer?)

The following statements are the basics of small talk and are indispensable when you're fairly new at a foreign language:

- **Je ne comprends pas.** *(zhuhn kohN-prahN pah)* (I don't understand.)

- **Je ne sais pas.** *(zhuhn seh pah)* (I don't know.)

- **Pardon/Excusez-moi.** *(pahr-dohN/eks-kew-zay-mwa)* (Excuse me.)

- **Je suis désolé/désolée.** *(zhuh sew-ee day-zoh-lay)* (I am sorry.)

Posing simple questions

Here's a list of simple questions that you may want to use when meeting someone. They all use the formal **vous** because, unless you're very young, you're more likely to use the **vous** when meeting someone for the first time:

- ✓ **Comment vous appelez-vous?** *(koh-mahN voo-zah-play-voo)* (What's your name?)

- ✓ **Quel âge avez-vous?** *(keh-lah-zhah-vay-voo)* (How old are you?)

- ✓ **Où habitez-vous?** *(oo ah-bee-tay-voo)* (Where do you live?)

- ✓ **Est-ce que vous êtes marié?** *(ehs-kuh voo-zeht mah-ryay)* (Are you married?)

- ✓ **Avez-vous des enfants ?** *(ah-vay-voo day-zahN-fahN)* (Do you have children?)

- ✓ **Qu'est-ce que vous faites (dans la vie)?** *(kehs-kuh voo feht dahN lah vee)* (What do you do [for a living]?)

- ✓ **Pour quelle compagnie travaillez-vous?** *(poor kehl kohN-pah-nyee trah-va-yay-voo)* (What company do you work for?)

- ✓ **Parlez-vous français?** *(pahr-lay-voo frahN-seh)* (Do you speak French?)

- ✓ **Aimez-vous voyager?** *(ay-may-voo vwa-yah-zhay)* (Do you like to travel?)

- ✓ **Quand partez-vous?** *(kahN pahr-tay-voo)* (When are you leaving?)

- ✓ **Quel temps fait-il aujourd'hui?** *(kehl tahN feh-teel o-zhoor-dwee)* (What is the weather like today?)

So Where Are You From?

After you've met new people, introduced yourself, and learned their names, you may want to know where they're from (what city, what country) and their nationality. To do all this, you need to get familiar with a very useful verb: **être** *(eh-truh)* (to be). This verb is irregular and admittedly a little difficult, but it's so important and so often used that you'll find putting some effort into memorizing all of its forms and practicing it over and over again is worthwhile. You want it to become second nature. Table 4-2 shows the conjugation of the present tense of **être.**

Table 4-2	Être
Conjugation	*Pronunciation*
je suis	zhuh sew-ee
tu es	tew eh
il/elle est	eel-ehl eh
nous sommes	noo sohm
vous êtes	voo zeht
ils sont	eel sohN
elles sont	ehl sohN

So the big question for this section is

D'où êtes-vous? *(doo eht voo)* (Where are you from?) or **D'où es-tu?** *(doo eh-tew)* (Where are you from?) [formal or informal]

You can answer along one of these lines, for example:

✔ **Je suis de New York. Et vous?** *(zhuh sew-ee duh New York ay voo)* (I am from New York. What about you?)

✔ **Nous sommes de Paris.** *(noo sohm duh pah-ree)* (We are from Paris.)

Sounds easy, doesn't it? But notice that the places mentioned in these examples (New York and Paris) are cities. It gets a little more complicated when you start talking about the country you come from because

in French a country can be masculine or feminine.
Table 4-3 presents a sample list of countries with their
genders:

Table 4-3	Genders of Countries	
French	*Pronunciation*	*English*
Feminine:		
La France	lah frahNs	France
La Suisse	lah sew-ees	Switzerland
La Belgique	lah behl-zheek	Belgium
L'Allemagne	lahl-mahNy	Germany
L'Italie	lee-tah-lee	Italy
L'Espagne	lehs-pany	Spain
L'Angleterre	lahN-gluh-tehr	England
L'Algérie	lahl-zhay-ree	Algeria
L'Inde	land	India
Masculine:		
Le Canada	luh kah-nah-dah	Canada
Le Danemark	luh dahN-mahrk	Denmark
Le Portugal	luh pohr-tew-gahl	Portugal
Le Japon	luh zhah-pohN	Japan
Le Maroc	luh mah-rohk	Morocco
Le Sénégal	luh say-nay-gahl	Senegal
Le Liban	luh lee-bahN	Lebanon
Les États-Unis	lay-zay-tah-zew-nee	The United States

Notice that all feminine countries end with the letter *e.*
One exception is **le Mexique** *(luh mehk-seek)* (Mexico)
which, even though it ends in *e,* is masculine.

Paying attention to the gender of countries helps you to understand the variations in the following statements:

- ✔ **City: Je suis de Paris.** *(zhuh sew-ee duh pah-ree)* (I am from Paris.)

- ✔ **Feminine country: Il est de France.** *(ee leh duh frahNs)* (He is from France.)

- ✔ **Masculine country: Vous êtes du Canada.** *(voo zeht dew kah-nah-dah)* (You are from Canada.)

- ✔ **Plural: Nous sommes des Etats-Unis.** *(noo sohm day zay-tah-zew-nee)* (We are from the United States.)

Of course sometimes, instead of saying where you're from, you simply want to say where you are. In this case, you use **à** for a city and a different preposition for a country (depending on whether it's masculine or feminine):

- ✔ **City: Je suis à Paris.** *(zhuh sew-ee ah pah-ree)* (I am in Paris.)

- ✔ **Masculine: Montréal est au Canada.** *(mohN-ray-ahl eh to kah-nah-dah)* (Montreal is in Canada.)

- ✔ **Feminine: Elle est en Suisse.** *(ehl eh tahN sew-ees)* (She is in Switzerland.)

In French, as in English, you can say "I come from" as well as "I am from." For this sort of expression, you use the verb **venir** *(vuh-neer)* (to come). (See Chapter 2 to find out how to conjugate this regular **-ir** verb.) For example, you can ask:

D'où viens-tu/D'où venez-vous? *(doo vyaN-tew/doo vuh-nay-voo)* (Where do you come from?) [informal and formal]

and the answer may be, for example:

Je viens de Montréal. *(zhuh vyaN duh mohN-ray-ahl)* (I come from Montreal.)

Describing cities

Suppose you want to have a longer exchange with a person about the city that he or she is from: Is it large, small, pretty, international, or . . . ? Here are some conversation starters:

- ✔ **De quelle ville êtes-vous?** *(duh kehl veel eht-voo)* (Which city are you from?)

  De quelle ville es-tu? *(duh kehl veel eh-tew)*, which is the informal form of the previous question.

- ✔ **Où est Montréal?** *(oo eh mohN-ray-ahl)* (Where is Montreal?)

- ✔ **Comment est Montréal/Bruxelles/Paris?** *(koh-mahN eh mohN-ray-ahl/brew-sehl/pah-ree)* (How is Montreal/Brussels/Paris?)

- ✔ **Est-ce que c'est une petite ville?** *(ehs-kuh seh tewn puh-teet veel)* (Is it a small town?)

And here are some possible answers that you may get:

- ✔ **Montréal est une ville internationale.** *(mohN-ray-ahl eh tewn veel aNtehr-nah-syo-nahl)* (Montreal is an international city.)

- ✔ **C'est au Canada.** *(seh-to kah-nah-dah)* (It is in Canada.)

- ✔ **Ce n'est pas une petite ville; c'est une très grande ville.** *(suh neh pah zewn puh-teet veel seh tewn treh grahNd veel)* (It's not a small town; it's a very large city.)

Words to Know

Où est . . . ?	oo eh	Where is . . . ?
une petite ville	ewn puh-teet veel	a small town

continued

Words to Know (continued)

une grande ville	ewn grahNd veel	a big city
une ville internationale	ewn veel aN-tehr-nah-syo-nahl	an international city

Getting down to the address

As people get more friendly, they may want to make "where are you from?" a little more personal and ask: **Où habitez-vous?** *(oo ah-bee-tay-voo)* (Where do you live?). Or maybe even:

- ✔ **Quelle est votre adresse?** *(keh-leh voh-tra-drehs)* (What is your address?)

- ✔ **Donnez-moi votre numéro de téléphone.** *(doh-nay-mwa voh-truh new-may-ro duh tay-lay-fohn)* Give me your phone number.

You may occasionally talk about your home. These words and phrases come in handy:

- ✔ **Nous habitons dans une maison.** *(noo-zah-bee-tohN dahN-zewn meh-zohN)* (We live in a house.)

- ✔ **Moi, j'habite dans un appartement.** *(mwa zhah-beet dahN-zaN-nah-pahr-tuh-mahN)* (I live in an apartment.)

Words to Know

le nom	luh nohN	last name
le prénom	luh pray-nohN	first name

l'adresse	lah-drehs	address
le numéro de téléphone	luh new-may-ro duh tay-lay-fohn	phone number
vous voulez?	voo voo-lay	do you want?
le code postal	luh cohd pohs-tahl	zip code
Pourquoi pas?	poor-kwa pah	Why not?

Making Small Talk on the Job

What you do for a living is almost always part of small talk. The following are some useful job terms and job-related expressions:

- **Qu'est-ce que vous faites dans la vie?** *(kes-kuh voo feht dahN lah vee)* (What do you do for a living?)

- **professeur** *(pro-feh-suhr)* (high school teacher or college professor)

- **informaticien/informaticienne** *(aN-fohr-mah-tee-syaN/aN-fohr-mah-tee-syehn)* (computer scientist)

- **secrétaire** *(suh-cray-tehr)* (secretary)

- **médecin** *(mayd-saN)* (physician)

- **infirmier/infirmière** *(aN-feer-myay/aN-feer-myehr)* (nurse)

- **avocat/avocate** *(ah-vo-kah/ah-vo-kaht)* (lawyer)

- **ingénieur** *(aN-zhay-nyuhr)* (engineer)

- **serveur/serveuse** *(sehr-vuhr/sehr-vuhs)* (waiter/waitress)

- **dentiste** *(dahN-teest)* (dentist)

- **retraité/retraitée** *(ruh-treh-tay)* (retired person)

In French, when you state your profession, you just say: **Je suis professeur** *(zhuh sew-ee proh-feh-suhr)* (I am a teacher or a professor), or **il est ingénieur** *(ee-leh-taN-zhay-nyuhr)* (he is an engineer), without using an article **(un)** like you would in English (I am a teacher; he is an engineer).

Here's a conversation that you could have about someone's work:

- **Amanda: Où travaillez-vous?** *(oo trah-va-yay voo)* (Where do you work?)

- **Patrick: Mon bureau est à Paris, mais je vais souvent à Nice en voyage d'affaires.** *(mohN bew-ro eh-tah pah-ree meh zhuh veh soo-vahN ah nees ahN vwa-yazh dah-fehr)* (My office is in Paris, but I often go to Nice on business trips.)

- **Amanda: Pour quelle compagnie travaillez-vous?** *(poor kehl kohN-pah-nyee trah-va-yay voo)* (What company do you work for?)

- **Patrick: Pour une compagnie d'informatique.** *(poo-rewn kohN-pah-nyee daN-fohr-mah-teek)* (For a computer science company.)

- **Amanda: C'est une grande compagnie?** *(seh-tewn grahNd kohN-pa-nyee)* (Is it a large company?)

- **Patrick: Non, elle est très petite. Il y a seulement dix employés.** *(nohN eh-leh treh puh-teet eel ee-yah suhl-mahN dee-zahN-plwa-yay)* (No, it is very small. There are only ten employees.)

Words to Know

le voyage d'affaires	luh vwa-yahzh dah-fehr	business trip
mon bureau	mohN bew-ro	my office

l'informatique	laN-fohr-mah-teek	computer science
une compagnie	ewn kohn-pah-nyee	a company
grand/grande	grahN/grahNd	big, tall, large
petit/petite	puh-tee/puh-teet	small, short
il y a	ee-lee-yah	there is/there are
un employé/une employée	aN nahN-plwa-yay/ew nahN-plwa-yay	an employee
un collègue/une collègue	aN koh-lehg/ewn koh-lehg	a co-worker

Speaking about Speaking

If you're stuck somewhere in a French-speaking country and are desperate for some help, you can always ask: Do you speak English? If you get a blank stare in return, go ahead, dive in, and **parlez français** *(pahrlay frahN-seh)* (speak French)! One of these phrases may help you express your situation:

> ✔ **Parlez-vous français?/Est-ce que vous parlez français?** *(pahr-lay voo frahN-seh/ehs-kuh voo pahr-lay frahN-seh)* (Do you speak French?) [formal and plural]

> ✔ **Je parle un peu français.** *(zhuh pahrl aN puh frahN-seh)* (I speak French a little.)

> ✔ **Je parle bien français.** *(zhuh pahrl byaN frahN-seh)* (I speak French well.)

> ✔ **Je ne parle pas du tout français.** *(zhuh nuh pahrl pah dew too frahN-seh)* (I don't speak French at all.)

Notice the way the French sentences above are built as compared to the English translation. The adverb (such as well, a little, or not at all) comes right after the verb instead of being thrown at the end of the sentence.

Here are a few conversation phrases with **parler:**

> ✔ **Mais tu parles très bien français!** *(meh tew pahrl treh byaN frahN-seh)* (But you speak French very well!)
>
> ✔ **C'est normal, je suis québécoise, alors ma langue maternelle, c'est le français.** *(seh nohr-mahl zhuh sew-ee kay-bay-kwaz ahlohr mah lahNg mah-tehr-nehl seh luh frahN-seh)* (It's nothing special, I am from Québec, so my mother tongue is French.)
>
> ✔ **Mais tu parles aussi l'anglais probablement.** *(meh tew pahrl o-see lahN-gleh proh-bah-bluh-mahN)* (But you probably also speak English.)
>
> ✔ **Moi je le parle.** *(mwa zhuh luh pahrl)* (I speak it.)

Words to Know

mon ami	mo-nah-mee	my friend (male)
mon amie	mo-nah-mee	my friend (female)
mais	meh	but
alors	ah-lohr	so
ma langue maternelle	mah lahNg mah-tehr-nehl	my mother tongue

moi/toi/lui/elle	mwa/twa/ lew-ee/ehl	I/you/he/she
moi aussi	mwa o-see	me, too
bien sûr	byaN sewr	of course
seulement	suhl-mahN	only
maintenant	man-tuh-nahN	now
il faut parler	eel fo pahr-lay	we/you have to talk/speak

How's the Weather?

Another great topic for small talk is, of course, **le temps** *(luh tahN)* (the weather). As a matter of fact, one way to designate small talk in French is **parler de la pluie et du beau temps** *(pahr-lay duh lah plew-ee ay duh bo tahN)* (Literally: to talk about the rain and the nice weather). Here are some useful phrases:

- ✔ **Quel temps fait-il?** *(kehl tahN feh-teel)* (What is the weather like?)
- ✔ **Il fait chaud.** *(eel feh sho)* (It's warm/hot.)
- ✔ **Il fait froid.** *(eel feh frwah)* (It's cold.)
- ✔ **Il fait doux.** *(eel feh doo)* (It's mild.)
- ✔ **Il fait beau.** *(eel feh bo)* (The weather is nice.)
- ✔ **Il fait mauvais.** *(eel feh mo-veh)* (The weather is bad.)
- ✔ **Il fait du vent.** *(eel feh dew vahN)* (It's windy.)
- ✔ **Il fait du soleil.** *(eel feh dew soh-lehy)* (It's sunny.)
- ✔ **Il pleut.** *(eel pluh)* (It's raining.)

✔ **Il neige.** *(eel nehzh)* (It's snowing.)

✔ **La température est de 20 degrés.** *(lah tahN-pay-rah-tew-reh duh vaN duh-gray)* (It's 20 degrees.)

Try out this weather conversation:

✔ **Amanda: A Nice, il fait beau et chaud et la température est de 30 degrés.** *(ah nees eel feh bo ay sho ay lah tahN-pay-rah-tew-reh duh trahNt duh-gray)* (In Nice, the weather is nice and warm and the temperature is 30 degrees.)

✔ **Patrick: A Nice, il fait toujours beau!** *(ah nees eel feh too-zhoor bo)* (In Nice, the weather is always nice!)

✔ **Amanda: Même en hiver?** *(meh-mahN-nee-vehr)* (Even in winter?)

✔ **Patrick: En hiver, il pleut un peu, mais il fait doux. Et à New York?** *(ahN-nee-vehr eel pluh aN puh me-zeel feh doo ay ah New York)* (In winter, it rains a little, but it is mild. And in New York?)

✔ **Amanda: En hiver, il fait très froid et il neige, et en été il fait très chaud et humide.** *(ahN-nee-vehr eel feh treh frwa ay eel nehzh ay ahN-nay-tay eel feh treh sho ay ew-meed)* (In winter, it's very cold and it snows, and in summer it's very hot and humid.)

✔ **Patrick: Et au printemps et en automne?** *(ay o praN-tahN ay ahN-no-tohn)* (What about spring and fall?)

✔ **Amanda: Le temps est agréable.** *(luh tahN eh-tah-gray-ahbl)* (The weather is pleasant.)

How Is Your Family?

If you're going to talk about your family, you need to know these common words:

✔ **le mari** *(luh mah-ree)* (husband)

✔ **la femme** *(lah fahm)* (wife)

✔ **les parents** *(lay pah-rahN)* (parents)

✔ **le père** *(luh pehr)* (father)

✔ **la mère** *(lah mehr)* (mother)

✔ **les enfants** *(lay-zahN-fahN)* (children)

✔ **le fils** *(luh fees)* (son)

✔ **la fille** *(lah fee-y)* (daughter)

✔ **le frère** *(luh frehr)* (brother)

✔ **la soeur** *(lah suhr)* (sister)

✔ **les petits-enfants** *(lay puh-tee-zahN-fahN)*
(grandchildren)

In the following conversation, two people talk about
their families:

✔ **Patrick: Votre fille habite en France?** *(vohtruh
fee-y ah-bee-tahN frahNs)* (Does your daughter
live in France?)

✔ **Amanda: Oui, son mari est français.** *(wee sohN
mah-ree eh frahN-seh)* (Yes, her husband is
French.)

✔ **Patrick: Et vous, êtes-vous française ou améri-
caine?** *(ay voo eht-voo frahN-seh-zoo ah-may-ree-
kehn)* (And you, are you French or American?)

✔ **Amanda: Les deux! Mon père est américain et
ma mère est française.** *(lay duh mohN pehr eh-
tah-may-ree-caN ay mah mehr eh frahN-sehz)*
(Both! My father is American, and my mother
is French.)

✔ **Patrick: Alors vous parlez bien l'anglais et le
français?** *(ah-lohr voo pahr-lay byaN lahN-gleh
ay luh frahN-seh)* (Then you speak English and
French well?)

✔ **Amanda: Bien sûr et mes enfants et mes petits-
enfants aussi.** *(byaN sewr ay may-zahN-fahN ay
may puh-tee-zahN-fahN o-see)* (Of course, and my
children and grandchildren too.)

✔ **Patrick: Quelle chance! Moi je parle seulement
français.** *(kehl shahNs mwa zhuh pahrl suhl-mahN
frahN-seh)* (How lucky! I only speak French.)

Words to Know

habiter	ah-bee-tay	to live
les deux	lay duh	both
quelle chance!	kehl shahNs	how lucky! (Literally: what luck)
seulement	suhl-mahN	only

In French, two verbs correspond to the English to live: **habiter** *(ah-bee-tay)* and **vivre** *(veevr)*. Most of the time, you can use these verbs interchangeably, but **habiter** is limited to space, whereas **vivre** refers to time as well as space.

Chapter 5

Enjoying a Drink and a Snack (or Meal!)

. . . .

In This Chapter

▶ Asking for your bread and butter

▶ Eating out

▶ Paying the check

. . . .

*E*xploring the food and eating habits of another country is one of the most pleasant ways to discover its culture. When the subject is French food and restaurants, this exploration is especially enjoyable. Whether you want to eat in a fancy two- or three-star restaurant or eat bread and cheese sitting on a park bench, you need to know how to select, order, and then enjoy (which we promise will be easy)!

All about Meals

What better way to enjoy what you are going to eat than to start with an empty stomach? Then you can say **"J'ai faim"** *(zheh faN)* (I'm hungry) or **"J'ai soif"** *(zheh swaf)* (I'm thirsty), and the glorious world of French gastronomy is yours!

French-speaking people like to emphasize the way they feel. So, instead of simply saying "I am very hungry" or "I am very thirsty," they tell you that they're dying of hunger or thirst: **Je meurs de faim** *(zhuh muhr duh faN)*, **je meurs de soif** *(zhuh muhr duh swaf)*.

The meals

The French-speaking world has a few varients on the names of meals:

- ✔ The word for "breakfast" is

  le déjeuner *(luh day-zhuh-nay)* in Québec

  le petit déjeuner *(luh puh-tee day-zhuh-nay)* in France

- ✔ The word for "lunch" is

  le dîner *(luh dee-nay)* in Québec

  le déjeuner *(luh day-zhuh-nay)* in France

- ✔ The word for "dinner" is

  le souper *(luh soo-pay)* in Québec

  le dîner *(luh dee-nay)* in France

  These nouns are also verbs; to have lunch or dinner is **déjeuner, dîner,** or **souper.**

- ✔ Other times when you may eat are

  le goûter *(luh goo-tay)* (midafternoon snack)

  un casse-croûte *(aN kahs-kroot)* (a snack; literally, break the crust)

Setting the table

As in North America, the biggest meal of the day in most French homes nowadays is dinner. The following list includes the items that you use to **mettre le couvert** *(meh-truh luh coo-vehr)* (set the table):

- ✔ **une assiette** *(ewn ah-see-yeht)* (a plate)
- ✔ **un verre** *(aN vehr)* (a glass)
- ✔ **les couverts** *(lay koo-vehr)* (silverware)
- ✔ **une fourchette** *(ewn foor-sheht)* (a fork)
- ✔ **une cuillère** *(ewn kwee-yehr)* (a spoon)
- ✔ **un couteau** *(aN koo-to)* (a knife)

✔ **une serviette** *(ewn sehr-vee-yeht)* (a napkin)

✔ **le sel et le poivre** *(luh seh-lay luh pwavr)* (salt and pepper)

After dessert, people move away from the table to have their coffee. They then use the following:

✔ **une tasse** *(ewn tahs)* (a cup)

✔ **une soucoupe** *(ewn soo-koop)* (a saucer)

✔ **une petite cuillère** *(ewn puh-teet kwee-yehr)* (a teaspoon)

✔ **le sucre** *(luh sewkr)* (sugar)

Going Out to Eat

You may not be lucky enough to share a French family's dinner, but the words from the preceding section may come in handy when you go to a restaurant. The following sections walks you through every aspect of dining out.

Getting a reservation

Many popular or well-known restaurants require a reservation — as much as two months in advance, in some cases! You may come across these phrases when making your reservation:

✔ **Bonjour, je voudrais réserver une table pour samedi prochain.** *(bohn-zhoor zhuh voo-dreh ray-zehr-vay ewn tah-bl poor sahm-dee pro-shan)* (Hello, I would like to reserve a table for next Saturday.)

✔ **D'accord, pour déjeuner ou pour dîner?** *(dah-kohr poor day-zhuh-nay oo poor dee-nay)* (Very well, for lunch or dinner?)

✔ **Pour combien de personnes?** *(poor kohn-byand-pehr-sohn)* (For how many?)

✔ **Et à quelle heure?** *(ay ah-keh-luhr)* (And at what time?)

✔ **C'est à quel nom?** *(seh-tah kehl nohN)* (What is the name?)

Ordering at the restaurant

When you arrive at the restaurant, these phrases come in handy:

✔ **Bonsoir, nous avons une réservation au nom de Miller.** *(bohN-swar noo-zah-vohN ewn ray-sehr-vah-syohN o nohN duh mee-lehr)* Good evening, we have a reservation under the name of Miller.

✔ **Votre table est là-bas à côté de la fenêtre.** *(voh-truh tahb-leh lah-bah ah ko-tay duh lah fuh-nehtr)* (Your table is over there next to the window.)

✔ **Et voici le menu et la carte des vins.** *(ay vwa-see luh muh-new ay lah kahr-tuh day vahn)* (Here is the menu and the wine list.)

After you're seated, you need to converse with your waiter. Here are some of the waiter's questions and statements:

✔ **Vous voulez boire quelque chose?** *(voo voo-lay bwar kehl-kuh shoz)* (Would you like something to drink?)

✔ **Voilà vos boissons.** *(vwa-lah vo bwa-sohn)* (Here are your drinks.)

✔ **Vous êtes prêts?** *(voo-zeht preh)* (Are you ready to order?)

Don't address the waiter as **garçon** *(gahr-sohN)*, which is considered condescending because it means "boy," but as **monsieur** *(muh-syuh)* (sir). In case it's **une serveuse** *(ewn sehr-vuhz)* (a waitress), you say **madame** *(mah-dahm)* (ma'am) or **mademoiselle** *(mahd-mwa-zehl)* (miss) if she's young.

Words to Know

Nous sommes fermés.	noo sohm fehr-may	We're closed.
d'accord	dah-kohr	okay; all right
C'est à quel nom ?	seh-tah kehl nohn	What's the name?
là-bas	lah-bah	over there
à côté de . . .	ah ko-tay duh	next to . . .
la fenêtre	lah fuh-nehtr	the window
parfait	pahr-feh	perfect

Of course, deciding what you actually want is another issue. In most restaurants in France, you may order from a **menu à prix fixe** *(muh-new ah pree feeks)* (set-price menu) or **à la carte** *(ah-lah kahrt).* You usually have several set menus to choose from, with a selection of between two and four appetizers, entrées, and desserts. When you order à la carte, you may choose anything.

You can ask your waiter to explain something on the menu with the following phrases:

✔ **Qu'est-ce que c'est . . .?** *(kes-kuh-seh)* (What is this?)

✔ **C'est bon?** *(seh bohN)* (Is it good?)

✔ **C'est délicieux. C'est une spécialité de la maison.** *(seh day-lee-syuh seh-tewn-spay-syah-lee-tay duh lah meh-zohN)* (It's delicious. It's a house specialty.)

You can also ask for the waiter's recommendation by saying **"Qu'est-ce que vous recommandez?"** *(kes-kuh voo ruh-koh-mahn-day)* (What do you recommend?)

When you're all set and ready to order, you need to have these phrases handy:

✔ **comme entrée, je prends . . .** *(koh-mahn-tray zhuh prahn)* (for the first course, I'll have . . .)

✔ **je voudrais . . .** *(zhuh voo-dreh)* (I would like . . .)

✔ **pour moi . . .** *(poor mwah)* (Literally: for me . . .)

✔ **et ensuite . . .** *(ay ahn-sweet)* (and then . . .)

✔ **et comme boisson . . .** *(ay kohm bwa-sohn)* (and to drink . . .)

✔ **et comme dessert . . .** *(ay kohm day-sehr)* (and for dessert . . .)

The first phrase of the previous list uses the verb **prendre** *(prahndr)* (to take), which you can use to order food or drink. **Prendre** is an irregular verb, as Table 5-1 shows.

Table 5-1	Prendre
Conjugation	*Pronunciation*
je prends	zhuh prahn
tu prends	tew prahn
il/elle prend	eel/ehl prahn
nous prenons	noo pruh-nohn
vous prenez	voo pruh-nay
ils/elles prennent	eel/ehl prehn

The following lists give you a sample of some of the things that you may find in a French restaurant. Remember, different restaurants may give these things different names, so if you're unsure, ask the waiter. First, **les entrées** *(lay-zahn-tray)* (appetizers):

✔ **le pâté/la terrine** *(luh pah-tay/lah teh-reen)* (pâtés; meat paste)

✔ **le saumon fumé** *(luh so-mohn few-may)* (smoked salmon)

✔ **la salade verte** *(lah sah-lahd vehrt)* (literally, green salad; salad with lettuce only)

✔ **les crudités** *(lay krew-dee-tay)* (mixed raw vegetables)

After the appetizers comes **le plat principal** *(luh plah pran-see-pahl)* (the main course):

✔ **les viandes** *(lay vyahnd)* (meats):

le boeuf *(luh buhf)* (beef)

You can order your steak **saignant** *(seh-nyahn)* (rare), **à point** *(ah pwan)* (medium), or **bien cuit** *(byan kwee)* (well done).

le veau *(luh vo)* (veal)

le poulet *(luh poo-leh)* (chicken)

le porc *(luh pohr)* (pork)

l'agneau *(la-nyo)* (lamb)

les poissons *(lay pwa-sohn)* (fish)

✔ **le riz** *(luh ree)* (rice)

✔ **les pâtes** *(lay paht)* (pasta)

What a difference an accent can make! **Le pâté** *(luh pah-tay)* is a meat paste, usually made from pork meat and spices, which is eaten as an appetizer with bread. On the other hand, **les pâtes** *(lay paht)* are pasta.

✔ **les légumes** *(lay lay-gewm)* (vegetables):

les pommes de terre *(lay pohm duh tehr)* (potatoes)

les haricots verts *(lay ah-ree-ko vehr)* (green beans)

les petits pois *(lay puh-tee pwa)* (peas)

les **champignons** *(lay sham-peen-yohN)* (mushrooms)

✔ les **fromages** *(lay fro-mahzh)* (cheeses)

✔ les **desserts** *(lay deh-sehr)* (desserts):

la **glace** *(lah glahs)* (ice cream)

la **crème** *(lah krehm)* (pudding)

le **gâteau au chocolat** *(luh gah-to o sho-ko-lah)* (chocolate cake)

la **tarte aux pommes** *(lah tahr-to-pohm)* (apple pie)

Words to Know

les poireaux	lay pwa-ro	leeks
Vous voulez . . . ?	voo voo-lay	Do you want . . . ? [formal, plural]
Tu veux . . . ?	tew vuh	Do you want . . . ? [informal]
la boisson	lah bwa-sohn	drink
et ensuite . . .	eh ahn-sweet	and then . . .
C'est bon!	seh bohn	It's good!
C'est délicieux!	seh day-lee-syuh	It's delicious!

Going out for breakfast

Heading out to a **pâtisserie** *(pah-tees-ree)* (confectioner's shop) or **boulangerie** *(boo-lahn-zhree)* (bakery) in the morning can be a wonderful thing. Here are some of the items you may want to order:

- ✔ **le café** *(luh kah-fay)* (coffee)

- ✔ **le café au lait** *(luh kah-fay o leh)* (coffee with hot milk)

- ✔ **le café crème** *(luh kah-fay crehm)* (coffee with a little milk)

- ✔ **le thé nature** *(luh tay nah-tewr)* (plain tea)

- ✔ **le thé au lait** *(luh tay o leh)* (tea with milk)

- ✔ **le thé au citron/le thé citron** *(luh tay o see-trohn/luh tay see-trohn)* (tea with lemon)

- ✔ **le pain** *(luh pahN)* (bread)

- ✔ **le pain grillé** *(luh pahN gree-yay)* (toast)

- ✔ **les tartines** *(lay tahr-teen)* (slices of bread with some kind of spread)

- ✔ **le beurre** *(luh buhr)* (butter)

- ✔ **la margarine** *(lah mahr-zhah-reen)* (margarine), not as popular as butter but used, nevertheless

- ✔ **la confiture** *(lah kohn-fee-tewr)* (jam)

- ✔ **le croissant** *(luh krwa-sahN)* (croissant — crescent-shaped)

- ✔ **le pain au chocolat** *(luh pan o sho-ko-lah)* (same dough as a croissant but a different shape and with a chocolate bar inside)

- ✔ **le chausson aux pommes** *(luh sho-sohN o pohm)* (applesauce-filled danish)

- ✔ **le pain aux raisins** *(luh pahN o ray-zan)* (a sort of raisin bread)

Getting a Drink

The questions **Qu'est-ce que vous voulez boire?** *(kes-kuh voo voo-lay bwar)* and **Qu'est-ce que vous voulez comme boisson?** *(kes-kuh voo voo-lay kohm bwa-sohn)* both mean "What do you want to drink?" And the verb in both questions is the irregular verb **boire** *(bwahr)* (to drink). Check out the conjugation in Table 5-2.

Table 5-2	Boire
Conjugation	*Pronunciation*
je bois	zhuh bwa
tu bois	tew bwa
il/elle boit	eel/ehl bwa
nous buvons	noo bew-vohn
vous buvez	voo bew-vay
ils/elles boivent	eel /ehl bwav

Here's a list of drinks people commonly order in a restaurant or cafe:

✔ **un verre de vin** *(aN vehr duh van)* (a glass of wine)

✔ **une bouteille de bière** *(ewn boo-tehy duh byehr)* (a bottle of beer)

✔ **une carafe d'eau** *(ewn kah-rahf do)* (a carafe of water)

✔ **un double express** *(aN doob-lehks-prehs)* (a double espresso)

✔ **un grand crème** *(aN grahn krehm)* (a large coffee with milk)

✔ **un déca; un décaféiné** *(aN day-kah; aN day-kaf-fay-ee-nay)* (a decaf coffee)

✔ **une tasse de thé** *(ewn tahs duh tay)* (a cup of tea)

People seldom order wine by the glass in France. More often, they order wine as **un quart** *(aN kahr)* (25 centiliters (cl), or a quarter of a liter), **une demi-bouteille** *(ewn duh-mee boo-tehy)* (33cl), or **une bouteille** *(ewn boo-tehy)* (75cl). They order the house wine in **une carafe** *(ewn kah-rahf)* or **un pichet** *(aN pee-sheh)* (a jug).

You usually don't have water on the table unless you say, **"Une carafe d'eau, s'il vous plaît"** *(ewn kah-rahf do seel-voo-play)* (A pitcher of water, please). Many people prefer bottled water and ask for it by its brand name, **une bouteille d'Evian, de Vittel, ou de Perrier** *(ewn boo-tehy day-vyahN duh vee-tehl oo duh peh-ryay)*.

Paying the Bill

In France, don't expect the waiter to come to you with the check if you haven't asked for it. The French consider bringing the check before you ask pushy and impolite. When you're ready, you can use these phrases to pay your bill:

- ✔ **L'addition, s'il vous plaît.** *(lah-dee-syohn seel voo play)* (The check, please.)

- ✔ **Vous prenez les cartes de crédit?** *(voo pruh-nay lay kahrt duh cray-dee)* (Do you take credit cards?)

- ✔ **Le pourboire est compris.** *(luh poor-bwar eh kohn-pree)* (The tip is included.)

Words to Know

un tas de . . .	aN tah duh	a lot of . . .
cher/pas cher	shehr/pah shehr	expensive/ cheap
d'accord	dah-kohr	all right; okay
quelque chose	kehl-kuh shoz	something
		continued

Words to Know (continued)

Vous êtes prêts?	voo-zeht preh	Are you ready?
la même chose	lah mehm shoz	the same thing
l'addition	lah-dee-syohn	the check
le pourboire	luh poor-bwar	the tip
laisser un pourboire	leh-say an poor-bwar	to leave a tip
la carte de crédit	lah kahr-tuh duh cray-dee	credit card
accepter	ah-ksehp-tay	to accept

Chapter 6

Shop 'Til You Drop!

• •

In This Chapter

▶ Finding the right stores and the right clothes

▶ Visiting the food markets

▶ Purchasing your finds

▶ Comparing apples and oranges

• •

Le shopping *(luh shoh-peeng)* — what a fun thing to do! Of course, you have to hit the markets — either because you can't resist all those fresh vegetables and wonderful crusty baguettes or because you spent all your money on the designer perfume and now need some frugal food. This chapter helps you navigate your way through the French shopping experience.

Heading Out on the Town

If you don't know where to start, or even if you don't have the slightest idea of what you want to buy, **un grand magasin** *(aN grahN mah-gah-zaN)* (a department store) may be a good choice. Here are some other possibilities:

✔ **Les centres commerciaux** *(lay sahN-truh ko-mehr-syo)* (shopping malls)

✔ **La boutique** *(lah boo-teek)* (boutique)

✔ **La librairie** *(lah lee-breh-ree)* (the bookstore)

> ✔ **La bijouterie** *(lah bee-zhoot-ree)* (the jewelry store)

> ✔ **Le bureau de tabac** (France), **la tabagie** (Québec) *(luh bew-ro duh tah-bah, lah tah-bah-zhee)* (the tobacco shop).

> ✔ **La dépanneuse** (Québec) *(lah day-pah-nuhz)* (the convenience store)

Getting around the store

When you decide to go shopping, you probably want to call ahead to find out about the store's hours. These questions can help:

> ✔ **A quelle heure ouvrez-vous/fermez-vous?** *(ah keh-luhr oo-vray-voo/fehr-may-voo)* (At what time do you open/close?)

> ✔ **Quelles sont vos heures d'ouverture?** *(kehl sohN vo-zuhr doo-vehr-tewr)* (What are your opening hours?)

> ✔ **Etes-vous ouverts le dimanche?** *(eht voo oo-vehr luh dee-mahNsh)* (Are you open on Sundays?)

After you find out when the store is open, you decide to go take a look; no buying, just browsing:

> ✔ **Je peux vous aider?** *(zhuh pew voo-zayday)* (Can I help you?)

> ✔ **Non, merci, je regarde seulement.** *(nohN mehr-see zhuh ruh-gahrd suhl-mahN)* (No thank you, I am just looking.)

Words to Know

le magasin	luh mah-gah-zaN	the store
le rez-de-chaussée	luh ray duh sho-say	first floor

les rayons	lay ray-yohN	the stands in a store
une vendeuse	ewn vahN-duhz	saleslady
les renseignements	lay rahN-seh-nyuh-mahN	the information counter
les escaliers roulants	lay-zehs-kah-lyay roo-lahN	escalator
l'ascenseur	lah-sahN-suhr	elevator
la caisse	lah kehs	the cash register
les soldes (France)	lay sohld	sales
l'aubaine (Québec)	lo-behn	sales

Time to get more serious! You have that long shopping list to get through. But this store is a maze, and you need some help finding your way around:

- **Pouvez-vous m'aider, s'il vous plaît?** *(poo-vay voo may-day seel-voo-play)* (Can you help me, please?)

- **Je voudrais un renseignement.** *(zhuh voo-dreh aN rahN-seh-nyuh-mahN)* (I would like some information.)

- **Je cherche . . .** *(zhuh shehrsh)* (I am looking for . . .)

- **Pardon, madame, où sont les parfums?** *(pahr-dohN mah-dahm oo sohN lay pahr-faN)* (Excuse me, ma'am, where are the perfumes?)

✔ **Ici, au rez-de-chaussée.** *(ee-see o ray duh sho-say)* (Here, on the ground floor.)

✔ **Les vêtements pour dames, s'il vous plaît?** *(lay veht-mahN poor dahm seel voo pleh)* (Ladies' clothes, please.)

✔ **C'est au troisième étage.** *(seh-to trwa-zyeh-may-tazh)* (It is on the third floor.)

✔ **Excusez-moi, je cherche les compact disques.** *(eks-kew-zay-mwa zhuh shehrsh lay kohN-pakt deesK)* (Excuse me, I'm looking for CDs.)

✔ **Ils sont au sous-sol, à côté des livres.** *(eel sohN-to-soo-soh-lah-ko-tay day leevr)* (They're in the basement, next to the books.)

Words to know

attendez un instant	ah-tahN-day aN-naNs-tahN	wait a moment
aider	ay-day	to help
essayer	ay-say-yay	to try
les cabines d'essayage	lay kah-been day-say-yazh	the fitting rooms
au fond	o fohN	in the back
à gauche	ah gosh	on the left
à droite	ah drwaht	on the right
un peu	aN puh	a little
trop	tro	too much
pas du tout	pah dew too	not at all
tant pis	tahN pee	too bad

Shopping for clothes like a pro

Clothes shopping involves all kinds of issues, like finding the right size, the right material, and the right color.

Finding the right fit

In French, size is **la taille** *(lah ta-y)*. But, often, you don't even have to say the word, as in these examples:

- ✔ **Je fais du 36.** *(zhuh feh dew trahNt-sees)* (I am a [size] 36.)

- ✔ **Je voudrais essayer une robe en 40.** *(zhuh voo-dreh ay-say-yay ewn roh-bahN kah-rahNt)* (I would like to try a dress in [size] 40.)

- ✔ **Est-que vous l'avez en plus petit?** *(ehs-kuh voo lah-vay ahN plew puh-tee)* (Do you have it in a smaller size?)

Of course, if everything else fails, you can always ask for **petit** *(puh-tee)*, **moyen** *(mwa-yaN)*, **large** *(lahrzh)*, or **extra-large** *(ehks-trah lahrzh)* (small, medium, large, or extra large).

English has only one word for clothes and shoe sizes, but French has two words: **la taille** works for height and clothes, and **la pointure** *(lah pwaN-tewr)* is for shoes.

Use the following phrases to describe how something fits. This phrase varies, of course, according to the person you're talking about. You can say:

- ✔ **Ça me va.** *(sah muh vah)* (It fits me.)

- ✔ **Ça te va bien.** *(sah tuh vah byaN)* (It fits you well.) [informal]

- ✔ **Ça lui va mal.** *(sah lwee vah mahl)* (It fits him/ her poorly.)

- ✔ **Ça ne nous va pas.** *(sah nuh noo vah pah)* (It does not fit us.)

✔ **Ça vous va très bien.** *(sah voo vah treh byan)*
(It fits you very well.) [formal]

✔ **Ça ne leur va pas du tout.** *(sah nuh luhr vah pah dew too)* (It does not fit them at all.)

Describing color and material

When talking about materials, you use **en** after the verb or **de** after the noun, as in these examples:

✔ **Cette veste est en laine. C'est une veste de laine.** *(seht vehs-teh-tahN lehn seh-tewn vehst-uh duh lehn)* (This jacket is [made] of wool. It's a wool jacket.)

✔ **Je voudrais un foulard de soie.** *(zhuh voo-dreh aN foo-lahr duh swa)* (I would like a silk scarf.)

✔ **Est-ce que ces chaussures sont en cuir?** *(ehs-kuh say sho-sewr sohN-tahN kweer?)* (Are these shoes [made of] leather?)

By the way, here's a list of clothing materials, just in case you need to know them:

✔ **la laine** *(lah lehn)* (wool)

✔ **la soie** *(lah swah)* (silk)

✔ **le coton** *(luh ko-tohN)* (cotton)

✔ **le velours côtelé** *(luh vuh-loor kot-lay)* (corduroy) (France)

✔ **le corduroy** *(luh kohr-dew-rwah)* (corduroy) (Québec)

✔ **le cuir** *(luh kweer)* (leather)

When you're picking out clothes, what's more important than **la couleur** *(lah koo-luhr)* (the color)? See Table 6-1.

Table 6-1	Colors	
Color	*Pronunciation*	*Translation*
noir/noire	nwahr	black
marron	mah-rohN	brown
blanc/blanche	blahN/blahNsh	white
bleu/bleue	bluh	blue
rouge/rouge	roozh	red
vert/verte	vehr/vehrt	green
jaune	zhon	yellow
orange	oh-rahNzh	orange
foncé	fohN-say	dark
clair	klehr	light-colored

The adjective of color always follows the noun:

- ✔ **un pantalon noir** *(an pahN-tah-lohN nwahr)* (black pants)
- ✔ **des chaussures vertes** *(day sho-sewr vehrt)* (green shoes)

And when you find the perfect item (or if the salesperson's ready to make a sale), you'll hear

- ✔ **Ça vous va à merveille.** *(sah voo vah ah mehr-veh-y)* (It looks great on you.)
- ✔ **C'est à la mode.** *(seh-tah lah mohd)* (It's in fashion.)

Dressing: From hat to shoes

Table 6-2 lists **vêtements pour dames** *(veht-mahN poor dahm)* (women's clothes).

Table 6-2	Women's Clothing	
French	*Pronunciation*	*Translation*
une robe	ewn rohb	a dress
une jupe	ewn zhewp	a skirt
un tailleur	aN tah-yuhr	a suit
une veste*	ewn vehst	a jacket
un pantalon*	aN pahN-tah-lohN	slacks
un jean*	aN zheen	jeans
un manteau	aN mahN-to	a coat
un imperméable*	aN-naN-pehr-may-ahbl	a raincoat
un chemisier	aN shuh-mee-zyay	a blouse
un foulard	aN foo-lahr	a scarf
une chemise de nuit	ewn shuh-meez duh nwee	a nightgown
une robe de chambre	ewn rohb duh shahNbr	a dressing gown
un maillot de bains	aN mah-yo duh baN	a bathing suit (France)
un costume de bains	aN kohs-tewm duh baN	a bathing suit (Québec)
des sous-vêtements* (m.)	day soo-veht-mahN	underwear

These terms also are used for men's clothing.

And now for the **vêtements pour hommes** *(veht-mahN poo-rohm)* (men's clothes) in Table 6-3.

Table 6-3	Men's Clothing	
French	*Pronunciation*	*Translation*
un complet	aN kohN-pleh	a suit (France)
un habit	aN-nah-bee	a suit (Québec)
un veston	aN vehs-tohN	a suit jacket
un blazer	an blah-zehr	a blazer
une chemise	ewn shuh-meez	a shirt
une ceinture	ewn saN-tewr	a belt
des chaussettes (f.)	day sho-seht	socks
un pardessus	aN pahr-duh-sew	an overcoat
un chapeau	aN sha-po	a hat
une cravate	ewn krah-vaht	a tie

French has borrowed many English words for clothes. But those words sometimes have a different meaning. Here are a few:

- ✔ **le tee-shirt** *(luh tee-shuhrt)* (T-shirt)
- ✔ **le sweat** *(luh sweet)* (sweat shirt)

  Notice the pronunciation.

- ✔ **le jogging** *(luh zhoh-geeng)* (warm-up suit)
- ✔ **le pull** *(luh pewl)* (sweater)
- ✔ **le slip** *(luh sleep)* (underpants)

Now for shoes:

- ✔ **les sandales** *(lay sahN-dahl)* (sandals)
- ✔ **les bottes** *(lay boht)* (boots)
- ✔ **les chaussures à talons** *(lay sho-sew-rah tah-lohN)* (high-heeled shoes)
- ✔ **les baskets** *(lay bahs-keht)* (sneakers)

 ✔ **les chaussons** *(lay sho-sohN)* (slippers)

 ✔ **une paire de chaussures** *(ewn pehr duh sho-sewr)* (a pair of shoes)

Words to Know

étroit	ay-trwah	narrow
large	larzh	wide
un autre	aN-notr	another
Combien coûte . . . ?	kohN-byaN koot	How much is . . . ?
joli	zho-lee	pretty
aujourd'hui	o-zhoor-dwee	today
absolument	ahb-so-lew-mahN	absolutely

Hitting the Market and the Pâtisserie

From outdoor markets to supermarkets to a multitude of specialty shops, the following sections get you out finding the fish for tonight's dinner or that delectable pastry that you've been craving.

Fresh air, fresh food: The outdoor market

Outdoor markets are a delight. They're especially nice in small, country villages, where you can enjoy the local fare and delight in the noises, smells, and accents. The largest places and many small town squares also have **les halles** *(lay ahl)* (an indoor market). What better way to try out your French?

Vendors in an outdoor market sell almost everything. Table 6-4 is a brief list of things that you may find at a local market.

Table 6-4	Market Items	
French	*Pronunciation*	*Translation*
la viande	lah vyahnd	meat
le poisson	luh pwa-sohn	fish
les fruits	lay frwee	fruit
la pomme	lah pohm	apple
la banane	lah banan	banana
la poire	lah pwar	pear
la pêche	lah pehsh	peach
l'orange (f.)	lor ahnzh	orange
la fraise	lah frehz	strawberry
les légumes	lay lay-gewm	vegetables
la laitue	lah leh-tooeh	lettuce
la tomate	lay to-maht	tomato
la carotte	lah kah-roht	carrot
l'oignon (m.)	loyhn-ohN	onion
la fleur	lah fluhr	flower

Here are some phrases that you may hear or want to try out in the market:

✔ **Qu'est-ce que tu aimes comme fruits?** *(kes-kuh tew ehm kohm frwee)* (What kind of fruit do you like?)

✔ **Tous! Mais à cette saison, je préfère les pêches.** *(toos meh ah seht seh-zohn zhuh pray-fehr lay pesh)* (All of them, but at this time of year, I prefer peaches.)

✔ **Est-ce qu'il y a des pêches ici?** *(ehs-kee-lee-yah day peh-shee-see)* (Are there peaches here?)

✔ **Oui, mais là-bas, elles sont plus belles et moins chères.** *(wee meh lah-bah ehl sohn plew beh-lay mwan shehr)* (Yes, but over there, they're nicer and cheaper.)

✔ **Donnez-moi un kilo de pêches, s'il vous plaît.** *(doh-nay mwa aN kee-lo duh pesh seel-voo play)* (Give me two pounds [literally, 1 kilogram] of peaches, please.)

✔ **Choisissez!** *(shwa-zee-say)* (Take your pick!)

✔ **Voilà madame, et avec ça?** *(vwa-lah mahdahm ay ah-vehk sah)* (Here you are, ma'am, anything else?)

✔ **C'est tout. Ça fait combien?** *(seh too sah feh kohn-byan)* (That's all. How much is it?)

Finding food stores large and small

When you don't have time to go to the outdoor market, the supermarket comes in handy. France has some huge supermarkets that line the highways as you enter a city. Some of them are so large that they're called **hypermarchés** *(ee-pehr-mahr-shay)* (hypermarkets) rather than **supermarchés** *(sew-pehr-mahr-shay)* (supermarkets). But if you visit France and have some time on your hands, go discover the little food stores. You're sure to enjoy them.

Following are some of **les petits magasins** *(lay puh-tee mah-gah-zaN)* (the little [food] stores):

- ✔ **la boulangerie** *(lah boo-lahn-zhree)* (the bakery)
- ✔ **la pâtisserie** *(lah pah-tees-ree)* (the confectioner's shop)
- ✔ **la boucherie** *(lah boo-shree)* (the butcher shop)
- ✔ **la charcuterie** *(lah shahr-kew-tree)* (butcher shop [specializes in pork and prepared foods])
- ✔ **l'épicerie** *(lay-pees-ree)* (the grocery store [more like a general store])
- ✔ **la crémerie** *(lah kraym-ree)* (the dairy product and cheese store)
- ✔ **le marchand de fruits et légumes** *(luh mahr-shan duh frew-ee zay lay-gewm)* (the produce vendor)

Here are examples of this vocabulary in action:

- ✔ **On achète du pain à la boulangerie.** *(oh-nah-sheht dew pan ah lah boo-lahn-zhree)* (Bread is bought at the bakery.)
- ✔ **L'épicier vend du café, du thé, et des épices.** *(lay-pee-syay vahn dew kah-fay dew tay ay day-zay-pees)* (The grocer sells coffee, tea, and spices.)

Weighing and Measuring

French-speaking countries use the metric system. The basic unit of weight is the gram, and you usually buy fruit, vegetables, or meat in multiples of the basic gram:

- ✔ **un gramme** *(aN gram)* (1 lb. = 453.60g)
- ✔ **un kilogramme/un kilo** *(aN kee-lo-grahm/aN kee-lo)* (1kg = 1000g, about 2.2 lb.)
- ✔ **une livre** *(ewn leevr)* (a pound = 500g, about 1.1 lb.)

As far as liquid measures go, the basic unit is **le litre** *(luh leetr)* (the liter), which equals 1.06 quarts. A liter is equal to 100cl, **centilitres** *(sahn-tee-leetr)* (centiliters).

When talking about unspecified quantities, French uses an article that we don't have in English. It's called the **partitif** *(pahr-tee-teef)* because it describes a "part" of a quantity. You construct it by combining the preposition **de** (of) with the definite article **le, la, les:**

- **de** + **le** = **du** *(dew)*
- **de** + **la** = **de la** *(duh lah)*
- **de** + **les** = **des** *(deh)*
- **de** + **l'** = **de l'** *(duhl)*

You can translate these constructions as "some," as in this example:

> **Je voudrais du carburant.** *(zhuh voo-dray duh kahr-bew-rahN)* (I would like *some* gas.)

Paying for Your Prize

Credit cards are widely accepted in French-speaking countries. However, you can't necessarily count on being able to use them outside big cities, and if you can use credit cards, you may just happen to be carrying the wrong kind. So you'd better have cash on hand, either from traveler's checks or out of an ATM (see Chapter 3 for more about money matters). Here's the vocabulary that you need to make that shopping spree your very own:

- **C'est combien?** *(say kohN-byaN)* (How much is it?)
- **Combien coûtent celles-ci?** *(kohN-byaN koot sehl-see)* (How much are these?)
- **C'est bon marché.** *(say boN mar-shay)* (It's a good deal.)

> ✔ **C'est un peu cher, mais je les prends.** *(say-taN puh shehr meh zhuh lay prahN.)* (It's a little expensive, but I'll take them.)

> ✔ **Est-ce que vous acceptez les cartes de crédit?** *(es-kuh voo ak-sep-tay lay kart duh kray-deet?)* (Do you accept credit cards?)

The equivalent of the English expression "I need change" (small coins) is **J'ai besoin de monnaie** *(zheh buh-swaN duh mo-nay)* in French.

Be careful not to accidentally translate the English word "money" to **monnaie** just because "money" and **monnaie** look and sound so much alike. The word "money" corresponds with **argent** *(ahr-zhahN)* in French.

In France (in a coffee bar for example, when the employee wants you to pay in a smaller denomination than a 20-franc bill), you may be asked:

Avez-vous de la (petite) monnaie? *(ah-vay voo duh lah puh-teet moh-nay)* (Do you have [small] change?)

In Québec, however, you may be asked in the same situation:

Avez-vous du p'tit change? *(ah-vay voo dew p'tee shahNzh),* meaning exactly the same thing.

Or you may hear in Québec:

Je voudrais faire du change. *(zhuh voo-dray fehr dew shahNzh)* (I would like to get some change.)

In France, you'd say:

Je voudrais faire de la monnaie. *(zhuh voo-dray fehr duh lah moh-nay),* meaning exactly the same thing as the preceding example.

Words to Know

tous	toos	all of them
là-bas	lah-bah	over there
celui-ci (m.)/ celle-ci (f.)	suh-lwee-see/ sehl-see	this one
celui-là (m.)/ celle-là (f.)	suh-lwee-lah/ sehl-lah	that one
voilà	vwah-lah	there you go
et avec ça?	ay ah-vehk sah	anything else?
c'est tout	seh too	that's all

Comparing Better and Best

Money's limited, so you have to be discerning when you're shopping — like deciding what's good, what's better, and what's best.

Making comparisons

To make a comparison between two objects or two people, the French language uses the following for all adjectives and adverbs, whether long or short:

- ✔ **plus . . . que** *(plew . . . kuh)* (more . . . than)
- ✔ **moins . . . que** *(mwan . . . kuh)* (less . . . than)
- ✔ **aussi . . . que** *(o-see . . . kuh)* (as . . . as)

Here are a few examples:

- ✔ **La France est moins grande que le Canada.** *(lah frahn-seh mwan grahnd kuh luh kah-nah-dah)* (France is smaller than Canada.)

✔ **On mange plus souvent des fruits en été qu'en hiver.** *(ohn mahnzh plew soo-vahn day frwuh-ee ahn-nay-tay kahn-nee-vehr)* (A person eats fruit more often in summer than in winter.)

✔ **Les poires sont aussi chères que les pêches.** *(lay pwahr sohN-to-see shehr kuh lay pehsh)* (Pears are as expensive as peaches.)

You can't use the **"plus"** construction for the adjective **bon** *(bohN)* (good). Just as in English, it has its own form, **meilleur** *(meh-yuhr)* (better).

Les fruits du marché sont meilleurs que les fruits du supermarché. *(lay frew-ee dew mahr-shay sohN meh-yuhr kuh lay frew-ee dew sew-pehr-mahr-shay)* (Fruit at the market is better than fruit at the supermarket.)

Using superlatives

When you want to say something is the best — or the most awful — you use a superlative:

✔ **le/la/les plus . . .** *(luh/lah/lay plew)* (the most)

✔ **le/la/les moins . . .** *(luh/lah/lay mwaN)* (the least)

You construct superlatives in French either with the adjective before the noun or with the adjective after the noun.

When the adjective precedes the noun

When the adjective goes in front of the noun (see Chapter 2 for the placement of adjectives), the construction is pretty much the same as in English. For example:

✔ **C'est la moins jolie robe.** *(seh lah mwaN zho-lee rohb)* (It's the least pretty dress.)

✔ **Eaton's est le plus grand magasin de Montréal.** *(Eaton's eh luh plew grahN mah-gah-zaN duh MohN-ray-ahl)* (Eaton's is the largest department store in Montreal.)

When the adjective follows the noun

The superlative construction is slightly different when you use one of those adjectives that follow the noun. For example:

- ✔ **C'est le garçon le plus intelligent de l'école.** *(seh luh gahr-sohN luh plew-zan-teh-lee-zhahN duh lay-kohl)* (He is the most intelligent boy in the school.)

- ✔ **Elle achète la robe la moins chère de la boutique.** *(eh-lah-shet lah rohb lah mwaN shehr duh lah boo-teek)* (She buys the least expensive dress in the store.)

Just as in English, you may not use "the most" or "the least" for the adjective "good" in French. French's special word for this superlative is **le meilleur** *(luh meh-yuhr)* (the best). Here is how you use it:

On trouve le meilleur chocolat en Suisse. *(ohN troov luh meh-yuhr sho-ko-lah ahN sew-ees)* (The best chocolate is found in Switzerland.)

Verbs for the Active Shopper

When shopping, you frequently use the verbs **acheter et vendre** *(ah-shuh-tay ay vahndr)* (to buy and to sell). **Acheter** is a regular verb with a slight irregularity: **Il achète** *(ee-la-sheht)* (He buys). (See Chapter 2 for more on verb conjugations.)

Vendre is an irregular verb and is conjugated in Table 6-5.

Table 6-5	Vendre
Conjugation	*Pronunciation*
je vends	zhuh vahn
tu vends	tew vahn

Conjugation	Pronunciation
il/elle vend	eel/ehl vahn
nous vendons	noo vahn-dohn
vous vendez	voo vahn-day
ils/elles vendent	eel/ehl vahnd

Aimer *(ay-may)* (to like; to love) is a very important verb for shopping, and as a regular **-er** verb, you can conjugate it easily (see Chapter 2).

Préférer *(pray-fay-ray)* (to prefer) is also an **-er** verb, but it has a slight irregularity: The **je, tu, il,** and **ils** forms make the second syllable sound like *eh* rather than *ay*. For example, **je préfère** *(zhuh pray-fehr)*.

Here are some other verbs that you may find helpful:

- **aider** *(ay-day)* (to help)
- **chercher** *(shehrsh-ay)* (to look for)
- **choisir** *(shwa-zeer)* (to choose)
- **donner** *(do-nay)* (to give)
- **essayer** *(ay-say-yay)* (to try on)
- **montrer** *(mohN-tray)* (to show)
- **payer** *(pay-yay)* (to pay)
- **porter** *(pohr-tay)* (to wear)
- **voir** *(vwahr)* (to see)
- **vouloir** *(voo-lwahr)* (to want)

Chapter 7

Making Leisure a Top Priority

In This Chapter
▶ Enjoying city cultural life
▶ Getting outdoors
▶ Playing sports

The French work hard, but they also know how to relax. France has something for everyone. From going out to museums and nightclubs to getting outside to play or watch sports, you're sure to have a good time if you know some of the language.

Going Out on the Town

When you visit a new city or town, have fun trying out as much of the local entertainment as possible.

Visiting museums

You can visit many different museums in Paris. And buying **Carte Musées et Monuments** *(kahrt mew-zay ay mohN-yoo-mehN)* (a museum pass) can be the best way to see them. Here's a short list of a few of the famous museums that you may want to check out:

- **Le Louvre** *(luh loo-vruh):* Home to some of the most famous sculptures and paintings in the world, the Venus de Milo, and Leonardo da Vinci's Mona Lisa (**La Joconde**) *(lah zhoh-kohNd).*

- **Musée d'Orsay** *(myew-zay dor-say):* Home to the world's finest collection of van Gogh *(vahn guhg)* paintings outside of the Van Gogh Museum in Amsterdam.

- **Versailles** *(vayr-si):* Louis XIV turned it into the official residence of the French monarchy. You may visit the State Apartments, the Hall of Mirrors, and the Royal Chapel.

- **Fontainebleau** *(fohN-tehn-bloh):* Napoléon set up court here in the early 19th century. The emperor also signed his abdication papers here in 1814.

While touring museums, please remember that many works of art weren't made to withstand the intensity of modern tourism. That's why you see the warning **"Photos au flash interdites"** *(foto oh flash aN-tehr-deet)* (no flash photography). Sometimes, complete rooms or even wings may be closed, and you'll see signs posted that read **"Défense d'entrer"** *(day-fahNs dahN-tray)* (no admittance).

Here are some phrases that may help you get the most out of your museum trip:

- **Y a-t-il des réductions pour des étudiants?** *(ee ah teel day ray-dewk-syohN poor dayzay-tewd-ee-ahN)* (Are there any discounts for students?)

- **Si vous avez votre carte d'identité, c'est moitié prix.** *(see vooz ahvay vohtruh kahrt dee-dehN-tee-tay-say mwah-tyay pree)* (If you have your ID card, it's half price.)

- **Avez vous un guide en anglais?** *(ahvay voo aN geed ahN nahN-glay)* (Do you have a guidebook in English?)

✔ **À quelle heure est la prochaine visite guidée?** *(ah kehl uhr ay lah proh-shehn veez-eet gee-day)* (What time is the next guided visit?)

✔ **Elle commence dans . . . minutes.** *(ehl kohm-aNs dahN meen-ewt)* (It starts in . . . minutes.)

✔ **Deux adultes et un étudiant, s'il vous plaît.** *(duhz ahd-ewlt ay aN nay-tew-dyahN seel voo play)* (Two adults and one student [ticket] please.)

Words to Know

Y a-t-il des réductions pour . . . ?	ee ah teel day ray-dewk-syohN poor	Are there any discounts for . . . ?
carte d'identité	kahrt dee-dehn-tee-tay	identification card
moitié prix	mwah-tyay pree	half price
la prochaine visite guidée	lah proh-shehn veez-eet gee-day	the next guided tour

Going to the theater

French theater has been world famous for centuries and offers something for every taste and budget, from classical productions to the **avant-garde** *(ahv-ahNt gahrd)* (modern). Four of France's five national theaters are located in Paris. (The fifth one is in Strasbourg.) You should make reservations at one of the national theaters at least two weeks in advance, unless you plan on trying to pick up some last minute "rush" tickets.

Men and women are expected to "dress" to go to the theater. Men should wear dark suits and women should wear dresses. Openings call for more formal attire, such as tuxedos and long dresses.

Here are some phrases that you may consider when thinking about the theater:

> ✔ **Je veux aller au théâtre ce soir.** *(zhuh vuhz ahl-ay oh tay-ahtruh suh swahr)* (I'd like to go to the theater tonight.)
>
> ✔ **Qu'est-ce qu'on joue?** *(kes kohN zhoo)* (What's playing?)
>
> ✔ **Je ne connais pas beaucoup le français. Ça va me plaire?** *(zhuh nuh kohNay pah boh-koo luh frahN-say sah vah muh plehr)* (I don't know a lot of French. Will I like it?)
>
> ✔ **À quelle heure commence-t-elle?** *(ah kehl uhr kohm-ahNs tehl)* (What time does it start?)

Words to Know

le théâtre	luh tay-ahtruh	the theater
un drame	aN drahm	drama
triste	treest	sad
une comédie	ewn kohm-ay-dee	comedy
rigolo	ree-goh-loh	funny

After you know what play you want to see, you can buy tickets **au guichet** *(oh gee-shay)* (at the box office) from **"le monsieur"** *(luh muh-suhr)*, the ticket seller.

> ✔ **Je voudrais deux places à l'orchestre, s'il vous plaît.** *(zhuh voo-dray duh plahs ah lohr-kes-truh seel voo play)* (I'd like two orchestra seats, please.)
>
> ✔ **Tout est complet à l'orchestre.** *(toot ay kohm-play ah lohr-kes-truh)* (The orchestra seats are sold out.)

✔ **Il y a deux places au premier rang au balcon.** *(eel ee ah duh plahs oh prehm-ee-ay rahN oh bahl-kohN)* (There are two seats in the front row of the balcony.)

✔ **Combien coûtent les billets?** *(kohm-byaN koot lay bee-yay)* (How much will the tickets be?)

✔ **Le lever du rideau est à quelle heure?** *(luh luh-vay dew ree-doh ayt ah kehl uhr)* (What time does the curtain go up?)

Words to Know

la place	lah plahs	seat
à l'orchestre	ah lohr-kes-truh	orchestra seats
au balcon	oh bahl-kohN	balcony
tout est complet	toot ay kohm-play	sold out
le premier rang	luh prehm-ee-ay rahN	front row
Le rideau se lève.	luh ree-doh suh lehv	The curtain goes up.
l'entracte	laN-trahkt	intermission

Going to the movies

Sometimes after a hectic day of sightseeing, it's very relaxing to go to the movies and just sit. The cinema, invented by Frenchmen Auguste *(oh-gewst)* and Louis Lumière *(loo-ee lew-mee-ehr),* had its debut in Paris. The French cinema is so popular that more than 300 films are shown in Paris per week; that's more than

any other city in the world. So after you answer the
following question:

> **Voulez-vous aller au cinéma?** *(voolay vooz
> ahlay oh see-nay-mah)* (Do you want to go to the
> movies?)

you can finish this sentence:

> **Je voudrais voir . . .** *(zhuh vood-dray vwahr)*
> (I want to see . . .)

Of course, your options are nearly unlimited, but here
are a few choices:

- ✔ **Un dessin animé** *(aN day-sehn ahn-ee-may)* (a
  cartoon)

- ✔ **Un documentaire** *(aN doh-kyoo-mehn-tahr)* (a
  documentary)

- ✔ **Un film d'aventure** *(aN feelm dah-vehn-tyoor)*
  (an adventure film)

- ✔ **Un western** *(aN vestehrn)* (a Western)

When films are marked **VO** *(vay oh)* **(version
originale)** *(vehr-zee-ohN ohr-eezh-ee-nahl),* it
means that the film is shown in its original
language, with French subtitles.

Enjoying a concert

No matter what language you speak, music is international. If you're feeling overwhelmed by having
to speak French all the time, try going to a concert.
However, you may need a little French to decide
which concert to go to.

- ✔ **Quel type de musique aimes-tu?** *(kehl teep duh
  mew-seek ehm tew)* (What type of music do you
  like?)

- ✔ **J'adore la musique classique.** *(zhah-dohr la
  mew-seek klah-seek)* (I love classical music.)

✔ **Il y a une symphonie de Mozart au parc ce soir.
Veux-tu y aller?** *(eel ee ah ewn saN-fohn-ee duh
mo-zahr oh pahrk suh swahr vuh tew ee ahl-ay)*
(There's a Mozart symphony in the park tonight.
Do you want to go?)

Words to Know

une symphonie	ewn saN-fohn-ee	a symphony
la musique classique	lah mew-seek klah-seek	classical music
la musique moderne	lah mew-seek moh-dehrn	modern music
la musique rock	lah mew-seek rohk	rock music
la musique de jazz	lah mew-seek duh zhahz	jazz music
la musique techno	lah mew-seek tehk-no	techno music
le rap	luh rahp	rap music
un orchestre de chambre	aN ohr-kes-truh duh shahNbr	a chamber orchestra
aimer	eh-may	to like
ennuyeux	ahN-nwee-yuh	boring
bizarre	beez-ahr	weird, bizarre
bruyant	brew-ee-yahN	noisy
moderne	moh-dehrn	modern

Don't shout **"Encore!"** *(ahN-kohr)* at a French concert unless you want the performers to play the entire piece again. Instead, say **"Bis"** *(bees),* which means that you want them to play some more.

The verb **jouer** *(zhoo-ay)* is a regular **-er** verb, meaning "to play." When you use **jouer** when talking about instruments, you use the preposition **de.** You use the preposition **au** when referring to playing games or to theatrical, cinematic, or musical performances. See Table 7-1 for some examples of the use of **jouer.**

Table 7-1	Using the Verb Jouer (To Play)	
Word	*Pronunciation*	*Translation*
Je joue du piano.	zhuh zhoo dew pee-ahnoh	I play the piano.
Tu joues de la guitare.	tew zhoo duh lah gee-tahr	You play the guitar.
Nous jouons aux échecs.	noo zhoo-ohN ohz ayshek	We play chess.
Vous jouez de la trompette.	voo zhoo-ay duh la trohN-peht	You play the trumpet.
Elles jouent du violon.	ehl zhoo dew vee-oh-lohN	They play the violin.

Words to Know

le piano	luh *pee-ahn-oh*	piano
le violon	luh *vee-oh-lohN*	violin
la trompette	lah *trohN-peht*	trumpet

la guitare	la *gee-tahr*	guitar
les échecs	lays *ayshehk*	chess
les dames	lay *dahm*	checkers

Getting wild at a nightclub

If you're not exhausted after a full day of sightseeing, you may want to try visiting a more lively setting. Most large cities have plenty of nightclubs that offer everything from live music to dancing.

Europeans also tend to dress up more for a night on the town than do their North American counterparts. Wearing black is **de rigeur** *(duh ree-guhr)* (compulsory).

Ready for some practice phrases before you hit the nightclubs?

- ✔ **Veux-tu aller en boîte? Nous pouvons danser.** *(vuh too ahl-ay ahN bwat noo poo-vohN dahn-say)* (Do you want to go to a disco? We could go dancing.)

- ✔ **Allons au club pour regarder une revue.** *(ahl-ohnz oh kloob poor ruh-gahr-day ewn ruh-vew)* (Let's go to a club to watch a show.)

- ✔ **Faut-il réserver?** *(foh-teel rayz-ehr-vay)* (Do we need reservations?)

- ✔ **Nous allons devoir faire la queue.** *(noozah-lohN duh-vwahr fehr lah kuh)* (We'll have to stand in line.)

- ✔ **À quelle heure commence le spectacle?** *(ah kehl uhr kohm-ahNs luh spehk-tahk-luh)* (What time does the show start?)

Words to Know

danser	dahN-say	to dance
une disco/ discothèque	ewn dees-koh/ dees-koh-tehk	a disco
un club	aN kloob	a club
une revue	ewn ruh-vew	a review/show
Faut-il réserver?	foh-teel ray-zehr-vay	Is a reservation necessary?

In addition to tipping the usher at a concert, theater, or movie, you're also expected to tip the attendant in the public restrooms. This attendant is such a familiar character of the French scene that she has a name: **dame pipi** *(dahm pee-pee).*

Enjoying the Great Outdoors

Getting outside gives you a great place to pick up some new vocabulary — especially some active verbs.

Going skiing

Whether you're in Switzerland, France, or Canada, you can find plenty of opportunities for both **ski** *(skee)* (downhill) and **ski de fond** *(skee duh fohN)* (cross-country).

Words to Know

un forfait	aN fohr-fay	a lift pass
les conditions	lay kohN-dee-see-ohN	conditions (ski)
la neige	lah nehzh	snow
poudreuse	pood-ruhz	powdery
rester	rehs-tay	to stay
acheter	ahsh-tay	to buy

Just saying these phrases out loud will have you on the slopes in no time:

- **Il fait très froid aujourd'hui.** *(eel fay treh frwah oh-zhood-wee)* (It's really cold today.)

- **Il y a beaucoup de neige.** *(eel ee ah bo-koo duh nehzh)* (There's a lot of snow.)

- **La neige est poudreuse, aussi.** *(lah nehzh ay pood-ruhz oh-see)* (The snow is powdery, too.)

- **Les conditions sont excellentes.** *(lay kohN-dee-see-ohN sohN tay-ksay-lahNt)* (The conditions are excellent.)

- **Je voudrais deux forfaits pour une journée, s'il vous plaît.** *(zhuh voo-dray duh fohr-fay poor ewn zhoo-nay seel voo play)* (I would like two one-day lift passes, please.)

- **Je voudrais louer des skis.** *(zhuh voo-dray loo-ay day ski)* (I'd like to rent some skis.)

- **Voulez-vous des leçons de ski?** *(voo-lay voo day luh-sohN duh ski)* (Will you need lessons?)

Words to Know

Je voudrais . . .	zhuh voo-dray . . .	I'd like . . .
louer	loo-ay	to rent
l'équipement	lay-keep-mahN	equipment
les leçons de ski	lay luh-sohN duh skee	skiing lessons
les skis	lay skee	skis

Hitting the beach

Feel like playing in the surf? Swimming is quite safe because lifeguards supervise most beaches. But if you see a sign posted that reads **"Baignade interdite"** *(bah-nyahd aN-tehr-deet),* beware. That means no swimming!

If you do something to or for yourself, you use a reflexive verb. Reflexive verbs are regular verbs that attach a pronoun to show who received the action of the verb. The action of a reflexive verb is always performed by the subject. The pronoun is usually implied in English. Table 7-2 shows the use of the reflexive verb **se baigner** *(suh-beh-nyay)* (to swim).

Table 7-2	Se Baigner
Conjugation	*Pronunciation*
je me baigne	zhuh muh beh-ny
tu te baignes	too tuh beh-ny

Conjugation	Pronunciation
il/elle se baigne	eel/ehl suh beh-ny
nous nous baignons	noo noo beh-ny-ohN
vous vous baignez	voo voo beh-ny-ay
ils/elles se baignent	eel/ehl se beh-ny

Here are a couple other examples of beach-related uses of reflexive verbs:

- ✔ **Les enfants s'amusent sur la plage.** *(layz ahN-fahN sah-mewz sewr lah plazh)* (The children have fun on the beach.)

- ✔ **Nous nous promenons au bord de la mer.** *(noo noo proh-mehn-ohn oh bohr duh lah mehr)* (We walk [ourselves] along the beach.)

Try out these phrases before heading to the water:

- ✔ **Allons à la plage!** *(ahlon ah lah plahzh)* (Let's go to the beach!)

- ✔ **Nous allons nager.** *(noo zah-lohN nah-zhay)* (We're going swimming.)

- ✔ **Attendez! Vous oubliez la crème solaire.** *(ah-tahN-day vooz oo-blee-ay lah krehm soh-lehr)* (Wait! You forgot your suncreen.)

- ✔ **Regarde les très grandes vagues!** *(ruh-gahrd lay tray grahnd vahg)* (Look at those really big waves!)

- ✔ **As-tu mon tuba et mes palmes?** *(ah-tew mohN tew-bah ay may pahlm)* (Do you have my snorkel and flippers?)

- ✔ **Je vais bronzer.** *(zhuh veh brohnzay)* (I'm going to work on my tan.)

Words to Know

les vagues	lay vahg	waves
nager	nahzh-ay	to swim
oublier	oo-blee-ay	to forget
se dépêcher	suh day-pehsh-ay	to hurry
bronzer	brohn-zay	to tan
la crème solaire	lah krehm soh-lehr	sunscreen
le tuba	luh tew-bah	snorkel
les palmes	lay pahlm	flippers
la plage	lah plazh	the beach
s'amuser	sah-mew-zay	to have fun

Setting up camp

Camping is a great way to get away from it all. Traditionally in France, the months of July and August are when the French, especially the Parisians, head to the hills, so to speak. Most campsites have showers and restaurants, as well as separate sites for bicycles and tent campers. Many are situated along the beaches.

Off-road camping is illegal. However, you may want to try asking a local farmer for permission to pitch your tent on his land. **Pouvons-nous camper ici, s'il vous plaît?** *(poo-vohN noo kahN-pay ee-see seel voo play)* (May we camp here, please?). He just may let you, provided that you leave the site as you found it and aren't too noisy or destructive.

Words to Know

monter la tente	mohN-tay lah tahNt	to pitch the tent
les allumettes	layz ahl-ewm-eht	matches
faire un feu de camp	fehr aN fuh duh kahN	start a campfire
un sac de couchage	aN sahk duh koosh-ahzh	sleeping bag
les douches	lay doosh	showers
les toilettes	lay twah-leht	toilets
les services	lay sehrv-ees	facilities
Nous sommes arrivés.	noo sohmz ahr-ee-vay	We're here. (We've arrived.)
se lever	suh luh-vay	to get up

Ready for some practice? Try these sentences out:

- ✔ **Montons la tente.** *(mohNt-ohN lah tahNt)* (Let's pitch the tent.)
- ✔ **Quels services y-a-til?** *(kehl sehr-vees ee-ah-teel)* (What facilities do they have?)
- ✔ **Il y a des toilettes et des douches.** *(eel ee ah day twah-leht et day dewsh)* (There are toilets and showers.)
- ✔ **Voilà les sacs de couchage.** *(vwah-lah lay sahk duh koosh-ahzh)* (Here are the sleeping bags.)
- ✔ **Trouves-tu les allumettes?** *(trewv too layz ahl-ewm-eht)* (Have you found the matches?)
- ✔ **Je vais faire un feu de camp.** *(zhuh veh fehr aN fuh duh kahN)* (I'll start a campfire.)

Words to Know

aller	ahl-ay	to go
pêcher	pehsh-ay	to go fishing
Je n'aime pas . . .	zhuh nehm pas	I don't like . . .
lire	leer	to read
attrapper	aht-rah-pay	to catch
le poisson	luh pwah-sohN	fish
la canne à pêche	lah kahn ah pehsh	fishing pole
les vers	lay vehr	worms
dégoûtant	day-gewt-ahnt	disgusting

Going fishing is a fun thing to do while camping.

- ✔ **Je vais pêcher.** *(zhuh vay pehsh-ay)* (I'm going fishing.)

- ✔ **J'espère attraper des poissons pour le dîner.** *(zhehs-pehr aht-rah-pay day pwah-sohN poor luh deenay)* (I hope to catch some fish for dinner.)

- ✔ **Tu as ta canne à pêche?** *(tew ah tah kahn ah pehsh)* (Do you have your fishing pole?)

- ✔ **Oui, et des vers aussi.** *(wee ay day vehr o-see)* (Yes, and some worms, too.)

- ✔ **Dégoûtant! Allez!** *(day-gewt-ahnt ah-lay)* (Disgusting! Go away!)

Sports, Sports, Sports

Today, the French are much more sports minded than in the past. Young people regularly join teams and compete in sports, such as those in Table 7-3:

Table 7-3	Sports	
French	*Pronunciation*	*Translation*
le basket	luh bahs-keht	basketball
le football	luh foot-bol	soccer
le rugby	luh rewg-bee	rugby
la natation	lah nah-tah-see-ohN	swimming
le tennis	luh teh-nees	tennis
la randonnée	lah rahN-doh-nay	hiking
le cyclisme	luh see-kleez-muh	cycling
la voile	lah vwahl	sailing
la planche à voile	lah plahNsh ah vwahl	windsurfing

Words to Know

le basket (ball)	luh bahs-keht (bol)	basketball
le football américain	luh foot-bol ah-may-ree-kaN	American football
le coup d'envoi	luh koo dahN-vwah	kick-off

continued

Words to Know (continued)

un club de sport	aN kluhb duh spohr	a sports club
une equipe	ewn ay-keep	a team
gagner	gahn-yay	to win
marquer un point	mahr-kay aN pwaN	to score a point
manquer	mahN-kay	to miss
un but	aN bewt	a goal
égalité	ay-gah-lee-tay	tied score

The French use two different verbs when talking about playing sports: **faire de** *(fehr duh)* for individual sports and **jouer au** *(zhew-ay o)* for team sports. **Faire** *(fehr)*, an irregular verb, uses the preposition **de** *(duh)* and its variants, whereas **jouer** *(zhew-ay)*, a regular **-er** verb, uses the preposition **au** *(o)* and its variants. See Table 7-4 to conjugate **faire**. **Jouer** is conjugated in the "Enjoying a concert" section earlier in this chapter.

Table 7-4	Faire	
Conjugation	**Pronunciation**	**Translation**
Je fais du tennis.	zhuh fay dew teh-nees	I play tennis.
Tu fais du tennis.	too fay dew teh-nees	You play tennis.
Elle fait du tennis.	ehl fay dew teh-nees	She plays tennis.

Conjugation	Pronunciation	Translation
Nous faisons du tennis.	noo fayz-ohN dew teh-nees	We play tennis.
Vous faites du tennis.	voo feht dew teh-nees	You play tennis. [formal/plural]
Ils font du tennis.	eel fohN dew teh-nees	They play tennis.

Chapter 8

When You Gotta Work

. . . .

In This Chapter

▶ Making a phone call

▶ Arranging meetings and doing business

▶ Using the Internet

. . . .

*N*ot all foreign travel is purely for pleasure's sake.
If this is your first business trip to a French-
speaking country, be assured that everyone wants to
make your visit pleasant. And making an effort with
your French will impress them — who knows, maybe
it will seal the deal. This chapter helps you navigate
the basics of business activities.

Picking Up the Phone

Making — or receiving — a phone call in French can
be nerve-wracking, but the best thing to do is take a
deep breath and don't hesitate to ask the person on
the other end to speak more slowly by saying **"Parlez
plus lentement, s'il vous plaît"** *(pahrlay ploo lahn-tuh-
mahN, seel voo play)* (Speak more slowly, please.).

French has two words for hello. You use **allô**
(ah-loh) when answering the telephone and
bonjour *(bohN-zhoor)* when greeting people
elsewhere. Also, in French, a telephone says
drin, drin *(dreen, dreen)*, not "ring, ring."

The following list covers some basic phrases used in phone conversations:

- ✔ **Allô.** *(ah-loh)* (Hello.)

- ✔ **C'est Pierre.** *(seh pee-her)* (It's Pierre.)

- ✔ **Ça va?** *(sah vah)* (How are you?)

- ✔ **Est-ce que Monique est là?** *(ehs kuh moh-neek eh lah?)* (Is Monique there?)

- ✔ **Un moment, s'il vous plaît.** *(aN moh-mahN seel voo play)* (One moment, please.)

- ✔ **Ne quitte pas.** *(nuh keet pah)* (Don't hang up.)

- ✔ **Au revoir.** *(ohr-vwahr)* (Good-bye.)

- ✔ **À bientôt.** *(ah byaN-toh)* (See you later.)

Many times, the people you're trying to reach aren't available. The following dialog shows you how to leave a message with someone else:

- ✔ **Christine: Âllo?** *(ah-loh)* (Hello?)

- ✔ **Pierre: Âllo, Christine? C'est Pierre. Ça va?** *(ah-loh krees-teen seh pee-ehr sah vah)* (Hello, Christine? It's Pierre. How are you?)

- ✔ **Christine: Ça va bien. Et toi?** *(sah vah byaN ay twah)* (I am fine. And you?)

- ✔ **Pierre: Bien. Est-ce que Marc est là?** *(byaN ehs kuh mark eh lah)* (Fine. Is Mark there?)

- ✔ **Christine: Non, il fait les courses.** *(nohN eel fay lay koors)* (No, he's shopping.)

- ✔ **Pierre: Dommage! Dîs-lui que j'ai téléphoné.** *(dohm-ahzh deet lew-ee kuh zhay tay-lay-foh-nay)* (Darn! Tell him that I called.)

- ✔ **Christine: Bien sûr. Salut, Pierre.** *(byaN sewr sah-lew pee-her)* (Sure. Bye, Pierre.)

- ✔ **Pierre: Salut, Christine.** *(sah-lew krees-teen)* (Bye, Christine.)

Words to Know

Dîs-lui que j'ai téléphoné.	dee lew-ee kuh zhay tay-lay-foh-nay	Tell him that I called.
Il fait les courses.	eel fay lay koors	He's shopping.
salut	sah-lew	good-bye (slang)
un répondeur	uhn ray-pohN-duhr	an answering machine

Meeting at the Office

The following sections give you some vocabulary so that you can make business appointments and then conduct the meeting.

Making an appointment

Businesses in both France and Belgium consider it polite to schedule appointments several weeks in advance. Also, don't expect French secretaries to be able to schedule appointments. Most of them don't have access to their bosses' schedules or planners. Your best bet is to directly contact the person with whom you're trying to meet.

✔ **Bonjour. Dan Thompson à l'appareil. Passez-moi M. Seiffert, s'il vous plaît.** *(bohN-zhoor Dan Thompson ah lah-pah-rehy pah-say mwah muh-syuh see-fehr seel voo play)* (Hello. This is Dan Thompson calling. Please transfer me to Mr. Seiffert.)

✔ **Un instant. Ne quittez pas.** *(aN aNs-tahN nuh kee-tay pah)* (One moment. Don't hang up.)

✔ **Il est dans son bureau. Je vous le passe.** *(eel ay dahN sohN bew-roh zhuh voo luh pahs)* (He's in his office. I'll transfer you to him.)

✔ **Je vais à Nice le 14 juin.** *(zhuh vay ah nees luh kah-tohrz zhwaN)* (I will be in Nice on the 14th of June.)

✔ **Je voudrais fixer un rendez-vous pour discuter . . .** *(zhuh voo-dray feek-say aN rahN-day voo poor dees-koo-tay)* (I would like to arrange a meeting to discuss . . .)

✔ **Je consulte mon calendrier.** *(zhuh kohN-sewlt mohN kahl-ahN-dree-ay)* (I'll consult my calendar.)

✔ **Ça va, je suis libre le 14 juin à 15h30.** *(sah vah zhuh swee lee-bruh luh kah-tohrz zhwaN ah kaNz uhr trahNt)* (Yes, I'm free June 14th at 3:30 p.m.)

✔ **Malhereusement, je ne peux pas.** *(mahl-huhrz-eh-maN zhuh nuh puh pah)* (Unfortunately, I can't.)

✔ **Je suis pris.** *(zhuh swee pree)* (I'm busy.)

✔ **Je suis en déplacement.** *(zhuh sweez aN day-plahs-eh-maN)* (I'm away on business.)

Conducting a meeting

A business meeting may involve the following phrases:

✔ **Asseyez-vous.** *(ah-say-ay voo)* (Have a seat.)

✔ **Vous avez reçu mon message électronique?** *(vooz ahvay ruh-sew mohN meh-sazh ay-lehk-troh-neek?)* (You received my e-mail?)

✔ **Je l'ai reçu.** *(zhuh lay ruh-sew)* (I received it.)

✔ **Vouz pouvez l'expliquer?** *(voo poo-vay layks-plee-kay)* (Will you explain it?)

✔ **Puis-je utiliser votre téléphone?** *(pwee zhuh oo-teel-ee-zay voh-truh tay lay-fohn)* (May I use your phone?)

✔ **Je me mets d'accord . . .** *(zhuh muh meh dah-kohr)* (I agree to do . . .)

✔ **Je signe.** *(zhuh saNy)* (I sign.)

Words to Know

l'accord	lah-corh	agreement
l'affaire	lah-fahr	deal
pendant	pahn-dahN	during
une idée	ewn ee-day	an idea
pratique	prah-teek	practical
télécopier	tay-lay-koh-pee-ay	to fax
faire les copies	fayr lay koh-pee	to make copies
le déjeuner d'affaires	luh day-zhuh-nay dah-fahr	business lunch
la poignée de main	lah pwo-nyay duh maN	handshake

Surfing the Internet

In French, the World Wide Web is sometimes called **la toile** *(lah twahl),* which literally means "the Web." More often, French-speaking people call it **Le Web** *(luh web)* or even **W3** *(doo-bluh-vay trwah* or *doo-bluh-vay kewb).* See Table 8-1 for some common terms.

Table 8-1	Computer Terms	
Phrase	*Pronunciation*	*Translation*
surfer le Web	suhr-fay luh web	to surf the Web
un site	aN seet	a Web site
un login	aN lohg-in	a login
envoyer des messages électroniques	ehN-voy-yay day may-sahzhay-lehk-trohN-eek	to send e-mail
l'adresse électronique	lah-dreh-say-lehk-tro-neek	e-mail address
s'abonner	sah-bohn-ay	to subscribe
cliquer	klee-kay	to click
une icône	oon eek-ohn	an icon

French also has a word for that little sign now so familiar to most of us: @. The French call it **aroba** *(ah-ro-bah)*. But hardly anybody uses this word; they prefer to say **à** or simply "at." Finally, the dot (in "dot-com") is **point** *(pwaN),* which means, among many other things, the period at the end of a sentence.

In Europe, each Internet address ends with the letters that identify the country that hosts the address. In France, these two letters are .fr. For example, if you want to connect to the French Yahoo! site, you type www.yahoo.fr. Be forewarned — this site is entirely in French!

Chapter 9

I Get Around: Transportation

. . . .

In This Chapter

▶ Choosing transportation

▶ Getting through customs

▶ Asking directions

. . . .

*W*hen you find yourself in any French-speaking country, you're instantly surrounded by a flood of French language: The porter, the taxi driver, and the customs people all address you in French. Don't worry — this chapter can help you navigate your way through the airport, train station, or subway system, rent a car or flag down a taxi, and ask directions.

On the Move: Transportation

You need to be able to get around in any French-speaking place you land. So how do you do that? The following sections give you some basic phrases to get you moving.

Taxis

Whether you're just leaving the airport and need assistance in finding the taxis or you're trying to get around the city, you may need to know the following phrases to help you get oriented:

✔ **Où sont les taxis, s'il vous plaît?** *(oo sohn lay tak-see seel voo play)* (Where are the taxis, please?)

✔ **Vous voyez un porteur ou un chariot?** *(voo vwah-yay aN por-tuhr oo aN shar-yo)* (Do you see a porter or a cart?)

✔ **Bruxelles, hôtel Gillon, s'il vous plaît.** *(brew-sehl o-tehl zhee-lohn seel voo play)* (Brussels, Hotel Gillon, please.)

✔ **Avec plaisir. C'est dans quelle rue?** *(ah-vehk pleh-zeer seh dahN kehl rew)* (With pleasure. On which street is that?)

✔ **Voyons . . . c'est 22 rue Albert. C'est combien?** *(vwah-yohN seh vaNt duh rew ahl-behr seh kohn-byaN)* (Let's see . . . it's 22 Albert Street. How much is it?)

✔ **Qu'est-ce que c'est le tarif normal?** *(kehs kuh seh luh tah-reef nor-mahl)* (What's the normal rate?)

✔ **Je mets les valises dans le coffre?** *(zhuh meh leh vah-leez dahN luh kohfr)* (I put the suitcases in the trunk?)

✔ **Je garde mon sac à dos avec moi.** *(zhuh gahrd mohN sah-kah do ah-vehk mwah)* (I'm keeping my backpack with me.)

Words to Know

le séjour	luh say-zhoor	stay
les affaires (f.)	leh zah-fehr	business
la semaine	lah suh-mehn	week
vous sortez	voo sor-tay	you exit
vous voyez	voo vwah-yeh	you see
la porte	lah pohrt	door

le chariot	luh shar-yo	cart
la rue	lah rew	street
je mets	zhuh meh	I put
la valise	lah vah-leez	suitcase
le coffre	luh kohfr	trunk
le sac à dos	luh sah kah do	backpack

Trains

Train stations around the world are always busy, noisy, and confusing, but you can usually find helpful people around, such as the police and station employees, that you can turn to for direction. Here are some useful phrases to know:

✔ **Pardon, où sont** *(pahr-dohN oo sohn)* (Pardon, where are)

  les guichets? *(leh gee-sheh)* (the ticket windows?)

  les quais? *(leh keh)* (the platforms?)

  les renseignements? *(leh rahN-sehn-yuh-mahN)* (the information desks?)

✔ **Excusez-moi, où est** *(eks-kew-say mwah oo eh)* (Excuse me, where is)

  la consigne? *(lah kohN-seenyuh)* (the baggage room?)

  la salle d'attente? *(lah sahl dah-tahN)* (the waiting room?)

  le bureau des objets trouvés? *(leh bew-ro day-zohb-zheh troo-vay)* (the lost-and-found?)

✔ **Je voudrais un billet pour Versailles, s'il vous plaît.** *(zhuh voo-dreh aN bee-yeh poor vehr-sahy seel voo play)* (I would like a ticket to Versailles, please.)

✔ **Aller-simple ou aller-retour?** *(ah-lay saNpl oo ah-lay ruh-toor)* (One way or round trip?)

✔ **Aller-retour. Deuxième classe.** *(ah-lay ruh-toor duh-zyehm klahs)* (Round trip. Second class.)

✔ **Est-ce que je dois changer de train?** *(ehs-kuh zhuh dwah shahN-zhay duh traN)* (Do I have to change trains?)

✔ **Vous avez une correspondance à Issy.** *(voo zah-vay ewn koh-rehs-pohN-dahN-sah ee-see)* (You have a connecting train in Issy.)

✔ **De quel quai part le train?** *(duh kehl keh pahr luh traN)* (From which platform does the train leave?)

Words to Know

le train (pour)	luh trahn (poor)	train (to)
la gare	lah gahr	train station
la ville	lah veel	town
il prend	eel prahN	he takes
le billet	luh bee-yeh	ticket
un aller-simple	aN nah-lay sahNpl	one-way (ticket)
un aller-retour	aN nah-lay ruh-toor	round-trip (ticket)
la correspondance	lah koh-rehs-pohn-dahNs	connection (train/bus)
la place	lah plahs	seat
la fenêtre	lah fuh-nehtr	window

Bus

If you have time, the bus is probably the most wonderful way not only to get an impression of the different **quartiers** *(kahr-tyay)* (neighborhoods) of a city, but also to experience that city's people a bit.

By the way, you must always **composter le billet** *(kohN-pohs-tay luh bee-yeh)* (validate your ticket) in a machine that's installed for that purpose on the bus. It gets awfully expensive when a **contrôleur** *(kohN-troh-luhr)* gets on and checks everybody. And they do!

Here are some helpful phrases for finding the right bus:

- ✔ **Excusez-moi. C'est bien le bus pour l'hôtel de ville?** *(eks-kew-say mwah seh byaN luh bews poor loh-tehl duh veel)* (Excuse me. Is that the correct bus to City Hall?)

- ✔ **Non, il faut prendre le bus numéro 67.** *(nohN eel foh prahNdr luh bews new-may-roh swah-sahN seht)* (No, you have to take bus number 67.)

- ✔ **À quelle heure est-ce qu'il arrive?** *(ah keh luhr ehs keel ah-reev)* (What time does it come?)

- ✔ **Il passe tous les quarts d'heure, mais il est souvent en retard.** *(eel pahs too leh kahr duhr meh eel eh soo-vahN ahN ruh-tahr)* (It comes every 15 minutes, but it's often late.)

- ✔ **Et c'est à combien d'arrêts d'ici?** *(ay seh tah kohN-byaN dah-reh dee-see)* (And how many stops is it from here?)

- ✔ **Ce n'est pas très loin. C'est le prochain arrêt.** *(suh neh pah treh lwaN seh luh proh sheh-nah-reh)* (It's not very far. It's the next stop.)

Subway

Paris, Brussels, Lille, and Lyon, as well as Montreal, all have subway systems. Big maps in each station make the systems easy to use. In these cities, the fare is standard, irrespective of the distance you travel.

You can also get **métro** *(may-troh)* maps from kiosks. The following phrases may help you out when you're riding the subway:

- ✔ **Bonjour. Est-ce que vous avez un plan de métro?** *(bohn-zhoor ehs-kuh voo zah-vay aN plahN duh may-troh)* (Hello. Do you have a metro map?)

- ✔ **Pour la Grande Place, c'est quelle ligne?** *(poor lah grahN plahs seh kehl leen-yuh)* (To Grande Place, which line is it?)

- ✔ **C'est direct avec la ligne 3.** *(seh dee-rehkt ah-vehk lah leen-yuh trwah)* (You can go directly with line 3.)

- ✔ **Combien de temps est-ce qu'il faut?** *(kohn-byaN duh tahN ehs-keel foh)* (How long does it take?)

Rental cars

If you like driving and have an inquisitive nature, renting a car may be the ultimate pleasure. You can stop wherever you want, change plans according to the weather or your mood, and not worry about interfering with anyone else's plans. And besides, you'll be confronted with another chance to practice your French.

The first place is the car rental office:

- ✔ **Nous avons une réservation pour une voiture.** *(noo zah-vohN zewn ray-zehr-vas-yohN poor ewn vwah-tewr)* (We have a reservation for a car.)

- ✔ **C'est pour dix jours?** *(seh poor dee zhoor)* (It's for ten days?)

- ✔ **Nous n'avons pas besoin d'assurance tous risques. C'est couvert avec la carte de crédit.** *(noo nah-vohN pah buh-zwaN dah-sew-rahns too reesk seh koo-vehr ah-vek lah kahrt duh cray-dee)* (We don't need full insurance. That's covered with the credit card.)

- ✔ **Dans quels pays allez-vous conduire?** *(daN kehl peh-ee ah-lay voo kohN-dweer)* (In what countries are you going to drive?)

✔ **On met quoi comme carburant?** *(ohN meh kwah kohm kahr-bew-rahN)* (What do we use for fuel?)

✔ **Du sans-plomb.** *(dew sahN plohN)* (Unleaded.)

✔ **Voulez-vous rendre la voiture remplie ou vide?** *(voo-lay voo rahNdr lah vwah-tewr rahN-plee oo veed)* (Do you want to return the car full or empty?)

✔ **Nous rendons la voiture où?** *(noo rahN-dohN lah vwah-tewr oo)* (We return the car where?)

✔ **Voilà vos papiers et les clés.** *(vwah-lah voh pah-pyeh ay leh klay)* (Here are your papers and the keys.)

Words to Know

il arrive	eel ah-reev	he/it arrives
il passe	eel pahs	he/it comes by
à l'heure	ah luhr	on time
en retard	ahN ruh-tahr	late
un arrêt	aN-nah-reh	a stop
la ligne	lah leen-yuh	line
il aide	eel ehd	he/it helps
le jour	luh zhoor	day
une assurance	ewn ah-sew-rahNs	full insurance
le pays	luh peh-ee	country
conduire	kohN-dweer	to drive
rendre	rahNdr	to return (something)

Most gas stations seem to be self-service in Europe and North America, but then, of course, some aren't. The following little phrases can help you out in case of the unexpected:

- ✔ **Où est-ce qu'il y a une station service?** *(oo ehs keel-yah ewn stas-yohN sehr-vees)* (Where is there a gas station?)

- ✔ **Est-ce qu'il y a une station-service près d'ici?** *(ehs keel-yah ewn stas-yohN sehr-vees preh dee-see)* (Is there a gas station near here?)

- ✔ **Le plein, s'il vous plaît.** *(luh plaN seel voo pleh)* (Fill it up, please.)

- ✔ **du super/de l'ordinaire/du sans plomb/du diesel** *(dew sew-pehr/duh lohr-dee-nehr/dew sahN plohn/dew dy-ay-zehl)* (super/regular/ unleaded/diesel)

- ✔ **Où est le compresseur pour l'air?** *(oo eh luh kohN-preh-suhr poor lehr)* (Where is the air compressor?)

Passing Passport Control

The first part of successfully getting through passport control is to make sure that you have the right documents to begin with. Here are a few phrases that you need to find out this information:

- ✔ **Bonjour. C'est le consulat français?** *(bohN-zhoor seh luh kohN-sew-lah frahN-seh)* (Hello. Is this the French consulate?)

- ✔ **Est-ce qu'il faut un visa pour aller en France?** *(ehs-keel foh-taN vee-zah poor-ah-lay ahN frahNs)* (Do you need a visa to go to France?)

- ✔ **Il faut un passeport valide et c'est tout.** *(eel foh taN pahs-pohr vah-leed ay seh too)* (You need a valid passport and that's all.)

Read the following phrases to get an idea of what passport control may ask and how to reply:

✔ **Bienvenue en France. Allez-vous rester en France pendant votre séjour?** *(byaN-vuh-new ahN frahNs ah-lay voo reh-stay ahN frahNs pahN-dahN vohtr say-zhoor)* (Welcome to France. Are you going to stay in France during your stay?)

✔ **Non, je vais aussi à . . .** *(nohN zhuh veh zoh-see ah)* (No, I am also going to . . .)

✔ **Et la raison de votre voyage?** *(ay lah reh-zohN duh vohtr vwah-yazh)* (And the reason for your trip?)

✔ **C'est pour les affaires et le plaisir.** *(seh poor leh zah-fehr ay luh pleh-zeer)* (It's for business and pleasure.)

✔ **Combien de temps restez-vous en tout?** *(kohn-byaN duh tahN rehs-tay voo ahN too)* (How much time are you staying altogether?)

✔ **Je vous souhaite un bon séjour!** *(zhuh voo soo-eht aN bohN say-zhoor)* (I wish you a nice stay!)

When you're talking about staying in a city, you use **à** *(ah)* to express the English "in." For countries, it's usually **en** *(ahN)* because most countries are feminine, such as **la France** *(lah frahNs),* **la Suisse** *(lah swees),* **l'Italie** *(lee-tah-lee),* and so on. For the few country names that are masculine, such as **le Canada** *(luh kah-nah-dah),* **le Portugal** *(luh pohr-tew-gahl),* **les États-Unis** *(leh-zay-tah-zew-nee),* and so on, you use **au(x)** *(o)* to mean "in." For example, you may say:

✔ **Je vais en France, en Suisse, en Italie.** *(zhuh vay zahN frahNs ahN swees ahN-nee-tah-lee)* (I'm going to France, to Switzerland, to Italy.)

✔ **Je vais au Canada, au Portugal, aux États-Unis.** *(zhuh vay zo kah-nah-dah o pohr-tew-guhl o zay-tah-zew-nee)* (I'm going to Canada, to Portugal, to the United States.)

For more details, see Chapter 4.

Words to Know

contrôle des passeports	kohN-trohl duh pahs-poh	passport control
douane	doo-ahn	customs
rien à déclarer	ryaN nah day-klah-ray	nothing to declare
marchandises à déclarer	mahr-shahN-dee zah day-klah-ray	goods to declare
marchandises hors taxe	mahr-shahN-deez ohr tahks	duty-free goods

Most likely, you won't even get stopped by the customs officer except to hand him your customs slip, but in case he does pick you out for further questioning, here's what you may expect:

- ✔ **Avez-vous quelque chose à déclarer?** *(ah-vay voo kehl-kuh sho zah day-klah-ray)* (Do you have something to declare?)

- ✔ **Non, rien.** *(nohN ryaN)* (No, nothing.)

- ✔ **Avez-vous des appareils électroniques?** *(ah-vay voo deh zah-pah-rehy ay-lehk-tro-neek)* (Do you have electronic items?)

- ✔ **Seulement pour mon usage personnel.** *(suhl-mahN poor moh new-zazh pehr-soh-nehl)* (Only for my personal use.)

- ✔ **Pouvez-vous ouvrir votre sac?** *(poo-vay voo zoo-vreer vohtr sahk)* (Can you open your bag?)

- ✔ **Qu'est-ce que c'est que ça?** *(kes-kuh seh kuh sah)* (What is this?)

- ✔ **C'est mon ordinateur portable.** *(seh mohn ohr-dee-nah-tuhr pohr-tahbl)* (That's my laptop.)

✔ **Branchez-le là-bas, s'il vous plaît.** *(brahN-shay luh lah bah seel voo play)* (Plug it in over there, please.)

Asking for Directions

You may find yourself in a French-speaking city or town and in desperate need for directions. (Where's the nearest bus stop? Bank? Bathroom?) The following sections give you some common phrases that can help you find yourself again.

Asking "where" questions

Where questions are made the same way in French as they are in English. The verb most often connected with the question word **où** *(oo)* (where) is the verb to be: **être** *(ehtr)*.

✔ **Où est le Louvre?** *(oo eh luh loovr)* (Where is the Louvre?)

✔ **Où est la place Victor Hugo?** *(oo eh lah plahs veek-tohr ew-go)* (Where is Victor Hugo Square?)

✔ **Où sont les toilettes?** *(oo sohN leh twah-leht)* (Where is the bathroom?)

Another verb, **se trouver** *(suh troo-vay)* (to be located) is very frequently used in this context:

✔ **Où se trouve le Louvre?** *(oo suh troov luh loovr)* (Where is the Louvre?)

✔ **Où se trouve la place Victor Hugo?** *(oo suh troov lah plahs veek-tohr ew-go)* (Where is Victor Hugo Square?)

✔ **Où se trouvent les toilettes?** *(oo suh troov lay twah-leht)* (Where is the bathroom?)

You see in either case that **où** is followed by the verb, which is followed by the subject.

You can use this sentence structure for all other verbs that you choose to connect **où** with:

> ✔ **Où va ce bus?** *(oo vah suh bews)* (Where is this bus going?)

> ✔ **Où mène cette rue?** *(oo mehn seht rew)* (Where does this road lead?)

Answering "where" questions

Asking questions is always easy — answering them can sometimes be tricky. As a rule, you can use the preposition **à** *(ah)* meaning "to," "in," or "at" when you want to say that you're going to or staying in a city. For example:

> ✔ **Je vais à Lille.** *(zhuh vay ah leel)* (I'm going to Lille.)

> ✔ **Ils sont à Montréal.** *(eels son tah mohN-reh-ahl)* (They're staying in Montreal.)

However, when you want to talk about going to or staying at places in general, such as museums, cathedrals, or churches, you need to add an article after **à**. This addition can seem tricky because **à** contracts with the masculine, and only with the masculine **le** *(luh)* and the plural **les** *(leh)*. The following examples show how **à** combines with each of the articles:

> ✔ **Sylvie va au (à + le = au) musée.** *(seel-vee vah oh mew-say)* (Sylvie is going to the museum.)

> ✔ **Guy veut aller à la cathédrale.** *(gee vuh tah-lay ah lah kah-tay-drahl)* (Guy wants to go to the cathedral.)

> ✔ **Les Martin vont à l'église St. Paul.** *(lay mahr-tahN vohN tah lay-glees sahn pohl)* (The Martins go to St. Paul's church.)

> ✔ **Allez aux (à + les = aux) feux!** *(ah-lay oh fuh)* (Go to the traffic lights!)

Sometimes, you can get a really quick answer, especially when the place you're asking about is right in front of you. So you may ask for the post office or some other location, and someone may tell you:

> ✔ **Voici la poste . . . le musée . . . l'université!** *(vwah-see lah pohst luh mew-zay lew-nee-vehr-see-tay)* (Here is the post office . . . the museum . . . the university!)

> ✔ **Voilà les bureaux!** *(vwah-lah lay bew-roh)* (There are the offices!)

But even more likely, you get one of these simple phrases for an answer:

> ✔ **Le voici!** *(luh vwah-see)* (Here it is.)

> ✔ **La voilà!** *(lah vwah-lah)* (There it is.)

> ✔ **Les voilà!** *(lay vwah-lah)* (There they are.)

The **le, la,** or **les** replaces the noun that was mentioned in the question, but remember to put them in front of the **voici** or **voilà**.

Words to Know

ils restent	eel rehst	they stay
elle mène à	ehl meh-nah	it leads to
ce bus	suh bews	this bus
cette rue	seht rew	this street
il se trouve	eel suh troov	it is (located)
la place	lah plahs	square
les toilettes	leh twah-leht	bathroom
le musée	luh mew-zay	museum
		continued

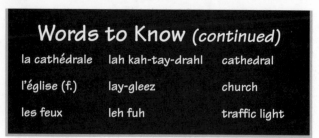

Words to Know *(continued)*

la cathédrale	lah kah-tay-drahl	cathedral
l'église (f.)	lay-gleez	church
les feux	leh fuh	traffic light

Getting direction about directions

What if you don't understand the directions because the person to whom you're speaking is talking too fast or mumbling or has a strong accent? Before you find out how to get directions in more detail, think about what you're going to say if this confusion happens. The following phrases can really help you:

- **Excusez-moi!** *(ehx-kew-say mwah)* (Excuse me.)
- **pardon** *(pahr-dohN)* (pardon)
- **Je ne comprends pas.** *(zhuh nuh kohN-prahN pah)* (I don't understand.)
- **Est-ce que vous pouvez répéter, s'il vous plaît?** *(ehs-kuh voo poo-vay ray-pay-tay seel voo play)* (Can you repeat that, please?)
- **Parlez plus lentement.** *(pahr-lay plew lahN-tuh-mahN)* (Speak more slowly.)
- **Qu'est-ce que vous avez dit?** *(kes-kuh voo zah-vay dee)* (What did you say?)

Words to Know

le centre-ville	luh sahNtr veel	downtown
près/loin (de)	preh/lwahN (duh)	close to/far (from)

allez!	ah-lay	go!
la gare	lah gahr	train station
là-bas	lah bah	over there
prenez . . . !	pruh-nay	take . . . !
la station de métro	lah stas-yohN duh may-troh	subway station
à deux minutes	ah duh mee-newt	only two minutes away
il y a	eel yah	there is/are
la station-service	lah stas-yohN sehr-vees	gas station
à gauche	ah gosh	left
suivez!	swee-vay	follow!
la rue	lah rew	street
à droite	ah drwaht	right
j'ai besoin de	zhay buh-zwaN duh	I need
le croisement	luh crwah-zuh-mahN	intersection
tout droit	too drwah	straight ahead
au bout (de)	o boo (duh)	at the end (of)

✔ **Nous voulons aller à pied à Notre Dame. Est-ce que c'est loin?** *(noo voo-lohn zah-lay ah pyeh ah nohtr dahm ehs-kuh seh lwahN)* (We want to walk to Notre Dame. Is it far?)

✔ **Non, c'est à 15 minutes peut-être. Vous sortez de l'hôtel, tournez à gauche et continuez tout droit.** *(nohn seh tah kahNz mee-newt puh-tehtr voo sohr-tay duh loh-tel toor-nay ah gosh eh kohN-tee-new-ay too drwah)* (No, it's 15 minutes, maybe. You leave the hotel, turn left, and keep going straight ahead.)

✔ **Et ensuite?** *(eh ahN-sweet)* (And then?)

✔ **Vous allez voir la cathédrale après le Pont Neuf.** *(voo zah-lay vwahr lah kah-teh-drahl ah-preh luh pohN nuhf)* (You'll see the cathedral after the Pont Neuf.)

Words to Know

nous voulons	noo voo-lohN	we want
à pied	ah pyeh	by foot
peut-être	puh-tehtr	maybe
vous sortez	voo sohr-tay	you leave
vous tournez	voo toor-nay	you turn
vous continuez	voo kohN-tee-new-ay	you continue
ensuite ·	ahN-sweet	then
vous allez voir	voo zah-lay vwahr	you'll see
après	ah-pray	after

Using commands

When someone directs you to a location, that person is giving you a command. It's understood that *you* are being addressed, but because you can say *you* in two different ways in French (the familiar **tu** and the polite **vous**), you get two different command forms:

- **Va au centre!** *(vah o sahNtr)* (Go to the center!)

- **Allez tout droit!** *(ah-lay too drwah)* (Go straight ahead!)

For **-er** verbs only, drop the final **-s** from the **tu** form in all commands, as in Table 9-1.

Table 9-1	Command Form (Informal)	
Infinitive (-er)	*Tu Form*	*Command Form*
aller *(ah-lay)* (to go)	tu vas *(tew vah)*	va! *(vah)* (go!)
continuer *(kohN-tee-new-ay)* (to go on)	tu continues *(tew kohN-tee-new)*	continue! *(kohN-tee-new)* (go on!)

Expressing distances

You can use the **à** for time expressions, such as "see you in 15 minutes, tomorrow, next week," but you can also use it for distance away from you, as in the following:

- **à deux minutes** *(ah dew mee-newt)* (it takes only two minutes)

- **à cent mètres** *(ah sahN mehtr)* (only 100 meters farther)

- **C'est à cent mètres (d'ici).** *(seh tah sahn mehtr [dee-see])* (It's 100 meters [from here].)

- **C'est à deux kilomètres.** *(seh-tah duh kee-loh-mehtr)* (It's 2 kilometers away.)

Going north, south, east, and west

If you're roaming around a French-speaking country by car, this section gives you some pointers on how to ask for directions or get out of a jam if you get lost.

First, you may need to know the cardinal points of the compass. See Table 9-2.

Table 9-2	Compass Directions	
Direction	*Pronunciation*	*Translation*
nord	nohr	north
nord-est	nor-ehst	northeast
est	ehst	east
sud-est	sew-dehst	southeast
sud	sewd	south
sud-ouest	sew-dwehst	southwest
ouest	oo-ehst	west
nord-ouest	nor-wehst	northwest

When you ask or give directions, always add **au** or **à l'** *(o* or *ahl)* (to the) in front of the cardinal point, as in the following examples:

- ✔ **Paris est au nord de Nice.** *(pah-ree eh to nohr duh nees)* (Paris is north of Nice.)

- ✔ **New York est au sud de Montréal.** *(noo york eh to sewd duh mohn-rey-ahl)* (New York is south of Montreal.)

- ✔ **Madagascar est au sud-est de l'Afrique.** *(mah-dah-gahs-kahr eh to sew dest duh lah-freek)* (Madagascar is southeast of Africa.)

> ✔ **La Belgique est à l'est de la France.** *(lah behl-zheek eh tah lehst duh lah frahNs)* (Belgium is east of France.)

Because **ouest** begins with an *o*, which is a vowel, you use **à l'** rather than the contracted **au (à+le=au).**

For example:

> ✔ **Où est le château de Versailles?** *(oo eh luh shah-toh duh vehr-sahy)* (Where is the castle of Versailles?)

> ✔ **Il se trouve à l'ouest de Paris.** *(eel suh troov ah lwest duh pah-ree)* (It's west of Paris.)

> ✔ **C'est loin?** *(seh lwahN)* (Is it far?)

> ✔ **C'est à une heure en voiture, à peu près.** *(seh tah ewn uhr ahN vwah-tewr ah puh preh)* (It's one hour by car, roughly.)

Words to Know

le château	luh shah-toh	castle
N'est-ce pas?	nehs pah	Isn't that so?
une heure	ewn uhr	hour
en voiture	ahN vwah-tewr	by car
à peu près	ah puh preh	roughly
nous pouvons	noo poo-vohN	we can
On va se téléphoner.	ohN vah suh tay-lay-foh-nay	We'll telephone.
avant	ah-vahN	before
Adieu!	ah-dyuh	Bye-bye (casual)!

Asking questions when you're lost

What if you get lost on your way to Versailles, for example? Or maybe, at some point of weakness, you just want to make sure that you're on the right track, wherever you may be going. Here are some helpful questions that you can ask:

> ✔ **Est-ce que c'est la bonne route pour Versailles?** _(ehs-kuh seh lah bohn root poor vehr-sahy)_ (Is this the right way to Versailles?)

> ✔ **Où va cette rue?** _(oo va seht rew)_ (Where does this street go?)

> ✔ **Comment s'appelle cette ville?** _(koh-mahN sah-pehl seht veel)_ (What's the name of this town?)

And here are some answers that you can expect:

> ✔ **Allez au rond-point.** _(ah-lay o rohN pwahN)_ (Go to the traffic circle.)

> ✔ **Passez les feux.** _(pah-say lay fuh)_ (Go through the traffic lights.)

> ✔ **Après le bois, prenez à gauche.** _(ah-preh luh bwah, pruh-nay ah gosh)_ (After the woods, turn left.)

Chapter 10

Laying Down Your Weary Head: House or Hotel

● ●

In This Chapter

▶ Getting around the house

▶ Arriving at a hotel

▶ Getting a room (and giving it back)

● ●

*W*hether you've been working at the office, shopping, or traveling, at the end of the day, you need a place to lay your head. This chapter gives you the phrases you need to get around your house or to find a hotel.

Making a Home

Whether you just want to know how to get around your house in French or you're visiting a French home, the vocabulary and phrases in this section get you going.

Table 10-1 lists rooms and places:

Table 10-1	Places around the House	
Word	*Pronunciation*	*Translation*
la maison	lah meh-zohN	house
l'appartement (m.)	l'ah-part-mawN	apartment
la cuisine	lah kwee-zeen	kitchen
le living/le salon	luh lee-veeng/ luh sah-lohN	living room
la salle à manger	lah sahl ah mawN-zhay	dining room
la chambre	lah shawm-bruh	bedroom
la salle de bains	lah sahl duh bahN	bathroom
la pièce	lah pee-ehss	room
le grenier/ la mansarde	luh grun-eeay/ lah mahn-sard	attic
le couloir	luh kool-wahr	hallway
le sous-sol	luh soo-sole	basement
l'escalier (m.)	les-cahl-ee-ay	stairs
la penderie	lah pawnd-ree	closet
l'étage (m.)	lay-tahzh	floor
le rez-de-chaussée	luh rayd-show-say	ground floor
la cheminée	lah shu-mee-nay	chimney
le toit	luh twah	roof
le garage	luh gah-rahzh	garage
la route	lah root	driveway
la terrasse	lah teh-rahss	terrace, patio
le porche	luh porsh	porch

Of course, having all those rooms empty isn't acceptable. Table 10-2 helps you fill them with furniture:

Table 10-2   Things around the House

Word	Pronunciation	Translation
l'étagère (f.)	lay-tah-zhehr	shelf
le bureau	luh bewr-oh	desk
la chaise	lah shehzh	chair
la commode	lah koh-mode	dresser
le lit	luh lee	bed
le couvre-lit	luh koo-vruh-lee	bedspread
l'oreiller	loh-ray-ay	pillow
la table de nuit	lah tah-bluh duh nwee	nightstand
le placard	luh plah-car	closet
le tapis	luh tah-pee	rug
la lampe	lah lahmp	lamp
la canapé/le sofa	lah kah-nah-pay/ luh soh-fah	couch/sofa
le fauteuil	luh foo-tuhee	armchair
la pendule	lah pahN-dewl	clock
la télé(vision)	lah tay-lay (vee-zee-ohN)	television
la télécommande	lah tay-lay-koh-mahnd	remote control
la table (basse)	lah tah-bluh (bahss)	(coffee) table
l'évier (m.)	lay-veeay	sink
le réfrigérateur	luh ray-free-zhay-rah-tir	refrigerator
le congélateur	luh kon-zhay-lah-tur	freezer
la cuisinière	lah kwee-zeen-yehr	stove
le four	luh foor	oven
le lave-vaisselle	luh lahv-veh-sell	dishwasher

(continued)

Table 10-2 *(continued)*

Word	Pronunciation	Translation
le four à micro-ondes	luh foor ah mee-kroh-ohnd	microwave
la baignoire	lah bahn-wahr	bathtub
la douche	lah lah doosh	shower
la corbeille	lah kor-bayee	waste basket
le lavabo	luh lah-vah-boh	bathroom sink
le miroir	luh mee-rwahr	mirror
la machine à laver	lah mah-sheen ah lah-vay	washing machine
le sèche-linge	luh sesh-lahNzh	clothes dryer
le plafond	luh plah-fohN	ceiling
le plancher	luh plawN-shay	floor
le rideau	luh ree-doh	curtain
la fenêtre	lah fuh-neh-truh	window
la porte	lah port	door

In French, there's a difference between **la salle de bains** *(lah sahl duh baN)* and **les toilettes** *(lay twah-leht)*. **La salle de bains** literally means bathroom, or a place to bathe. It does not necessarily have a toilet. If you are looking for the restroom, be sure to ask for either **les toilettes** or the **W.C.** *(doo-bluh-vay say)* or "water closet."

Here are some phrases you may hear around the house:

✔ **Vous devez m'aider à faire le ménage.** *(voo duh-vay may-day ah fehr luh may-nazh)* (You must help me clean the house.)

✔ **Je fais mon lit.** *(zhuh fay mohN lee)* (I'll make my bed.)

✔ **Je range ma chambre.** *(zhuh rahNzh mah shahNbr)* (I'll clean up my room.)

✔ **Je passe l'aspirateur dans la salle de séjour.** *(zhuh pahs lahs-peer-ah-tuhr dahn lah sahl duh say-zhoor)* (I'll vaccuum the living room.)

✔ **Je nettoie la salle de bains et les toilettes.** *(zhuh neht-wah lah sahl duh baN ay lay twah-leht)* (I'll clean the bathroom and the toilet.)

Words to Know

faire le ménage	fayr luh may-nazh	clean the house
Je fais mon lit.	zhuh fay mohN lee	I'll make my bed.
Je range ma chambre.	zhuh rahNzh mah shaNbr	I'll clean my room.
passe l'aspirateur	pahs lahs-peer-ah-tuhr	vacuum
la salle de séjour	lah sahl duh say-zhoor	living room
nettoie la salle de bains et les toilettes	neht-wah lah sahl duh bihn ay lay twah-leht	clean the bathroom and the toilet
Mettez la table.	meh-tay lah tah-bluh	(You two) Set the table.
fais la cuisine	fay la kwee-zeen	make dinner
fais un gâteau	fay aN gah-to	make a cake
fais la vaisselle	fay lah veh-sehl	do the dishes

Scoping Out the Hotel

You have several options when it comes to finding a hotel:

- ✔ **Hôtels** *(o-tehl)* (hotels) or **hôtels de tourisme** *(o-tehl duh too-reez-muh)* (tourist hotels)
- ✔ **Hôtel garni** *(o-tehl gahr-nee)* (bed and breakfast)
- ✔ **Maison de logement** *(meh-sohN duh lohzh-mahN)* (small hotel [Canada])
- ✔ **Pension (de famille)** *(pahN-syohN [duh fah-meey])* (small family hotel [Europe])

  Also called a **logis** *(loh-zhee)* or **auberge** *(o-behrzh)*.
- ✔ **Châteaux-hôtels** *(shah-to o-tehl)* (luxury hotels)
- ✔ **Gîtes ruraux** *(zheet rew-ro)* (furnished holiday cottages or flats)

You may wonder how to address the hotel staff at the place you're staying, especially when you inquire about a room. Male members of hotel staff are called **Monsieur**; female members, **Madame** or **Mademoiselle**. These names also apply to waiters and waitresses, as well. Many people nowadays regard the word **garçon** *(gahr-sohN)* (boy) as old-fashioned and improper.

Here are some phrases that you may use or encounter when inquiring about a room:

- ✔ **Je voudrais une chambre pour deux personnes.** *(zhuh voo-dreh ewn shahNbr poor duh pehr-sohn)* (I would like a room for two people.)
- ✔ **Je regrette. L'hôtel est complet.** *(zhuh ruh-greht lo-tehl est kohN-pleh)* (I'm sorry. The hotel is booked.)
- ✔ **Est-ce qu'il y a un autre hôtel près d'ici?** *(ehs-keel-yah an-notr o-tehl preh dee-see)* (Is there another hotel nearby?)
- ✔ **C'est combien par nuit?** *(seh kohN-byaN pahr nwee)* (How much is it a night?)

✔ **Est-ce qu'on peut voir la chambre?** *(ehs kohN puh vwahr lah shahNbr)* (Can we see the room?)

✔ **Nous voulons une chambre avec des lits jumeaux.** *(noo voo-lohN zewn shahNbr ah-vek deh lee zhew-moh)* (We want a room with twin beds.)

✔ **Je veux une chambre double avec douche (ou avec baignoire).** *(zhuh vuh ewn shahNbr doobl ah-vehk doosh [oo ah-vehk behn-ywahr])* (I want a double room with shower [or with a bathtub].)

✔ **Côté cour ou côté rue?** *(koh-tay koor oo koh-tay rew)* (Looking out on the yard or the street?)

✔ **Le rez-de-chaussée nous convient.** *(luh rayt-sho-say noo kohN-vyaN)* (The ground floor suits us fine.)

Words to Know

la chambre	lah shahNbr	room
complet	kohN-pleh	booked
près d'ici	preh dee-see	near here
un autre	an notr	another
par nuit	pahr nwee	per night
une chambre double	ewn shahNbr doobl	double room
des lits jumeaux	deh lee zhew-mo	twin beds
la douche	lah doosh	shower
la baignoire	lah behn-ywahr	bathtub
		continued

Words to Know (continued)

un lit	aN lee	bed
côté cour	koh-tay koor	facing the yard
Je vérifie.	zhuh vay-ree-fee	I am checking.
ça coûte	sah coot	that costs

Checking In and Checking Out

When you arrive at a hotel, you probably have to fill out the registration form, which asks you for the items in Table 10-3.

Table 10-3	Registration Items	
Word	**Pronunciation**	**Translation**
nom/prénom	nohN/pray-nohN	name/first name
lieu de résidence	lyuh duh ray-zee-sahNs	address
rue/numéro	rew/new-may-roo	street/number
ville/code postal	veel/kohd pohs-tahl	city/zip code
état/pays	ay-tah/peh-ee	state/country
numéro de téléphone	new-may-ro duh tay -lay-fohn	telephone number
nationalité	nasyoh-nah-lee-tay	nationality
date/lieu de naissance	daht/lyuh duh neh-sahNs	date/place of birth
numéro de passeport	new-may-ro duh pahs pohr	passport number

Word	Pronunciation	Translation
signature	seen-yah-tewr	signature
numéro d'immatriculation de la voiture	new-may-roh dee-mah-tree-kew-las-yohN duh lah vwa-tewr	license plate number

When you're ready to take a room, these phrases can help out:

✔ **Nous prenons la chambre au troisième étage.** *(noo pruh-nohN lah shahNbr o trwah-zyehm ay-tahzh)* (We'll take the room on the fourth floor.)

✔ **Veuillez remplir cette fiche, s'il vous plaît, et j'ai besoin de vos passeports.** *(vuh-yay rahN-pleer seht feesh seel voo pleh ay zhay buh zwaN duh vo pahs-pohr)* (Would you please fill out this form, and I need your passports.)

✔ **L'ascenseur est à gauche.** *(lah-sahN-suhr eh tah gosh)* (The elevator is on the left.)

✔ **À quelle heure fermez-vous la porte principale?** *(ah keh luhr fehr-may voo lah pohrt praN-see-pahl)* (What time do you close the main door?)

✔ **À quelle heure faut-il libérer la chambre?** *(ah keh luhr fo teel lee-bay-ray lah shahNbr)* (At what time do we have to vacate the room?)

The next morning at checkout, you may hear or use some of the following:

✔ **Je peux laisser mes bagages ici jusqu'à seize heures?** *(zhuh puh leh-say meh bah-gahzh ee-see zhews-kah seh-zuhr)* (Can I leave my luggage here until 4 p.m.?)

✔ **Voulez-vous la note maintenant?** *(voo-lay voo lah noht maN-tuh-nahN)* (Would you like the bill now?)

🖛 **Vous acceptez les cartes de crédit, n'est-ce pas?**
(voo-zahk-sehp-tay leh kahrt duh kray-dee nehs-pas) (You accept credit cards, don't you?)

🖛 **Pouvez-vous m'appeler un taxi, s'il vous plaît?**
(poo-vay voo mah-puh-lay uhN tah-ksee seel voo play) (Can you call a taxi for me, please?)

Words to Know

veuillez remplir	vuh-yay rahN-pleer	would you please fill out
la fiche	lah feesh	registration form
j'ai besoin de	zhay buh-zwaN duh	I need
à quelle heure?	ah kehl uhr	at what time?
vous fermez	voo fehr-may	you close
la porte principale	lah pohrt praN-see-pahl	main door
à minuit	ah mee-nwee	at midnight
toujours	too-zhoor	always
vous pouvez sonner	voo poo-vay soh-nay	you can ring
il faut libérer la chambre	eel faut lee-bay-ray lah shahNbr	we have to vacate the room
avant midi	ah-vahN mee-dee	before noon

je peux laisser	zhu puh leh-say	I can leave (behind)
le bagage	luh bah-gahzh	baggage
jusqu'à	zhews-kah	until
là-bas	lah bah	over there
au coin	o kwaN	in the corner
la note	lah noht	bill
un coup de téléphone	uhN koo duh tay-lay-fohn	telephone call
vous acceptez	voo zahk-sehp-tay	you accept
le reçu	luh ruh-sew	receipt
vous pouvez appeler	voo poo-vay ah-puh-lay	you can call

Chapter 11

Dealing with Emergencies

● ●

In This Chapter

▶ Taking care of medical emergencies

▶ Dealing with run-of-the-mill health concerns

▶ Asking for help from the police

● ●

*T*his chapter deals with those unfun situations, emergencies. First, the health section deals with health problems, emergency, and everyday stuff; and then the legal section deals with matters of the law.

Surviving Health Emergencies

No matter where you are, you'll find that people, in a case of emergency, tend to be helpful and caring. They usually do their best to get you help and try to use whatever English they know or rush to find someone who has a better grasp of your native language.

At the scene of an accident

The following list gives you some key French phrases that you need to know in an emergency:

  ✔ **Est-ce qu'il y a quelqu'un qui parle anglais?**
    (ehs keel yah kehl kaN kee pahrl ahN-gleh)
    (Is there someone who speaks English?)

✔ **Est-ce qu'il y a un docteur/une infirmière qui parle anglais?** *(ehs keel yah aN dohk-tuhr/ewn ahn-feer-myehr kee pahrl ahn-gleh)* (Is there a doctor/nurse who speaks English?)

✔ **À l'aide! Vite!** *(ah lehd veet)* (Help! Fast!)

✔ **Au secours!** *(oh suh-koor)* (Help!)

✔ **Au feu!** *(oh fuh)* (Fire!)

When you're on the scene of the accident, these phrases can be essential:

✔ **Pouvez-vous nous aider, s'il vous plaît?** *(poo-vay voo noo zeh-day seel voo play)* (Can you help us, please?)

✔ **Appelez un docteur!** *(ah-puh-lay uhn dohk-tuhr)* (Call a doctor!)

✔ **Cet homme est blessé.** *(suh tohm eh bleh-say)* (This man is hurt.)

✔ **Il saigne et il a perdu connaissance.** *(eel sehn-yuh ay eel ah pehr-dew koh-neh-sahNs)* (He's bleeding, and he's unconscious.)

✔ **Il s'est évanoui.** *(eel seh tay-vah-noo-ee)* (He fainted.)

✔ **Qu'est-ce qui s'est passé?** *(kes kee seh pah-say)* (What happened?)

✔ **Il y a eu une collision.** *(eel yah ew ewn kohl-lee-syohN)* (There was a collision.)

✔ **Où avez-vous mal?** *(oo ah-vay voo mahl)* (Where does it hurt?)

✔ **Ne bougez pas.** *(nuh boo-zhay pah)* (Don't move.)

✔ **Est-ce que ça fait mal?** *(ehs-kuh sah feh mahl)* (Does that hurt?)

✔ **Je vais appeler une ambulance.** *(zhuh veh ah-puh-lay ewn ahN-bew-lahNs)* (I'll call an ambulance.)

Here are a few extra pieces of vocabulary that you may need to know:

✔ **un hôpital** *(uhn oh-pee-tahl)* (hospital)

✔ **les urgences** *(leh zewr-zhahns)* (emergency room)

✔ **le/la secouriste** *(luh/lah suh-koo-reest)* (paramedic)

Qu'est-ce qui s'est passé? *(kehs kee seh pah-say)* (What happened?) is an idiomatic expression that you probably want to memorize because French speakers use it so frequently. **Ça fait mal!** *(sah feh mahl)* (That hurts!) is another expression that you may want to memorize because it comes in quite handy at times.

In French, you use the definite article **(le, la, les)** in front of body parts, contrary to English, where you use possessives. For example:

✔ **Il ouvre les yeux.** *(ee loovr lay zyuh)* (He is opening his eyes.)

✔ **Il s'est cassé la jambe.** *(eel seh kah-say lah zhahNb)* (He broke his leg.)

When you want to say that a body part hurts, you can use this construction: **j'ai mal à/au/aux** *(zheh mahl ah/oh/oh)* + any body part. You're using the verb **avoir** *(ah-vwahr)* (to have) plus the preposition **à** *(ah)*. Here are some examples:

✔ **J'ai mal à la jambe.** *(zheh mahl ah lah zhahNb)* (My leg hurts.)

✔ **Il/Elle a mal aux yeux.** *(eel/ehl ah mahl oh zyuh)* (His/Her eyes hurt.)

See Table 11-1 for a list of body parts:

Table 11-1	Body Parts	
Word	**Pronunciation**	**Translation**
le bras	luh brah	arm
la main	lah mahN	hand

(continued)

Table 11-1 *(continued)*

Word	Pronunciation	Translation
le doigt	luh dwah	finger
le nez	luh nay	nose
les côtes (f.)	lay koht	ribs
le pied	luh pyeh	foot
la figure	lah fee-gewr	face
un œil, les yeux	aN nuhy, leh zyuh	eye, eyes
la oreille	lah oh-rehy	ear
le cou	luh koo	neck
la épaule	lah ay-pohl	shoulder
la poitrine	lah pwah-treen	chest
le genou	luh zhuh-noo	knee
le orteil	luh ohr-teh-y	toe

At the hospital

Check out the following phrases for after you're at the hospital and being examined by a doctor:

- **La coupure n'est pas grave.** *(lah koo-pewr neh pah grahv)* (The cut isn't serious.)

- **Nous allons faire une radio de la jambe.** *(noo zah-lohN fehr ewn rah-dyo duh lah zhahNb)* (We'll take an X-ray of your leg.)

- **Voilà la fracture. Oui, vous vous êtes cassé la jambe.** *(vwah-lah lah frahk-tewr wee voo voo zeht kah-say lah zhahNb)* (Here is the fracture. Yes, your leg is broken.)

- **Il vous faut un plâtre.** *(eel voo fo taN plahtr)* (You need a cast.)

Be sure to tell attending medics and doctors if complicating factors exist in your or your companion's medical history, such as:

- ✔ **Je suis cardiaque.** *(zhuh swee kahr-dyahk)* (I have a heart condition.)

- ✔ **J'ai eu une crise cardiaque il y a deux ans.** *(zheh uh ew kreez kahr-dyahk eel-yah duh zahN)* (I had a heart attack two years ago.)

- ✔ **J'ai de l'hypertension.** *(zhay duh lee-pehr-tahn-syohn)* (I have high blood pressure.)

- ✔ **Je suis diabétique/allergique à . . .** *(zhuh swee dee-ah-bay-teek/ah-lehr-zheek ah)* (I am diabetic/allergic to . . .)

Words to Know

un bleu	aN bluh	bruise
une égratignure	ewn ay-grah-teen-yewr	scrape
une brûlure	ewn brew-lewr	burn
une fracture	ewn frahk-tewr	fracture
une coupure	ewn koo-pewr	cut

Dealing with a Nonemergency

Suppose you just want to make an appointment with a doctor in a nonemergency situation?

For a cold, a cough, indigestion, or diarrhea, go talk first to a pharmacist. In France, pharmacists are allowed to suggest medication for you. When you go there, you can say any of these things:

✔ **Pourriez-vous me donner un conseil?** *(poo-ree-ay voo muh doh-nay uhN kohN-sehy)* (Can you give me some advice?)

✔ **J'ai très mal à la tête.** *(zhay treh mahl ah lah teht)* (I have a very bad headache.)

✔ **J'ai le nez bouché.** *(zhay luh nay boo-shay)* (I have a stuffy nose.)

✔ **J'ai un gros rhume.** *(zhay aN groh rewm)* (I have an awful cold.)

✔ **J'ai la diarrhée.** *(zhay lah dee-ah-ray)* (I have diarrhea.)

✔ **Je suis constipé(e).** *(zhuh swee kohN-stee-pay)* (I am constipated.)

Also, if you need to see a doctor, pharmacists can gladly give you the address of one or call a doctor's office for you, if you like. Here are some phrases that you and the doctor may use at the office:

✔ **Est-ce que je pourrais prendre rendez-vous le plus tôt possible?** *(ehs-kuh zhuh poo-reh prahndr rahn-day voo luh plew toh poh-seebl)* (Can I have an appointment as soon as possible?)

✔ **De quoi souffrez-vous?** *(duh kwah soo-fray voo)* (What are you suffering from?)

✔ **Pouvez-vous venir tout de suite?** *(poo-vay voo vuh-neer toot sweet)* (Can you come in right away?)

✔ **Depuis quand vous sentez-vous comme ça?** *(duh-puis kahN voo sahN-tay voo kohm sah)* (How long have you been feeling like this?)

✔ **Avez-vous perdu l'appétit?** *(ah-vay voo pehr-dew lah-pay-tee)* (Have you lost your appetite?)

✔ **Reposez-vous bien pendant quelques jours.** *(ruh-poh-zay voo byaN pahN-dahN kehl-kuh zhoor)* (Take it very easy for a few days.)

✔ **Est-ce que vous prenez des médicaments?** *(ehs-kuh voo pruh-nay deh may-dee-kah-mahN)* (Do you take any medication?)

✔ **Je suis allergique à l'aspirine.** *(zhuh swee zah-lehr-zheek ah lahs-pee-reen)* (I am allergic to aspirin.)

✔ **Voilà une ordonnance . . . en cas de douleurs.** *(vwah-lah ewn ohr-doh-nahNs . . . ahN kah doo-luhr)* (Here is a prescription . . . in case of pain.)

✔ **Prenez un comprimé toutes les quatre heures et revenez dans trois jours.** *(pruh-nay uhn kohN-pree-may toot lay kaht ruhr ay ruh-vuh-nay dahN trwah zhoor)* (Take one pill every four hours and come back in three days.)

Table 11-2 lists other symptoms or illnesses that you may have.

Table 11-2	Illnesses	
Word	*Pronunciation*	*Translation*
une maladie	ewn mah-lah-dee	illness
la grippe	lah greep	flu
les amygdales	lay zah-mee-dahl	tonsils
une appendicite	ewn ah-paN-dee-seet	appendicitis
une intoxication alimentaire	ewn aN-toh-ksee-kahs-yohN ah-lee-mahN-tehr	food poisoning
s'étouffer	say-too-fay	to choke
la rougeole	lah roo-zhohl	measles
une apoplexie	ewn ah-poh-plek-see	seizure
une sciatique	ewn see-ah-teek	sciatica
une insolation	ewn aN-soh-lahs-yohN	sunstroke
l'asthme	lahsm	asthma

(continued)

Table 11-2 (continued)

Word	Pronunciation	Translation
l'arthrite	lahr-treet	arthritis
un torticolis	tohr-tee-koh-lee	a stiff neck
une rage de dents	ewn razh duh dahN	violent toothpain
la douleur	lah doo-luhr	pain
une commotion cérébrale	ewn koh-moh-syohN say-ray-brahl	concussion

If you need to visit the dentist, these phrases may be useful:

- ✔ **Cette dent me fait mal.** *(seht dahN muh feh mahl)* (This tooth hurts.)

- ✔ **Le plombage est tombé.** *(luh plohN-bazh eh tohN-bay)* (The filling fell out.)

- ✔ **Pourriez-vous le remplacer tout de suite?** *(poo-ree-ay voo luh rahN-plah-say toot sweet)* (Can you replace it right away?)

- ✔ **Je peux seulement vous donner un traitement provisoire.** *(zhuh puh suhl-mahN voo doh-nay uhn treht-mahN proh-vee-zwahr)* (I can only give you a temporary treatment.)

- ✔ **Faites-moi une anesthésie locale.** *(feht mwah ewn ah-nehs-tay-zee loh-kahl)* (Give me a local anesthetic.)

- ✔ **Vous pouvez vous rinser, s'il vous plaît.** *(voo poo-vay voo raN-say seel voo play)* (You can rinse, please.)

- ✔ **Ne mangez pas pendant quatre heures.** *(nuh mahN-zhay pah pahN-dahN kahtr uhr)* (Don't eat anything for four hours.)

Words to Know

Vous souffrez.	voo soo-fray	You are suffering.
Je me sens bien.	zhuh muh sahN byaN	I feel well.
tout de suite	toot sweet	immediately
depuis hier	duh-pwee yehr	since yesterday
quelques jours	kehl-kuh zhoor	several days
provisoire	proh-vee-zwahr	temporary
une ordonnance	ewn ohr-doh-nahNs	a prescription
un comprimé	aN kohN-pree-may	a pill
une piqûre	ewn pee-kewr	an injection
un calmant	aN kahl-mahN	a sedative
un généraliste	aN zhay-nay-rah-leest	a general practitioner
un dentiste	aN dahN-teest	a dentist
une de mes lentilles de contact	ewn duh may lahN-teey duh kohN-takt	one of my contact lenses
les lunettes (f.)	lay lew-neht	glasses
un verre	aN vehr	a lens

Meeting the Law

If you're traveling abroad, most likely, you'll never have a need for your consul, but you need to know this fact: While you're in a country that's not your own, the laws of that country override the laws of your own. And it's your consul who's really on your side, more so than any local lawyer or police.

Accidents

Hopefully, you'll never find yourself in an accident in a French-speaking area. But you may want to have all these helpful phrases handy so that you can pick from them in the event of an accident:

- **Il y a eu un accident. . . .** *(eel yah ew aN nak-see-dahN)* (There has been an accident. . . .)

  sur l'autoroute *(sewr loh-toh-root)* (on the highway)

  sur la route *(sewr lah root)* (road)

- **Appelez . . . !** *(ah-puh-lay)* (Call . . . !)

  une ambulance *(ewn ahN-bew-lahNs)* (an ambulance)

  un docteur *(aN dohk-tuhr)* (a doctor)

  les pompiers *(lay pohN-pyeh)* (the fire brigade)

  la police *(lah poh-lees)* (the police)

When the police arrive, they usually ask a great many questions, such as:

- **Est-ce que je peux voir votre . . . ?** *(ehs-kuh zhuh puh vwahr vohtr)* (Can I see your . . . ?)

  permis de conduire (m.) *(pehr-meet kohN-dweer)* (driver's license)

certificat d'assurance *(sehr-tee-fee-kah dah-sew rahNs)* (insurance certificate)

carte grise (f.) *(kahrt greez)* (vehicle registration document)

✔ **Quel est votre nom et adresse?** *(kehl eh vohtr nohN ay ah-drehs)* (What is your name and address?)

✔ **À quelle heure est-ce que ça s'est passé?** *(ah keh luhr ehs kuh sah seh pah-say)* (At what time did this happen?)

✔ **Est-ce qu'il y a des témoins?** *(ehs keel ee ah day tay-mwaN)* (Are there any witnesses?)

They may also say phrases such as the following that you should understand:

✔ **Vos feux ne marchent pas.** *(voh fuh nuh mahrsh pah)* (Your lights are not working.)

✔ **Vous devez payer une amende.** *(voo duh-vay peh-yay ewn amahNd)* (You have to pay a fine.)

✔ **Vous devez venir au commissariat pour faire une déposition.** *(voo duh-vay vuh-neer oh koh-mee-sah-ree-ah poor fehr ewn dees-poh-zees-yohN)* (You need to make a statement at the station.)

And then, maybe you want to say a few things, too? Some of the following phrases may help you explain:

✔ **Il m'est rentré dedans.** *(eel meh rahN-tray duh-dahn)* (He ran into me.)

✔ **Elle a conduit trop vite/près.** *(ehl ah kohN-dwee troh veet/preh)* (She drove too fast/close.)

✔ **J'ai fait . . . kilomètres à l'heure.** *(zhay feh . . . kee-loh-mehtr ah luhr)* (I was doing . . . kilometers per hour.)

✔ **Je voudrais un interprète/un avocat.** *(zhuh voo-dray aN nahN-tehr-preht/aN-nah-voh-kah)* (I would like an interpreter/a lawyer.)

Robbery, theft, and aggression

Here are words to cry out to get just anyone's attention:

- **À l'aide!** *(ah lehd)* (Help!)
- **Au secours!** *(oh suh-koor)* (Help!)
- **Arrêtez-le/la!** *(ah-reh-tay luh/lah)* (Stop him/her!)
- **Au voleur!** *(oh voh-luhr)* (Catch the thief!)
- **Police!** *(poh-lees)* (Police!)

You should report to the **commissariat de police** *(koh-mee-sah-ree-aht poh-lees)* in major cities or to the **gendarmerie nationale** *(zhahn-dahr-muh-ree nahs-yoh-nahl)* in smaller towns. You may need to ask this question of a stranger:

> **Où est le commissariat de police le plus proche?** *(oo eh luh koh-mee-sah-ree-aht poh-lees luh plew prosh)* (Where is the closest police station?)

When you get to the police station, you may need some of these phrases:

- **Est-ce qu'il y a quelqu'un qui parle anglais?** *(ehs keel ee ah kehl kaN kee pahrl ahN-gleh)* (Is there anyone who speaks English?)
- **Je veux signaler . . .** *(zhuh vuh seen-ya-lay)* (I want to report . . .)

    un accident *(uh nak-see-dahN)* (an accident)

    une attaque *(ew nah-tahk)* (an attack)

    une agression *(ew nah-grehs-yohN)* (a mugging)

    un viol *(aN vee-ohl)* (a rape)

    un cambriolage *(aN kahN-bree-oh-lazh)* (a burglary)

    un vol *(aN vohl)* (a theft)

- **Mon enfant a disparu.** *(moh nahn-fahN ah dees-pah-rew)* (My child has disappeared.)

✔ **Voilà une photo.** *(vwah-lah ewn foh-toh)* (Here is a photo.)

✔ **Quelqu'un me suit.** *(kehl kahN muh swee)* (Someone is following me.)

If someone has stolen things from you, the following list gives you the French equivalents for the most likely items:

✔ **On m'a volé . . .** *(ohN mah voh-lay)* (They stole . . .)

mon appareil photo *(moh nah-pah-rehy foh-toh)* (my camera)

mes cartes de crédit *(meh kahrt duh kray-dee)* (my credit cards)

mon sac *(mohN sahk)* (my bag)

mon argent *(moh nahr-zhahN)* (my money)

mon passeport *(mohN pahs-pohr)* (my passport)

mon porte-monnaie *(mohN pohrt-moh-neh)* (my wallet)

ma montre *(mah mohNtr)* (my watch)

ma bicyclette *(mah bee-see-kleht)* (my bicycle)

ma voiture *(mah vwah-tewr)* (my car)

The police may then ask for more details, as in the following questions:

✔ **Qu'est-ce qui vous manque?** *(kehs kee voo mahNk)* (What is missing?)

✔ **Ça s'est passé quand?** *(sah seh pah-say kahN)* (This happened when?)

✔ **Où logez-vous?** *(oo loh-zhay voo)* (Where are you staying?)

✔ **Où étiez-vous à ce moment-là?** *(oo ay-tyay voo ah suh moh-mahN lah?)* (Where were you at that moment?)

✔ **Pouvez-vous décrire la personne?** *(poo-vay voo day-kreer lah pehr-sohn)* (Can you describe the person?)

✔ **C'était quelqu'un . . .** *(say-teh kehl-kahN)* (It was someone . . .)

aux cheveux blonds/bruns/roux/gris *(oh shuh-vuh blohN/braN/roo/gree)* (with blond/brownish/red/gray hair)

un peu chauve *(uhn puh shohv)* (balding)

grand/petit/mince/gros *(grahN/puh-tee/mahNs/groh)* (tall/short/skinny/fat)

d'environ . . . ans *(dahN-vee-rohN . . . ahN)* (of about . . . years [of age])

As a person not fluent in the language, you may feel overwhelmed and welcome some help. You can ask to do one of the following things:

✔ **J'ai besoin d'un avocat qui parle anglais.** *(zhay buh-zwahn daN nah-voh-kah kee pahrl ahn-gleh)* (I need a lawyer who speaks English.)

✔ **Je dois contacter le consulat.** *(zhuh dwah kohN-tahk-tay luh kohN-sew-lah)* (I have to contact the consulate.)

✔ **Je voudrais téléphoner à un/e ami/e en ville.** *(zhuh voo-dreh tay-lay-foh-nay ah aN/ewn ah-mee ahN veel)* (I would like to call a friend in town.)

Chapter 12

Ten Favorite Expressions

After you get tuned into French a little, you may suddenly hear people use these little very French expressions that seem to just sort of slip out on any given occasion. You may even have heard some of these phrases already; now it's time to casually use them yourself.

C'est un fait accompli.

(seh taN feh tah-kohN-plee)

The literal translation is "It's an accomplished fact." What it means (beautifully expressed in a few words!) is this: a thing done and therefore no longer worth opposing.

Quel faux pas!

(kehl foh pah)

The literal translation is "What a false step!" You can use it, however, to comment on a slip-up in conduct, speech, and manners, or a breach of etiquette, a blunder, or a gaffe.

Comme il faut.

(koh meel foh)

The translation of this phrase is "As it should be," meaning the proper way to do something or just the way people expect it to be done.

Bon appétit!

(bohN ah-pay-tee)

This phrase literally means "Good appetite!" However, it certainly isn't commenting on anyone's good or bad appetite. It's what you wish each other when you begin to eat or when you see someone eating, much like the English "Enjoy!" except that the French say **"Bon appétit!"** much more freely.

Quelle horreur!

(kehl oh-ruhr)

This phrase means "What a horror!" The French use it not only for real horrors, but also to express any kind of disgust, as in these expressions: "What a terrible thought!" "How nasty!" and "I can't believe it!"

Oh là là! La catastrophe!

(oh lah lah lah kah-tahs-trohf)

This expression translates as "Oh gee, the catastrophe!" French speakers often use it facetiously, when a situation seems terrible to one party but not really to the other.

À tout à l'heure!

(ah too tah luhr)

The literal translation of this phrase is "Until right away." You only use this expression when you really expect to see the departing person within the hour or so.

C'est la vie!

(seh lah vee)

This expression translates as "That's life!" and implies "Oh well, what are you going to do about it?"

Comme ci, comme ça.

(kohm see kohm sah)

Literally, this phrase means "Like this, like that" or "so-so." The phrase means not great and not terrible but in-between. Generally, you use this expression in answer to someone asking you how you're feeling.

C'est le ton qui fait la musique!

(seh luh tohN kee feh lah mew-zeek)

This expression literally translates as "It's the tone that makes the music." It basically means that what counts is the way you say things, not necessarily what you say.

Chapter 13

Ten Phrases That Make You Sound French

• •

*T*hese expressions are so very French that you may even pass for a native French speaker when you use them.

Ça m'a fait très plaisir! or C'était génial!

(sah mah feh treh pleh-zeer) or *(say-teh zhay-nyahl)*

With this phrase, you're saying "I really liked that!" or "That was fantastic!" Here are two ways to express your excitement and really get it across, too. You also can speak for your partner (whose French is nonexistent) by just changing the pronoun: **Ça lui a fait très plaisir!** *(sah lwee ah feh treh pleh-zeer)* (He/She really liked that!)

Passez-moi un coup de fil!

(pah-say mwa aN koot feel)

This phrase means "Give me a call." You can say of course: **Appelez-moi!** *(ah-puh-lay mwah)* or **Téléphonez-moi!** *(tay-lay-foh-nay mwah),* but that wouldn't sound as sophisticated!

Some possible variations are:

- **Passez-nous un coup de fil!** *(pah-say noo aN koot feel)* (Give us a call!)

- **Je vais vous/lui/leur passer un coup de fil.** *(zhuh veh voo/lwee/luhr pah-say aN koot feel)* (I am going to call you/him/her/them.)

On y va! or Allons-y!

(oh nee vah) or *(ah-lohN zee)*

This phrase means "Let's go there!" You can also send someone off somewhere with the latter one: You can say **Allez-y!** *(ah-lay-zee)* (Go ahead!) or **Vas-y!** *(vah-zee)* for the familiar form, if you want to get a little insistent about it.

Je n'en sais rien.

(zhuh nahn seh ree-ahn)

This phrase translates as "I don't know anything about it." In casual speech, you can also say (and this is what you hear most of the time) **J'en sais rien** *(jahn seh ree-ahn)*. Technically, this phrase is grammatically incorrect, but then so is "I don't know nothing" in English.

Mais je rêve!

(meh zhuh rehv)

With this expression, you exclaim, "Oh, I don't believe it!" Literally, this phrase means "But I am dreaming!" and is an expression that has become incredibly popular in recent years, probably because it works on every level of excitement. You can use **mais tu rêves!** *(meh tew rehv)* (You must be crazy!).

Quel amour de petit garçon!

(kehl ah-moor duh ptee gahr-sohn)

This phrase means "What an adorable little boy!" Or you can just say, pointing to a little kid, a pet, or a toy, **Quel amour!** *(kehl ah-moor)* and everyone around you will be so impressed not only with your beautiful French but also with your object of admiration!

Vous n'avez pas le droit.

(voo nah-vay pah luh drwah)

This phrase translates as "You don't have the right." It simply means "It is forbidden," but this phrase says it ever so much more elegantly.

Tu cherches midi à 14h.

(tew shehrsh mee-dee ah kah-tohrz uhr)

This has to be the best phrase of all. Try to translate this and what you come up with is "You are looking for noon at 2 p.m." It means that so-and-so is making things more difficult than necessary, that he or she is sort of off the mark and has lost perspective: **Il/Elle cherche midi à 14h.** You can also practice saying **"Il ne faut pas chercher midi à 14h."** *(eel nuh foh pah shehrsh-shay mee-dee ah kah-torz ahr)* (You shouldn't get so obsessive about it.)

Je veux acheter une bricole.

(zhuh vuh ash-tay ewn bree-kohl)

With this phrase, you're saying "I want to buy a little something, a doodad." It's the word **bricole** that makes

you sound so in-the-know. The word actually derives
from the verb **bricoler** *(bree-koh-lay),* which means to
do odd jobs.

Prenons un pot!

(pruh-nohn aN po)

"Let's take a pot"? If you stretch your imagination a
bit, it means "Let's have a drink!"

Index

Notes

FOR DUMMIES®

The easy way to get more done and have more fun

TRAVEL

0-7645-5453-0 0-7645-5438-7 0-7645-5444-1

Also available:

America's National Parks For Dummies
(0-7645-6204-5)

Caribbean For Dummies
(0-7645-5445-X)

Cruise Vacations For Dummies 2003
(0-7645-5459-X)

Europe For Dummies
(0-7645-5456-5)

Ireland For Dummies
(0-7645-6199-5)

France For Dummies
(0-7645-6292-4)

Las Vegas For Dummies
(0-7645-5448-4)

London For Dummies
(0-7645-5416-6)

Mexico's Beach Resorts
For Dummies
(0-7645-6262-2)

Paris For Dummies
(0-7645-5494-8)

RV Vacations For Dummies
(0-7645-5443-3)

EDUCATION & TEST PREPARATION

0-7645-5194-9 0-7645-5325-9 0-7645-5249-X

Also available:

The ACT For Dummies
(0-7645-5210-4)

Chemistry For Dummies
(0-7645-5430-1)

English Grammar For Dummies
(0-7645-5322-4)

French For Dummies
(0-7645-5193-0)

GMAT For Dummies
(0-7645-5251-1)

Inglés Para Dummies
(0-7645-5427-1)

Italian For Dummies
(0-7645-5196-5)

Research Papers For Dummies
(0-7645-5426-3)

SAT I For Dummies
(0-7645-5472-7)

U.S. History For Dummies
(0-7645-5249-X)

World History For Dummies
(0-7645-5242-2)

HEALTH, SELF-HELP & SPIRITUALITY

0-7645-5154-X 0-7645-5302-X 0-7645-5418-2

Also available:

The Bible For Dummies
(0-7645-5296-1)

Controlling Cholesterol
For Dummies
(0-7645-5440-9)

Dating For Dummies
(0-7645-5072-1)

Dieting For Dummies
(0-7645-5126-4)

High Blood Pressure For Dummies
(0-7645-5424-7)

Judaism For Dummies
(0-7645-5299-6)

Menopause For Dummies
(0-7645-5458-1)

Nutrition For Dummies
(0-7645-5180-9)

Potty Training For Dummies
(0-7645-5417-4)

Pregnancy For Dummies
(0-7645-5074-8)

Rekindling Romance For Dummie
(0-7645-5303-8)

Religion For Dummies
(0-7645-5264-3)